PREDATORY NATURES

BY AMY GOLDSMITH

Those We Drown

Our Wicked Histories

Predatory Natures

PREDATORY NATURES

AMY GOLDSMITH

INK ROAD

First published in the UK in 2025 by
INK ROAD
an imprint of Bonnier Books UK
5th Floor, HYLO, 105 Bunhill Row, London EC1Y 8LZ

Copyright © Amy Goldsmith, 2025

All rights reserved.
No part of this publication may be reproduced, stored or transmitted in any form or by any means, electronic, mechanical, photocopying or otherwise, without the prior written permission of the publisher.

The right of Amy Goldsmith to be identified as author of this work has been asserted by them in accordance with the Copyright, Designs and Patents Act 1988.

This is a work of fiction. Names, places, events and incidents are either the products of the author's imagination or used fictitiously. Any resemblance to actual persons, living or dead, is purely coincidental.

A CIP catalogue record for this book is available from the British Library.

ISBN: 978-1-78530-886-4
Also available as an ebook and in audio

1

Interior design by Cathy Bobak
Printed and bound in Great Britain by Clays Ltd, Elcograf S.p.A.

The authorised representative in the EEA is
Bonnier Books UK (Ireland) Limited.
Registered office address: Floor 3, Block 3,
Miesian Plaza, Dublin 2, D02 Y754, Ireland
compliance@bonnierbooks.ie

bonnierbooks.co.uk/InkRoad

To those afraid to stay but afraid to leave:
There's light on the other side, I promise.

She wants to be flowers, but you make her owls.
You must not complain, then, if she goes hunting.
—Alan Garner, *The Owl Service*

An early spring breeze stirs the delicate buds on the trees as I gaze out over the ancient walled city of Carcassonne, deep in the south of France. Adjusting the vintage sunglasses I picked up in Milan last week, I take a final sip of my chocolat chaud *before heading back to the bustling market where Vincent is waiting for me, all floppy French hair and—*

"Attention all passengers. The *Banebury* will soon be arriving on platform thirteen."

The announcement crashes into my dream. I flip my glossy magazine shut with a grin and shove it into my backpack. The article I was reading is titled "Secret Escapes"—which is fitting—and soon that will be *me*, lapping up the scenery as I make my way across Europe. My phone's already bookmarked with historic sites I'm dying to see and directions to all the best beaches. Clicking my phone to selfie mode, I force a smile and shake back my curls, appraising myself. I *got* this. Lara Williams, reinvented. Lara Born Anew. My fresh start (Lara's Version). I'm friendly, professional . . . *relaxed*. If I say it enough times, who knows, maybe I'll start believing it. Picking up my Frappuccino, I tug my case toward the platform, weaving between hordes of distracted commuters.

I'm expecting the *Banebury* to be grand; after all, it's five-star luxury accommodation. But though I've checked out the glossy photos on the website countless times, I audibly gasp as the train slides into Cardiff Central station. I mean, okay, I knew it wasn't going to be anything like the crappy commuter train I used to take to school, all crazy '80s prints on the seats and perfumed with stale piss, but this . . . *this* is an entirely different beast.

It glides effortlessly along the platform like some magnificent stallion, its sleek black paintwork glistening, its windowpanes glittering like diamonds in the February sun. And for a moment, I think I must have got it wrong, that this is an entire echelon above the train someone like me is due to work on, but no, there's the name, painted on the side of the carriages in glorious golden, looping letters:

The Banebury

Through the windows, I spy plush crimson seating, acres of polished wood, and delicate crystal light fittings.

This is some fancy shit.

I'm early—I always am—wanting to scope out my surroundings and the people I'll be working with in advance. As the train finally stills, I wait to see if anyone disembarks, but the doors remain stubbornly closed, with no sign of any passengers within. I hesitate outside the carriage nearest me, wondering if I should knock. But seconds later, there's movement behind the window, and a tall, serious-looking woman with neat black braids opens the door. She squints down at me.

"Lara, yeah?" Her accent is pure South London. I smile, relaxing immediately—the image of the sneery old posh guy I'd pictured as my boss thankfully dissolving.

"Hey! Yeah, that's me."

"Recognize you from your photo. I'm Shoshanna. Well done for being early—good start." She steps aside and, with a flourish of her white-gloved hand, gestures into the darkened interior of the carriage. "And *welcome* . . . to the *Banebury*."

At her invitation, I climb on, clumsily hauling my suitcase behind me.

"Leave that here a minute," she says, gesturing at my case, "while we wait for the others. I'll give you a quick tour so you can orient yourself. Follow me."

Together we step into what must be a dining carriage, the air expensively fragranced with a fresh floral scent. Roses, I think—my grandparents are big gardeners. My shoes sink deep into a plush carpet that is the color of ripe plums. What I notice first is how *warm* everything is, how welcoming. From the yellow-toned gold of the fixtures to the amber-colored wooden surfaces, all polished within an inch of their life, everything in this carriage glows with its own internal light. Elegant crystal glasses stand regimentally on mirrored shelves below fussy glass lamps that peer out from the walls like curious, long-necked swans. Upon a magnificent sideboard, inlaid with mother-of-pearl in checkerboard patterns, are several etched-silver champagne buckets. Velvet-padded seats in a vibrant peacock print sit politely beneath tables draped in white cloths, each bearing its own delicate little Tiffany-style lamp.

"*Wow*," I say, my voice hushed with awe. I genuinely have no words. Shoshanna snorts. "I know, right?"

As she leads me through the train, the luxury seems to increase with each subsequent carriage. Through the dining room is a shimmering bar topped with milky, gold-veined marble, behind which is an expansive art deco mirror etched with candy-pink stained-glass feathers. Rose-gold stools topped with plump cushions in a playful shade of watermelon stand in a perfectly spaced arc about the bar.

"So this is the Dahlia Bar . . . and then through here . . . the Cedar Lounge."

The lounge is a cozy but opulent space crammed with pillowy burgundy couches and low tables stacked with pricey-looking tomes on fashion and architecture. Arched windows framed in gold are accentuated with tapestry drapes, and the floor is a carpenter's marvel: upon it, delicate polished stars interlink, each composed of three kinds of wood.

"Next, we've got the Azalea Coffee Lounge."

Shoshanna's meager words do not remotely do justice to this sumptuous homage to dark academia, complete with an antique, globe-style drinks trolley and artfully disheveled leather armchairs. A fully stocked coffee bar is discreetly hidden within carefully crafted bookshelves, each stuffed with leather-bound tomes imprisoned behind delicate gold filigree mesh, presumably to prevent them from flying off once the train starts moving. Gazing balefully down from the higher shelves are several slightly eerie, although well-kept, examples of taxidermy.

In sharp contrast, the following carriage is a sleek, airy viewing lounge in cool shades of cream, sage, and heather. Delicate settees and chaise longues face crystal-clear picture windows. In the next and final carriage, a lustrous black grand piano dominates, surrounded by a scattering of chic golden tables and black-leather stools. A gold-etched sign decrees it the Orchid Lounge.

Shoshanna stops here and gestures about. "So . . . as you can see, we've got all the usual things you'd expect on a train like this—dining carriage, bar, couple of lounges . . . there's an onboard chef, so you don't have to worry about making meals or anything like that. As we make our way back through the train, I'll show you the sleeper cars and the staff quarters, where you can dump your suitcase and get changed."

At the other end of the train, past the communal areas, is a series of darker, narrower corridors carpeted in gold-flecked navy. On one side is a row of closed doors set into glossy dark wood, each bearing some ridiculously convoluted name engraved onto a brass plaque: the Amaryllis Suite, the Jacinda Suite, the Oleander Suite.

Shoshanna unlocks a door at random and gestures for me to look inside.

"Pretty swish, huh? You'd want it to be . . . for the price."

It's like peering into an intricate jewelry box. A bottle-green leather couch faces an enormous picture window, beside which is a low glass table bearing several crystal decanters in the shape of swans. Beyond that, half obscured by the swoop of an emerald-velvet drape, is a king-size bed that takes up the entire width of the room. Crisp white sheets peek out beneath an embroidered coverlet. For a moment, I'm outrageously jealous that people are allowed to travel like this.

"I'll tell you how to make up the cabins once everyone's here. For now, let me show you where you'll be bunking."

We pass through another carriage of passenger suites until Shoshanna unlocks a door leading to a more utilitarian-looking area. Here the space is much plainer, the walls a dirty off-white. As in the previous carriage, there is a row of closed doors to our left, although the gaps between them are noticeably narrower. Shoshanna stops outside the first door, gray and unadorned. No brass plaques here.

"And this is you. You're lucky, actually. Usually, staff have to bunk together, but as you already know, *this* is a limited journey—skeleton staff, fewer passengers than usual—until we get to Tallinn and pick up the regular staff and full-paying customers."

Her words send cold reality crashing over me—a reminder that this was the only reason I managed to score such a good job. I applied for the opportunity the very first moment I heard about it last fall, along with some of my old school friends. Back then, it seemed like the perfect way to spend our first summer after graduation—working for the first few weeks but in *luxury*, then backpacking home across Europe.

Somewhat unsurprisingly, due to my complete lack of any relevant experience, my application was almost immediately rejected. Until a few weeks ago, that is, when, several dull months into an unexpected gap year, I was contacted by the company and offered a similar position on one of their off-season trains. Two weeks' work for a pretty decent sum of money—enough to get me back home in style. I accepted mere seconds after opening the email. To quote my friend Casey: For once, the planets seemed to have aligned. After a long run of nothing but bad luck, here was the perfect opportunity to turn things around while I waited to re-sit my exams in May. It wasn't as if I had much else to do, and I hoped that working would take my mind off the fact that my social life had recently dwindled to nothing, leaving me festering in my bedroom watching *Supernatural* reruns and consoling myself with the odd tub of ice cream.

Anyway, *off-season* actually sounds much more my speed than the original offer. From what I can gather, I'll be strictly making up the numbers as the *Banebury* ambles across Europe to its official starting point, Tallinn, where the professional staff get on, along with all the millionaires. I'll be leaving the train there and traveling back to Wales, hopefully catching some early spring sun on the way.

"Right, then, I'll leave you to get sorted while I look out for the others," Shoshanna says. Once I've retrieved my case, she hands me a neat stack of monochrome clothes and checks her watch. "Team meeting in the Cedar Lounge in about half an hour, okay?"

Opening the door, I shrug off my heavy backpack and scope out where I'll be staying for the next couple of weeks. There's a narrow, metal-framed bunk bed that gives me prison vibes, a chipped fold-down table beneath a meager slit of a window, and a slim built-in armchair. Opposite the bunk, a door leads to an imaginatively small bathroom containing a toilet and a mini sink. No shower—but I assume they're shared—and at least I have my own toilet. Besides, anything is going to look disappointing after the opulence I've just walked through.

Heaving my suitcase onto the bottom bunk, I splash my already sweaty face with water, apply a quick slick of mascara, and pull my unruly blond curls into an approximation of a neat bun. Next, I get changed into the uniform Shoshanna handed me. It isn't exactly something I'd *choose* to wear: a black knee-length pencil skirt (that, in all honesty, is probably a size too small) and a starchy-collared white blouse, all topped off with a fussy burgundy scarf that conveniently matches a lot of the train's upholstery. A badge declaring my name is the finishing touch. Tucking a loose strand of hair behind my ear, I smile, close-lipped, into the mirror, barely recognizing the professional-looking person staring back at me.

"You *got* this," I remind my reflection sternly.

A loud bang comes from the cabin beside mine—the sound of a door being flung open too exuberantly—and I jump. Attaching the old-fashioned set of keys Shoshanna gave me to my belt loop, I go to see what the noise is all about, narrowly avoiding walking directly into a tall, rangy figure with a tangle of dark hair shoved beneath a baseball cap. Immediately, I catch his eye, and time seems to slow.

"Oh," I say, momentarily lost for words. "It's you."

2

"Well, that's quite the welcome," muses Rhys in his familiar singsong Welsh drawl. "Yeah, I'm doing good, Lara. Happy to be here, thanks for asking and all."

I falter at the sight of him, finding myself unwillingly pulled into a whirlpool of complicated emotion.

"Sorry," I murmur. "I'm just surprised to see you here, that's all."

Honestly, I shouldn't be. After all, we initially applied for the position together. Rhys was the one who'd found the ad way back when we'd all been planning out our summer with giddy excitement. In the before-times, when we were still friends gazing out at that glorious stretch of freedom together before heading off to university and whatever awaited us beyond.

Of course, it *had* crossed my mind when I accepted the job that Rhys might well have been offered this second opportunity, too. I knew that like me, he'd ended up taking a gap year. Not because he was retaking exams, like I was—Rhys would *never*—but to save some money before he took up his deferred place at Cambridge. Still, just the sight of him dredges up a tangled skein of feelings that I hadn't wanted to examine too closely unless I was forced to. Wariness, uncertainty . . . and even *hope*.

"Guess you got the email, too?" he asks. "I was going to call and ask you, actually, but . . . uh, yeah."

To my relief, he leaves it there.

He's like a stranger before me, despite the fact that up until recently, we were close friends, and had been for over a year. I don't know where to look or what to do with my face as he stands there expectantly, waiting for some kind of response.

As the seconds tick by, my neck slowly heats. I know I should have called him the moment I got the job—before that even—but every time I tried, the words I wanted to say became an unknown language, impossible to speak.

Get it together, Lara. Just act normal.

I clear my throat.

"Yeah—yeah, I got the email. I mean, this opportunity is too good to miss, right?"

Adventure . . . distraction. But more than that, *escape*. *That's* what I'm here for. Well, it'll be harder to escape now that there's a permanent reminder of my recent past chilling in the next cabin.

He nods at my outfit.

"I barely recognized you, to be honest; it's been so long. Still, I've got to say, the air-hostess vibe kind of suits you."

Unsurprisingly, there's a tinge of resentment in his tone. I chew my lip. I can't exactly blame him for it.

"Yeah, well. I guess we've both been busy," I say breezily. "I've been working double shifts at the bakery, saving for the trip back."

His reply is drowned out by the door to the other end of the carriage opening, revealing what must be our first three passengers, all decked out in expensive goose-down jackets and carrying skis.

"No, we can't be staying here, Cass. This area is obviously for the plebs—"

The speaker—lanky, blond, and blandly attractive, with an expensive-looking tan—spots me and stops, apparently not at all embarrassed by his faux pas. "Oh . . . hey there."

Rhys turns to me with a pained wince.

"Good morning, and welcome to the *Banebury*," I say, smiling sweetly as if I haven't heard him. "Are you looking for the passenger suites?"

"Ye-es, actually. Need to offload these babies." He gestures at the skis. "We're on our way to Zurich to catch the last of the powder, y'know."

I do *not* know. He draws out the words, his voice bored as if it's paining him to speak to me.

The pair behind him are similarly attractive: a beachy-looking, freckled blond girl, likely related to the speaker, and a moody-faced guy with decent cheekbones and neatly gelled black hair.

Shoshanna looms up behind them, a professional-looking mask on her face. "Allow me, sir," she says, gesturing for them to follow her—which is good, because I've already forgotten where the passenger cabins are.

"So . . . remind me, how many passengers are going to be on this thing?" I ask Rhys, in a pathetic attempt at normality, once the skiers are out of earshot. "This is meant to be off-season, right? Easy money and all that?"

Rhys nods. "Sure is. Shoshanna says we're starting with around thirteen passengers, but most aren't staying for the whole trip—and there are five of us staff. Pretty healthy ratio for the service industry."

We dutifully join the rest of the staff in the Cedar Lounge, sinking into the deep wine-colored couches, the dull gray light from the station soaking through the vast windows. Joining Rhys and me is a confident-looking girl with a ready laugh and large doe eyes, her thick black hair woven into an intricate French braid. Beside her slouches a tanned older guy with short gray hair shoved behind a paisley bandanna, who radiates a could-not-give-a-fuck attitude, yawning as he scrolls noisily through his phone.

Shoshanna sits at the head of the walnut coffee table in a wingback armchair, an enigmatic smile on her face, looking immensely pleased with the power she wields over us. I give her a wary glance. I've seen teachers with that expression before; they're always dangerous. After passing us all a sheaf of thick cream-colored paper with *The Banebury* etched into the header in gold, she settles comfortably back into her chair.

"Right, everyone, welcome to Team *Banebury*. You guys

got lucky, being booked for this trip. Believe me: It's going to be an easy ride *all* the way to Tallinn."

I absently flick through the papers, which I discover is the roster of all the guests, along with basic info about them, such as allergies and food preferences, as well as some poorly printed photos. "In my experience, that all depends on the *guests*," the older guy murmurs gruffly. I am hazarding a guess that he is the chef. Ignoring him, Shoshanna introduces us all.

"As you already know, I'm Shosh. We've also got Lara and Rhys on service; believe you guys know each other already, right?" She gives us both a comedy wink, and I stare fixedly at my shoes, unable to meet Rhys's gaze. "And Samira here, also on service, and finally, Carlos, our chef."

We all wave and mumble awkward hellos.

"There's also Terrance, our driver, who's already settled in. I've worked with him before—a very experienced gentleman. You probably won't see him much; he's got his own quarters right next to the cab and tends to keep himself to himself."

She continues: "Now, more importantly, on to our *guests*. So we've got three skiers who are leaving the train in Zurich: Cassandra Montague, Theodore Montague, and Xavier Henley-Richards. They're already on board. Points to note: Theo is gluten intolerant, and Cassandra is vegan. None of that should pose a problem, *especially* to an experienced chef." I catch Carlos rolling his eyes.

"Next, there's a *baroness*—apparently—Carlotta Winterbourne and her niece-slash-assistant, Rebecca. Our dear baroness also has a very limited diet. Chef, I'll talk to you about that in a bit. Then we've got the Chao family—they're only staying until we get to London—and the Marriotts, newlyweds, who'll be leaving us in France. Finally, we have a pair of siblings—Gwendolyn and Gwydion Llewellyn. They'll join us a little farther down the line, before we cross the border into England."

The faces of the last pair stare mournfully out at me from the paper, both so white-faced and dark-haired that the picture may as well have been black-and-white. Shoshanna wraps it up.

"So only thirteen passengers for the five of us to handle. As you all know, this is a limited charter—the *real* work will start when we reach Tallinn and pick up all the passengers paying full price for five-star service and the scenic route back to London." She nods at Rhys and me. "But you guys don't need to worry about that, as I believe you'll be leaving us then. I'll give you a run-through of your duties next, but it's nothing too taxing. Apparently, a few other guests dropped out at the last minute, you lucky things. Now let's all go grab a cup of tea, and I'll show you what to expect."

Rhys, Samira, and I spend the next few hours shadowing Shoshanna as she fastidiously demonstrates how to clean the cabins, each of which is more sickeningly luxurious than the last, with their silken coverlets in expensive shades of racing green or vermilion and polished gold bathroom fixtures. Immediately after, we get an exhausting speed run of how to restock the bar and the coffee lounge and lay the tables for meals.

Shoshanna clasps her hands and looks at us with satisfaction, evidently confident that we know exactly what we're doing. "Okay, on to service. Plan is that I'll do tonight's dinner service alongside Samira, who's got the most experience. You two can serve the drinks and take notes so you're ready to take over tomorrow."

I chew my thumbnail. Rhys, who's worked in his mum's café pretty much since birth, will undoubtedly ace this, while I have the (frankly, earned) reputation of being spectacularly clumsy.

The rest of the passengers are due to board within the next hour, and then we'll be setting off. Before they arrive, we are treated to a dismal lunch of microwaved lasagna in the staff lounge. It's a depressing little room, the last carriage before Shoshanna's office and the driver's cab, with dirty yellow walls and mismatched faulty or stained furniture from the main part of the train, haphazardly arranged on corporate blue carpet tiles. Shosh reels off another set of incomprehensible instructions, then rustles busily away, leaving us blankly looking at each other.

"This *train*." Samira exhales, throwing down her fork and shaking her head. "Can you believe it? How the other half live, am I right? I mean, I've worked at a couple of nice hotels before, but *this* is luxury."

"It's pretty lush," I agree distractedly, poking at my food, Rhys's presence still unsettling me.

"Understatement of the year," Samira replies. "D'ya reckon we'll get time off to, like . . . hang? Planning on getting some bougie content on here."

Rhys nods amiably as he flicks through pages on his Kindle. "Yeah, of course, although I doubt we'll be allowed to use the guest facilities. We're not paying customers, after all."

I frown a little. I hadn't thought about that. My room is so tiny that the thought of being confined to it for hours when I'm not working a shift gives me intense claustrophobia. They probably made the staff cabins that way on purpose to put an end to any slacking.

"Shosh seems cool, though," continues Samira chattily. She flicks a beautifully manicured finger across her phone screen. "I'm saving to do a cosmetology degree. What about you guys?"

I fill her in, shamefaced, about having to do exam re-sits later this year, and she nods sagely, patting my hand. "Hey, resilience is an underrated quality, you know. Getting back up and trying again."

I like Samira already, and I'm not usually this quiet, but being here, in such close proximity to Rhys after everything that's happened these past months, has got me tongue-tied.

Eventually, Samira gives up trying to make small talk, and for a few minutes, we all awkwardly listen to the sound of our own chewing, intermittently interrupted by the distant sound of slamming doors.

"Honestly, it is good to see you again, La," says Rhys eventually, with an inscrutable smile. But I still detect a hint of slyness or at least chastisement in it. "As I said, it's been a while. I half wondered if you'd be *allowed* to show up here."

"Come on, Rhys, give it a rest," I mutter uncomfortably. "You *know* all that's over with now."

Seeming to sense the immense tension that has fallen cleanly across the room like a guillotine blade, Samira clears her throat and excuses herself from the table with a knowing flash of her eyes, leaving us alone.

I fiddle aimlessly with my phone. He's right; it *has* been a while since we last saw each other—since I saw *anyone*, to be fair. And I thought about contacting him to ask if he was going on this trip—unsure of my feelings, whether I'd be glad or whether I'd want to cancel immediately if he was—but each time I selected his number, saw his face in my phone contacts, I managed to find some excuse not to call.

And anyway, the last time I saw him—a month or so ago—was one of the most excruciating moments of my life. We bumped into each other in the grocery store, where I'd picked up a few shifts in the bakery to help save for the trip—one way or another, I was getting away from here for a while. Truthfully, I'd clocked him first and was trying to fade into obscurity behind a bread oven before he noticed me in my highly unflattering uniform. He called my name three times before I realized I couldn't ignore him anymore without it being weird and greeted him with an awkward hello. We made small talk, initially so stilted it cracked my heart, until the rusted joints of our friendship slowly began to loosen.

"I heard about your re-takes," he said apologetically, studying the baguettes. "I'm sorry.... Maybe I could have helped if I'd known earlier."

I pulled a face. "Well, don't be. It's my own fault. Besides, I'm going to ace them second time around."

He looked up at me warily, and I waited for him to offer me some tutoring, to catch me up on all I'd missed, to tell me Stevie, Casey, and Aiden were always asking after me. That things could be how they used to be if I wanted. But he didn't. Why would he? I didn't deserve it. And anyway, before he could speak, his mum discovered us talking and launched into a ten-minute public tirade about how someone like *me* should be nowhere near her precious son.

"Anyway, you're looking ... well," I say now, forcing myself to be cool and collected. And I'm relieved to see that he does look well—*now*. Better than well, in fact, although it's weird to see him out of his usual uniform of rumpled plaid shirt and hoodie.

"Yeah, healed up pretty good," he says, absently patting the side of his face. Then he leans across the table, catching my eyes, his own preternaturally green in the sharp slant of sunlight that falls through the window. Something painful and long buried rises within me, and instinctively I swallow it back down.

"Honestly, La, I wasn't sure how I'd feel if you were here. I knew it might not be easy between us. But now that you *are* here ... I'm glad."

This time there's a sincerity to his words I can't help but smile at.

Might not be easy is the understatement of the year. But I still sense the ghost of that easiness between us, the patterns of teasing and relaxed banter we fall into, the firm foundations of our old friendship, and if he's willing to forgive me, then I'm more than willing to meet him halfway.

I open my mouth to reply, when the train gives a sharp lurch, rattling the cutlery on the laminate table like bones, followed by a piercing whistle. Rhys immediately shoots up, apparently even more relieved by the distraction than I am, and heads directly to the nearest window.

"Hey . . . looks like we're moving." He turns to me and grins, his eyes full of hope. "London . . . here we come!"

3

I'm surprised by the unexpected giddiness I feel, a confetti-cannon explosion of sunshine in my heart, as the train begins to tug forward, slowly leaving Cardiff station behind. I've been dreaming about this trip for weeks but never anticipated how good it would feel to actually *leave*, to watch the place that holds so many freshly unpleasant memories shrink away into the distance in real time, ready to be replaced by new and unfamiliar scenery.

Buoyant now, I follow Rhys through the softly swaying carriages—the movement of the train isn't spiky and jarring like the public transport I'm accustomed to but butter-smooth and rhythmic—and into the regal scarlet glow of the Cedar Lounge, ready to be introduced to our passengers. Shoshanna's confident voice floats down the carriage as I take my place beside Samira and peer curiously out at the guests.

A smiling family of four that must be the Chaos takes up a pair of facing couches; their youngest, an adorable toddler with chubby pink cheeks, is busy chasing banana slices around a porcelain bowl while the older child industriously doodles in a sketchbook. Then there's a moneyed-looking couple of guys sitting bolt upright on a plush love seat, sipping champagne: one stern-faced, in a brushed-wool coat, leather briefcase resting on his lap; the other grinning toothily in a fabulous neon-yellow bomber jacket. From the aura of bliss that surrounds them, I'm guessing these are our honeymooners, the Marriotts. At a smaller table, clinking a teacup against a saucer, is a dour-faced elderly lady with alarmingly flame-red hair and a scarf that looks suspiciously like fur, accompanied by a slender, blue-haired teen in a Metallica tee—the baroness and her niece. And then, of course, there are the skiers, who are—quite rudely, in my opinion—muttering all the way through Shosh's welcome speech.

Besides the old lady and the annoying skiers, it doesn't look like anything we can't handle between us. I'm thankful the train isn't full, though. I might be able to deal with the Karens at the supermarket, but an entire trainful of snooty people would be way out of my wheelhouse. As Shosh wraps up her welcome, I give the Chaos' youngest an enthusiastic wave, wincing a little as they take one look at me and immediately start to cry.

Most of the passengers dissipate once Shoshanna is done giving out information about breakfast times and laundry services, and I spend the next hour learning how to use the intimidatingly large steel coffee machine in the small atrium between the kitchen and the dining carriage, stacks of porcelain coffee cups clinking perilously over my head with the movement of the train.

"So how'd you wangle this job with zero experience?" asks Samira as she shows me how to use the grinder for the third time. While I'm a little surprised at her bluntness, she delivers it with a winning grin.

"Ah, you know . . . a few little creative tweaks to my résumé. They must have been desperate for staff," I confess in a low voice.

She grins and nods. "Yeah, not to be rude, but I think you're right. A slow, off-season train crawling through the ass end of Europe with a load of demanding toffs. Not like the pay's anything special either."

I laugh. "What do you mean, the ass end of Europe?"

I'm not exactly a seasoned traveler.

Samira shrugs. "I've worked on a couple of these old things before—we're not taking the usual fast route with all the views—y'know? We're not even stopping at the cool places you'd expect—no Paris, no Berlin, no Bruges. . . . Nah, this baby's basically saving money by taking the back rails to Tallinn, where the *proper* journey starts. Guarantee all the passengers on here got cut-price tickets." She opens the fridge below to get out the milk and shakes her head. "See, not even premium brands. They'll restock with the pricey stuff at the other end."

It makes sense. And honestly, I prefer it this way, less

pressure on me. All I really care about is reaching Tallinn and being set free—a bird flying from a cage—

Shosh puts her head around the door. "*Jesus*, girls, how long does it take to make a bloody cup of coffee? Dinner is in five minutes. Both of you get changed into your evening uniforms."

Despite Shoshanna radiating stress like a slowly leaking barrel of toxic waste, dinner service goes smoothly. Unlike the harried denizens of the supermarket I work in, everyone here is in holiday mode, relaxed and cheerful. And although entering the kitchen is accompanied by a barrage of Chef's creative cursing, his food looks (and smells) amazing. Surprisingly, I begin to find I enjoy satisfying our passengers. I discover how to lean into the movement of the train to minimize whacking my hips into the tables; I learn how casual Mr. Marriott likes his soda (two limes, no ice) and how business-mode Mr. Marriott takes his tea (lemon, no milk). I make fresh strawberry milkshakes for the Chaos' adorable children and admire the elder child's drawing of me, particularly the wild yellow corkscrews emerging from my head. Rhys has it a little harder than I do, and I grin at the sight of him hurrying back and forth between the bar and the dining carriage to fix the skiing trio's ever more elaborate cocktails.

As service draws to a close, I lean at the counter, chin in hand, watching through the windows as the sky slowly darkens from orange to dusky pink over the soft Welsh hills and, inside, the lights go up, giving the carriage a cozy yellow glow. Accompanying the genteel clink of glasses and the low murmur of conversation is a gentle background of classical string music. After dessert (a chocolate-and-hazelnut parfait that makes my mouth water), the guests drift away in small groups, some to their rooms, some to the bar, some to read in the lounge, and Chef and I begin to clear up.

Carlos is gruff but patient as he teaches me how to use the dishwasher and shows me where to put the dirty linen, complaining all the time, in a way that's quite endearing, that this is not what he's used to. When we're done, I stare with satisfaction at the once more picture-perfect carriage we have created between us, every surface gleaming, every crystal glass shining. Now my shift is over, my feet are sore—I'm already regretting the cheap ballet flats I chose to wear—and I smell strongly of spilled coffee, but I am also filled with a pleasing sense of achievement.

Leaving the passenger carriages, all glittering light and fragranced air, is like leaving a sumptuous party early, but I'm exhausted and have been given the early shift tomorrow. Back in my cabin, I wash up in the tiny bathroom and clamber into some sweats before picking up my book and trying to read, telling myself that things are going to be different now that I'm thoroughly distracted. But it's only minutes before I give in to that familiar itch in my brain and instead switch to my phone—which I am blissfully not allowed to use outside the staff areas.

With clumsy fingers, I maneuver to my contacts and stare

at Beckett's number, his golden face framed in a tiny circle, my finger poised over the word *unblock*. I won't actually do it. I'm not stupid, but my heart doesn't always understand this, and there are things I can't help but miss. The constant, conversational tone of a new message, for example. For months now, my phone has been as silent as the grave.

A soft knock at my cabin door makes me jump. As if caught in an illicit act, I swiftly shove the phone under a pillow and crack open the door. Rhys peers through, the soft cotton scent of the deodorant he always wears weirdly calming my nerves. He gives me a hesitant smile.

In return, I raise a wary eyebrow, remembering his earlier jibes.

"May I help you?"

His smile fades a little. "Thought you might want some company, since it's still kind of early?"

And that *is* all he means. Rhys doesn't do flirtatious, doesn't do seductive, and *definitely* doesn't do sleazy. And he's right; I *do* want some company. I feel strange here, like I'm straddling the space between two worlds: the Lara I used to be and want to be again—the Lara Rhys knows—and this uncertain and uneasy Lara I've become, always jumping at the things that I've learned hide in the shadows. But if we can manage to get over this strange stiltedness, maybe he can even help me find my way back.

I open the door wider and make a sweeping gesture.

"Sure. Welcome to my palatial lodgings."

He snorts and crashes onto the lower bunk, narrowly

missing hitting his head on the steel bar above. "I know, cozy, right? Mine's identical." He eyes the crumpled clothes spilling out of my suitcase, including, to my dismay, a graying bra. "But . . . uh . . . tidier. So how'd your first shift go?"

There's the tiniest hint of nerves in his voice. Does he feel responsible for me because he initially shared the job listing or something?

"A little hectic, I guess, but nothing I can't handle. Don't forget, I worked the late shift at McDonald's last year—the sights I've seen . . ." I give him a reassuring smile. "Hey, you know there's a *library* on this thing?"

He grins readily back. "Of course. Where'd you think I spent my break?"

JANUARY, LAST YEAR

I first met Rhys after relocating from London to a small town just outside Cardiff. Dad had been struggling to pay the rent on our flat after losing his job, so we'd had to up and move to Wales to live with my grandparents, a situation no one was particularly happy about except me, since it meant I wouldn't have to handle Dad's moods alone anymore. But if my home life had finally improved, I couldn't say the same for the rest of it. Starting a new school at sixteen had not been easy. I'd been pretty popular at my previous school, coasting along as your average B student, and initially I hadn't been too worried about fitting in. I figured coming from London, it would be easy to navigate a small-town school. But at Haerthton High, I soon discovered that everyone was in tight little friendship groups that had been established since first grade, and despite my usually outgoing nature, I found myself continually on the fringes and sidelines, eyed with suspicion as the fancy "up herself" London girl.

During the second week, I began to give up on the fruitless small talk and took to haunting the library at lunchtime so as not to sit self-consciously alone in the dining hall. I noticed Rhys before he noticed me. Objectively, he was cute, plaid-shirted, and bespectacled, with dark hair that curled at the edges, always busily reshelving books or tutoring younger kids with his warm, lyrical voice. I considered starting a conversation more than once—we shared a few classes, and he seemed friendly. But he radiated this intimidating confidence, perpetually acing his tests, the teachers always joking that he should be teaching their classes instead of them. That, along with the continual coldness I'd experienced since starting at this school, made me reluctant to get rebuffed again.

"Y'know . . . if you're researching mitochondrial exchange for Canning's class, this book's way better—that one's pretty outdated. By several decades, in fact."

Surprised, I looked up from my notes into Rhys's warm green gaze, for once lost for words.

"Huh. Well, that's quite the pickup line," I eventually replied. "Do you find it usually works for you?"

His cheeks pinked, and immediately I felt bad.

"We have biology together—" he began to explain, looking like he wished he'd never said anything.

Remembering my desperate need for a friend, I tucked my hair behind my ear and gestured for him to sit down. "Sorry, sorry. Bad joke. It's Rhys, right? I'm Lara . . . the new girl," I added resentfully.

He nodded, his head cocked in sympathy. "Can't be easy. We have history together, too. I've been meaning to say, actually, I enjoyed your essay on Roman women the other day."

No one else had. Delilah Barnes and her crew had spent the entire time smirking and passing notes about me.

Rhys, however, seemed genuine. "Thanks. I'm definitely flunking biology, though," I admitted, gesturing down at my notes, which were, in fact, just doodles of sleepy cats.

He shrugged easily. "Well . . . I could help with that . . . if you want . . . that is?"

Oh, I wanted, all right.

I gave him a warm smile. "That would be great, actually. If you could . . . uh . . . find time to fit me in."

Did that sound weird?

"Uh, I absolutely could fit you in." He paused, blushing again, something I was finding seriously endearing, and smiled back. A winning, genuine kind of smile.

The kind of smile that left me thinking that things might not be so bad here after all.

Rhys yawns, bringing me back to the present. "So how's your dad been?"

I look away. "Better, thanks. Gran's forcing him to attend AA meetings—like, literally driving him to the door—and he's been keeping to it. Sober, he's grumpy as hell, but I'll take that any day over him being grumpy and drunk."

Rhys nods and says no more about it.

"And how have *you* been?" I press gently. I'm curious.

"Yeah, pretty good," he says, stretching out, moving deeper into the bunk as if hiding from me. "You know, still busy tutoring and helping out at the café. Same old same old. You?"

I launch into a story about how two ten-year-olds held us all hostage in the supermarket the other week by hurling their scooters at the glass doors. He laughs, and as we continue to chat for a bit, it's almost like old times—if it weren't for the fact that we are both studiously avoiding *certain topics* and pretending that the last two months have not, in fact, happened.

"So are you planning on backpacking home?" I ask, not meeting his eyes.

He shakes his head. "Nah, I'm taking a flight straight back—need to help Mum out at the café. How about you?"

"Well, I don't have my re-takes until May, so I'm planning on taking my time getting back. Y'know, maybe do a little bar work, some club promo, fruit picking—whatever's available. And in my downtime, I'll be submerging myself in local culture and checking out the heady delights of Euro Tinder."

He chuckles. "Euro Tinder, is that right?"

I shrug, a little irritated at his amusement, but then he catches my eye, suddenly serious.

"I tried to call you, y'know. . . . As soon as I could . . . well, *after*. . . . You'd blocked my number."

Because your mum told me to. Because she told me to never speak to you again, to never approach you, to not even look at you. To turn in the opposite direction if I ever caught sight of you—

I don't say this, though.

"I . . . I did send you a message."

"I know. I read it."

The silence stretches between us like lengthening shadows. Outside it's fully dark, and we clatter through the dull greenery of the Welsh valleys, bare winter branches swiping longingly at the window.

I sigh.

"Rhys, would it be okay if . . . if we didn't talk about it? Not yet, anyway? Today's been a lot. . . ."

He nods, keeping his green eyes locked on mine, full of sincerity, making me glance away in shame.

"Of course. I'm sorry; I should have known better." He gets up. "I better go, actually. G'night, La."

4

I wake with that groggy, disoriented feeling of being wrenched out of a deep dream and having no idea where I am.

I'm on a train, I recall after a few moments, and I quickly realize that the reason I'm confused is that, for some reason, it isn't moving anymore. The gentle rocking motion that lulled me so sweetly to sleep is now entirely absent. My cabin is in total darkness, meaning it's still nighttime.

Why have we stopped?

I sit up, immediately cursing as I forget I'm in a top bunk and whack my head against the ceiling. At the same time, the train makes an odd juddering motion, lurching forward and then backward before stilling once more.

Yeah, we're definitely stationary.

Weird. Didn't Shoshanna say the first stop wasn't until London? Have we gotten there so soon? Considering the interminable crawl at which this train was traveling all evening,

I highly doubt it. Has something gone wrong? God, could we have *crashed*? Sure, I can be a heavy sleeper, but I wouldn't have slept through *that* . . . would I?

Climbing carefully down from my bunk, in case I'm caught off guard by another unexpected lurch, I push the slats of the window blind apart and peer out.

Well, London can definitely be ruled out by the green morass of trees that loom over the train and the complete lack of light pollution. It looks like we've stopped at a station somewhere deep in the countryside. I can make out the concrete platform outside, dimly lit by tall lights, the familiar yellow safety line demarcating its edge. A few feet away is what must be the ticket office, leprously peeling paint, the windows barred, utter darkness behind them, all locked up for the night—or, judging by its dilapidated state, forever. A little farther down the platform, I can see a rusting footbridge arcing over the track. I look out for the station name, but the boards that *should* be displaying it are all curiously empty. I mean, they're *there*, as at any other station, but they're displaying *nothing*—no words at all, just blank space.

Okay, *that* is a little weird.

I pick up my phone from where it's charging on the bottom bunk as the train continues to lurch drunkenly back and forth. Thankfully it doesn't look like we've crashed. The train is calm and silent, and now that I've shrugged off some of my sleepiness, I realize that the sensation is familiar to me: I've traveled on enough trains to understand that it means carriages are being either attached or detached. Checking the time, I see it's three a.m.—not exactly the most sociable hour to be stopping.

Yawning, I click open Google Maps, waiting for it to boot up with the limited signal I currently have. As expected, it looks like we're several hours outside London but also pretty far from the nearest town. The train is presently just a blue blob floating in the middle of a sea of green—and on the map, there's no sign of a station.

I look again at the chained-up waiting room and archaic footbridge, now realizing we've stopped at what is clearly an old, abandoned station. Maybe we needed to pick up some supplies or an extra set of passenger carriages, or are being held at a red light. . . . It isn't a big mystery.

I yawn again, my eyes closing for slightly longer than a blink.

Something thumps hard against the window, like a stray football, uttering a wild shriek as it flutters away.

Clutching a hand to my chest, I give a shocked laugh. Just a bird—probably an owl or something, judging by the sheer size of it. Muffled voices drift from the platform and I unlatch the window, sticking my head out to get a better view of whatever's happening out there.

Behind me, right at the very rear of the train, there's activity. My suspicions are correct; two or three new carriages have been attached to the back of the train, gleaming darkly in the distance. And on the shadowy platform stands a small huddle of people. Two are tall and thin, their faces hidden by the hoods of their dark coats in the dim yellow light, while the third is wearing what looks like a pair of overalls—their face covered by what appears to be a black fencing mask ... something like that. ... Or maybe they're wearing a beekeeper's suit. Besides the occasional warning hoot of the owl, the platform is quiet. The new passengers are standing in an eerily silent triangle as they wait for the carriages to be attached.

A few moments later, the shunting stops and Shoshanna steps off the train. I let out a breath as I see her, a reassuring symbol of normality—proof the train isn't being hijacked by rogue fencers. I debate whether or not to get dressed and see if she needs any help since I'm wide awake now, but something stops me. Passing off my gut feeling of reluctance as down to the lateness of the hour, I continue watching. Shoshanna briefly chats with the new guests, their voices too distant for me to catch any words, and then they follow her lead and climb on.

As the slamming door echoes down the train, I clamber back into my bunk and shut my eyes. I'm on the early shift tomorrow, so now would *not* be a good time for my brain to decide to keep me awake all night. After a minute or so, I can hear hushed voices softly drifting down the corridor, followed by the low rumble of Shoshanna's voice and a steady tread that goes past my cabin door. The insulation in these cabins is *not* the best. Then, minutes later, as I'm about to drift back into sleep, there come more footsteps—quieter this time, almost sneaky. It's probably just lucid dreaming or something, but they appear to pause directly outside my door. After a minute or two of straining to hear in the intense silence, I force myself out of bed again with a soft sigh. Better to reassure myself than spend the next hour lying in self-induced anxiety, wondering. Padding to the door, I peer through the peephole.

I was right: Someone *is* standing in the corridor just outside my room. I jump back in shock as soon as I spot them, but one glimpse is enough. Their eyes catch the moonlight pouring through the window, making them look golden—amber—while the rest of them is shrouded in absolute darkness.

I lean against the door, my heart pounding, then immediately back away from it, bizarrely afraid it will give way and send me tumbling out into the corridor, into the path of whoever (*or whatever*) is out there.

No one is out there, I tell myself harshly. *No one. That's ridiculous.*

Shaking a little, reminding myself that I'm safe, that I have my phone, and that Rhys is just next door, I force myself to look again. I have to, or I'll spend all night awake and wondering.

Tentatively, I raise my eye to the peephole once more.

There's no one there. Only the mop trolley resting against the wall opposite, and behind it, the moonlight reflecting off a golden lamp fitting, giving the illusion of eyes.

I huff a laugh, embarrassed at myself. But then, who can blame me? It's *dark*, I'm exhausted, it's three a.m., and we're stopped at some deserted, spooky station. As I lie back down, the train lurches into motion, and only moments later, I fall gratefully back to sleep.

* * *

Despite the slightly uncomfortable end to the previous evening, despite my curiously disrupted sleep *and* my alarm going off at the ungodly hour of five a.m., I wake feeling energized and refreshed.

Overnight we've left Wales behind and are now across the border in England, heading smoothly and steadily toward London, where we'll stop and lose the Chao family. I can't blame them for wanting to travel such a short distance in such grand style; I wouldn't use regular public transport either if I had the choice. From there we'll continue onward, taking the short trip across the English Channel and into France.

Outside my window, nameless gray towns and backyards flicker by, revealing fleeting glimpses of other people's lives: their trampolines and washing lines, their painted sheds and novelty planters. I'm still amazed at how much lighter I feel the more physically removed I am from my past.

Dawn is beginning to filter through the slatted blinds of the staff lounge as I wolf down some granola and coffee, scrolling my socials on my phone. Then, grabbing my robe and wash bag, I head to the communal staff shower—no luxury private bathrooms for us. Back in my cabin, feeling much fresher, I change into my uniform, apply minimal makeup, and tie back my curls with a red-velvet ribbon that matches my scarf.

I've been here less than twenty-four hours, but already the train is starting to feel familiar in the best possible way, especially once I leave the bland, monotone scrappiness of the staff quarters and step into the stately opulence of the passenger carriages. I pad softly down the narrow corridor of suites, shoes sinking pleasantly into the gold-speckled carpet, pausing now and then to tie back the heavy drapes while smirking at the occasional ragged snore that emanates from behind the polished door of the Jacinta Suite. Leaving the blinds half closed as instructed so our waking guests aren't blinded by the low winter sun, I head to the dining carriage to prepare for breakfast.

I call out a cheery good morning to Carlos, who is already banging away in the small kitchen area. He mumbles something darkly in response; I suspect he is not a morning person, but still, the sweet smell of fluffy pancakes and the rich, salty scent of crisping bacon drift out as I begin opening the drapes in here and laying the tables.

I'm a summer girl, the kind who lives for the beach and the feel of the sun warming my skin, so the fact that today the sun is beaming in a fresh blue sky raises my spirits. It's late February—not exactly warm—but hopeful silver-green buds are appearing on the trees in the flashing glimpses of parks and gardens, and a merry yellow spatter of daffodils adorns the grassy banks along the train tracks.

The swish of the automatic door alerts me to the first guests, and I am jolted by the sight of them. Even though I've never seen them before, they look familiar: the dark-haired siblings from the preference sheets Shoshanna handed us yesterday. It must have been them who boarded the train last night. It makes complete sense now—I remember her saying these two would join us later. I exhale, the anxiety I experienced last night melting away.

They are much more striking than their crappily printed pictures suggested, and not too much older than Rhys and me, at a guess. They share the same slender build and angular face. As they take their seats at one of the tables, the guy's mouth quirks in a small smile as he subtly beckons to me.

"Good morning!" I sashay over, beaming, professional mask firmly in place. "And welcome to the *Banebury*. We're very pleased to have you here! What can I get for you both?"

Up close, he is even more eye-catching. His sleek black hair is shorn short on the sides and left longer in a softly waved side part on top. But it's his eyes that are remarkable, so light and so blue they are glacial, and I can't help but stare. I'm surprised I'm close to blushing at his scrutiny. Everything about him is sharp—from his cheekbones to his aquiline nose. When he speaks, his voice is deep and clipped, with the faintest trace of a Welsh accent.

"A coffee, please, with cream if you have it."

"Of course. Anything else?" I ask, casting a curious eye at his companion.

She is busy typing frantically on a laptop, her pale face drawn. She has the same sleek black hair, currently pulled back from her face in a slick low bun, her octagonal gold-rimmed glasses perched on the same strong nose. She's wearing a simple but chic black shift dress, an eye-wateringly expensive quilted handbag perched on the seat beside her. Dangling from her neck on a chain is an ornate Tiffany-style key that occasionally catches the fleeting morning sunlight. She throws a split-second glance at me, accompanied by a frown of annoyance at my interruption.

"What? No, nothing. Uh, on second thought, some water."

"Wonderful choices," I reply, so brightly I'm aware I'm in danger of sounding sarcastic. "I'll be *right* back!"

As I fuss with the overly complicated coffee machine, Rhys enters the kitchen, stifling a yawn, through which he manages a "good morning." He gestures back to the carriage with a tilt of his head. "Where'd they get dug up from? I don't recall seeing them yesterday."

"They got on along with the new carriages last night," I mutter.

Rhys frowns. "*New* carriages? What do you mean?"

"Didn't you hear them being attached? God, Rhys, you must sleep like the dead."

He takes over the coffee machine, makes himself an espresso, and downs it. His sheer proximity in the small space is secretly thrilling, but I stand as far away from him as possible, afraid he might somehow sense this. "I knew we'd be getting a couple of new passengers, but not new *carriages*."

"Hmm, I hope we don't have to clean them," I mutter, thinking of my already packed schedule today.

Rhys grins. "Anyway, no way can they be worse than the skiers. I've just taken the most convoluted coffee order in the *world:* oat milk chai with extra hot water and extra steam, and oh my *god*, this is going to be a long trip. Y'know, they shouldn't even *be* here. From what I can work out, they missed their regular train and *bribed* Shosh to take them on this one so they didn't miss their hotel booking."

"Good for her, to be honest," I say, pouring the guy's coffee into an intricately filigreed coffee jug. "Get that money."

I rattle the breakfast tray into the carriage and place it delicately on our new arrivals' table.

"I'm Lara, by the way," I say, determined to kill them both with kindness, as I pour some coffee into a ridiculously twee porcelain cup. "I'll be one of your servers on this trip."

"Gwydion," replies the guy absently, watching what I'm doing with an intense look of concentration, as if waiting for me to slip up. He pronounces it as two lyrical syllables. *Gwyd-yun.* "And this is my sister, Gwen."

Gwen doesn't even bother to look up from her laptop as I belligerently push her water toward her.

"So, are you guys heading all the way to Tallinn with us?" I ask mildly, trying to fill the silence as I place the fiddly paper coasters, the sugar cubes, the hand-painted cream jug, a crystal glass, a mini ice bucket—all the ridiculous accompaniments that come with a simple cup of coffee and a water on the *Banebury*.

Gwydion catches my eye once more—I kind of enjoy the way he deliberately seeks it out—and gives me a thin smile.

"You know... you ask a lot of questions for someone who empties the bins."

I am so surprised at this casual cruelty I twitch and overfill his cup, watching in horror as the coffee flows over the saucer and onto the pristine white tablecloth beneath. Beside him, Gwen tuts irritably, scooting away her laptop.

For once, I have no words. If I ever thought my experiences over the past few months had made me tougher and more resilient, then I am wrong. Too ashamed to look up, I drift back to the kitchen in a trance, still holding the dripping coffeepot.

"Do they want anything else?" asks Rhys, busily heating up croissants. He turns at my silence and immediately takes the pot away from me, which is good, because it is in imminent danger of crashing to the floor. He casts a dark glance over my shoulder to where Gwydion is loudly fussing over the spilled coffee with a napkin. Rhys places a gentle hand on my shoulder, his voice softening.

"I'll deal with it," he says.

5

Once breakfast service is over, we are all summoned for a midmorning meeting in the staff lounge by a harried-looking Shosh.

I take a seat next to Samira, deliberately ignoring Rhys's concerned glance. I don't want his sympathy; what I *want* is to show him that I'm different now, back to the old Lara—the one he liked, not some victim to be pitied. Only I'm not doing a very good job of it.

"Just a quick one, guys," she says, rapping her clipboard efficiently on the table. "You may have noticed we had some new carriages attached to the train overnight. One of our new guests"—she glances down at her clipboard—"Gwendolyn Llewellyn, is a scientist, and the carriages contain some organic samples she's transporting to Eastern Europe."

"Ugh . . . great. Will they need cleaning, too?" asks Samira, reading my mind and not bothering to disguise her annoyance.

"Not yet," replies Shosh sternly. "Although if they change their minds, I don't expect any complaints. But as of now, there's no need for any of you to go into those carriages. They've brought an assistant on board who'll deal with everything, so no extra work for us."

"An assistant? We don't have enough food for unexpected guests," says Carlos matter-of-factly. "I am very exacting with my orders."

Shosh eyes Carlos murderously. "This assistant won't be staying long, so you don't need to count them among the dinner guests." She scans her clipboard one last time. "Oh, Samira, Lara: I know you're about to start on the cabins now, but we're under strict instructions not to enter the new passengers' rooms until they're unpacked and settled."

Beside me, Samira arches a curious eyebrow. "Fine with me."

"Organic samples?" mutters Rhys curiously as we leave. *"Interesting."*

Still embarrassed by my overreaction at breakfast, I follow Samira down the train to make up the passenger cabins, grateful for the chance to be alone for a bit and regroup. The silence in these grand, empty rooms is soothing, and happily, it looks as if most of our guests are fastidiously tidy. As the train gently rattles on toward London, I carefully polish surfaces and thump the crisp white pillows. There's a begrudging satisfaction to be found in a job well done. Listening to a podcast on the French Revolution as I work my way from suite to suite, I run a wistful finger over the quilted lambskin of Mrs. Chao's beautiful handbags, arranged like objets d'art on a lacquered shelf; fastidiously hang Mr. Marriott's admirable selection of designer puffer jackets; and peer suspiciously at the baroness's extensive collection of what appears to be genuine fur, sympathetically patting the head of an *actual* mink forced to exist forever as a ratty-looking scarf.

At lunchtime, sufficiently recovered, I find Samira in the staff lounge, digging into a bowl of leftover noodles that Carlos has set out for our lunch.

"How's it going, babe?" she asks, shaking sriracha sauce over her plate.

I sink opposite her at the table, relieved to be off my feet for a bit, and pile my own bowl high with noodles.

"Good . . . actually. Like, is it weird I enjoy cleaning the cabins?"

Samira wrinkles her nose. "You must have got lucky. I had the posh guys. It was like a *biohazard* in there. Lemme just say you can tell their mum does everything for them at home. *So* gross."

"More like their *staff*," I counter.

She snorts. "*Right?* Y'know, I always thought I'd marry into money, but looking at how these guys live, I'm having second thoughts."

I commiserate, and we spend the rest of our break snorting over Samira's desultory Tinder options.

Once I've loaded the dishwasher, I intend to head back to my cabin before dinner for a power nap to make up for last night's disturbed sleep. But halfway there, I stop, distracted, my thoughts drifting back to Shoshanna's mention of the new carriages. Ever since I woke this morning, there's been this strange itch beneath my skin. A whispered insistence to *see* them, like the sound of a TV turned down low.

Just a quick look, I tell myself. I slip past my cabin, through the sleeper cars and the polite morning hush of the lounges, the honeyed smell of freshly polished wood rich in the air, and on to the very end of the train.

I enter the Orchid Lounge, which until last night was the final carriage of the train. At this time of day, it's completely deserted, the still air smelling sweetly of perfume, the spring sunshine illuminating the floating dust motes. The lid to the piano is open, the keys seeming to smile encouragingly at my presence.

And up ahead, the door that once signaled the very end of the train is now open. It leads into a small antechamber and what must be the newly attached carriages.

Through here, I come face to face with a beautifully carved wooden door. This wood is much darker than the fittings of the *Banebury*, a deep, glossy brown that is almost black. Here, in the space between the carriages, the sound of the train is louder, almost deafening, its swaying more insistent. The door is a work of art, intricately etched with twisting patterns inlaid with gold leaf. At its center is a large brass doorknob. On either side of the door are two slender stained-glass windows in an art deco style, each depicting a single black bloomed flower set into green and yellow glass, both of which are fogged up and impossible to see through.

I knock lightly. After all, I work here; it's my job to check on the passengers. Maybe that assistant Shosh mentioned could do with a cup of tea—that's what I tell myself, anyway.

But there's no reply. There is no sound at all, in fact.

Now that I'm here, outside the carriages, my itch of curiosity should abate. There's no reason for me to stay any longer. But to my surprise, my hand slips over the doorknob.

Then I remember what I thought I saw last night. Those wide golden eyes—the dark figure standing in the corridor outside my room.

Do I really want to go inside? Alone? Curiosity did kill the cat, after all.

What if one of the new passengers—the third one, the masked one—was a total creep who stood outside women's cabins at night? Do I want to encounter them right now? I huff a nervous laugh at myself—I never used to be this anxious—and gently twist the handle.

But the door is firmly locked.

Back in my cabin, reclining in the small armchair, I stare, transfixed, at the window as the green spaces slowly thin out, replaced by gray high-rises and bleak car-park wastelands. Familiar station names soon flash by, ghosts of my past—Reading, Slough, Southall—until the high-rises become glittering skyscrapers, the car parks morph into stately rows of Victorian town houses, and we finally pull into the hubbub of London Victoria Station, our first official stop.

We wave off the Chao family reluctantly, and I find myself

almost in tears as I accept another Chao mini masterpiece: a stick-person Lara surrounded by hearts, flowers woven into my curls.

A little later, as the sun sets and we clatter through the gentle hills of the South Downs on our way to the coast, I change into my evening uniform—black shirt, black skirt, and burgundy scarf—readying myself for dinner service.

I'm early, and I sigh inwardly as I notice that Gwydion is already seated in the dining carriage, staring out the window at the passing fields, lounging in his seat like some elegant crow in loose black pants and crisp blue-striped shirt, the sleeves rolled carelessly up.

"Do you happen to have a wine list?"

His voice is whip-sharp, almost a reprimand. My shoulders sinking, I plaster my smile back on. It already feels worn and tattered.

"Good evening," I reply, tight-lipped. He is thirty minutes early. "Sorry to keep you waiting. Let me check; there should be someone on duty in the bar this time of the evening."

He stares at me, unblinking.

I can't exactly shoo him out of the carriage. Shoshanna has been clear that our level of service here is *yes, sir, of course, sir, anything within the realm of possibility, sir,* and I figure a good reference from her will help score some jobs on my travels back to Wales. Besides, who knows, maybe this entitled prick even tips.

Gwydion runs a hand through his hair with a loud sigh. I hover, sensing he is about to say something else. Somewhat resentfully, I notice that even from this distance, he smells good—some clean, expensive scent like winter pines, fresh and airy.

"Hold on. . . . Look, I want to apologize for what I said this morning. I'm not normally that rude."

"No problem at all," I lie, forcing the robotic smile to remain on my face. "It was my mistake. I shouldn't have spilled your coffee."

He raises his head slightly, chin in hand. "I'd say that was more a natural reaction to my beastliness. And drop the plastic smile. I don't actually need a wine list—any decent red will do. A Malbec, if you have it—and two glasses, please."

A little wrong-footed by this one-eighty in his attitude, I gladly drop the smile and head into the bar in the next carriage, hoping someone will be there to pass his order on to, but the place is deserted. Not wanting to piss him off further, now that we've reached a truce, I try to recall Shoshanna's wine-related instructions to Rhys. Hastily, I grab an ice bucket for the wine and larger glasses for red, as well as a cloth napkin and a bottle opener, and place it all on a silver tray.

Now that we've escaped the city's outer reaches, endless rolling green hills flash by the window already wreathed in twilight. I pause in the bar for a moment, soaking it all in. It is *so* beautiful—so different from the crowded terraced streets I grew up in, where the air permanently reeked of exhaust fumes and rancid cooking oil. According to the latest driver dispatch over the intercom, his voice robotic and stilted, as if he were reading off some script, we've reached the south of

England and are well on our way to Folkestone, and the tunnel through which we'll cross the channel into France and mainland Europe.

Back in the dining carriage, Gwydion is staring thoughtfully at the fleeting landscape. The window is open a crack, and a chill breeze laced with the fresh scent of salt water signals our proximity to the coast. After gently placing the tray on the table before him, I proudly display the bottle to him, label up, as I watched Rhys do the other night.

"Would sir like to try the wine first?"

He looks up at me with a wry grin. "I'm sure it's perfectly adequate. Also, Malbec's not typically served on ice—"

He stops himself, pinching the bridge of his nose and closing his eyes. I am now aware he appears to be experiencing some level of stress. He gestures at the chair opposite.

"God . . . I didn't even ask: Do you drink red?"

I raise both eyebrows in surprise. "Sir, I'm on duty—"

He smiles, and it is unexpectedly heart-stopping, changing his face from haughty and bleak into something sun-dappled and soft and really quite beautiful.

"*Please* stop calling me sir, especially when it's obvious the direct translation is *bastard*. And you're not exactly busy—there's no one in here yet except me. Exempli gratia, your colleague is currently playing *Animal Crossing* in the coffee lounge when she thinks no one's looking."

Awkwardly, I perch on the seat opposite. I may be new to this level of service, but basic common sense tells me I shouldn't be sitting drinking with the guests. Would Shosh's insistence that *nothing* is too much trouble cover this? Feeling trapped, I watch distractedly as Gwydion opens the wine with long, nimble fingers, slicing through the foil in a way I had no idea the bottle opener was capable of and pouring a decent few glugs of red wine into both glasses before pushing one in my direction.

"To fresh starts, *Lara*," he says, his eyes flicking to my name badge as he tips his glass to mine. We clink them together as the sun finally sinks behind the hills, and our reflections solidify in the dark glass of the window. "I'm sorry for being a dick." He nods to the opulent surroundings with distaste. "It's just . . . if I'm honest with you, this isn't a trip I particularly wanted to take. You see, I'm basically here to chaperone my sister, when really I have more pressing things to do. . . . But there was absolutely no need to take my frustrations out on you. I'm genuinely sorry. Forgive me?"

I take the teeniest sip from my glass, not wanting to dismiss his efforts at reconciliation outright, while keeping an eye on the door, ready to leap up if anyone walks in. The wine is strong—almost acrid. A chilled Diet Coke with a slice of lime would have been much more my style—but after the initial throat burn, I kind of enjoy how the warmth of it seems to seep into my bones, blurring my edges.

"Uh, of course," I say uncomfortably. Gwydion has this odd way of looking at me. As if everything I say is a lie and he is curious to find out the truth. "I mean, let's face it, I *do* empty the bins. Someone's got to."

"No, no—my tone was unforgivable. I have a regrettably sharp tongue."

He downs half his glass, and an awkward silence follows.

I am about to reply when the carriage door swooshes open and Rhys enters. I jump up from the table as if I've been electrocuted, nearly knocking over the entire bottle of wine.

"Not interrupting, am I?" he asks with mock innocence, his eyes flitting to the glass before me.

"Not at all," says Gwydion smoothly, his eyes still on me. "The lovely Lara here was just fixing an aperitif for my sister and me."

Rhys trails me into the kitchen as I go to collect the menus.

"*The lovely Lara*, hey?" he teases. "Seriously, though, you probably shouldn't let Shosh catch you drinking with the guests."

I turn to him, my expression pained. "He insisted. Anyway," I say, pouting playfully, "would you disagree?"

After all I put him through, the answer should immediately be *Yes, actually, you're kind of a bitch*. But all he does is shrug and turn to greet Carlos, who has arrived unnoticed and is dramatically sharpening his knives.

My second dinner service is more chaotic than I hoped. Despite the absence of the Chao family, without Shoshanna's clear and militant direction, drinks are mixed incorrectly, dishes are misplaced, and sauces are spilled, thanks to the somewhat violent rocking of the train as we speed through the claustrophobic darkness of the Channel Tunnel.

I'm glad I'm working with Rhys, though. Despite the terse

barking of the baroness and the lazy sarcasm of the skier bros, he remains calm and restrained, apart from the moments when we are alone together in the kitchen and he lets loose a volley of words I didn't even think he knew existed.

I am on my *third* attempt at making Baroness Winterborne's tea when the dining carriage finally begins to clear out. Honestly, I blame Shoshanna's bare-bones teaching. At home, I grab whatever mug currently has the fewest tea stains in it, add hot water to the bag, and then top it all off with a glug of two percent. On the *Banebury*, tea needs to come from actual *foliage* in a fussy porcelain pot.

Back in the dining carriage, the baroness takes a hesitant sip and nods, glowering, as if disappointed that her tea finally tastes acceptable. With her satisfied, I wander into the Dahlia Bar next door. By now, my feet are beginning to ache, and I am distinctly sweaty. Rhys is currently on service in here, busily shaking drinks as the trio of skiers sit around a nearby table, laughing uproariously. He sees me enter and subtly rolls his eyes.

"*God*, a quadruple tequila, please," I murmur, slipping behind the bar to unload the glass washer. "And don't skimp on the tequila."

"Coming right up—if I ever finish the world's most complicated set of cocktails," he mutters back with false gaiety, specs firmly back on as he leafs through a thick tome of drink recipes. "Y'know, I think I started making these about half an hour ago. No lie, one of them involves real gold."

"I'd help if I could," I commiserate.

He grins, elegantly balancing a delicately sculpted twist of lemon on the edge of a cocktail glass. "Impressed?"

"I'd give it a solid seven," I say, glancing darkly down the cocktail menu. Every drink involves eight different types of alcohol and up to five different garnishes. There might only be ten guests remaining on this train, but they all certainly seem intent on getting their money's worth. I asked Shosh earlier when the late shift finished, trying to stifle my yawns, and she gave me a thin smile in return. "The shift *ends* when the last guest decides to go to bed, my love."

Looking at the skiers, who are busily working their way through a full flight of exotic-looking shots, I think we could be in for a very long evening. Still, it's got to be better than the night shift, which Shoshanna is thankfully taking. I think of those stealthy footsteps last night and give an involuntary shiver.

"The baroness is having a final cup of tea, then she's off to bed," I let Rhys know.

"Cool, so just these guys we have to wait up for," he says quietly as he competently rattles a cocktail shaker full of ice. "But I got this, Lara. There are only three of them—no point in both of us staying up—plus you're no use to me anyway. Doubt they're planning on asking for a cappuccino at this time of night."

I eye him warily, wondering whether this is some kind of test. Either that or, deep down, he doesn't want me around. And while I can't exactly blame him for that, I'm surprised by how much the idea hurts.

"Seriously, La. You look like crap—"

"*Wow*," I say with a surprised smirk, whipping him beneath the bar with the dish towel I have permanently attached to the belt loop of my skirt. "Any other charming comments you'd like to make about my appearance?"

He smiles, and the act lights up his face, causing my heart rate to increase dramatically. "Come off it. What I *meant* is, you look tired."

I hesitate, experiencing a sudden moment of weakness. I don't want to leave him without some reassurance that things *will* be normal between us again, that there'll be no more of last night's awkwardness, that we can mend our friendship—but I know we're not there yet.

Before I head to my cabin, I remember I need to clean up the baroness's table in the dining room. Last night she lingered there for hours, as if to cause maximum annoyance for us staff. As I'm clearing the expensive porcelain onto a tray, my phone buzzes violently in my skirt pocket, making me jump. I'm not meant to have it on me—staff scrolling through their phones in front of passengers is *not* the look the *Banebury* is going for—but it's Dad's AA meeting today, and Gran promised to let me know he attended. Distracted, I quickly swipe the message to read it, not noticing until it is too late that the number it has been sent from is unfamiliar.

The words immediately sear into my brain, the impact exactly as if he were *here*, standing behind me in the gloom of the carriage, his words, unmistakably *his* words, whispered softly, sickeningly, into my ear:

—Seems you're still intent on blaming me for something we both know was all your fault. Can't believe I ever wasted my time on a dirty little nobody like you—

I drop the phone immediately, recoiling from it in disgust, leaning over the table as I try to steady my hastened breathing. I *hate* that he still has this effect on me, that he is still *allowed* it after everything he has done. His words stare up at me, accusatory, from the polished wooden floor.

—dirty little nobody—

—all YOUR fault—

Dimly, I realize that someone has entered the carriage behind me.

"La? You okay?"

I curse quietly, repeatedly. Out of everyone on this train, I most want Rhys to believe I'm okay now.

But the simple truth is, I'm not.

Slyly kicking my phone under the table, I pick up the tray full of tea paraphernalia.

"Yeah," I say as breezily as I can, hoping he won't catch the tremor in my voice. "Of course. Why?"

I forget how well he knows me. He doesn't fall for it.

"Wait—you're shaking. Let me grab that for you."

He's not wrong. I might be able to control my voice, but the tea set is chiming a delicate little warning tune in my trembling hands.

"No, I'm not; it's just the train," I mutter as he moves to take the tray. I twist away from him too quickly, catching the edge of it on an adjacent table and causing the entire thing to crash to the floor, the delicate tea set shattering into a million pieces.

For long seconds, there is silence, and I do nothing but stare down at the mess, the tiny fragments of bone-white porcelain like stars against the dark wood, the pieces as scattered as my thoughts.

Shit.

Face heating, I drop to my knees and scoop the shards into a haphazard pile, cursing under my breath as the sharp edges prick my palms, drawing blood.

"Hey." Rhys crouches opposite me, stilling my hand, his voice hushed. The warmth of his fingers is jolting, even though they are light on my skin, turning my hand with a gentleness that leaves me speechless. "Wait a minute—you've cut yourself."

Tears blur my vision, and I curse inwardly again. I don't *want* this. I don't want this gentleness, this pity, and least of all from him. I don't deserve it. Standing, I furiously brush my arm across my face and turn away, busying myself, looking for a dustpan and brush. "It's no problem. I'll clean it up," I say, clearing my throat, my pulse finally steadying now that I am far enough away from him.

"Lara . . . you seem . . . wound a little tight. . . . Did something happen? Do you . . . do you want to talk about anything?"

I begin brushing up the mess and force a brightness I absolutely do not feel into my voice.

"Honestly, Rhys, I'm fine! You know me, clumsy as ever! Um, I think someone's calling you from the bar?"

We both know it's a lie, but, god, *anything* to get him out of here. He hesitates in the doorway for a moment, and I continue brushing the now-cleared floor, knowing he's watching me, praying for him to leave.

And as I toss the broken crockery into the trash and retrieve my phone, it isn't the mishap with the tray I am thinking of, or even Beckett's cruel message. . . . It's the feel of Rhys's fingertips against my skin.

6

The narrow corridor of the sleeper car is silent and deserted; the globe lamps glow warmly, their light not quite reaching the thick shadows that gather in the corners. Outside, the darkened landscape flashes by, and the clatter of the train over the tracks is somehow reassuring. I trail a hand along the polished walnut walls, a jigsaw-like mosaic of light and dark wooden leaves running through the middle. Marquetry, Rhys says it's called.

In the staff carriages, I unlock my cabin door and change into my favorite cotton pajamas, remove my makeup, and apply a thick layer of moisturizer in the vague hope I'll look less rattled tomorrow. Sometimes I forget that Rhys knows the old Lara, not the Lara of now, always hollow-eyed and sleep haunted. I force myself to do the breathing exercises the therapist taught me. And as I slowly count my breaths in and out, as my pulse slackens and my brain quiets, I allow myself to hope. Hope that I'll have time to breathe on this train, in these beautiful surroundings. That I'll be able to fix all the things that have become broken in the last couple of months, including myself.

Before climbing into my narrow bunk, I retrieve my phone from where it sits on the armchair like a coiled snake. Still wary of it, I see there's currently no signal, and I let out a breath of relief. Quickly, I delete the message Beckett sent earlier and block this new number. But his messages are like invasive weeds; there'll be another emerging from the cracks soon enough. I switch off my phone. Tonight, at least, there'll be no further messages; there'll be nothing, nothing at all, and, safe in that knowledge, I gratefully fall asleep.

The dream is always the same.

There's something in that room.

Something he doesn't want me to see.

I slip from his bed, reassured by his soft, regular snoring, the dawn light mostly blocked out by the expensive slatted shutters, and tiptoe down the stairs. I know the house well by now. Know that his parents won't be back until next week. Know that the housekeeper doesn't arrive until eight. Know that the locked door is through the kitchen, past the utility room, with its constantly humming dryers and washing machines, and across a small, open courtyard with a marble bench flanked by spherical topiaries. Know that the key hangs from a hook to the left of the door.

I bend down and peer through the keyhole.

It's too dark to see. So I take the key and place it in the lock. The sky above me darkens as I turn the key and becomes filled with a sharp shrieking that rends my eardrums. Feathers drift to the ground all around me, tawny brown and tipped with red. And, from down the corridor, footsteps echo sharply.

"I took a chance and trusted you, and look what happened."

I have been caught.

Gasping, I sit bolt upright, bathed in a sticky sheen of sweat, the chill from the cracked-open window immediately making me shiver. For a moment, I consider tapping on the wall between Rhys's cabin and mine. Could he be awake, too? After everything that happened, is he plagued by nightmares as I am? But I hear nothing but silence from the other side of the wall.

Gathering myself, I slip out of my bunk and pull on some sweats. Maybe some hot milk will help. Or, if Samira's still on duty, she mentioned she had a stockpile of antihistamines, which, she assures me, make you drowsy.

Yawning, I quietly crack open the door to my cabin. In the narrow corridor, the lights are dimmed. Tiptoeing through the door and past the passenger suites, I press the button that opens the door to the dining carriage.

The door is caught. It tries to open, opens a little, but something stops it, catches it, causing a low mechanical clicking. Heavy drapes are pulled across on the other side, preventing me from seeing into the carriage. Frowning, I press the button again and again in frustration. Before long, I figure out that something is tangled at the bottom of the door. I crouch, thinking it must be the drapes, but am surprised to see it's some kind of stringy plant matter. I gently pull until whatever it is gives, then hold it up to the light.

It's ivy. The twining stems are yellow and new, the leaves delicate and barely formed.

I don't think much of it. Vases of fresh flowers are dotted here and there about the train. It's probably just errant foliage that got caught on someone's clothes and has been brushed off here.

I press the door button again, and this time it swishes cleanly open.

Pushing aside the heavy drape, I enter the dining carriage. As expected, it's deserted. The only illumination comes from the soft emergency lights sunk subtly into the floor. The only sounds the click of the train over the rails and the gentle chattering of the crockery stacked in the kitchen.

Something in here is different, though.

The tables are all where they should be, still and white-clothed like squat little ghosts. The plumply upholstered chairs pushed neatly beneath them. The polished walnut counter bears nothing but a stack of the morning's breakfast menus and several empty baskets waiting to be laden with fresh croissants and pains au chocolat. The purple carpet—

That's what's different. There is another thin strand of ivy trailing all the way down the center of the carriage.

Bemused, I bend, gently pulling it up as I travel through the room. It comes up stickily, like Velcro, the stems coated with thousands of tiny hairs that cling possessively to the woolen strands of the carpet. It creeps onward into the Dahlia Bar, snaking around the milky marble countertop and through to the Cedar Lounge, where I start to feel like Theseus in the labyrinth, unravelling his ball of string. Too curious to stop now, I follow the ivy all the way to the end of the train, right through to the austere glamour of the piano lounge.

The ivy leads to the new carriages, winding its way beneath the closed door.

I remember what Shosh said this morning in our meeting about Gwen and her *organic matter*. So these carriages contain plants?

I step into the alcove, thrust up the window in the exterior door of the antechamber, and throw out the sticky ball of weeds, shivering as the freezing air rushes in, shrinking back at the sharp rattle of steel over steel.

As I pull down the window and wipe my hands on my sweater, I notice a glowing band of light beneath the door of the new carriage. Is someone *in* there? Are they awake, too? Is this where Gwen and Gwydion are staying? Perhaps I should ask them about this rogue ivy? The warm orange light beckons me temptingly.

Instinctively, I grasp the handle and give it a gentle twist.

This time, the door opens.

It's like stepping into another world. Lucy through the wardrobe into Narnia. Alice through the looking glass. I assumed this was the siblings' private suite and expected to see leather couches, gold fittings, polished wood—another variation on the *Banebury*'s sumptuous lounges. Or, recalling Shosh's talk of organic matter, some clinical science lab, all white surfaces and stainless steel. But instead, I am standing in the middle of a dark, living crystal. The night sky crowds in through the vast windowpanes that make up the walls and ceiling of this carriage; constellations wink overhead like fairy lights. And the air is heavily perfumed: midnight jasmine, starlit rosebuds. And everywhere I look, every available inch of space is adorned with flowers.

I release an admiring breath. It is *beautiful*.

The floor beneath me is made of square stone tiles, and around the perimeter of the carriage runs a decorative gray stone planter, in which a myriad of species proudly bloom. It's like being in the middle of some fancy Victorian greenhouse like Kew Gardens. In the center of the carriage is an intricately patterned circular rug, upon which stands a round card table flanked by two moss-green armchairs. The golden legs of the table are carved to look like a bird's, knobbly and slender, with cruel-looking claws. Torch-style sconces are dotted about the carriage, welded to its curved wooden frame; their bases twisted glass stems, their bulbs glowing orange buds.

Feeling ever more like Alice, I drift around the carriage, heady with the scent of blooms, blissfully breathing it all in. Delicate wooden signs inlaid with mother-of-pearl helpfully spell out the names of the plants. Some I recognize, thanks to the many hours I've spent helping Granddad in the garden. There are rosebushes in glorious shades of autumnal orange and candy-floss pink; plush, football-sized heads of hydrangea in hazy watercolor shades of lilac and fuchsia; cheerful, bold chrysanthemums in mouthwatering peach and mango; a snowy lily, its petals like purest silk beneath my fingers.

Any vague hope that peeking in here would scratch the itch in my brain, quell the insistent voice in my head, or sate my curiosity is immediately squashed. There's no question of not continuing into the next carriage. There's a pressing need within me to see what's there—to see if it can possibly hold more beauty than this one. But before I turn the handle, I remember that our new guests may be within.

Again I knock quietly, politely, and again I am greeted with silence.

Stepping through, it becomes obvious that this is a different world altogether—darker and cooler. The structure of the carriage is the same as that of the one before, the same vast expanses of glass, but here the moonlight is obscured by spreading branches. In each corner are vast Grecian urns bearing trees heavily laden with pink and white blossoms, their branches spiderwebbing across the ceiling and strung with delicate paper lanterns, giving the carriage a feel of dark enchantment. Palm fronds splay themselves flat against the window, and fruiting bushes and flowering shrubs line the fringes of the carriage; I recognize the soft whisper of lavender and woody rasp of rosemary. A chaise longue takes up space before one of the less-obscured windows.

It is *quiet* in here. The only thing I can hear is the gentle rustling of the leaves overhead, stirring in some unknown breeze. I continue moving along the carriage, petals drifting down upon me like gentle snow.

At the very end of the room, two trees bend toward each other—willows, I think, from their drooping foliage—their branches interlacing like affectionate fingertips, creating a natural arch. The area beyond is darker than the rest of the carriage. I hesitate before entering, listening intently. The sound I initially thought was stirring leaves takes on a sibilance that makes me think more of whispering. Is there someone there, beyond the arch, watching me? Come to think of it, didn't I feel that odd sensation the moment I entered this carriage? Beyond the glass, clouds scud over the moon, and the room grows darker still.

It *does* sound like whispering.

"Hello?" I call tentatively, knowing I shouldn't be in here and hoping I am alone.

I pull my phone out of my pocket and switch on the flashlight, hoping to brighten the area beyond the arch. The branches create a private space behind them, which appears to be used as a reading nook or study. One side is crammed with shelves and leather-bound books, while on the other side squats a well-worn studded-leather armchair. Where the door to a further carriage might have been is instead a handsomely carved panel of polished wood.

I step closer.

This—this panel—is where the whispering appears to emanate from. I trace the carvings with my fingertips. At head height is a large circle composed of interlinked symbols:

Celtic knots. It's a common enough sight in Wales, printed on all the usual tourist knickknacks—key rings, bracelets, and the like. Within the circle is carved a pair of broad, open wings, done in a similar style, some feathers falling loose, and in the middle is a face—an owl, I think, with deep-seated golden eyes and a cruel, hooked beak.

I am reminded of the vision outside my cabin door last night.

—meadowsweet and broom and blossom of oak and—

I shake my head sharply. The whispering is soft and hypnotic, almost somnolent.

It's just a radio or a TV left on, I think.

Is this the end of the carriage? Or could there be something beyond the panel? Another carriage, perhaps? I didn't see exactly how many were attached the other night. The windows are too crammed with branches for me to be able to look out and see farther down the train, and anyway, it's too dark. I look in vain for any sign of a handle or keyhole on the panel, but there's nothing.

As I turn to leave, clicking off the flashlight, I notice the time and blink. An hour has passed since I stepped into these carriages.

Impossible . . . isn't it?

I yawn enormously. It feels as if the pollen I breathed in in the first carriage has some kind of sedative effect.

Impossible or not, I should be in bed, not creeping around our guests' private carriages. Yawning once more, I go back to my cabin.

My alarm has been going off for nearly forty minutes before I fully wake. My head feels heavy and thick, as if I'm recovering from some horrendous flu.

"Shit . . . *shit*," I utter under my breath, realizing I'm late for breakfast service.

After fumbling wildly to shut off my alarm, I half fall out of my bunk and pull open the drapes. Outside, the world is bright and clear, the morning sun glinting off the wide, flat expanses of frosted fields that flash past. A smile breaks across my face. I haven't traveled out of the UK since I was a kid—since Mum—and now here I am, in France.

There's no time to shower, so I quickly wash up, dress, shove my curls into a claw clip, and hurry out of my cabin. As I enter the dining carriage, Rhys, balancing a tray of tea in one hand and a rack of toast in the other, casts an annoyed glance in my direction. I scan the room, offering my sunniest smile to the passengers already settled in for breakfast.

The three skiers ignore me, carrying on some overly loud conversation about where the best slopes can be found, but I catch the eye of Gwydion.

He half raises his hand.

"Good morning!" I say, a little breathless, surreptitiously tucking in my shirt.

"I'm wondering what a person has to do to get a coffee around here?" he says, his eyes fixed on mine. "Your colleague seems a little . . . overwhelmed."

I raise my eyebrows in slight surprise but keep the sweet smile on my face.

"My sincerest apologies," I reply, hoping he doesn't complain, leaving me to explain to a displeased Shoshanna that I overslept. "He's . . . uh, new. Needs a little more training. Let me get that for you right away."

Rhys follows me into the kitchen.

"Where have you *been* for the past hour?" he hisses.

I give him an apologetic wince. "God, I am *so* sorry. I set my alarm . . . but I must have slept through it. . . . I just couldn't sleep last night and spent most of it wandering through the train. . . . I even checked out the new carriages, by the way."

He gives me a strange look. "I'm not sure sleepwalking through private parts of the train at night is strictly professional, but okay. And anyway, what do you mean, you checked them out? I thought you said they were locked?"

"They *were*. But they weren't last night. It's the coolest thing, Rhys. The carriages—they're full of *flowers*. . . . And—and the carriages are all made of *glass*, kind of like a conservatory or . . . or a mobile greenhouse."

He turns to me with a frown.

"The hell? *Plants?* Like a *greenhouse*? On a train? Are you sure you weren't dreaming? I thought Shosh said they were carrying scientific samples or something."

"Organic matter . . . so yeah, *plants*. And of course I'm sure. They're beautiful . . . stunning. You have *got* to check them out later. I bet they look even more impressive in the daylight! They must be for some event . . . like a flower show or—"

But Rhys is still looking at me like I'm suffering the effects of some hallucinogenic drug. "But *flowers* . . . really? I mean, it's barely even spring—"

"You'll see" is all I say.

After breakfast service is over, we obediently traipse into the staff room again for our now-familiar mid-morning meeting. I nod at Shosh's brisk greeting, secretly enjoying the routine of it all. Shosh gives us a generous smile as we settle down before dishing out the usual reminders about how to fold in the ends of a loo roll and how often we need to replace towels.

"Right, you've all managed to survive to day three, so now for a little bit of good news. As you already know, we'll be making a stop around four p.m. this afternoon in the medieval town of Domme to let the Marriotts off on their honeymoon . . . *and* thanks to your wonderful boss, the stop will coincide with a delivery of supplies to the train." She pauses, taking in our confused expressions. "What *that* means is you guys will have a couple of free hours in a beautiful walled city while Carlos and I unload and do a stock check."

Beside me, Samira pats my wrist excitedly as her eyes light up, and my own heart lightens, too. A few hours when I'm not meeting our guests' apparently endless needs or falling asleep on my feet sounds like bliss. It also crosses my mind that it will be the perfect opportunity to have a proper chat with Rhys.

"Use the time to soak up the sights, make all your phone calls, buy some tacky souvenirs . . . whatever you want. Strictly *no* alcohol, though, and timing is *key*. You'll have two hours, and two hours only. We won't be holding up the train for anyone, so make sure you're back *early*."

With that, Shosh calls the meeting to a close, and we emerge out of the carriage in a bubble of excitement.

Outside the train, the February morning is cloudy and still. Barren fields flash endlessly past the window, interspersed occasionally with quiet yellow-stone villages.

Lunch is a slightly less hectic affair than breakfast, despite its being just Rhys and I on service again. However, this time it's his turn to slip up, spilling Gwen's ice water over Gwydion's lap, thanks to a particularly violent lurch of the train; sharp words float into the kitchen, where I'm busily squeezing oranges. I like the Marriotts a great deal, but their insistence on fresh OJ every day is *testing* me.

"What a dick!" sings Rhys as he returns to the privacy of the kitchen bearing a handful of wet napkins.

I snort. "Which *one*?"

By now, the siblings are the only two left in the dining carriage, idling over glasses of water, and I, for one, have no desire to deal with them again. I cast Rhys a wicked look.

"What . . . ?" he says cautiously. "I know that look. It's dangerous."

I smile, then nod in the direction of our guests, their plates pushed away, both of them staring morosely out of the window. "They're done, right?"

He looks momentarily confused, and then it dawns on him.

"I think so. . . . But I'm not sure if we can just leave them. What if Shosh sees—"

"She's on her break—she was on the late shift last night. Besides, we'll be quick. And it's worth seeing, I promise. It's *gorgeous* in there."

After checking in with the siblings a final time—technically, lunch service finished twenty minutes ago anyway—we hustle down through the lounges in the direction of the newly attached carriages. Once we are away from any guests, I impulsively grab Rhys's arm in my excitement.

"Wait, Lara—wait a second. . . . Should we really be doing this?" asks Rhys, tugging the sleeve of his fusty jacket away from me and slowing down. "Shosh said there was no need for us to be in there."

A little wounded at his casual dismissal of my hand, I stop and turn to look at him, incredulous. "Listen to yourself—*Are we allowed in there?* Where's your sense of *adventure*, Rhys?"

Technically, I'm pretty sure we're *not* allowed back there, given that the carriages are usually locked, but this little act of defiance seems fun, like something the old Lara would do. I think Rhys senses that, too, as with only mild protestation he follows me down to the final carriages. He pauses before the door, giving a shake of his head.

"So weird . . . to think this was the end of the train just the other day."

I whirl around, wide-eyed, glad he finally appreciates my find.

"*Right?* And just wait until you see inside."

I grasp the handle and twist it, just as I did last night, but to my annoyance, the door is locked again.

"Ugh, *annoying*. It was definitely unlocked last night." I give the door handle another sharp tug, but it doesn't budge. "Anyway, inside ... the carriages are like a mini garden center or ... a decorative greenhouse ... or something. Honestly, it's stunning. There are even *trees*, for God's sake! I mean, *trees*? On a train? Can you *imagine*?"

Rhys nods. "Maybe it's some kind of traveling exhibition? They're probably on their way to the Estonian equivalent of the Chelsea Flower Show. Weird time of the year for it, though."

He's not wrong. This is the time of year Granddad begins planting seeds in his greenhouse, not harvesting vast amounts of flowers. Still, I suppose if the carriages are carefully climate-controlled, anything's possible.

Fleeting movement through one of the small windows on either side of the door catches my eye.

"Wait a sec—there's someone *in* there," I say, pushing my face against the window. Rhys mirrors me on the opposite side.

It's the person I saw on the station platform the other night, still wearing their dark beekeeper suit. I forgot all about them until now. They must be the assistant Shosh mentioned, but why are they still wearing that outfit? A cold chill creeps down my neck. Could there be something *dangerous* in those carriages? Some reason Shosh was so insistent that we avoid them? Like some special plant that requires special staff with special equipment. Why else would they be wearing protective clothing? Had I inadvertently put myself in some kind of danger last night, snooping around where I shouldn't have?

Beside me, Rhys staggers back, a look of shock stark upon his face.

"What?" I whisper urgently, backing away. "What is it? Did they see you? ?"

He blinks, running a hand briefly down his face, then attempts a reassuring smile. "No . . . no, it's nothing. They, uh, just surprised me, that's all."

I do *not* believe him. There has to have been something else. I know him well enough to know when he's lying.

"Why are they wearing a suit like that?" I push. "Rhys—do you reckon there could be something dangerous in there?"

Rhys is already ambling away, waving a hand in dismissal. "I *highly* doubt it—they'd have to warn us if there was, make us sign a waiver or whatever, or put up signs. Whoever it is probably has allergies or extreme hay fever. Look, I'm gonna chill in my cabin for a bit—you owe me one after this morning, remember?"

With a final wary look at the locked door, Rhys retreats down the train.

"Catch you later, La."

7

Remembering that I still need to clear up after lunch, I hurry back to the dining carriage. Now that we've crossed into mainland Europe, there's a fizz of anticipation in the air, like that first moment you step off a plane in a new country. As I pass through the train, I chat briefly with the Marriotts, enjoying a final coffee in the Azalea library, and check on the baroness and Rebecca, playing an intense-looking game of cards in the Cedar Lounge.

I expect the dining carriage to be empty, but to my mild annoyance, Gwydion still sits where we left him, writing notes in a book with an ostentatious gold fountain pen.

"What are you writing?" I muse as I clear the plates from his table. Whatever it is, it is clearly not for my eyes, as he immediately snaps the book shut at the sound of my voice.

"Oh, nothing important," he murmurs, for once avoiding eye contact, the slight pink flush to his pale skin making me wonder if it's some gloriously filthy fan fiction.

Gwydion downs the dregs of his cup, then rubs the back of his hand across his mouth. I glance at the title of the book, an ancient-looking thing bound in leather: *De Venenis Mysteriis*. A picture of a plant is etched on the cover, very on-brand for these two.

"What is with all the flowers?" I ask, momentarily forgetting I shouldn't have been in those weird carriages in my desperation to fill the silence. "You came on with them the other night, right?"

He looks at me curiously for a moment, then nods. "Flowers? You've seen inside the carriages?"

"Uh, only through the window," I clarify quickly. "Wasn't sure if the room needed a quick spruce, you know?"

It's scary how easy it is for me to lie these days.

He nods as if satisfied. "My sister, Gwen, is a scientist—a brilliant one. She's transporting them . . . for research purposes."

"Really? What's she researching?" I ask casually, hoping he's not about to say something like *deadly spores*.

Gwydion dabs delicately at his mouth with a napkin before replying. "Accelerated growth."

"Oh . . . that's interesting," I say mildly, thinking of the stray ivy last night. Makes sense, I guess.

Gwydion looks over my head at the scenery beyond. "Mmm. Gwen thinks if the cause can be isolated, then it might be beneficial to developing countries. Places where there's often drought or flooding, or where crops have failed."

I nod along, a little bored now. I've always had a hard time with science.

"And you have to chaperone her because . . . ?"

"She suffers from intense anxiety," he says, lowering his voice. "It's a wonder she leaves the house at all. Taking a trip of this magnitude alone would be . . . far too much for her."

"Well, it's kind of you to support her like that," I say, softening toward him a little.

He hides a sly smile beneath his hand like a magic trick. "Hmm. I suppose you could say that."

"And the other person you got on with?" I neglect to mention the bee suit; I don't need someone else laughing at me. "Your assistant. Do they need anything? I noticed they didn't come to breakfast. I could make them a tray?"

For a moment, his gaze sharpens, then he waves a hand in casual dismissal.

"Oh, no. They won't be needing anything."

Sensing this conversation is a dead end, I change the subject.

"What are you guys up to in Tallinn, then?"

He shrugs, cocky composure back in place. "Gwen will have her plants delivered to the lab, and while she works, I'll probably find a decent hotel to hole up in and spend the weekend indulging in mountains of coke and expensive strippers."

I give Gwydion a searching look, unsure if he's joking, only to find he's smirking. It is an intensely attractive smirk; there's no denying it. Nor is there any denying that he himself is intensely attractive, all sharp angles and intense eye contact.

"Kidding. I'll probably take in the sights. Catch up on some reading. Find myself wishing I had some company." He pauses, giving me a meaningful glance. Was he *flirting* with me? "What about you? Are you staying with the train?"

I snort. "No. That's when they pick up the *proper* passengers and the fully qualified staff." I realize I have vaguely insulted him. "Oh . . . sorry, I didn't mean—"

He smiles again. "No, please, it's fine. It was difficult enough to find a train willing to travel with all Gwen's . . . baggage. We had to have those carriages custom-made, you know."

After seeing inside them, I can well believe it.

"How will you be getting home?" he asks, prompting me.

"I'm planning on backpacking—kind of taking an extended holiday. Need some time to escape . . . regroup, that kind of thing."

He nods slowly as if he understands. "Sorry to hear that. Here—stay still a second."

He leans over the small table that separates us and plucks something out of my hair, holding it in the palm of his hand and examining it.

It is a heart-shaped white petal, a beautiful cherry-blush pink at its tip. My face turns the same color, and his eyes meet mine, glittering with realization. He *knows*. I curse the fact I didn't have the time to shower this morning.

"What is it they say about curiosity and cats again?" he murmurs.

"I—I *work* here," I stutter defensively. "The door was open, and I wondered if . . . if it needed cleaning. I was only in there a few seconds."

He sits back, the petal in the palm of his hand. Beneath the table, his leg brushes mine.

"Gwen doesn't like people touching her plants, Laura. I'd be more careful if I were you."

Deliberately, I touch my name badge, annoyed that he's already forgotten my name. As if he's summoned her, Gwen looms up behind him like some chic demon in her tight black jeans and oversized blazer, gold bangles chiming on her slim wrists. Immediately Gwydion snaps his outstretched hand shut.

Walking into the staff corridor to wash up after lunch, I jump as Rhys flings his cabin door open.

He winces as he catches sight of me. "Sorry. Hey, are you done with your shift?"

I wave away his concern. "Yeah, why?"

He gives me a crooked grin, a slight twinkle in his eye. "You and Gwydion seemed to be getting on well back there."

I flush slightly. "Um, it's part of our job to make the guests feel comfortable. Maybe you forgot that."

"Yeah, he certainly looked comfortable in your company."

"Jealousy's not a good look, Rhys."

Interestingly, his cheeks pink at this, but he flashes me a smile. "Eh, he's not really my type. Seriously, though, have you got a minute?"

I follow him into his cabin, leaving the door politely ajar, and perch on the chair opposite his bunk. Rhys has, of course, already unpacked all his stuff; a photo of his picture-perfect family, goofy-looking Labrador and all, is tacked beside his bunk; a neat pile of popular science books sits on the small table below the window, along with a bottle of water. Typical Rhys, as organized as ever. I think of my room, with the tangled vines of bras and chargers snaking untidily across the floor.

Rhys exhales, his mouth a tight line. I know that face. There's something on his mind.

"So, what's up?"

He gives me his wounded look. The look that says he's unsure whether to trust me or not. "I'm . . . I'm feeling a bit unsettled, I guess."

Honestly, I'm surprised at this admission of vulnerability. Rhys is the type of person who's guarded to a fault, forever acting as if nothing ruffles his laid-back exterior. I glance again at the photo. He's always been close to his family. Maybe he's missing them more than he lets on.

"Go on," I press gently. "What d'you mean?"

He sighs. "It's going to sound weird, but I feel like . . . the atmosphere on the train has changed or something. Since the other night."

"*Changed?* Changed how?"

He looks away. "I don't know, exactly. In fact, I'm probably imagining it. But it's like everything's gotten more tense. Like everyone's . . . on edge."

Is he talking about me? Admittedly, I *am* on edge, but that has little to do with being on this train and a lot to do with my history with the person standing in front of me. But I've been pretty pleased with the atmosphere on the train so far—it's a lot less stuffy and pretentious than I feared.

Rhys continues, carefully studying his hands: "Those carriages—the ones you saw attached the other night. When you were in there, did you notice anything . . . strange?"

I pause before saying no. Remembering that odd silence in the second of the carriages, the way time passed like fast-running water, and that persistent whispering sound.

Just the leaves stirring, La. You were half asleep.

"No, not really," I say carefully. "Okay, I wasn't exactly expecting them to be full of *plants*, but other than that, there was nothing out of the ordinary. Why?" I ask, but truly I'm not sure I want to know; everything has gone pretty smoothly up until now.

Rhys is quiet for a moment or two, then shoots a glance at me, his expression both curious and reluctant. "That person we saw in there earlier—the beekeeper/hazmat guy, whoever they were. Did you . . . did you see what they were doing when we looked through the window?"

I frown. "Well, yeah—looked to me like they were watering the flowers. Is that somehow a big deal?"

Rhys leans forward, his dark green eyes boring into mine. "*Yes*, but did you see what was coming out of the watering can? Did you see what they were watering them *with*?"

I stare at him, bewildered and half smiling. "Er . . . water?"

He gives a brief shake of his head. "*No*. And, La, I know how wild this sounds, but honestly, from what *I* saw . . . it looked—it looked an awful lot like they were watering them with *blood*."

* * *

We continue to stare at each other for a good few moments, my mind spooling back to an hour earlier. Yes, I saw someone watering the plants, and yes, they were wearing that weird black beekeeper suit, but they held a basic tin watering can, and I'm pretty sure I would have noticed if they were spraying blood about the place.

I laugh, more in surprise than amusement. "*Blood?* You're kidding, right?"

He stares at me warily for a few more seconds, then shakes his head, collapsing back onto the bunk and kicking off his shoes, his hands behind his head.

"You're right. I don't doubt what I saw, but whatever it was, I guess it wasn't blood."

I recall the spidery old plant shed in my granddad's garden—and the weird, unpleasant-smelling tubs he kept on its shelves: odd-smelling cardboard boxes labeled BONE-MEAL, or FISH, BLOOD, AND BONE.

"Exactly," I say. "Probably added some fertilizer or plant food to the water that gave it a weird color. Let's face it, you don't exactly come across a garden center on a train very often. They must need a lot of upkeep." I pause. "You really okay, Rhys? Is that all that's up?"

He yawns. "Just tired, I think. Still settling into the routine, getting used to the new normal."

I take a deep breath. "It's . . . it's just that it feels kind of awkward between us right now . . . that's all."

Those words were never going to span the gulf between us.

"Well, it's bound to be, isn't it?" he concedes easily, staring up at the top bunk. "At first, anyway. It's been ages since we've talked."

I shift uncomfortably in the armchair.

What I actually want is for him to yell at me. *Blame* me. Tell me he hates my guts, and with good reason. I want him to tell me he's disgusted by me. *Embarrassed* by me. But he won't. Whatever he truly feels is tightly sealed within him, secure within a stone sarcophagus, and I'm not going to be privy to it. And there's so much I want to say to him, *need* to say to him, but there's a dam within me holding back this tidal wave of words, and every time I try to open the floodgates, there's only ever silence or this, a few awkward platitudes that trickle uselessly into the dusty canyon between us. There's only ever his face, pale and bloodied in the flashing blue lights. There's only ever a hushed museum corridor, my back pressed against the wall. There's only ever myself, humbled, in a hospital waiting room.

And so even here, alone, in the close quarters of his cabin, the distance between us stretches on.

FEBRUARY, LAST YEAR

After our first meeting in the school library, my social life improved with indecent haste, and I was beckoned into the warm embrace of Rhys's group of friends, becoming the fifth member they never knew they were missing. There was Casey, a willowy blonde with a truly surreal sense of humor, forever insisting there was nothing her collection of healing crystals could not fix; Stevie, the brash hockey obsessive and provider of legendary baked goods, who could start drama with a lamppost; and Aiden, D&D dungeon master extraordinaire, with a caustic wit and immaculate style. And, of course, Rhys, reliable and clever, the patient heart of our little group.

"Personally, I was never averse to befriending you. . . . I just thought you were a little stuck-up," Stevie once confided through a mouthful of scone.

We were all seated around a table in Rhys's mum's café, the Cozy Cuppa, drinking hot chocolate—something that had developed into a blissful after-school routine.

"Oh my god, Stevie, you know you don't have to say every little thing that comes into your head aloud, right?" scolded Casey, flicking her straw at her.

"What? It's a compliment." Stevie turned to me apologetically, her large brown eyes beseeching. "You just have this, like, confident air about you that maybe comes across as . . . as superior to people who don't know you. That's all it is."

"Uh, what she means is, you have pretty privilege," Aiden interrupted matter-of-factly.

I rolled my eyes. "Guys, come on. I wasn't acting stuck-up; I was *terrified*. I was new here, had zero friends, and every time I tried to even make eye contact with anyone, I got told to fuck off back to London."

"Except by Rhys," Casey pointed out with a sly smile.

"Aw, Rhys, your mum must be so proud of you," Stevie teased.

He only smirked. "Oh, she is."

It would be fair to say I had a slight crush on Rhys by then. Not only did he have remarkably pretty green eyes, but beneath his endless supply of plaid shirts, I suspected he was hiding the strong but lean figure of a dedicated rugby player. It was much more than that, though. He was intimidatingly smart but never arrogant about it. There was a kindness, a steady maturity about him, that I was drawn to. The clear counterpoint to all my chaos. Sometimes when we were studying, I had this irresistible urge to reach up and twist my fingers through his dark curls—

"Huh?" I said, realizing that I had drifted into a daydream and was quite possibly staring.

"I said, are you guys going to Cecily Hunterson's birthday party?" Stevie repeated. "From what I hear, she's invited the entire class." She gave me a wicked grin and affectionately threw an arm over my shoulder. "I mean, she even invited Lara."

"No, but she's the *worst*," Aiden moaned. "Imagine having all that money and absolutely zero style. It's almost like some kind of fairy-tale curse. For starters, have you seen her house? You can't miss it. It's the giant McMansion with plaster pillars, fake Italian cypress, and stone lions on either side of the drive. It's so embarrassing."

"Have you seen her mum?" Stevie snorted. "Always decked out head to toe in fake designer labels."

"Um, I don't think they're fake, Stevie," said Casey.

"Yeah, me either," Rhys agreed. He looked at me. "Basically, Cecily's dad's the town real estate magnate and likes to act as if he runs this whole area. And I mean, to be fair, he probably does."

"Y'know, Cecily's not so bad," Casey chipped in. "I had to partner with her in chem once. A little superficial, sure, but it's her brother I'm always hearing about . . . ," she added darkly.

"No, but he is *gorgeous*, though," said Aiden wistfully. "He could treat me as badly as he wanted."

"Please, Aiden, have some standards," Stevie groaned.

"Well, whatever, I'm definitely going," said Casey. "I'm always down for a party. Lara, you're coming, too, right? You can get ready at mine."

Thanks to my gran's interminable stockpile of terrible soaps and my dad's heroic nightly beer consumption, I was always up for a reason to leave my house in the evenings. "You bet I am."

"And, Rhys?" asked Stevie. "I know how hard it is to drag you away from your tricked-out PC."

Rhys considered for a moment. "Sure, why not? I don't think I've got anything else going on that night."

A secret fizz of excitement sparked in me at his words, like my blood had been replaced by sherbet. Rhys was a difficult guy to get a read on at the best of times, often diverting any stabs at flirtatiousness I inserted into our tutoring sessions with a wry, world-weary smile, but I was starting to hope there might be something between us all the same. Something that was growing fast as summer ivy during those late-night, coffee-fueled chats as I precisely, carefully pried away the hard pieces of his carapace.

I was thinking of one Friday afternoon a couple of weeks ago in particular, when, unusually, it was just Rhys and I after school. Casey was out sick with the flu, and Stevie had an extra hockey practice that afternoon. I was still expecting Aiden to show, though, and was surprised when Rhys turned up alone, outside the gates, pink-cheeked and bright-eyed, like me, his coat powdered with a fine dusting of snow.

"Man, it's freezing today," he exclaimed, rubbing his gloved hands together. "I'm dying for a hot chocolate."

"Do you still want to go?" I asked, feeling nervous. At that point, I was less sure that Rhys felt the same way I did. Our intimate conversations, rather than heightening, had started to flatline lately as Rhys stressed about fitting in his tutoring with exam sessions. I didn't want him to feel awkward or that I'd somehow tricked him into a date.

"Um, yeah," he said, side-eyeing me with surprise. "Why wouldn't I?"

Rhys's mum's café was without doubt one of my favorite places. As usual, we had sequestered the slightly tatty pair of leather couches next to an overstuffed bookcase, two steaming mugs of hot chocolate on the low table before us.

"How are you feeling about the mock exams?" asked Rhys once he'd wiped the steam off his glasses. I sighed inwardly. It was admirable that he was so focused on his future, but I wished we could change the record every now and then, especially on the rare occasions we were alone.

"Utterly ambivalent. Okay, my turn. Rhys, if you could be anything, what would you be?"

He thought about this for approximately two seconds before replying, "Happy."

I rolled my eyes. "Oh my god, so lame."

"Okay, fair, but also true. How about you?"

I tried to take a seductive sip of my hot chocolate but only succeeded in gaining a chocolate-powder mustache.

"Happy's surely just a given. Who actively wants to be unhappy?" I paused, discreetly wiping my mouth. "What I really want is to be that woman on the BBC who gets paid thousands to dress up in period costumes and speculate about Henry VIII's wives."

He chuckled. "Okay, fine. If I could be anything, I'd be the new David Attenborough—but with better fits."

That made me cackle until my sides hurt, and so I excused myself to head to the bathroom. When I returned, satisfied with both my reflection and my investment in expensive lip oil, I made the choice to sit beside him rather than opposite. A bold move, but as hot fox Robin Hood once said, faint heart never won fair lady. While he looked surprised, to my relief, he didn't edge away or say anything. The sensation of my thigh firmly against his made me feel like I was about to spontaneously combust. Surely there was no way he wasn't feeling this, too? Could chemistry truly be so one-sided? I considered asking him; I mean, it was a science-based question, so he was bound to know the answer.

But I was played out at this point. If I went any further, chanced anything else, it would feel too weird and forced. We finished our drinks, and I quickly forgot about his proximity, instead losing myself in our conversation. I was sorry to leave, but the sky was darkening outside the window, and Gran had made me promise not to walk home alone at night.

"I could walk with you—or lend you my bike," said Rhys, looking at the sky sympathetically. "You gotta promise to look after my wheels, though. I don't lend them to just anyone."

"I'm good. Let me get the drinks, though," I said, pulling some change out of my pocket.

"No, I've got it," said Rhys. His hand closed firmly over mine for only a few seconds, but in those moments, my veins were pure gunpowder, and his touch sparked it off. As I walked home, I replayed those few seconds over and over again, a dreamy grin on my face, my mind racing through scenarios where he hadn't just cleared his throat and instantly removed his hand. . . .

But at the party . . . everything could change.

"So, Casey told me you guys broke up?"

I flinch, startled back into the present and assailed by a sudden flicker of memories, a vicious highlight reel of darkness. I am grateful, at least, that Rhys avoids saying his name.

A locked door. A wall crowded with photos. A dress I

don't belong in. A bright arc of sprayed blood. The festive glitter of party streamers. Flashing blue lights.

You may go anywhere within my house except this one room—

I push a hand through my hair and chew my lip.

—all YOUR fault—

"Yeah, we did. You *know* we did. Months ago—"

Rhys's turn to look awkward. "After the party?"

"Yes, after the party. *Immediately* after."

"Huh. I—I mean, *we*—kind of expected you to get in touch sooner. . . . You know—"

A sudden knock at the half-closed door makes us both jump. I stand immediately, remembering that this was meant to be a quick chat and that I'm still on shift. Honestly, I'm desperately glad of the interruption.

One of the skiers stands in the doorway, a fixed grin on his face. The blond one, Theodore Montague, with the golden tan and curling hair that give him a laid-back surfer appeal until he opens his mouth and those cut-glass vowels tumble out.

"Ahh, *so* sorry to disturb you guys in the middle of what looks like super important business, but I was wondering if we might get some, uh . . ." He gives a short roll of his eyes, his smile hardening. *"Service?"*

I stare back at him for a moment, itching to mention the fact that they have paid a pittance to be here and aren't exactly *entitled* to silver service. Then I remember how much I need each and every tip and return his smile glassily.

"Apologies! We had a, uh, minor emergency. Please, let me follow you out."

Looking disparagingly behind me, the skier gives me a nod and retreats down the corridor. Turning to pull a face at Rhys, I follow him. Besides, there's plenty of time for us to have *that* conversation later.

8

The rest of the afternoon passes quickly in a flurry of cabin cleaning. Again, I find myself enjoying restoring order to chaos, the repetitive nature of the work leaving me able to blissfully sink into my podcast and think of nothing else. Just after three, as scheduled, the train slows, then stops, and we regretfully wave off the Marriotts. The late-winter sun makes a special appearance at the newlyweds' arrival in a fairy-tale French town surrounded by high castle walls, and I'm sure I'm not the only one who's unspeakably jealous that they get to spend the next few weeks basking in the beautiful scenery of southern France, cycling down cobbled lanes and eating crusty bread topped with fancy pâté.

"Can't wait to hit you with one hundred and seventy facts you never knew about medieval France," I say to Rhys, hoping to chase away the awkwardness of earlier, once the couple have disappeared into their taxi. "*And* expensive Mr. Marriott told me this place has one of the best crepe stands in the whole of the country."

Rhys looks at me, surprised. "Oh . . . Sorry, La. I offered to stay behind and give Shosh a hand with the deliveries. I thought you and Samira would be off souvenir shopping or whatever. But you can bore me once you get back if you want."

My buoyant heart deflates with disappointment. Since the moment Shosh told us we'd have these precious hours off, I've been carefully planning what I'll say to Rhys once we're alone, all the ways I might make things easier between us. I don't know why I'm surprised, though. I try to tell myself it's not personal, that it's nothing to do with me, that he's *always* been chivalrous to a fault, but honestly, I don't know the truth of it, and either way, the rejection still stings.

By the time I collect myself and climb off the train, Samira has already disappeared into the crowds in a cloud of expensive perfume, talking animatedly to someone on FaceTime, and I'm left standing alone in the shadows of the station. I consider walking down the platform to take a closer look at the unusual carriages the Llewellyn siblings came with, but a quick glance in that direction tells me they're conveniently shrouded in a deep-set tunnel at the end of the station.

"Want some company?"

I whirl around to see Gwydion sloping elegantly down from the train. I blink, his presence catching me off guard—though not as much as his offer does. *Do* I want his company? I'm both flattered and nervous. There is a world-weary elegance to Gwydion that leaves me tongue-tied. Besides, is it professional to spend time alone with guests like this? If Shosh finds out, will I get in trouble? I think again of his casual cruelty that first time we met, and he seems to read this on my face.

"*Come on*. . . . Give me one hour to prove to you I'm not what you think I am," he implores, his face unguarded. "That's all I ask."

Technically, I'm off the clock, and I can't see how it would hurt. Besides, what else am I going to do? Go back to the train and mope in my cage of a cabin, or awkwardly wander the cobblestone streets a few paces behind him?

Against my better judgment, I smile. "Yeah? And what is it I think you are?"

He gives a noncommittal shrug. "After yesterday, an insufferable knob, probably."

This makes me laugh. "All right, then."

To my secret delight, Gwydion proves to be as informed a travel partner as Rhys would have been, our animated chatter bringing the cobbled streets and high walls to life with tales of crusades and a war that lasted a hundred years.

He's not at all as I expected him to be. As we chat, he becomes less unapproachable by the minute. It turns out he's closer to my age than I thought, only a year older at nineteen, and the fact that he's also an enthusiastic history obsessive *definitely* works in his favor.

Before long, we discover the crepe stand and take a seat at

a wrought-iron table in a picturesque town square. The wind is brisk, but the sun on my skin is warm with the promise of spring. I take a surreptitious glance at my watch. We only have half an hour left. Gwydion might be able to afford a private helicopter to catch up with the train, but if I'm late, I'll be stranded here.

"What's Gwen up to?" I ask.

"Probably sitting in her cabin, spinning a web, who knows." He rubs a hand over his face, and our eyes meet. I'm surprised at the change I see in him. His easy, laconic arrogance has vanished, and instead, his elegant features are solemn and pale.

"Oh? Are you guys not getting along or something?"

He gives a bitter laugh. "You might say that." He inhales lengthily. "It's difficult. . . . You see, I *want* to support her . . . but as I told you, I'm not exactly thrilled to be here, traipsing across Europe playing chaperone, but I *am* here all the same. And honestly, I wouldn't usually mind, but it's just . . . something's different about her lately. In fact, she's been different ever since she got the research grant from this lab."

I finish my milkshake with a rumble of bubbles and regard him seriously. "Different, how?"

Admittedly, I'm curious to learn more about Gwen. Yes, I'm intimidated by her cold beauty, her icy countenance, and the wealth she flaunts, but I'm in awe of her, too. So young but so poised, and a gifted scientist on top of all that. She also possesses the air of someone who genuinely does not give a shit what anyone else thinks of her.

Gwydion is silent for a few moments before answering, searching for the right words. "It's just . . . lately, she's been incredibly *secretive*. She's always been the quiet, studious type, but we used to share everything. Our hopes, our dreams, our secrets. . . . But these days, we barely talk at all. If she isn't whispering to her bloody plants, then she's got her face glued to her laptop, emailing the lab back and forth. I was hoping this trip might bring us together a bit, that it might be like old times between us, but now, I don't know. . . ."

Putting down his fork, he gives such a long, shuddery sigh I almost reach for his hand in consolation.

"We've probably just grown apart, you know . . . ? Can't be helped. She's always been the successful one, the hardworking, *tenacious* one. The one everyone's interested in. My parents' shining star, leaving me in shadow."

I think of Rhys, more interested in unpacking stock than spending time with me, even in this fairy tale of a location, and sort of understand how Gwydion feels.

"Still," he says, flicking those pale-blue eyes to mine, his mouth curled into a hopeful smile, "this trip isn't turning out to be a total waste of time."

It's *such* a line, and really, I should groan and kick him under the table, but there's something so sincere, so vulnerable, in his gaze that I don't.

"I get it, you know," I say quietly. "The whole growing-apart thing."

"Your friend Rhys," he says perceptively. I wince inwardly. Is it *that* obvious to everyone? "An ex, maybe?"

I shake my head. "No, an old friend. And honestly, I'm not even sure we're that anymore."

It's only when I say it aloud that I realize how true it is. Tears blur my vision, and I blink them back furiously.

"Let's change the subject," he says softly, *kindly*. "So, you say you're on a gap year? That's got to be fun. What else do you have planned?"

"Well, it's an enforced one, really," I admit. "I'd planned to go straight to university; I'm not the kind of person who has the money to just up and travel the world for a year. But last year was a difficult one for me, and long story short, I, uh . . . I ended up failing a couple of my exams. I'm re-sitting them in May, and then . . . hopefully I'll be off to uni to study history in the fall."

My voice trails off. Even though I've come to recognize it's not wholly my fault, there's always shame in admitting failure. He places a hand over mine for a brief moment. "Well, judging by our conversation earlier, you're clearly a natural, Lara. I'm sure you'll ace them this time."

We finish up and walk back to the train, people-watching and chatting comfortably. By now, the sun is sinking behind the city walls and the temperature has dropped considerably. I shiver in my thin jacket, and Gwydion pauses to take off his coat and drape it over my shoulders. It's made of a rich, expensive-feeling wool and smells as divine as he does.

As we climb back on board, we pass Rhys, who's busy arranging a fresh display of flowers in the corridor. I pause as Gwydion and I go our separate ways, thanking him and handing back his coat. Once he has disappeared into his cabin, Rhys raises an eyebrow. "Have a good time?"

He doesn't sound as if he's being facetious. Why would he be? He clearly doesn't care what I do.

I smile before replying, "Yeah, actually. I guess I did."

Shoshanna is overseeing dinner this evening; apparently, one of the guests has complained about yesterday's service, so under her careful scrutiny, Samira and I busy ourselves polishing glasses and shining cutlery. I glance about the dining car, wondering who the snitch is and somehow knowing it is Gwen.

Samira narrows her eyes and gives me a wicked grin. "Okay, hear me out—he is *stunning*, right?"

I hesitate for a second. Who is she talking about? Surely she doesn't mean Rhys?

"Gwydion. The guy with the spooky sister."

Oh. Gwydion.

I shrug. "If you like snarky posh boys . . . I guess."

She grins. "Posh? Bitch, he's from *Wales*."

I decide not to mention our earlier excursion. After all, it didn't mean anything; he was probably still trying to assuage his guilt, that's all.

"I dunno, the guy has a sharp tongue," I warn. "By the way, have you seen what they've come on with?" I ask. "Those carriages full of flowers?"

Samira wrinkles her nose. "*Flowers?* I thought they were

scientists. Damn, I have the worst hay fever. That's an immediate left swipe."

I give her a consolatory pat on the back. I like Samira a lot. There's a sharpness to her, an edge of rebellion, that appeals to me. Anticipating the rush, we lean against the counter, admiring our work.

A table of three is laid, ready for the skiers; Gwydion and his sister are already seated at their usual spot; and another table is set for the baroness and her niece. I find myself looking forward to seeing everyone together. It'll be nice to have some convivial atmosphere in here this evening. I already miss the cheery chatter of the Chao family and the loud joking of the Marriotts. With so few passengers aboard, the train has taken on a melancholy air of abandonment.

As if somehow knowing we are talking about him, Gwydion catches my eye in that playfully confident manner that seems designed to make me blush. I make my way over and take his order.

"And for you, Ms. Llewellyn?" I ask warily, wondering whether Gwydion told her I have illegally gazed upon her precious plants.

But as usual, she barely looks up from her laptop long enough to say, "Just water for now."

I pass their order to the chef and then head over to where the baroness and Rebecca have just been seated, tinny rock music emanating from Rebecca's headphones as usual.

"What can I get you both to drink?" I smile.

My heart sinks when the baroness yet again orders tea.

* * *

Hiding a yawn beneath my hand, I mentally urge the skiers to hurry up and retreat next door, where Samira patiently awaits them at the bar, so I can begin clearing up. Leaning against the counter, polishing glasses, I watch the three of them in the dark reflection of the window. Cass is flicking through her phone while the other two talk and bray with laughter. I've never met two guys with so many tedious travel stories. I appreciate that it might be my jealousy talking, but *still*.

Finally, after a long and borderline-offensive anecdote about the time he singlehandedly rescued eighteen donkeys from being mistreated by locals at a tourist trap, surfer dude Theo departs, leaving his dark-haired friend, *Xave*, and his sister alone. I'm about to head over and collect Theo's glass, but interestingly, the moment he leaves, the atmosphere in the room seems to increase several notches in intensity. Clearing my throat to indicate that I'm not listening, I turn back and begin to noisily stack menus as Xavier lowers his voice.

"Look, we've got to tell him sooner or later, Cass," he says. "And I'm pretty sure he won't mind. . . . To be honest, part of me thinks he already *knows*. Besides, he of all people can hardly talk about its being *inappropriate*. He made enough comments about my sister last time we were all together down at Soho Farmhouse—"

Cass sighs. "It'll get too complicated, Xave. If you don't mind, I'd much rather just put it all down to a . . . a drunken mistake."

Xavier gives a small gasp—pain or surprise. Probably both. There's no denying it: Cass is gorgeous.

"*Mistake?* You can't be serious, Cass?"

Even I have to feel sorry for Xavier; he looks like a kicked dog. But Cass only nods, looking anywhere but at him.

"Yeah, I'm sorry. . . . I—thought about it—a lot—and I don't feel the same, Xave. I just don't. So, like I said . . . it was a mistake. . . . I'm sorry."

Seconds tick by, and I rise, feeling for Cass and wondering how to help break the awkward silence. Xavier begins to rummage in his designer backpack and, from it, like a sideshow entertainer, whisks out an enormous bunch of fresh purple flowers. My eyes widen. There is only one place *they* could have come from.

"For *you*," he says, dropping them onto the table, an unappealingly sulky edge to his voice. I wait for him to leave, predictably thrusting his chair violently beneath the table like a spoiled toddler, then wander over to Cass, giving her a sympathetic smile. "Hey. Everything okay?"

"Guys, right?" She sighs, looking at the discarded flowers with distaste.

"Oh, believe me, I *know*," I agree.

She traces a finger over the hooded blooms, their vivid-purple petals already wilting and falling away to reveal an ugly mass of stamens beneath.

"I mean . . . they're not your stereotypical roses, at least?" I say.

She exhales resignedly. "It's Xavier all over. . . . He only ever likes the pretty parts of things."

"Want me to clear those away?"

She smiles up at me as if shaken from a dream. "*Please.* . . . Ugh, I think I'm going to lie down in my room for a bit."

I clear the table of crockery and glassware, then distractedly gather up the unusual-looking bouquet, the blooms a brilliant shade of deep violet and oddly bulbous.

"Aconitum," says a whisper of a voice from behind me.

I jump, clutching my chest. Behind me stands Gwen, her dark eyes huge behind her gold-rimmed glasses, her black hair hanging silkily down her shoulders.

"Oh! You scared me—"

"Also known as monkshood—for obvious, aesthetic reasons—devil's bane, and, my personal favorite, Queen of Poisons. They look unusually *fresh*. Where did you find them?"

More of an accusation than a question. Something about the odd way she's staring at me—unblinking, her eyes filled with a secretive light—is highly disconcerting, and for some reason, I decide it is imperative she doesn't think *I* have stolen them.

Gwen doesn't like people touching her flowers.

"Um, the skiers," I mutter. "Not exactly sure what the situation is there . . . looked a tad awkward, if you ask me, but I guess Xavier must have brought them with him. Part of some grand romantic gesture—failed, unfortunately."

I'm aware that I'm babbling, but Gwen nods, gently taking the bunch from me. I notice she's wearing plastic gloves, the type you see staff wear in hospitals.

"As for me, I've never understood the appeal of cut flowers," she says thoughtfully. "Why would you want something so beautiful to be *dead*? Cut down in its prime. Think about it.... If you did that to a *person*... just because you thought they looked appealing... decorative... *pretty*... well, you'd be considered a monster, right?"

I'm about to answer, but Gwen is already halfway across the carriage. "I'd wash your hands well," she calls out before she exits the room. "If you haven't already guessed from its many names, *Aconitum* is *extremely* poisonous."

LATE FEBRUARY, LAST YEAR

Well, turns out I'd been right and wrong about the party. After Cecily's Gatsby-themed birthday extravaganza, everything did change ... just not in a good way. Instead of my night ending in some kind of Cinderella fantasy, all my hopes regarding Rhys and me had turned out to be utterly unfounded. That night, he'd told me, not in so many words—and kindly, because it was Rhys we were talking about—that he wasn't into me, leaving me feeling embarrassed, confused, and monumentally friend-zoned.

Then, one bleak afternoon, a couple of weeks after the party—when the hills behind the school were wreathed in freezing mist and younger kids skidded all over the icy pavement like penguins—was the day it happened.

Back then, the five of us often walked home together

when we could, splitting up a mile down the road at the park to go our separate ways. Rhys and I would usually continue on, since his house was only a couple of streets over from mine, but lately he'd been staying later at school, helping with after-school tutoring, so I was on my own. And after everything that had gone down at the party, I couldn't say I was sorry about it.

My attention was directed intently at the pavement as I tried to avoid deadly patches of compacted snow, when a car slowed down beside me. Despite the early hour, it was already growing dark, and instinctively I increased my pace, recalling the stories Dad used to tell me about predatory cars creeping down empty streets, but a familiar voice called my name, and I stopped dead.

"Lara? I thought it was you. Want a lift home?"

Immediately I was flustered, trying to recall his name. He knew mine, after all, as clearly as I knew his face: his confident, easy grin, the casual way he pushed that wayward blond hair from his brow.

Beckett. I'd met him for the first time the night of Cecily's party—her gorgeous, golden older brother.

I was upset after the party. I supposed I'd read too much into things—I always did have an overactive imagination—and had inadvertently gotten hurt. Stevie left with me; it was already midnight. And as we stood in the taxi queue, me still sobbing dramatically, Stevie's arm around my shoulders, I noticed Beckett reclining against the wall outside, chatting on the phone. He caught my eye and grinned, cutting off his call and sending a billion butterflies loose in my stomach.

"Whoever they are, they are not worth it," he said in his clipped, smooth voice. He shook his head at the long line. "C'mon, I'll give you both a lift home."

Stevie nodded at the bottle of beer in his other hand. "Nah, we're good, mate. We'll get a cab, thanks."

He moved away from the wall and approached us, his eyes still firmly locked on mine. "I insist. I've only had the one—and not even finished it. Besides, I promised Ces I'll happily play taxi for her friends."

Thanks to Dad, I was very familiar with the signs of drunkenness when I saw them, and he didn't seem drunk to me—his eyes clear and focused, his speech lucid—so he took us home, driving at twenty miles per hour at Stevie's stern insistence but dropping her off first, even though she lived farther away. She gave me a warning look, mouthing *Call me* when she got out, but she needn't have worried. Beckett was the perfect gentleman, making pleasant small talk and throwing in some dad jokes, all to take my mind off my tears, before dropping me right outside my door and watching me go in.

I'd waited for him to ask me out then, but he didn't. And I remember being surprised by how disappointed I was. And now here he was again, only days later, peering at me from the open window of a sleek Mercedes.

"It's no bother. I'm going your way anyway."

Despite everything, I didn't jump in his car immediately.

Something made me hesitate—perhaps the odd convenience of this meeting. But those thoughts quickly drifted away with the Arctic winds. Since we'd met before, Beckett was hardly a stranger anymore. Besides that, the icy streets were treacherous. It would be weird to refuse.

"Sure."

"You looked a little like Red Riding Hood out there," said Beckett, grinning, as I slipped into the passenger seat. "In that coat."

Truthfully, I hated my coat. A slightly too-small, red woolen duffel. But he made it sound exotic, like I'd been conjured from a fairy tale.

I watched his large hands easily glide the car down narrow streets, cool and collected, utterly unlike my dad when he had to drive in this weather and his language made my ears bleed.

Before I got out of the car, he asked for my number. I gave it to him, half of me thinking that surely he was just being polite, the other half fervently hoping he wasn't.

A couple of days later, he invited me over to his house. The disappointment of the silent few days preceding his message resolved into an explosion of happiness, and I eagerly replied within minutes, forgetting the rules, forgetting the necessity of playing it cool. Rhys and I had a tutoring session planned for that evening, but lately these get-togethers had lessened in both frequency and intimacy, more focused on quadratic equations than banter, at his gentle insistence. And sure enough, Rhys's message came through mere seconds after I canceled: A smiley face. A friendly "Sure!" No sign of disappointment, no questions about why or what I might be doing instead. But this time, my own disappointment was brief.

My horizons were widening.

9

A loud flapping of wings wakes me.

Slowly I gather it isn't wings at all—that must have been a remnant from my dreams—but an irritating tapping directly against the wall of my bunk. Wiping my eyes, I sit up and check the time on my phone.

It's three a.m.

The tapping persists, directly next to my head.

"*Rhys?* What—what the *hell*? What's up?"

I hear a vaguely agitated mumbling from his cabin, and my phone buzzes angrily seconds later.

Open the vent

Climbing down, still swaddled by my blanket, I switch on the cabin light and squint at the dividing wall between our cabins. Beside the foot of the bottom bunk, I see what he's talking about: a rectangular golden vent with a catch. I slide it open.

"*Rhys,*" I hiss, rubbing my eyes as they adjust to the light. "This had *better* be good. You know I'm on early shift again tomorrow."

"My door's locked."

For someone on the other side of a thin wall, his voice sounds weirdly far away.

"*What?*"

"I said my cabin door's locked—I can't get out. Check yours. Can *you* get out?"

"Why would I *want* to? It's the dead of night," I huff, pulling the blanket tighter around me. Despite the deceptive hint of spring in the air earlier, it's freezing tonight.

"Says the person who spent the previous night on a midnight tour of the train. Can you check? Please. . . . For me."

Rhys needs to do something about his anxiety. Irritated, I twist the inside lock and tug on the doorknob.

It remains closed.

"Okay . . . ," I say, twisting the lock back and forth, rattling the handle, and pulling harder.

It doesn't budge.

"Okay . . . that's weird."

I hunker down and squint through the peephole. The corridor is thankfully deserted.

I hurry back to the sanctuary of my bunk and burrow down into the covers, seeking any residual warmth.

"Rhys, er, what the actual fuck? Why are we locked in?"

There's a long pause before Rhys finally answers. "I don't know. . . . I didn't exactly scrutinize the job description. . . . Maybe it's protocol?"

I stifle a yawn. "We can check with Shosh tomorrow. Where were you off to anyway at this time of night? Late-night booty call?"

His voice sounds farther away than ever: "I was going to meet Gwen."

My eyes widen to saucers in the darkness of the room. *Gwen?* Gwydion's creepy sister, who's barely uttered a word since she got on the train? I try to hide the surprise in my voice. "Wow, good going, Rhys."

I hear a drawn-out sigh.

"Don't be ridiculous; I barely know her. She wanted to talk to me about something."

"At *three a.m.*?"

"She said . . . she said it was important."

I give a derisive snort. "Rhys, does that not sound incredibly weird to you? If she wants to talk to you, why can't she just call you, text you, or better yet, talk to you in daylight hours like a normal person? Why does she want you creeping about in the middle of the night? Like, is she under a curse? Does she only speak past midnight or something?"

There's a long silence before Rhys speaks, his voice now thick with sleep.

"Yeah . . . I guess you've got a point. . . . Anyway, no, I don't have her number."

"Rookie mistake, Rhys—rookie mistake."

And lying back on my narrow bed, I shut my eyes once more but leave the vent open, listening to the sound of Rhys's soft and even breathing.

FEBRUARY, LAST YEAR

After that second ride home, the relationship between Beckett and me progressed quickly. Texts turned into calls, calls turned into long walks talking about anything and everything, setting the world to rights. I was surprised by how often Beckett agreed with me, how charming he was, how complimentary. Being with him made me feel I was standing on a pedestal.

And while Aiden might have sneered at it, to me, Beckett's house—or, more accurately, mansion—was a marvel. The windows gleamed in the golden light of the setting sun, their brightness hurting my eyes. Stepping through the huge entrance for the first time was akin to being swallowed by a mirror ball, pristine and sparkling, my reflection staring back at me from every surface.

We were going to the cinema tonight—our very first date after several weeks of more casual hangouts at his house, watching movies or Netflix. Some flashy, over-the-top thriller, nothing I'd usually be interested in if I'm honest, but I'd made sure to dress up in my favorite jeans and DMs, a slinky black camisole top beneath my favorite cashmere cardigan, soft and tattered, the color of moss.

Beckett ushered me in, and I gazed at myself in the foyer's enormous gold-framed mirror: my unruly blond curls straightened within an inch of their life to a sleek river that hung obediently down my back, my brown eyes made catlike with a flick of eyeliner, the way he'd said suited me. He stood behind me, equally pretty, as if hewn from gold and marble, but his expression was stern, like a reproachful member of club security.

"Babe, you look beautiful—you always do—but . . . you're not really planning on going out in that, are you? No offense, but it's a little . . . uh, cheap-looking."

My mouth tightened. Heat flushed my cheeks, and my eyes darted away from my reflection, ashamed. Why hadn't I thought more carefully about what to wear? About what he would like? Having no idea what to say, I followed Beckett silently into an expansive, open-plan kitchen, perching awkwardly on a tall suede stool before an immense marble island, gray streaked with silver. I felt like a tacky vase in an expensive department store. A mirror across from me betrayed a different, more honest reflection. I was paler there—anxious. My eyes ringed with too much liner, my hastily applied concealer unpleasantly chalky.

"You know," Beckett said, "owning the biggest agency in town, Dad could pretty much choose any property he wanted, but I think he's done a good job on this place, right? The old Hunterson magic, as he calls it."

Sometimes I found Beckett's hero worship of his father—a loud, red-faced man I'd only seen shouting into his phone—a little cringe. In this town, he might have been a big-deal estate agent, but in London he'd be nothing but small change. I'd never tell Beckett this, of course.

I knew he was waiting for me to speak my approval of the place into existence, wanted to watch it spill out from my lips like honeyed milk, so I didn't disappoint. I trailed soft fingers over cold marble surfaces; I marveled at the intricate wallpaper—silver trees etched onto a midnight-blue sky, each bearing golden pears—and pulled something else from my database of compliments, something about the ridiculous amount of glass in the chandelier above me or the giddying height of the ceiling it hung from. It was a little wearying, this feeling that I needed to keep feeding him this or else he might tire of me.

But thankfully he seemed satisfied as he spoke to some complicated AI system, filling the room with slow, seductive R&B.

"Here. I've got something for you. It was going to be a present, but it actually might work for tonight. Something a little more . . . appropriate, you know."

Moments later, he passed me a stiff paper bag, a satisfied smile on his face, confident he'd fixed everything. I recognized the department store it was from—an expensive one, so expensive I was afraid to accept it. Worried it would tie me into some Faustian bargain. And perhaps it did, in a way.

I murmured my thanks. When I emerged from the bathroom, he led me back to the mirror, slipping my cardigan from my shoulders.

"Ready? You don't need this old thing; ruins the look."

Beneath it, I wore the dress he'd given me: high-necked and black and closely fitted. It was designer and something I'd never have chosen for myself. As I was changing, I'd felt wrong in it, too different. Like I was cosplaying someone older and glamorous. But in the mirror, in his eyes, he reassured me I was worthy.

"Yes, that's much better," he said, tucking a strand of my hair behind my ear, his eyes sparkling with approval. "Now you look perfect."

Wishing there was a way to forget all this, to rewind the past, erase the darkness, the memories that always seep back when the night is quiet, I finally fall into a fitful sleep.

My alarm shrills beside me, slicing my dreams into ribbons. Head unpleasantly heavy, I sit up and yawn, hurriedly switching off the relentlessly cheerful tune while my brain catches up with my body. I have the breakfast shift again, and when I twist the latch to leave my cabin, the door opens smoothly. Curious, I check the other side to see if there is any kind of outer bolt that might have kept us in last night, but there's nothing. It must have been someone with a key. Strange.

When I get to the dining carriage, it's still in utter darkness. Chef is supposed to start his shift an hour before me to prep, but I've already noted that he works to his own schedule. I switch on the lights, then pull open the thick damask drapes, tying them back with their heavy cords. It's been a disappointing start to spring so far, and it's raining this morning; the windows are fogged and spattered with mirror-like droplets, rendering the fleeting fields a mossy blur. Turning back to the carriage, I see that vases of cloudlike white flowers have been placed on all the tables, giving the room a delicate, greenish perfume.

I lay the tables absently, thinking over what Rhys said last night about our being locked in, all the while carefully making sure the *Banebury*'s logo, stamped onto all the crockery, is precisely at twelve o'clock and ensuring that the cutlery is free of smears. Minutes later, Carlos mumbles a grumpy "Morning" to me, looking as bleary-eyed as ever, then bustles off into his gray cell of a kitchen.

Once everything is ready, I make myself and Carlos a coffee. At present, I'm finding I need at least three to get me through the morning—it takes considerable energy to uphold this cheerful façade. Just inside the kitchen, where the hot drinks are made, someone has placed a large stone planter of trailing greenery, filling the space with their fragrance. They must have come from the greenhouse carriages—a gift from Gwen and Gwydion, maybe, presumably not poisonous.

Coffee made, I slip out of the carriage and down to the staff room. As I wait for the morning meeting to start, I pull my phone from my pocket, doom-scrolling social media as per my usual routine. Since we arrived in France, my service has been patchy, some unfamiliar French communications company's name now appearing in the signal area.

"The breakfast carriage is looking great—you're a quick learner, Lara."

Shosh enters the carriage, all business as usual, clipboard in hand. I bask in her praise as the others file in behind her.

"Any other stops today?" asks Samira hopefully. "I mean, since we're in France and all, I'm thinking maybe Cannes, Saint-Tropez, Biarritz..."

"Not a chance," says Shosh with a grin. "However, we *have* got something slightly different going on this evening. The Llewellyn siblings want to hold a fundraiser tonight. Not sure how many funds they're hoping to raise with a grand total of five other passengers on board, which is probably why they're insisting we all attend, too—"

"Yes, night off!" shouts Samira.

"Not *exactly*. Someone's still got to serve the food and drinks and clear up, and that someone is you guys. But if you want to donate, I'm sure they'll be grateful."

"Donate to what exactly?" asks Rhys.

Shosh shrugs. "Uh, plant science... research... I think. I'm sure they'll explain later. So, girls, you're both on dinner service tonight, and, Rhys, you'll serve drinks. Any other business before we get on?"

Samira sneezes dramatically, then raises her hand. "Yeah, who keeps putting those bloody flowers everywhere?"

Shosh shakes her head. "On a high-class train like this, guests expect fresh bouquets, I'm afraid. It's part of the aesthetic."

As Samira leaves, I hang back, glancing at Rhys, hoping he realizes what I'm about to ask.

"Hey, Shosh.... Last night Rhys and I were locked in our cabins. Is that... um, is that normal? Seems a bit dangerous. What if there was a fire or something?"

She frowns at me, evidently confused. *"Locked in?"* she says dubiously. "What do you mean by that—surely you've been locking your door from the inside at night? I mean, I know we're among friends here, but you can never be too careful."

I nod along nervously. "Yeah, of course, but the thing is, when we tried unlocking the doors during the night, neither of them would budge."

"In the middle of the night, you say?" She pauses, looking at me, then at Rhys, narrowing her eyes, and I blush, realizing what is coming next. *"Guys.* . . . I shouldn't need to tell you this, but there's not to be any . . . funny business happening on this train, not while we have guests present. You can save all that up for when we—"

"That's *not* what was happening," Rhys mutters quickly, staring fixedly at the ground and no doubt wishing it would swallow him whole.

"No?" says Shoshanna, looking entirely unconvinced. "Well, good. Let's keep it that way, hmm? Look, I'll have Carlos check your locks after he's prepped for dinner. They probably just need oiling. Right, now if that's all, let's get started."

Somewhat mortified, I make my way back to the dining carriage. Loud voices float down the corridor ahead of me.

Fabulous. The skiers. Do they ever sleep?

Theo is leading the way, bleating on about how he became besties with a llama while on a backpacking trip to South

America, about eighty decibels too loudly for this hour of the morning, while his companions dutifully nod along.

"Good morning, guys!" I greet them brightly. Xavier, apparently still sore about yesterday's events, frowns thunderously at me while Theo continues his story—although louder—obviously annoyed that I interrupted him. Cass gives a weary shake of her head in his direction and mutters, "Good morning."

Out of sight in the kitchen, I down my coffee as they settle, wondering if Theo will ever stop talking about "always eating where the locals do" long enough to let me take their order when Gwydion and Gwen enter the carriage from the opposite direction.

"Hey, is it possible we could get some service here?" calls Theo as I emerge. "Or do we all need to wait for you to finish your coffee first?"

"Theo, for *God's* sake," says Cass sternly.

I consider telling him I was waiting for him to finish his endless monologue but decide to go with "My sincere apologies. What may I get you?"

As I begin taking their order, Xavier emits a loud hacking cough into a tissue. I jump, recoiling a little. We're all a little too close for comfort for anyone to get sick.

"Apologies," he mutters. "Not feeling the best this morning. Just a cold, I think."

I pass their breakfast order to the chef, who takes one look at it and mumbles colorful expletives under his breath, then head over to Gwydion and Gwen.

"Good morning," says Gwydion with a pleasant smile. "And how is the lovely Lara this morning?"

Today he has a formal white shirt on beneath a cozy-looking forest-green sweater and dark-brown cords, giving him the vibe of a hot hobbit.

I glance curiously at Gwen and wonder what she had to say to Rhys that could only be communicated in the darkness and silence of three a.m., which inadvertently led him to discover we were locked in. Or were we? Maybe it was just rusty hinges, like Shosh said.

The door opened fine this morning, though. . . . I shake my head, pushing the intrusive thoughts aside.

After taking their order—black coffee for Gwen, eggs Benedict for Gwydion—I head over to the baroness and Becca, who have just taken a seat. I feel weirdly deflated today for the first time since boarding—probably due to the weather, which is definitely not what I was hoping for. Behind me, Xavier gives another impressively loud cough, causing the baroness to mutter something darkly under her breath.

The carriage seems muted this morning, like someone has turned the brightness down. I ponder what Rhys said yesterday about the atmosphere changing. But to me it's pretty apparent the downturn in joviality is because we've said goodbye to six of our guests.

Once the passengers are finished with breakfast, I'm beginning to clear away plates when Gwydion stands, pretentiously tapping his crystal juice glass with a butter-smeared knife. The murmur of conversation immediately stops, and we all turn to look at him.

"Good morning, everyone," he begins with all the relaxed ease of a breakfast show presenter. "My sister, Gwen, and I would like to invite you all to a little gathering this evening—in the Orchid Lounge, starting around six."

As he says "everyone," he looks directly at me—fat chance of *that*. I'll be in and out of the kitchen all night.

"Gwen and I are launching a charity called Abundance. We aim to help improve crop production in developing countries. All donations to our cause shall be gratefully received."

There's a momentary, confused silence, and then the baroness speaks.

"Well. Hear! Hear! I like the idea of a little soiree, and especially one in aid of a good cause."

Beside him, Gwen is oddly stiff, staring fixedly down at the table before her. Her obvious awkwardness endears her to me. Maybe I've judged her too harshly, taken Gwydion's words too literally. Siblings fall out all the time, and there's every chance she's just *shy* or reserved, not cold or stuck-up. I remember how everyone at school immediately judged me based solely on my previous geographical location, and I debate whether to make more of an effort to get to know her.

Rhys appears behind me in the kitchen doorway, absently tucking in his shirt. I nod subtly in the direction of the skiers and lower my voice: "Um, I'd keep my distance if I were you. One of them sounds like he has the plague."

As if on cue, Xavier releases another volley of hacking,

phlegmy-sounding coughs. There's an odd smell coming from the direction of their table, too. Slimy, almost like compost. It could be that the table decorations need changing. I make a mental note to mention it to Shosh.

Remembering myself, I do another round of the carriage to see if the guests need anything else. After a chorus of murmured noes, I turn, then nearly jump out of my skin. Gwen is standing immediately behind me, blocking my exit. Close up, she looks unwell. Her skin dull, her eyes ringed with large circles.

"Oh, hey . . . there. Can . . . Can I get you something?"

She shakes her head and looks past me.

"I was hoping to speak to *you*, actually," she says quietly, looking over my shoulder to Rhys. I raise my eyebrows, a little offended.

"Okey dokey, then," I say quietly, leaving them to it.

Back in the kitchen, I bang the coffee machine around with unnecessary violence, causing Carlos to reel off something aggressively in Spanish. I don't know why I'm so bothered about their little exchange.

Samira enters the kitchen behind me, sniffing juicily. I turn and see that her eyes are red and leaky.

"Oh my god, what's wrong?" I ask, immediately concerned. "Are you okay?"

She smirks. "Some bastard decided to turn their cabin into a garden; *that's* what's wrong."

She chucks a tissue into the bin, then scoops up the pile of dirty linen that's waiting for her to launder. "Don't worry;

I've taken an antihistamine. I'll be fine in a few minutes. Can't get away from this shit since the Addams twins boarded. Seriously, take a look at what's growing in Wednesday's cabin next time you're in there. It's *revolting*."

After the skiers leave the dining carriage, I go to clear their table. Among the detritus of breadcrumbs and eggshells, I notice that Xavier has also left the tissues he was busily coughing into all morning, lying discarded on the table.

"Ugh. How *delightful*."

Wrinkling my nose, I pick them up, glad of the silicone gloves I've been provided with. As I do, their contents spill out onto the polished table. I start, dropping them hurriedly and clasping my clean hand to my mouth. It's not as disgusting as I feared, but much more *unexpected*. Clumps of delicate, moist white petals laced with pink, a blood-red dot at their center, spill out from the tissues and onto the table.

10

The crackle of old-time jazz seeps beneath the walnut door of the Orchid Lounge: a piano skittering freely, accompanied by the deep, hollow bellowing of a sax. Instead of excitement, though, I feel uneasy. The sweetly perfumed air, the clink of crystal glasses, the low lighting—it all takes me back to the places I went with *him* where I simply did not belong.

I adjust my black pencil skirt, which clings to my hips more tightly than I'd like. Jesus, I cannot wait to get off this train and slip into something comfortable.

Inside the piano lounge, the old-fashioned glass lamps cast golden shadows and the passengers chat quietly, sipping champagne from elegant crystal coupes. Despite the shortage of guests, the carriage seems oddly full tonight. The skiers are laughing away at a table, hands of cards laid before them, their chatter regularly interspersed with Xavier's dramatic coughing. Not going to lie—I hoped he'd stay in his cabin tonight.

Every available surface has been decorated with a generous spray of flowers. I scrutinize them briefly for any sign of the Queen of Poisons but happily find none. The arrangements here consist of exotic-looking lilies in various shades of white and pink, beautifully accenting the sophisticated black-and-gold decor of the carriage.

I'm probably imagining it, but Rhys looks different tonight; smarter than usual. In fact, I do a sly double take to check that it's really him. His usually unruly brown curls are swept into a neat side part, and he wears a crisp white shirt and dark slacks, accompanied by what I believe is a cravat in the same wine color as my pointless scarf. When he sees me, his face breaks into a friendly smile, and again I self-consciously tug my skirt down.

"I'd say we both scrub up pretty well, hey, La," he says, giving me a polite once-over.

I roll my eyes. "Um, I'm dressed like my *gran*. Always knew you had a crush on her, to be fair."

Shosh notices us and immediately heads over with a tray of champagne.

"Ah, thanks," I joke, whisking away a glass with a smirk.

She immediately swipes it back and pushes the tray at me. "Not on my watch. Now"—she spins an immaculately manicured finger in the air—"*circulate.*"

"I'm not even meant to be working this shift," I quietly protest.

Shosh gives me a toothy grin, a wicked glint in her eye. "You'll be singing a different tune once you see what's in the envelope the goth twins handed us to host this little shindig—which will, of course, be divvied up at the end. Oh, speak of the devil."

Gwydion enters the carriage, causing everyone to stop and look at him. He's dressed in an old-fashioned black velvet blazer over a waistcoat embroidered with leaves in subtle shades of gold and green. An olive-green scarf with gold tassels completes the look.

The baroness, who I suspect has developed a crush, stands and gives him a dainty round of applause with her lace-gloved hands. Everyone else follows suit, albeit half-heartedly.

Beside me, Samira smirks. "Yeah, the guy's hot, but that look is *not* it. Why does he keep dressing like he's just been dug up from a different century?"

"Please, you're embarrassing me," Gwydion says once the clapping has died down, not looking the least bit embarrassed. "Save that for my charitable sister, Gwen."

If I'm not mistaken, a layer of sarcasm coats his words like sticky tar.

Gwen enters the room behind him, and rather than clap, it seems we all draw a breath. She's wearing what looks like a shimmering black cobweb that clings daringly to her slender frame and trails along the floor. Her thick black hair is a sleek, artfully rumpled river combed to one side, the wine tint of her lips the only color apparent on her face. She says nothing, does not acknowledge the thinning applause, only heads to an empty table, her swinging curtain of hair hiding her expression.

After I've done a few persuasive rounds with the champagne, the mingling magically begins.

"You're looking even more delightful than usual," says Gwydion, appearing beside me. He *smells* even better than usual—a light fragrance, like summer meadows or early roses. Like the first awakening of spring.

"Champagne, sir?" I ask airily, thrusting out the mirrored tray that has been surgically attached to my hand for the past thirty minutes.

"Wouldn't say no," says Gwydion with a world-weary flutter of his dark lashes. "But you'll have to have one with me." He takes my tray from me, discards it elegantly on a walnut sideboard, and hands me a glass. "It's only polite. *Relax* a little. We're all here to celebrate—I *insist*. People can help themselves now."

Not sure that Shoshanna will see it that way, but I don't want to argue with him, either. Still, I won't be drinking on duty—I can't stomach champagne anyway—so I place the glass discreetly back on the tray.

"You should have told me you were underage," he says mildly.

"I'm not," I say, feeling oddly as if I've disappointed him somehow, my face heating at his words. "I don't like the taste."

He looks at me a moment longer, as if he's weighing up my reasons, the pale blue of his eyes almost translucent in the light above us, then drains his glass.

"It gives me reflux," I add unnecessarily.

"I sense there are layers to you, Lara," he muses, a half smile on his face. "Untold stories."

He's right, but unfortunately they're not stories anyone would want to hear.

"Like lasagna," I reply soberly, looking him straight in the eye.

He chuckles, and the tension between us lessens. After a couple of minutes of pleasant chitchat, Shoshanna appears at my shoulder.

"*Busy,* Lara?"

I redden, immediately picking up the tray again.

"Now, Shoshanna, I was explaining to Lara that you must *all* join us," implores Gwydion, putting his TV-host voice back on, different from the hushed, intimate tone he uses with me. "There's so few of us on this train, it's barely a celebration. And we can easily push the tables together in the dining carriage for dinner."

Shosh raises a quizzical eyebrow. "Okay, in theory, loving the idea . . . but who's going to serve the food?"

Gwydion grins. "Chef is going to serve it family style; I've already cleared it with him—then he can join us, too."

Shoshanna looks as if she's about to object, but no doubt reminded of the envelope's contents, she gives a resigned nod. "If you *insist*—"

"Er, *waitress*?"

I turn to see Theo looking at me and tapping his empty glass. Inwardly rolling my eyes, I pick up the bottle of champagne and dutifully refill the skiers' glasses. Returning the bottle, I look around for Rhys, since he's the one who's actually meant to be on dinner service tonight.

I catch sight of him behind the bar at the other end of the lounge. Gwen is elegantly draped over one of the gold barstools, her glittering gaze fixed on his. He looks happier than I've seen him in ages, his green eyes twinkling with merriment as he laughs at something she says. A delicate hand flutters over her mouth as she laughs along.

They're just talking, I reassure myself. *It's his job to be polite, to schmooze the guests.*

And, granted, I've not seen him in a while, but Rhys was never a *dating* kind of guy, preferring to spend any spare time gaming on the rare occasions when he wasn't surrounded by piles of dusty textbooks, inscribing endless note cards with his pleasingly precise handwriting.

Or so I thought.

I bite my lip. But maybe I don't know Rhys as well as I think I do.

About an hour later, we follow Chef into the dining carriage, giving a collective gasp as we enter.

Several giant urns containing magnolia and cherry trees have been moved into the room, and their blossoms hang over our heads like a silken curtain. They must have been relocated from the flower carriages, by the siblings' mystery assistant perhaps. Remembering them suddenly makes me wonder if they're still on board—to my knowledge, we haven't set aside any meals for them.

Regardless, once I sit down to dinner, sandwiched comfortably between the combined confidence of Shoshanna and Samira, I finally start to relax.

I'm not sure how he's achieved it with a kitchen that appears to be fitted out with nothing more than a microwave and a toaster oven, but Carlos has made a delicious starter of deep-fried courgette flowers (or so Theo informed everyone before Carlos himself could get a word out) filled with creamy cheese. Admittedly, they resemble something from the Little Shop of Horrors, but they taste amazing. The main is a Spanish frittata, delicately spiced with smoked paprika, followed by a ginger-biscuit cheesecake. To my utter delight, a cheese board is brought out at the very end, each cheese a specialty of one of the countries we'll be passing through. *Definitely* an upgrade from the lukewarm ramen noodles I "enjoyed" in the staff lounge at lunchtime.

Sipping my soda, I kick Rhys under the table and grin at him. He's sitting beside Gwen, who seems comfortable in his company, even breaking into a smile now and then at some rambling story Rhys is telling her.

"This is pretty fancy, huh?" I say, leaning toward him.

Rhys grins back. "Yeah, can't say I expected *this* when I filled out the application form. Chef's killing it. I think I finally understand why they employ him."

A crystalline chiming slowly silences the table. Gwydion is standing at the head of the table, once again tapping his glass with a knife.

"Before we all move on to coffee, I'd like to thank you all

for attending our little gathering and to invite my sister to give a speech."

Gwen's previously relaxed expression turns thunderous. Gwydion clicks his tongue with impatience: "Come now, Gwen, don't be *shy*. . . . Everyone has come here with the express intention of supporting you."

Gwen shifts uncomfortably in her seat at the attention, then, slowly, she rises, like some witchy leviathan, a dark look etched on her sharp features. As she daintily puts down her glass, I notice that her thin hands shake.

"All right," she says quietly, "all right. If that's really what you want, Gwydion?"

Her words seem more of a threat than an acquiescence. Immediately the table hushes. I notice there is now something oddly blank about her expression. As if she's retreated behind it, like a shield, so terrible is the secret she's about to divulge. We all lean closer. Waiting.

But before she can speak, Xavier, whose coughing appeared to have abated a little during the meal, suddenly begins loudly clearing his throat as if trying to rid himself of something stuck there. Gwydion shoots him a mildly irritated look.

"You okay, man?" asks Theo, patting Xavier on the back.

Xavier nods, waving his hands, since he still can't speak, but his incessant throat clearing swiftly descends into a hoarse and grating wheeze, like the bellowing of a crazed bull. His face is now an alarming shade of livid red.

"Shit!" says Cass, standing up, her voice urgent, her chair toppling to the ground. "I think—I think he's choking!"

Shoshanna stands immediately, bustles over in her no-nonsense fashion, and puts her broad arms firmly around his waist from behind as we all watch helplessly.

She begins thrusting up from beneath his rib cage. Xavier no longer seems to have the energy to cough and is now hopelessly wheezing and gasping for breath, his mouth wide, his face an unpleasant shade of purple. Time seems to stretch and slow like an elastic band held taut. The people around me seem to speak and move as if I am watching them from underwater; vowels elongated, movements drifting and drunken. Everyone is doing *something:* searching in bags for mobile phones, trying to call the emergency services, frantically googling how to help someone who's choking . . .

But I can do *nothing*. Nothing but stare at Xavier, tears blurring at the corners of my eyes at my uselessness as I grasp the deadly impact of every passing second, because I have been here before: unable to look away from the horror unfolding before me, unable to do anything to help as I watch someone suffer. My brain is telling me to leave, that I can't be here again. That I can't add yet more fuel to the conflagration of my nightmares. But my body won't listen.

Xavier's mouth is open in an unnaturally wide O, his eyes bulging wildly, his lips a livid purple blue. From my unique position, directly opposite, only I have a clear view of what is emerging from the cavernous depths of his mouth—something dark and writhing. Is it what he's choking on? Could it be a bone? It looks *huge*. Or is it something much worse—is he coughing up a lung or some other internal organ? Bile rushes into my mouth at the thought of it.

I don't want to look, but I can't stop.

Shoshanna continues her efforts, her face grim, her brow beaded with sweat as her arms thrust up beneath his ribs.

"Clear out," murmurs Gwen softly but firmly. Her eyes are fixed on Xavier. "Everyone . . . leave. I'm a doctor."

"Yes," Gwydion agrees, rising hastily. "Quickly, everyone, out. We need to give them some space."

But I cannot stop staring at Xavier because something is *happening* to him. As Shoshanna heaves him up repeatedly, both arms hooked under his ribs, something long and thick is emerging from his mouth with each and every thrust, flopping down his chin, something thick and green and stringy and—

"*La*— C'mon. We need to try and call for help—"

Rhys's hand lands on my upper arm, attempting to pull me up from the table, but I wrench fiercely away from him, caught up in this monstrous spell.

I cannot *believe* what I am seeing.

Because I see now it isn't a piece of lung; it isn't his tongue or any other type of internal organ that Xavier is trying to hack up. No, it looks like . . . *plant matter,* like several thick, snakelike vines. And whether it is only Shoshanna's desperate motions that make it look like the vines are writhing or whether they actually are, they are emerging ever farther, with each violent thrust, like some revolting vivid-green sprawl of *tentacles.*

"What . . . ? What the *fuck*—"

A pale face looms in front of me, eyes so wintry and so

cold they are arctic chasms, a voice as clean and sharp as a scalpel: "Leave, *now*. I'm a doctor, or did you not hear me? We *need* space."

Gwen.

Swallowing, the spell finally broken, I allow Rhys to drag me up from the table and out of the carriage.

11

"Wh-what the hell was *that* . . . ?" I whisper to Rhys once we're safely ensconced in his cabin. I sit, shaking, in the chair. My voice is ragged, barely even there.

He passes me a cup of sugary tea and shrugs. "Looks like he choked on something. Poor guy. I reckon he'll be okay, though. Shoshanna and Gwen looked like they knew what they were doing. Here—drink this; you look like you're about to pass out."

We sit silently for a few moments as I force down the tea and try to convince myself I didn't see anything. Xavier could have been choking on a large piece of asparagus, swallowed too many green beans—

No. You know *what you saw—*

I make myself look at Rhys. Need his calm reassurance. "You really think so?"

Rhys is quiet before he answers. "Well, hopefully, Gwen

knows what she's doing. . . . She did say she was a doctor, remember."

I frown. "But Shosh told us Gwen was a scientist. And Gwydion said she was a botanist or something. Being a scientist doesn't exactly qualify her to deal with a choking patient, does it? Plus, how the hell is she a *doctor*? She's not much older than we are." My tone is more scathing than I intended.

"Gwen mentioned to me earlier that she was a medical student for a year before she swapped courses to plant science. She's *incredibly* smart—like, skipped-several-grades smart. I'm willing to bet she has more expertise with this than anyone else onboard this train."

Gwen, Gwen, Gwen, Gwen—

"Okay, but that still doesn't make her a *doctor*, does it?" I say darkly. "And besides, Shosh is *qualified* in giving first aid—"

Rhys continues as if he hasn't heard me. "Man, it's moments like this that hit home, isn't it. . . . How fleeting everything is. How everything can be snatched away from you out of the blue like that. Even if you spend your whole life being careful, playing it safe, avoiding any overtly dangerous situations, never step foot on a plane, a boat, or even a train . . . you can still get taken out by—by your own dinner."

I shift awkwardly in the chair, wondering if he is indirectly referring to what happened last summer. It's still a barricade between us, a barbed-wire fence, an uncrossable trench.

"Rhys—"

He looks up, startled, as if unaware he has been speaking aloud.

The silence is thick between us, as if it's holding back a deluge. I am shaky and on edge, nerves stretched tight like cheap cellophane. I sense that Rhys wants to reassure me, wants to be the steadfast friend he used to be, but he doesn't know how. It's been months since we've spent any prolonged period of time alone. He clears his throat.

"Lara—"

I cut him off. "Look, please—let me just say it." I swallow hard before speaking, the words cement-thick on my tongue. "I hope you know how sorry I am, Rhys. About what happened. About . . . about your eye . . . and . . . well, everything."

My voice, stilted and cold, refuses to match my intention, and I don't *mean* it to be that way, but that's how it comes out. It's impossible to look at him as I say those words. A month later, his face is perfect again. The bruises faded, the swelling vanished—those arresting dark-green eyes of his wide open once more.

"I know," he says quietly and *far* too reasonably. "I know. You messaged me, you said as much—"

I shake my head. "It wasn't enough, though, was it? I should have tried harder to come see you—" I stare belligerently at the floor. "I *wanted* to, but it was all such a . . . well, a mess. And—"

And I couldn't bear it if you told me you hated me. So I hid.

I can't say this, though, so the silence elongates.

I stand. "Look, I can't just sit here and wait. . . . I'm going to see if there's any news."

Rhys says nothing, doesn't try and stop me from leaving.

Outside his cabin, the narrow passageway is dark and silent. Momentarily I bury my face in my hands. The pale blur of my reflection in the dark window opposite reminds me of that painting *The Scream*. Hurriedly I rattle the drapes across the window. Fixing my professional demeanor back in place, I pass through the deserted expanse of the Cedar Lounge and into the dining carriage. Samira and, surprisingly, Gwydion are busily stacking the plates full of half-eaten food and rearranging the tables in industrious silence.

"God, *sorry*, guys. . . . Here—let me help—"

"My mum always says it's best to keep busy in times of crisis," says Samira, scraping a plate noisily into the bin.

"Do we know how he is?" I venture, looking at Gwydion. "Is he okay? I mean . . ."

Is he dead?

That's what I really want to ask.

"'Okay' is probably a step too far," replies Gwydion, running a distracted hand through his hair. "But thankfully, he's alive. . . . He's recovering in his cabin—Gwen had to perform an emergency tracheotomy. He's breathing again, but he needs to get to a hospital, and fast."

"*Jesus*," I reply.

I remember reading stories about tracheotomies being performed in emergencies, like on planes, shoving a jagged pen tube into a person's throat below an obstruction so they can get air to their lungs. I swallow, shutting off *those* delightful thoughts.

"Lucky for us, we've got your sister on board," says Samira, giving Gwydion a smile that reveals all her teeth.

Gwydion returns it wanly.

"So she is a *doctor* doctor, then?" I ask. "I thought she was the scientific kind?"

He turns to me with a quizzical look. "Surely *all* doctors are the scientific kind?"

"You know what I mean. I thought she was more like . . . into research. You said she studied plants, not people."

"Gwen's *prodigiously* smart. She was planning on becoming a surgeon before she switched courses. She got sidetracked . . . became obsessed with natural remedies, the whole history of medicines and plants—toxicology, that kind of thing. Father was disappointed; he'd hoped she'd follow in his footsteps. Even so, she's still far less of a disappointment than I am."

I ignore Gwydion's bid for pity. "I'm going to check on them—see if they need anything," I murmur.

I head for the passenger cabins. Shosh and Cass are standing outside Xavier's cabin in the narrow hallway; Cass is red-eyed and clutching a mug of tea. Shosh is talking to her in a low voice.

"It's all in hand now," Shosh says. Her voice is reassuringly calm and measured, but there is a haunted, almost vacant look in her eyes that unnerves me. "We're going to stop the moment we reach the next viable station. Gwen's already rung ahead and spoken to the hospital. Xavier's stable now, thank God. He's out of any immediate danger, okay, love?"

Cass gives a shaky sob and steps toward the closed cabin door. "Can—can I see him?"

Shosh puts a hand on her shoulder, stilling her. "Gwen says it's best not to, babe. It's apparently not . . . not pretty. But he's lucky, Cass. He's going to be okay, thanks to her. Just . . . just go back to your cabin for now and try to get some rest. I'll wake you the moment the train stops—promise."

With her words, much of the uneasiness I've been feeling slips away like oil on water. Everything *is* going to be okay. Whatever it was I saw, it was unlikely to be *vines*—but even if he did decide to eat a bowl of them as an afternoon snack and then choke them up at dinner, the hospital will sort him out; they'll know exactly how to fix him up.

And those petals I saw crushed up in his tissue? Just strays tidied from the drooping table displays.

The train is stopping, Xavier's going to hospital, and everything will be okay.

I unlock the door, exhausted after this evening's unexpected drama—at least I shouldn't have any trouble sleeping tonight. Playing these guessing games, trying to work out what I did or didn't see in a moment of heightened stress, isn't going to provide me with anything other than yet more stress. Still, I'll be glad when Xavier's off the train and delivered into the safe hands of the hospital staff.

The moment I step into the cabin, I immediately clap my hands over my nose. There is now an overpowering stench in here. Not entirely unpleasant but not exactly enjoyable either. It's like the time Gran accidentally whacked her lavender plug-in air freshener up to the max setting. Or when their aging terrier did a wee on the carpet and Dad went overboard with an entire bottle of Febreze. But this smell isn't artificial. No, it's more complex, floral. If I had to guess, I would say . . . roses.

Thrusting up the window a few inches, I shrug it off. Shoshanna was on cabin-cleaning duty today. Maybe she did ours, too, and overdid it with the deluxe room spray or whatever they use here.

A welcome rush of fresh air wafts in, and that now-familiar rhythmic sound of the train clattering over the rails makes me sleepy. I trace my hazy reflection in the window with a finger, the lamplight giving me a fuzzy amber halo.

Then, with a yawn, I climb into bed and let the train's rhythm rock my exhausted body into a deep sleep.

12

MARCH, LAST YEAR

As it turned out, my horizons didn't just widen under Beckett's attention; whole new worlds opened up to me, and I reveled in them, loved that for once the focus was solely on me. This was a feeling I'd been sorely missing ever since Mum passed and Dad discovered the twin wonders of alcohol and dating apps.

And I loved Beckett, too. Or at least, I thought I did. Could stare at his perfect, symmetrical face for hours, listen to his deep, clever voice, run my hands through his soft golden waves.

For the first time in a long while, I had someone who listened. To everything I said. My boring day-to-day worries, my struggles with fitting in at school, my concern I was still flunking biology, and my anguish about how Dad was still using alcohol as a crutch for his loneliness. My complaints about how I was solidly average at everything except history. My confusion about how I might ever channel my passions into any kind of job. Beckett laughed at all my jokes and made me feel witty, funny—even clever. He indulged my wilder flights of fantasy; whispered that my night fears were justified instead of talking me down with a playful laugh like Rhys and Casey did.

Then there was the fact that he was older and more mature, always offering to pay for the things we did together, speaking to fussy waiters and sneery shopkeepers with a lazy confidence I'd never witnessed before. Together we did the things I'd always wanted to do but that were too pricey to be within my reach: crazy golf, Sunday-morning movie matinees, late-night theme park trips. He said that he didn't mind at all, that being with me was something money couldn't buy.

Then he stopped only paying for things and began to buy me things. Limited-edition Jordans. That bougie backpack I'd had my eye on forever. A ridiculously expensive makeup palette I'd lusted after for ages. Things I'd never dreamed of owning. He told me I deserved them for all the joy I brought him. And I was so grateful for them and for him that I wanted to *feel* deserving.

I wanted to earn them, was willing to do anything he asked.

We pulled up at school one Monday after a blissful weekend together, only to see Rhys waiting in his usual spot outside the gates, reading a battered copy of *The Brothers*

Karamazov, two coffees balancing on the wall beside him, hair mussed over his eyes, glasses sliding down his nose. We had the same first class, and we'd usually meet beforehand for a quick chat (lately so Rhys could prime me on all the studying I hadn't done). He caught my eye through the car window and gave me a casual wave. But for the very first time, I wished he hadn't waited. Wished he wasn't there.

I shrunk a little in my seat, hoping Beckett hadn't noticed.

"Huh? Him again," Beckett said as I unclipped my belt and made to get out of his car. I loved it when he dropped me at school. The interior of his Mercedes—a proper car— always smelled so adult and expensive—warm leather and pine air freshener. Not sour milk and rotting banana skins, like Dad's.

Something in his tone made my stomach drop. I put my hand on his arm in reassurance. "Ugh, believe me, he is strictly an acquaintance," I said, my skin crawling not only with the lie but with the casual betrayal of my friend. I leaned over and kissed Beckett full on the lips. "Besides, I need to steal his notes. I didn't get any studying done yesterday, thanks to you."

But Beckett said nothing, only arched a single golden eyebrow before driving off at excessive speed. He then spent the remainder of the day deliberately ignoring my calls.

After that morning, things began to change. I'd answer my phone—95 percent of the time, it was only Dad—but the echo of that male voice made Beckett's own that little bit tenser, frostier, once I hung up. Soon I began to see there was some punishment associated with these perceived slights. "Forgetting" to pick me up when it was pouring rain, returning from Starbucks with only a drink for himself. "Oh, I didn't know you wanted anything." Canceling dates last minute. Not answering my calls. The affectionate caress around my throat as we kissed, turning almost to a grip.

It was just because he cared about me, I reassured myself. Wanted me more than anyone else ever could. I should feel grateful that he was jealous. If he didn't act this way, then maybe it meant he didn't care.

After a while, the gifts became more extravagant but also somehow less meant for me. A fussy double string of pearls more suited to my gran, a pair of lethal-looking red-soled pumps that I couldn't even walk in but that he assured me were far more flattering than those "clumpy black boots you always wear." He didn't tell me outright that he disliked my natural hair but would always joke about my curls looking "disheveled" or "wild," then heap praise upon me when I made the effort to straighten it, iron it flat, the way he liked.

I'd try to tell him that these things weren't really me, but I didn't want to appear ungrateful, and anyway, he didn't want to hear it.

"You could be so perfect," he'd say, staring at me with those intense blue eyes of his, "with just a few adjustments here and there."

On the few occasions we argued, there was an underlying viciousness to him that frightened me. His eyes would change in a second from warm and playful to some frigid wasteland; his barbed comments became instantly too personal—about the state of my dad or why Mum died or some jibe about the neighborhood I lived in.

So I went along with what he wanted. It was easier that way. And he was worth it, after all. There were plenty who'd love to be in my place. Beckett was caring, good-looking, had the prestige, the car, the money. . . . Undeniably, he was the whole package.

Wasn't he?

I wake with a hushed gasp, my skin bathed in a cool sheen of sweat. As I sit up, I'm aware that something is wrong in that primal way the ancient part of your brain knows but can't put into words. In seconds I see the problem: the door to my cabin is ajar. Weird, I must have forgotten to lock it. Immediately I climb down, shutting the window—the wind must have nudged open the door, and the breeze has grown chilly—then cross the cabin to close the door, still half asleep.

Something stops me in my tracks.

Directly outside my cabin is a small pile of pink rose petals. Their scent lingers in the narrow corridor, although not as overpowering as before. A scattered trail of petals continues down the low-lit passage, past Rhys's door, and ends at the entrance to the sleeper carriages. I hesitate, unsure what to make of this. The ridiculous idea that Gwydion has set up some romantic trail for me briefly flashes into my mind, but

I quickly push the idea away. It would be madness for anyone to be in a romantic mood after the events of this evening, and at this time of night, the action is much more *sinister* than romantic. Besides, whatever's between us is barely even a flirtation right now.

The lights glow in their elegant glass globes; the dark-paneled walls make the space shadowy. I remember childhood stories about people following trails, the kind that led children deeper and deeper into the woods, and those stories rarely ended well.

But curiosity gets the better of me. It always does. So, shutting my cabin door quietly behind me, I pad softly down the passage.

The trail leads away from the gentle snores of our sleeping guests, through the stately dining room where I can hear Samira still clinking plates in the kitchen, wrapping up the night shift, and past the glittering bar.

This is the way to the greenhouse.

But of course it is.

The trail of petals gets more and more apparent the closer I get. There are lots of them now, stuck together in lurid pink clumps. I reach the end of the train and pause, peering through one of the small side windows of the greenhouse carriage. It's dark inside. And it will be locked at night. Most importantly, I'm not meant to be here—Gwen doesn't like people touching her flowers. This has been a wasted journey. I'm glad I have no option but to return to my bed.

Come closer.

Two words, softly spoken, seemingly kindly meant, and also, *not* spoken. An echo inside my head, as if someone is speaking directly within my brain, their words stirring the nerve endings, cajoling, beckoning me nearer.

My hand closes over the brass door handle, and I am unsurprised when the door opens smoothly. I am also unsurprised to see that the carriage is occupied. Gwydion sits on one of the high-backed armchairs in the flower room, directly facing the door, his face as smooth and impassive as if carved from marble. His dark hair is a little harried; his pale eyes glint like stars. He does not look remotely surprised to see me.

Around him, the flowers and flowering shrubs are lusher than ever—rudely fecund, crowding the windows and blocking out the night. I gag. The scent here is no longer sweet and delicate; it is intense, *sickening*.

"Lara," he says, his face breaking into a secretive smile.

There are a lot of things I want to ask him.

Is he going to sweep all those petals up before morning? Because that looks like a hell of a job. Did he *mean* to lead me here? *Was* this some over-the-top romantic gesture? Because I'm pretty sure we aren't there yet. If he wanted my attention, a simple knock on my cabin door would have been sufficient—

"They took the blossoms of the oak, and the blossoms of the broom, and the blossoms of meadowsweet, and from them, produced a maiden, the fairest and most graceful that man had ever seen."

He speaks the words beautifully, says them like a prayer

or, more accurately, a spell, his voice low and lilting, lips lovingly forming the words. I want to ask him what he means, but cannot.

"Follow me," he says, rising, turning, and exiting the carriage, moving deeper into the greenhouse through the door at the other end. "There's someone who wants to meet you."

But when I reach the second carriage, he isn't there; the plants in it have grown monstrous, the space now a dense jungle, ivy and creepers utterly obscuring any view of the outside world.

And at the end of the carriage where the strange panel was yesterday is now an open door. A door that leads to a third, previously concealed car.

Gwydion isn't through there either, but something else is.

Whatever it is waits at the very end, shrouded in darkness, the space behind it a dark morass of thorns that gives the impression of a throne. Its eyes are deep gouges that glint with an iridescent amber light, like a deer's eyes caught in headlights.

Then the whispering begins.

I was conjured from the loam and clay, my bones dank peat and soil.
My beauty stolen from the blossoms of the meadow.
He told me I was perfect, made only for him.
He knew me better than myself. Fixed me, molded me.
Made me whole.
Made me his.
Come here. Come closer.

There is an unpleasant ring of familiarity about some of this, but I can't deny that the tone the words are spoken in is gentle, reassuring—protective, even.

Something soft drifts onto my skin, making me jump—a petal. I glance up. The ceiling is laced with overhanging branches, and despite the earliness of the season, they are heavy with white blossoms that drift to the ground and lie thick on the floor like freshly fallen snow. I wade through them, the petals unpleasantly sticky against my skin, the floor slanting sharply beneath my feet, so that soon I am waist-deep, almost swimming through them.

I stop, wanting to go back. Their scent fills my nostrils, sickly sweet, not dissimilar to rotting flesh, and I gag as they drift onto my face, stick to my lips.

"Gwydion?" I say, although by now I sense this is nothing but a dream. His voice is in my ear, familiar, coaxing.

"Keep going," he tells me, his voice harsher now, unpleasantly insistent. "She is waiting for you."

The petals are almost to my neck, and there is something unpleasant beneath this sea of blossoms, something hidden, something sharp and thorny that scratches at my skin.

"No—no—I want to go back," I say, turning. Because soon I will be choked by the petals, drowned by them, as they fill my lungs with their cloying perfume. "I want to—I want to stop."

"But . . . I need you," he replies, and it is no longer Gwydion speaking. I turn to see Beckett, shuddering at the unwelcome sight of his face. I see he is made of thorns, cruel and wickedly barbed, marring his perfect features. His hand stretches for my wrist, tearing at my skin, and wrenching me closer. "You're mine, Lara. Let me love you, like you need to be loved. It was I that molded you; made you perfect. You belong to me. *Mine.*"

He advances on me, kissing me, only his tongue is like the vine I thought I saw at dinner; thick and florid green as it invades my mouth, my throat, and I gag as the air begins to leave my lungs, choking me, my eyes bulging and—

The drone of my alarm and an insistent knocking at my door wrenches me from my dream—or, more accurately, my *nightmare*. I rub my hands over my sweating face and groan, struggling for my phone and immediately silencing the jangling music.

"God's *sake*," I murmur, trying to slow my breathing. Up until now, the nightmares had stopped, and I'd thought I wouldn't need to take the medication prescribed by my doctor anymore—especially not while I'm here, away from everything that caused them—but now I'm not so sure.

"La?"

It's Rhys. I throw on a hoodie, wrench open the door, and manage a gruff, "Hey. . . . What's up?"

"Are you okay? I thought I heard, like"—he hesitates and gives me an apologetic grin—"some kind of moaning."

"Just a bad dream," I murmur, red-faced.

Rhys slips past me and sprawls on the armchair before the window, gesturing for me to close the door.

"Okay, whatever Carlos did to 'fix' the doors yesterday didn't work. We were locked in *again* last night. Weird thing is, I don't think the door was *locked*, exactly. I checked, but I couldn't see an extra bolt or anything; it was more like something was blocking it. I even waited up, and there was no sound—no turn of a key, not even any footsteps. Don't you think that's weird? I mean, did you hear anything last night?"

I stifle a yawn. After last night, I'm *really* not in the mood for Rhys's creepypasta stories.

Then I remember the trail of petals in the corridor outside my cabin.

"No . . . wait a minute. I wasn't locked in. I—"

Hold on. That wasn't real. That was a dream. I pause, clearing my throat and collecting myself. "I don't actually know, Rhys. Because I was *asleep*, like a normal person. Not creeping around my cabin, searching out conspiracies."

Rhys nods, unfazed. "I know it sounds a bit deranged . . . I don't know. . . . After last night—what happened to Xavier—I'm just a bit . . . weirded out, I guess."

Immediately the sight of Xavier gagging helplessly on plant matter fills my vision.

"Hey, do you ever have those dreams within dreams?" I ask absently. "Like fever dreams . . . where you wake up, in your dream, and you think it's reality—but then something mad happens, and you realize that no, it's *still* a dream and—"

I realize I'm rambling and stop, but I'm surprised to see

Rhys nodding in understanding, a sober expression on his face. "Yeah, those are the worst, because why are they always nightmares?"

"Exactly! In my dream, I woke up here, or at least I *thought* I did, and there was this trail of petals outside my door that led to the greenhouse carriages. . . . They were open, and Gwydion was inside—"

"Um, do I *want* to hear the rest of this dream?" Rhys interrupts with a wry smile.

"It wasn't like that," I say quickly, embarrassed. "There was something weird at the end of the carriage—something with orange eyes—or cat's eyes . . . and these thorns . . . and . . . and *vines* . . ."

I trail off.

"I wouldn't read much into it," says Rhys dismissively. "I had some properly weird dreams myself. I think it's all the stress of last night. That or the cheese board."

Reassured, I recall what Shoshanna told us about stopping to let Xavier off. "Hey—did you notice if we stopped at all last night, so Xavier could get to the hospital?"

Rhys perks up a bit. "Yeah, didn't it wake you up? It was only a couple of hours ago. He was stretchered off the train— Shoshanna was there. . . . Saw Gwen talking to the paramedic. Hopefully, the guy's going to be okay."

My heart feels lighter immediately. Xavier is alive, and we're five days in, getting ever closer to our final destination and my freedom. After everything that happened in the past months, the doctor warned me I might still have intrusive thoughts and uncomfortable dreams. But spring is on its way, signaling a new beginning, as Gran always says, and things will get better.

Rhys stands. "Well, we should get going. Unfortunately, breakfast isn't going to make itself."

13

Now wide-awake, I quickly shower, change into my uniform, and follow Rhys to the still-empty dining carriage. After swiping one of Carlos's delicious pastries—there are so few passengers now, I'm confident it won't be missed—I take a temporary seat at an empty table.

"Those are *meant* for guests."

"I'll give you a hand this morning . . . if you want," I say, ignoring Rhys's chastisement. My offer's not as selfless as it seems. Lately I've spent too much time cooped up in my cabin, alone with my thoughts. It doesn't feel healthy. But Rhys dispenses with the snark and instead gives me a smile, and once again I realize how much I've missed the sight of it.

"Nice," he replies. "Go Team Wales and all that. . . . I'm even prepared to overlook the fact that you're an interloper for now."

I grin wickedly despite myself. "Oh, c'mon, I'm *half* Welsh on Dad's side. Besides, I know you *love* my London accent."

It might be my imagination, but I swear the delicate flush of his skin deepens.

Cass and Theo enter the carriage moments later, and I stand up immediately to greet them while Rhys ducks into the kitchen. Unsurprisingly, they are quieter than usual. I smile at them both in a way I hope is reassuring.

"Hey . . . how are you guys feeling this morning?"

"Ah, you know," murmurs Cass. "A little down after last night, but at least Xavier's being looked after now."

I nod. "Yeah, I heard he was taken to hospital this morning—that's good news. Do you guys have any idea what happened yet? Has the hospital been in touch? Was he really choking, or was it to do with that cold he had?"

Something Gwen said to me yesterday pops unwelcomely into my mind.

Aconite. Queen of Poisons.

I blink the thought away.

"I don't know. They haven't actually been in touch yet. Gwen seems to think it might have been an allergic reaction." Cass slumps back in her seat. "But as far as I'm aware, he isn't allergic to *anything*." She sighs. She looks rattled, dark circles around her eyes, her usually perfect golden waves lank. "Anyway, after breakfast, I'm gonna call the hospital again—or maybe even him, if he's up to talking."

With a concerned nod, I take their order.

It's obviously my imagination, but Gwydion seems to give me a secretive smile as he enters the carriage today, loitering behind his sister, his eyes bright. Almost as if he knows he was in my dreams last night.

"You're sta-ring," murmurs Rhys behind me in a singsong voice.

I flush a little. "No, I'm not. Okay, maybe I am—a little. But can you blame me?"

He snorts in response. "Well, sure, he's a total arse. Of course, you find him attractive." I blink at his acidic tone, but he carries on regardless. "You all right to grab Samira? I think she's making coffees in the library, but Shosh says she's needed on laundry."

As I walk down the train toward the austere coffee lounge, I hear a faint sound over the rhythmic clattering of the train—like a song playing on a distant radio. Someone's alarm or phone left in one of the rooms, no doubt. Curious, I follow the music down the train. The Azalea Coffee Lounge is deserted, and there's no sign of Samira. But that tinny, somehow familiar music persists. With a sense of dull inevitability, I realize where it's coming from, and it isn't long before I'm staring through the small, slender windows into the greenhouse carriage.

The music is definitely coming from in there.

And now that I'm closer, I realize why I recognize the sound. I recognize it because Xavier's phone was obnoxiously ringing nonstop at lunch the other day.

Beethoven's Fifth.

Why would Xavier's phone be in there?

The answer is, it wouldn't be. . . . It *must* just be a radio.

Maybe the bee guy is doing a bit of weeding and chilling to some classical tunes. I peer through the window again, but it's too fogged up to see, so I rattle the handle and knock politely on the door.

But the carriage is locked, and though I wait for a full minute, no one answers. Eventually the music stops, but not before I've made up my mind to investigate further.

Samira looks tired when she opens her cabin door.

"Sorry, babe," she says, stifling a yawn. "I must have slept through my alarm. It's . . . it's really not like me."

And it isn't. Samira is always early, always willing to do the most.

"That's okay," I reassure her. "Shosh thinks the sun shines out your— Shosh loves you. Plus, you look like you needed the rest. Must have been a late one last night?"

"Not too late. Everyone was exhausted after all the drama. But I couldn't get to sleep for ages. And when I did finally drop off . . . I had the *weirdest* dreams. . . ."

"God, I hear you." I peer behind her. The cabin looks as untidy as mine, her bunk rumpled and unmade. A large bouquet of beautiful orange chrysanthemums rests on the fold-down table under the window. They strike me as somewhat familiar. Are they from the flower carriages? Why would they be in here?

Samira sneezes violently, making me jump. It's then that I notice how red her eyes are, streaming with tears.

"Are you really okay, Sam? I can do the laundry if you're feeling sick. I've got time?"

Samira gives a businesslike shake of her head. "Nah, bless you, Lara. It's just my allergies again. I'll pop another antihistamine and be grand. Wait a sec—"

She bustles back into her cabin and hands me the flowers. "Here, these were a gift, but you take them. I think they are *literally* killing me."

A gift. Who could they be from, I wonder? Gwydion? A small lick of envy ripples through me. I thank her, but still unable to forget Gwen's whole Queen of Poisons spiel, I decide to dispose of them the moment I'm alone. Then, that eerie ringtone still playing in my head, I go to find Shosh and, hopefully, the key to the greenhouse.

Shosh is in her cramped office, flicking through the screens on an old-fashioned black-and-white monitor. Compared with the fanciness of the train, the tech on board seems antiquated. She starts when I tap on the window, quickly clicking off the screen so it flickers to a small dot.

"Ey, Lara. Everything okay?"

I nod nonchalantly, the lie sliding easily from my tongue. "Yeah, all good, but the Addams twins want their conservatory swept, and I, uh, don't have a key."

It's a long shot, mainly because I'm not even sure if Shosh herself *has* a key, so I'm surprised when she stands and begins rummaging through a nearby drawer.

"Don't lose it; we've only been given the one," she says distractedly, her gaze falling intently back to the switched-off monitor in a way that makes me slightly uncomfortable.

Well, that was easy. Almost *too* easy. To the point where I wonder why I am dicking about, snooping around empty carriages, when I could be doing something useful, like giving Chef a hand with prepping for lunch. But something about the previous evening, what I thought I saw while Xavier was choking, combined with the highly coincidental sound of his ringtone in there, impels me right through to the end of the train again.

With a gently trembling hand, I unlock the door and step inside.

The greenhouse is as lush as I remember, although thankfully nowhere near as fecund as it was in my dream, and less ethereal in the soft filter of daylight. The plants are all neatly staked and labelled, their perfume only delicately lacing the air as I creep through, looking for signs of the phone I heard.

The bird-footed card table in the center of the room is empty; the chairs are plush and inviting. I sink into one for a minute, listening.

It's peaceful here. It's a tragic waste not to open these carriages up to the rest of the passengers. Effort and thought have been put into how the flowers are arranged in their impressive stone planters. Color has been used intelligently. Cornflower blues mingle with vibrant magentas; a sizeable central planter, shaped like a diving fish, its tail molded around a shallow bowl, holds fiery marigolds and red-hot pokers. Trellises are nailed neatly to every available surface, the floor tiles covered with a rich gold-green rug that complements the foliage. The windows are all open, just a crack, and in the thin rays of sunlight that dapple the carriage, I can see a million motes of pollen drifting like gold dust.

No wonder Samira hasn't dared step in here—she'd probably require immediate hospitalization.

Resting my head against the back of the velveteen cushion, I shut my eyes just for a second. They've been heavy all morning, my brain full of bees, but in here, everything seems to move at a slower pace. The gentle warmth of the weak winter sunshine filtering through the large windows, the absorbent effect of the thick foliage, the soft, supple perfume of the lilies all conspire to shut out noise.

It isn't long before I hear it. That whispering sound. Soft, sibilant, and just out of earshot, like a radio turned down low or someone murmuring sweet nothings to a lover in the next room. What *is* it? At first I passed it off as just rustling leaves, but it's plainer than ever that's not all it is. Am I losing my mind? *Where* is it coming from?

Not for the first time, I'm reminded of Lewis Carroll's Alice. Honestly, I never liked those books as a kid; I didn't find them cute or whimsical, as everybody else did, but *nightmarish*, to the point where I begged Dad to stop reading them at bedtime. And *that's* what the whispering reminds me of: Alice in the garden of live flowers, who were far crueler and cattier than seven-year-old me had ever expected flowers to be, more unpleasant, odd denizens of Wonderland who spoke in cold and unhelpful riddles.

Reminding myself why I'm in here, I rise and enter the second carriage. The darker, colder one. Placing my ear to the door, I listen, remembering Rhys's somewhat eerie description of the bee guy's activities and am less keen than I was to go in. There's been absolutely no sign of them on the train since the first day these carriages were attached.

"*Hel*-lo?" I call softly.

Something about this green carriage, as I decide to call it, is decidedly less welcoming than the first. For some reason, I think of a pitcher plant. The previous carriage offers that sweet entrance, dripping with golden nectar, designed to lure in unwary insects; the next chamber holds their damp, dark doom.

Still, I open the door.

If possible, it's even quieter in here—apart from the occasional drip of water; these plants are well cared for—but the whispering has ceased. It is an intense, pregnant silence, though, as if the carriage and all the plants within are holding their breath, waiting for me to pass by.

"Is anyone in here?" I call out anyway, knowing no one will answer.

I amble around, peering closely at the plants, hoping to spot Xavier's phone lying forgotten among the foliage, and not wanting to return just yet to all the noise and bustle of the train, where once again I'll have to put on that fake smile and pretend to be something I'm not.

Instead of the decorative scrolling and beading of the first carriage's stonework, I notice for the first time that quotes are inscribed onto the planters here.

"IN MOST GARDENS," THE TIGER-LILY SAID, "THEY MAKE THE BEDS TOO SOFT—SO THAT THE FLOWERS ARE ALWAYS ASLEEP."

Do flowers sleep? This room has been made dark by the ivy that grows everywhere. In the corners, the stems are so thick they have formed hardened, twisted branches. It drips from the ceiling and creeps over the trellises, clinging with tiny spines, its bottle-green foliage obscuring the windows. How fast does it grow? Every time I come in here, the space seems darker than before.

This carriage even *smells* darker, mossy and dank, like an unloved pond. I crouch down and look beneath the only furniture in the room, a damp chaise longue embroidered with autumn leaves. There's nothing there but shadows. Tired, I straighten and sit on its cushions, closing my eyes for a blissful few seconds. Goose bumps dapple my arms; it's chilly in here.

Then the whispering starts again, closer this time, and I get the sense that the room is growing darker around me. After a moment or so, though, I realize I've been mistaken. The whispering I've been hearing isn't whispering at all. No, it's the sound of ivy stems *creeping*. Slinking silently over each other like thick, ripe veins, steadily rippling across the floor toward me. They wrap around my wrists like restraints, slowly tighten about my waist, leaving me trapped here, a sacrificial offering to—

I snap my eyes open.

Of course, I am imagining this. The ivy behaves itself, meters away, and unmoving, I am sitting on the chaise longue, untouched and unharmed. But I get up, unnerved now. My head is thick and heavy, my eyes are itchy and sore, and in the gloom, I can see something glinting at me at the far end of the carriage, at the very back of the train, the place farthest away from the passengers.

I walk over.

The noise shatters the heavy silence so violently I nearly scream. Beethoven's Fifth. Xavier's phone, and the reason I am in here. I shake myself—in my pollen-drenched stupor, I'd almost forgotten. The sound is bright and artificial, entirely unsuited to its surroundings, and is coming from directly ahead.

Before me is the darkened antechamber laden with books and that strange carved panel.

Except today it isn't a panel. Today it hangs open at a narrow angle, revealing a dark gap through which the music shrilly sounds.

Today the panel is a doorway, just as it was in my dream.

A thrill charges through me, immediately overriding any unease. I feel like I am in one of my mum's old Nancy Drew books I cherished as a child, about to solve a delicious mystery. Pushing the panel wider, I peer through.

The music stops at precisely the same time I realize that behind the door is an entire other carriage. One that is in complete and utter darkness. Fumbling for my phone in my back pocket, I switch on the flashlight. Its beam barely penetrates the immense black space beyond. I hesitate. I'm not scared of the dark, but it's sensible to be scared of what might hide in it. And the darkness here has a strange quality—thick and impenetrable, even in daylight. I have no idea what could lie within. I think of a carriage entirely swallowed by poison ivy. I think of that mass of thorns from my nightmare—

Intrusive thoughts; that is all.

The drapes or blinds in here must be shut. Stepping a little farther in, I direct my phone's flashlight to the nearest adjacent wall, where the light switches are usually found. The light reveals thick, spruce-colored anaglypta wallpaper above polished oak paneling, the kind of thing you might see in a Victorian gentleman's study. But where the light switch would usually be is a wrought-iron sconce in the shape of an outstretched hand, the palm dripping with candle wax. Unsurprisingly, I am not carrying a candle.

I shouldn't go any farther into this vast black space alone. God knows what's in there. Likely more plants, but darker things crawl from my overactive imagination. Some mad scientist's lab where Gwen grows snapping Venus flytraps with a hunger for human flesh, or Xavier's dead body, now entirely animated by tentacular vines—

Jesus, Lara, stop it.

In defiance of my brain, I force myself to take another step into the cabin, shuffling toward the left to find the drapes. It's midmorning; there should be *some* daylight inching through the cracks. But as I get closer, I discover there *are* no windows. Only that polished wood paneling, inlaid with glorious Celtic knots and lavish sprays of leaves.

A carriage with no windows? What the actual fuck? What kind of plant grows in utter darkness?

My flashlight catches on something that glimmers at the end of the carriage. From where I stand, it looks unnervingly like a pair of eyes. I think again of that dark-clothed figure standing at the station the night these carriages were attached, their face entirely obscured by a black mask.

Don't be stupid, Lara. No one is going to be silently standing in a dark, locked carriage. Honestly—

Not unless they're hiding. Not wanting to be seen.

Swallowing, I take a few more steps forward. It is so *quiet* here, the walls, the drapes, the plants absorbing all sound.

"Hell—hello?"

I listen intently for sounds of breathing, but there is nothing—only the sullen rumble of the train. When my eyes finally decide to adjust to the darkness, I let out a sigh of relief. What I thought were eyes are actually part of some old statue dumped at the end of this windowless space.

From what I can make out, it is made of gray stone, weather-beaten and spotted with lichen. Stepping closer, my flashlight held out before me like a ward, I see it is tall—taller than me, practically touching the carriage roof—the stone carved into an effigy of some vaguely humanoid *bird*. And, judging by its scrawny, hunched-over shape, a hungry one. Half owl, half vulture, its wings held out high and arched in a way that weirdly reminds me of old-school depictions of Dracula, cloak held aloft like the wings of a bat. I can make out a cruelly carved beak and crude etchings on the surface that give an approximation of feathers. The most distinctive features are its huge eyes, buried deep in the stone and made of some shiny dark material—onyx, perhaps? Reaching out a hand, I impulsively touch it.

—meadowsweet and briar and blossom of oak and—
—my beauty is terrible, powerful, and born of this earth beneath us. A sight that leaves men sickened with lust and longing.
I was made to be HIS—
An object to crave—a prized possession

I snatch my hand back as if burnt. It's as if someone close to me was whispering directly into my ear. Red-faced and embarrassed, I stagger around, half expecting to see the masked assistant standing directly behind me. My phone flashlight dances wildly across the walls, creating crazed patterns, but the room is as still and empty, as devoid of movement, as before.

I stifle a scream as that familiar ringtone crashes into the silence of the carriage once more, its light now flashing directly beneath me. With a shaking hand, I direct my light to the source of the sound.

Before me are large piles of delicate cherry blossoms, lying like discarded candy wrappers, like the swept-up remnants of last night's dream. They're spread upon a low stone plinth the size of a tomb, as my brain helpfully informs me.

But as I bend to take a closer look, I realize that these aren't haphazard clumps. No; the blossoms seem to form the shape of a supine person lying deathly still beneath the statue, like an offering, arms politely resting by their sides. It reminds me somewhat of the mummies I've seen in the British Museum, faceless, forever still, and very, very dead. There are even subtle indents where the eyes, the nostrils, and the mouth should be.

And beneath the petals, where a person's heart would be, is the glowing screen of Xavier's phone.

14

"No, seriously, you *have* to see this," I say, my voice hushed as I propel Rhys through the deserted piano lounge. "It's . . . it's properly *weird*."

I'm starting to find that ornate, shut door at the very end of the train increasingly sinister. It's as if the busy world around me recedes, the sound of the train switched to low, whenever I approach it.

I wrench at the door handle of the first greenhouse carriage—I need someone else to witness this, if only to confirm I'm not crazy—and almost tumble headfirst into it.

"*Jesus,*" breathes Rhys, stepping in behind me. "What *is* this place?"

I forget he hasn't been in here before. I half-assumed Gwen had already shown him the sights, maybe during one of their weird three a.m. chats.

"I already told you. These carriages—they're full of plants. Something to do with Gwen's research or whatever."

"It's . . . it's *beautiful*. . . ."

"Right?"

I pause, impatiently waiting for him to take it all in, watching as he stoops to read the beautifully carved names on the polished wooden stakes, his nimble fingers stroking the silken petals of a beautiful blush-pink flower. Seconds later, he snatches his hand back, wiping it on his trousers.

I look at him quizzically, and he nods down at the stake.

"Belladonna," he says, as if that explains everything.

"Okay, and?"

"It's Italian for 'beautiful lady,' but it's more commonly known as deadly nightshade."

"So it's poisonous?"

I think back to Gwen and her Queen of Poisons.

He nods, looking discomfited. "Yeah . . . well . . . only if you eat it."

"Wow, I can see why you and Gwen get along so well," I mutter blithely. "Come on. What I want to show you is through here—in the last carriage."

"That explains why this place is kept locked all the time, at least," Rhys continues evenly as we pass into the second carriage. "Especially since there were kids on the train earlier."

By now it's late afternoon, and the light is failing, what little there is, is filtered through heavy palm fronds and spirals of trunklike ivy. I hesitate. The door ahead is now shut and resembles a carved panel again. Did *I* close it? I exhale in frustration, pushing at it, but it doesn't budge.

"So this—this was—*is* a door," I say.

Rhys examines the wooden panel, tracing the carved knots with his fingertips. "What do you mean?"

"Well, earlier . . . the panel was open. It leads into another carriage—that was what I wanted to show you."

I nudge him out of the way, fumbling around the edges of the panel. There must be *something*—a catch or a lock or a spring trigger—that releases the door.

Rhys stands back, arms folded, surveying the entire wall. "What *is* that? Is it meant to be an owl, d'ya think?" he asks, staring at the weird winged carving with its giant, baleful eyes.

"Yeah," I say, on my knees now, pressing and prodding random bits of the carving like it's one of those frustrating puzzle boxes I can never figure out. "I think so. And just wait until you see what's through here. Why would this door be disguised?" I wonder aloud.

"Could just be a . . . vibe. I mean, look around you—the old books, the wingback chair. The person who designed this carriage is clearly a fan of dark academia."

He begins pulling random books off the shelf to our left. Understanding what he's doing, I yank at one of the sconces to the left of the door, perhaps a little too hard, as it comes off in my hand.

"Crap," I murmur, attempting to reattach it.

Feeling desperate, I begin poking at the panel again. Irritated by the sardonic stare of the owl, I jab viciously at its eyes with both fingers. There's a neat mechanical click, and the lower part of its beak drops open, revealing a small keyhole.

"Oh . . . *nice*," Rhys says appreciatively.

"Except we don't have a *key*," I snipe. I think then of the ever-present key around Gwen's neck. Maybe it's more than an ostentatious show of wealth.

As I stand there, I hear that damn whispering start up again. I glance at Rhys, wondering if he hears it, too, but he is oblivious, still poking around the bookcase, pulling out titles at random and flicking through them, apparently now more interested in the desiccated books than in anything I might have to show him.

"Hey, do you hear that?"

He looks up, his face bland. "What?"

It's that random jumble of words again.

Meadowsweet and broom and blossom of oak and—

"Never mind."

Frustrated, I again stare at the stupid etching of the owl, whose golden eyes seem to be mocking me. And the more I look at its wings, the more the shape of them reminds me of a pair of fanned-out hands. On impulse, I place my palms into the indents, where they fit perfectly, as if this carving were made specifically for me, and push—hard.

The door swings open immediately with a smooth clunk, revealing the room beyond, now lit by flickering candlelight.

"What the *hell*?" Rhys utters behind me, to my satisfaction.

"Someone must have been in here since," I murmur, a little alarmed. "It was dark before."

In the low orange flicker of candlelight, I can see that the room is, as I'd already guessed, entirely windowless. Smooth polished panels inlaid with knots and leaves line the lower half of the walls, while the upper portion is covered in thick green wallpaper. In this light, the artifact looks even eerier now, its shadows deepening, and utterly incongruous with the smooth old-world glamour of the room, which is mostly empty except for that odd stone plinth and two withered saplings in planters on either side of the statue.

Disappointment seeps through my veins as I gaze down at the petals, which are no longer arranged artfully on the plinth but are now in an untidy heap in the corner of the room, as if someone has just finished sweeping them up.

Rhys stares at the statue, eyes wide. Do I detect a hint of fear in them?

"What—what the *hell* is that?"

"Believe it or not, that's not even what I wanted to show you," I say, gesturing in frustration at the pile of blossoms. He gives it a once-over.

"Okay . . . granted, that's a lot of petals, but the carriages before this are crammed with blossoming trees. . . . Someone's just swept them up, that's all."

"You don't understand," I mutter, frustrated. "When I first came in here, they were . . . in the shape of—of a body. A *life-sized* body."

"Is that right? A literal human body?"

Rhys doesn't even try to hide the skepticism in his voice.

"Yes, I am fully aware that that sounds ridiculous, but I saw what I *saw*."

Rhys smiles a little. "Do you remember last summer, we were lying in the park, and you were convinced you saw Taylor Swift's face in the clouds and thought it was a sure sign she was dropping a new album?"

Ignoring him, I peer at the pile more closely. It's a shapeless mess—not even close to resembling what it did before. Frustrated, I pull Xavier's phone from my pocket, my trump card. "Whatever. But this—this was in the middle of it all. It's Xavier's. Don't you think that's *weird*?"

He takes it from me gently and examines it. Annoyingly, the phone perfectly reflects Xavier's personality, bland and dull, in its unremarkable blue plastic case. Even the lock screen displays nothing but the time and date against a generic background of swirls. He turns it over.

"Are you sure it's Xavier's? Why would it be in here?"

"Well, no, I'm not *sure* sure—but it has the same ringtone he does," I say distractedly. "Beethoven's Fifth."

Rhys looks unconvinced. I can understand why. It's a common enough generic ringtone, and there's nothing else about the phone that links it to Xavier.

"It probably belongs to Gwen or Gwydion," says Rhys, not unkindly. "We best give it to one of them."

I can't exactly put my finger on why, but for some reason, this sounds like a monumentally bad idea.

"I'll hand it to Shosh," I say. "If she agrees it might be Xavier's, maybe she can get it to him somehow."

It *is* Xavier's; I know it is. Did Gwen take it from him when they were alone in her cabin the evening he choked?

Did she bring him in here? Did she *do* something to him later that night?

He was taken off the train, I remind myself sternly. *He's safe in the hospital now.*

We stand awkwardly for a moment, both staring down at the untidy pile of blossoms.

"Okay, but again, you know what is *actually* weird?" says Rhys, stepping carelessly through the pile of petals. "*This.* This is weird."

In the guttering candlelight, he examines the statue more closely. It looms out of its nook, its eyes deep, glimmering pits, a jagged crack I hadn't noticed before almost splitting its impassive face in two. From within the crack emerge tiny wavering stems, like weeds between paving stones.

"I know, right? I mean, why bring it on a train? Looks damn heavy, for one thing."

Rhys moves closer, studying it intently. "Looks like something you'd find in a graveyard, maybe."

"What, you mean a headstone?"

He shakes his head, tracing his fingers along the creature's beak. "More like a monument to someone who died. Or to some old god. It could be Anglo-Saxon, maybe. Or . . . or Celtic?"

"I'm surprised Gwen hasn't told you all about it," I fail to stop myself from muttering resentfully.

He turns to give me a bemused little smile, then continues to trace his fingers over its rough surface while I look nervously back at the door. It is *too* quiet here, as if the plants are listening . . . or watching.

"We should probably be getting back. . . ."

"One sec," he says, crouching down to examine the base the thing stands on. "There's something carved here." He begins gently pulling away tiny tendrils of ivy and brushing off moss, and something primal within me wants to warn him not to mess with it, not to touch it; he's right—it's *ancient*, perhaps it's cursed. He leans back, gets out his phone, and begins carefully typing the letters into his Notes app.

"*Yma y gorwedd* Blodeuwedd."

"Is that a code?" I wonder aloud, my Nancy Drew fantasies roaring back to life.

Rhys snorts. "No, Lara, it's *Welsh*."

"Okay, genius," I snap, feeling foolish. "Then what does it mean?"

Rhys frowns a little, still looking intently at the statue in a way that creeps me out.

"I don't know . . . and there's no signal here to look it up either."

I decide to ask Shosh about it when I hand her the phone. Something about this situation, this entire carriage—even Gwydion, and especially Gwen—makes me decidedly uneasy.

"So . . . last night, right?"

Shosh's opening words at the staff meeting lead to a few

awkward chuckles. Due to the events of the previous evening, the meeting has been pushed back to the afternoon.

"Honestly, it's unusual for a situation like that to occur on one of our trains, but I want to say well done, everyone. You kept your cool, and it was really gratifying to see how you all supported each other."

"Is there any update on Xavier's condition?" I ask quietly.

Shosh shakes her head. "Not yet. But we got him off to hospital safely, and I've asked Cass to keep us in the loop."

Xavier's phone is burning a hole in my pocket, and the moment Shosh calls an end to the meeting, I hang back, wanting to speak to her alone. Thankfully, she seems fully recovered after yesterday's events. The haunted, almost catatonic look I saw in her eyes last night is now absent.

"Everything all right, Lara?"

I nod. "Mhm, I think so. It's just, earlier, while I was sweeping the greenhouse carriages, I heard a phone ringing. I went to take a look and, well"—I pull the phone from my pocket—"I found this in there, under a pile of petals. I think it's Xavier's."

She frowns, a tiny line appearing in her forehead, and takes the phone from me, staring at the anonymous lock screen.

"Xavier's? How do you know it's Xavier's?"

"The ringtone. It kept on ringing the other day at dinner. You remember—" I hum a half-hearted rendition of Beethoven's Fifth, and Shosh grins, turning the phone over and examining the bland blue cover.

"Have *you* been in those carriages?" I press, curious to see what Shosh makes of them.

"Yeah, I did a brief inspection once they were attached. Why?"

I wrinkle my nose. "Don't you think they have a weird... vibe? And did you see that statue, that bird *thing,* in the end carriage? It's creepy as hell. I thought Gwen was meant to be transporting organic samples, not haunted statues."

Shosh chuckles. "Uh-oh, we've got a regular Miss Marple on our hands. Love, those two are *rich*-rich. Take it from me: I've seen much stranger things in well-off people's cabins. It's probably just some overpriced piece of modern art or something. Believe me when I tell you, in this job, ignorance is *bliss*." She narrows her eyes. "Did they actually want their cabin swept earlier, or did you just fancy snooping around?"

I blush. *Busted.* "I—I heard the ringtone and went to see what it was...."

Shosh pockets the phone and pats me affectionately on the shoulder. "Look, I'll make sure this gets back to the right person, but from now on, keep focused on your shifts, all right?"

It's good advice; I'd be wise to take it. But something still doesn't feel right to me. I'm so permanently aware of the location of my phone, it may as well be an additional limb. So why was Xavier's found discarded on the floor at the end of a series of locked carriages?

* * *

Later I am just finishing up mopping the floor of the staff lounge when Rhys enters. He grabs a bottle of water from the fridge and then flops down at the table, pulling out his phone.

"Okay, so . . . I *finally* managed to get a signal—took a while—and I found out what it means."

I glance over at him, confused. I've been busy scrubbing floors for the past hour, blissfully lost in a Bravo podcast.

"What what means?"

"The *Welsh* . . . on that statue we saw earlier, obviously."

I've been so caught up in the mystery of Xavier's phone, I forgot all about the strange inscription on that hideous statue. We're alone in the room, so I throw my cloth into the sink and sit opposite him. Rhys is always happiest when investigating something or other, going down endless internet rabbit holes about weird rituals, cryptids, and conspiracies.

"Okay, what's the deal?" I say. "What does it mean? Wait, let me guess: 'Abandon hope, all who gaze upon me'?"

"Nothing so dramatic. It says, 'Here lies Blodeuwedd.' I told you it looked like something out of a graveyard, right?"

I nod. "Okay, cool. So what's a Blodeuwedd when it's at home?"

Rhys grins a little, clearly pleased that I asked.

"Blodeuwedd is this beautiful maiden from an old Welsh legend. Her name means 'Flower Face.' Basically, a magician conjures her out of flowers for this guy, Lleu Llaw, as a get-around for the fact he's been cursed never to have a human wife. However, this being a legend, things don't go to plan, and she winds up falling for someone else. In the end, her lover and her husband fight, and she's turned into an owl out of spite by the magician who created her."

Something about the story is vaguely familiar, and a second later, I place it: My dad read it to me when I was a child. I vividly remember the illustration in the book: a woman magicked from flowers, ethereal and unearthly.

"Wait, wait—*she* ends up being turned into an owl?" I say, my attention snapping back to the conversation. "For what reason? Typical feminist legend, I see. So that's what that monstrosity was meant to be? Another woman getting done over by men and then immortalized as a giant, ugly owl beast for her troubles? How wonderful."

Another one to join the ranks of the daughters deserted in forests by jealous stepmothers, sisters trapped in cages and thrown into ovens, queens murdered by faithless kings—

I go to get up.

"Don't you think it's *strange*, though?" Rhys says. There's something steely in his voice that makes me sit back down.

"What?"

"That a statue or—or monument—whatever it is, dedicated to a mythical person made of flowers, is in a carriage full of flowers?"

I think about this for a moment.

"Let's be real: the whole *thing* is strange, Rhys," I say, lowering my voice. "Why attach all these fancy Chelsea Flower Show carriages to the train when all you're doing is heading off for a bit of scientific research? Surely all Gwen needs to bring is a couple of those stainless-steel cases of dry ice you see in sci-fi movies? Why take a *train*?"

Rhys smiles. "That's very specific. Anyway, they might have had trouble getting that thing through airport security."

"You know what I mean, though. And that's before we even get to the mystery of their so-called assistant—the disappearing bee guy—the owl beast statue, and weird petal people."

"I dunno," says Rhys, glugging his water. "From what I can tell, Gwen and Gwydion look like they have some serious money. It's probably just some wild rich-person shit like that billionaire guy from Cardiff who always flies direct to Italy to get pizza. Personally, I'd rather have taken my custom private jet to the lab, but maybe plants don't fly well. Maybe they're planning on taking the owl thing to a museum or auction. . . . There are a thousand reasonable explanations."

"Did Gwen say anything about it to you? You know, anything that would help make this seem a little more normal?" I press, wanting to be reassured.

His cheeks flush a little.

Does *Rhys have a crush?*

"No. No, she didn't mention it at all."

"So what *do* you guys talk about?" I push. "I'm curious."

He flushes further; the pink tint to his cheeks would be almost endearing if it weren't the delightfully personable *Gwen* he was talking about. "Nothing, La. Honestly, I've barely spoken to her, and the times I have, it's just been chat—y'know, professional small talk. You'd be better off pressing Gwydion if you're looking for answers."

But he refuses to meet my eyes, and I wonder if he's telling me the whole truth.

15

That evening, while turning down the passenger cabins, I'm in full detective mode, eyeing stains on discarded clothing, checking under beds, and peering into cupboards, like some hyperactive Sherlock. But I find nothing out of the ordinary. The only exceptions are the brazen smell of weed that emanates from Becca's hoodies and the revolting-looking carnivorous plant that Gwen is curating in her room. It's a vast, fleshy green thing that resembles a giant, ugly urn—a pitcher plant—the mournfully buzzing flies in the jar beside it tipping me off to its nature. Gwydion's cabin looks barely inhabited, revealing not a single clue to his personality other than a pristine copy of Kafka's *Metamorphosis* beside his bed. The bed has been neatly made; the towels have been artfully folded, his possessions either neatly hung in the closet or locked within his designer suitcases.

Disappointed, I go back to my cabin to get changed for

dinner service. Even though it's only six p.m., the sun is already pooling onto the horizon like molten yolk, the expansive picture windows revealing nothing but the bleak, flat stretches of French autoroutes, making me grateful for the train's cozy interiors. As I pad through the sleeper carriages, I bump into Shosh doing her final checks.

"The cabins are looking great, Lara—nice work."

I beam. Coming directly from Shosh, this feels good. Maybe I'm not as useless at this job as I thought.

"And while I'm at it, well done on finding that phone. Gwen's been looking for it since yesterday. I guess we should have guessed it was hers straightaway." She gives me a conspiratorial wink. "Don't worry, I didn't tell her *where* you found it."

I stop dead. *"Gwen's?"*

What were the chances of her and Xavier both having the same ringtone? Besides, there's no way that bland, utilitarian phone case belongs to Madame *Gwen*, with her personal library of Chanel's finest quilted purses. Something was wrong here.

"Yeah, she was really pleased. When you think it through, why would it be Xavier's? Those guys have never set foot in the Llewellyns' private space."

I recall Xavier, a bunch of drooping purple blooms in his hand. No—he, at least, was well versed in the contents of those carriages.

"Anyway," Shosh continues, already sashaying down the corridor, "don't let me stop you from getting to dinner service!"

The dining carriage has been set up immaculately, and the sounds of amiable conversation drift out of the kitchen. I pop my head round the door and greet Samira and Carlos, who are busy prepping dinner and chatting about England and Spain's relative chances in the World Cup.

"Hey, La, have you got a sec?"

I whirl around to find Rhys standing directly behind me in the drinks area of the kitchen, a cramped space only a couple of feet square. He reaches past me and pulls the door to the dining carriage closed.

"What's up?" I say, not sure what I'm most alarmed by, his hushed and secretive tone or his sheer proximity. I chew my lip, finding it difficult to maintain eye contact.

"I spent most of my break trying to get a signal on my phone again—involved some interesting gymnastics in my cabin, I can tell you," he says, his voice so hushed I have to lean in closer to hear him. "But what you said earlier . . . it stuck in my head. So I googled Gwen and Gwydion, and turns out—well—I'd rather show you. Can you come to my cabin after we're finished with service?"

A prickly edge of panic creeps across my skin like nettles. "Oh god . . . is it bad?"

Mug shots of Gwen and Gwydion flash before my eyes, my brain already composing the lurid headlines, but Rhys gives a subtle shake of his head. "No, not exactly bad, but . . . *weird.*"

"Any orders yet, guys?" shouts Carlos from where he's juggling pans on the hob, evidently overhearing our hushed whispering. Rhys casts a nonplussed look in his direction, and I follow him out into the dining carriage.

The baroness and Becca are first to arrive for dinner and eat their meal with little fuss and minimal cups of tea. I'm clearing their plates when Cass and Theo enter. They, too, eat in relative silence, to the point that I'm seriously considering launching into some impromptu karaoke just to lighten the dour mood. This idea is immediately quashed when Gwen and Gwydion step into the carriage, seeming to deliberately sit as far away from the other pair of siblings as possible.

The moment Theo finishes eating, he leaves the dining carriage, all the while fiddling with his phone. Looks like everyone is dealing with the same shitty cell service on this train. I make my way over to Cass.

"Hey, Cass . . . how are you feeling?"

She looks at me as if startled from a bad dream, white-faced and frail, shrinking away from me, closer to the window.

"Oh, Lara. It's you. Sorry—I'm all right, I guess." She doesn't elaborate.

"Can I get you anything else?"

"Uh, I'd love a cup of tea, please. Um, oat milk and two sugars."

I quickly fix her drink and hover beside her.

"Did—did you guys manage to get hold of Xavier at the hospital yet?"

I already know the answer but ask anyway.

She rubs her eyes. "*No.* It's fucking frustrating. I even tried his mobile a few times, hoping he'd recovered enough to answer, but his phone's now permanently switched off. Battery, I guess."

I think it has more to do with the fact that Xavier's phone is probably only a few feet away from us, at the bottom of Gwen's crocodile Birkin. I briefly consider telling Cass this, but something stops me. First, I don't think Shosh would view this as particularly professional, and second, the longer I stand chatting with Cass, the stronger the sensation I have that someone is *watching* me. I angle my body slightly, casting a wary eye down the carriage, but Gwen is staring fixedly down at her dinner plate, picking at her food like a fussy heron.

"Crap," I breathe. "But he definitely got off to hospital okay?"

Truth is, after seeing that odd. . . . *petal corpse*, I'm asking more for my own reassurance than hers.

"Yeah. . . . Obviously, none of us slept a wink last night, but when the train stopped, Shosh came and got us to see him off like she said she would. . . . She's been fab. Still, I don't know if you were awake, but the place we stopped at was some little backwater town. I was expecting a city. . . . And I . . . I wanted to go with him, but I wasn't allowed. I—"

She breaks off to cough into a tissue—a grating series of wet barks that do *not* sound healthy. I have the mad urge to ask her if I can peek inside at the contents, but she crumples the tissue and stuffs it in the pocket of her dress. She casts a glance at the other end of the carriage, and I turn, too. Gwen still has her head down. Gwydion is sipping his wine and staring at the orange sun still sinking into the fleeting hills.

"You weren't allowed? What do you mean?"

She lowers her voice. "My French isn't the greatest, but they indicated it was best we came later. And obviously we wanted to do what was best for Xave. But I was expecting, y'know, an ambulance to pick him up, but what was waiting for us was more like a private taxi . . . with the windows all blacked out."

"Okay, but that's probably for privacy? Some French protocol about treating patients with respect," I reassure her.

She shrugs and lowers her voice to almost a whisper, shooting another dark look over to the corner booth where Gwen is finishing her plate. "Yeah, I suppose you're right. Apparently, he's at some private hospital that Gwydion and Gwen's family are familiar with. Gwen's offered to pay all his medical expenses, since it happened at their charity dinner."

This actually goes a little way to reassuring me. For starters, it explains why there wasn't a proper ambulance on the scene.

"Well, that's good—that's a nice gesture, right?"

She coughs again, grimacing and swallowing hard.

"Yeah. Yeah, I guess. And Shoshanna's been great, but—" She gives a deep, shaky sigh that turns into a sob. "It's just all happened so fast. And—and when they took him away, I couldn't *see* him, Lara. They'd covered him up—covered his face. And—you don't understand—the last time we spoke, things between us were—were—"

She melts down on the table, quietly sobbing into the safety of her hands. I scootch over to her side of the table and wrap my arm about her.

"He'll be okay, y'know," I say, wishing I could sound more convincing, gently stroking her hair, still unable to get that nightmarish image of his mouth crammed full of vines out of my head.

She raises her head and gives me a hopeful look.

"You think so? I can't stop *thinking* about that evening . . . reliving it. . . . It was all so strange. Like a fever dream, or . . . or like I was watching it all unfold miles away, as if I were removed somehow . . . as if I were seeing it from a great height."

She rubs at her face. Not only is she pale, but her skin is tinged with gray, and beads of sweat form pinpricks on her brow.

"Are *you* okay, though?" I ask, resisting the urge to shuffle away from her as she once more releases a volley of coughs. A dark part of me imagines an enormous vine springing from her mouth and flopping down onto the table in front of us like some monstrous tongue. "Look, don't take this the wrong way, but you don't sound that great."

She stifles a yawn. "Yeah, on top of all this, I'm coming down with a cold." She picks up her tea. "Anyway, thanks for noticing. I'm gonna take this back to my room and try to grab a few hours of sleep."

I nod, promising to check on her in a while.

"How is she?" Gwydion asks as I arrive at his table, cocking his head sympathetically in the direction of Cass.

"Not great, unsurprisingly," I reply a little frostily, looking at Gwen, who has finished her plate and is now staring down at her laptop screen. For a gleeful few seconds, I imagine violently slamming the lid down on her fingers. "She wanted to go with Xavier to the hospital last night, but they wouldn't let her. Do you guys know why? Apparently your family is familiar with the hospital?"

Gwen clicks the laptop lid closed and gives me a hard stare. "She's got her wires crossed. We're not *familiar* with it; it's just the closest private hospital in the area, according to Google. And I have no idea why they wouldn't let her attend—why would I? Are you questioning all the guests like this, or just us?"

I blush furiously, immediately wishing I hadn't said anything. Gwen's right. I'm not paid to play detective; I'm here to serve guests.

Before I can apologize, she stands, hoisting her bag over her shoulder. "Look, sorry for snapping, but I'm a little tired after spending most of yesterday saving someone's life. I guess I'll go and get some sleep and leave you two to get better acquainted."

She flounces out of the carriage, a thunderous look upon her face.

"Um, wow," I say awkwardly.

Gwydion blinks, looking as embarrassed as I feel. "Sorry about that. Like she said, she's tired. . . ."

Apart from the two of us, the carriage is now deserted, so I sink down opposite him. There's more I want to know about Gwen-Queen-of-Poisons. I recall what Gwydion said about her the other day, about how she's become more secretive lately.

"Is that *really* all?" I press, looking around once more to make sure we're alone.

He looks at me, his clear blue eyes studying mine, for so long I begin to feel my skin heat under his scrutiny. Then he leans across the table, a playful smirk playing about his lips that makes me forget all about his sister. "Yes—of *course* it is. We're all on edge today, are we not? You know, sometimes I feel you're hung up on the wrong sibling."

I raise an eyebrow. "I'm not hung up on *anyone*, thanks."

He gives an easy laugh and collapses back into his seat.

"Why does Gwen's assistant wear that mask?" I ask impulsively. "It was like a fencing mask. . . . Is there something dangerous in those carriages?"

Gwydion shrugs off my question, as if bored now. "I don't know. I think it's just because of all the pollen or something," he says, staring out the window. The sun has almost disappeared, melting slowly into the sea of fields flashing by, turning them blood-red. "From what I understand, they were only here to ensure the conditions were correct for the plants. I think they left a while back."

I try a different angle. "So, uh, what does Gwen think is causing this . . . accelerated growth she wants to study?"

He gives an exasperated groan. "Now, that one I *really* can't answer. Science bores the shit out of me."

Honestly, he's not alone. Biology class has always been my kryptonite. And I don't really want to *learn* about the science either. But I *do* want to check that we're not in any potential danger.

"Okay, same. But I was sweeping the Llewellyns' carriages earlier, and I noticed that the door at the very end was open. You know, I hadn't even realized it *was* a door—I didn't know there were three carriages—and then—"

Oh, and Gwydion is listening *now*, his glassy blue eyes firmly fixed on mine—his wine, the darkening horizon beyond the window, all forgotten. I begin to feel uneasy. If that *was* Xavier's phone lying there like some kind of offering beneath that quite frankly disturbing statue, it wasn't necessarily *Gwen* who put it there.

"Sorry, the door was *open*, you say? Specifically, the door to the carriage containing the statue?"

"Yeah . . . what's that about? I mean, what's with that thing?"

"'Thing.'" He smiles as he repeats the word back to himself as if I've told a particularly amusing joke. "Honestly, you shouldn't have been in there, Lara. The door should have been locked. It's always kept locked. Gwen wears the key around her neck. It's unlike her to be so . . . negligent."

"*Negligent?* Why?" I press, chilled by his words. "Is it . . . is it dangerous in there? Is it to do with the plants? The poisonous ones?"

Because, Gwydion, you should know, I did open the door.
I always *open the door.*

"They're only poisonous if you're stupid enough to eat them, but that third carriage, well . . . *that* one might be dangerous," he says, his eyes seeming to gleam with a secretive light. "Especially at night. You see . . . that's when she goes hunting."

I swallow. "*Hunting?* What? *Who?* Do you mean Gwen?"

There's no *way* he's talking about the creepy statue. No way. Reminded of those golden eyes I thought I saw glinting at me through the peephole of my cabin door the first night they boarded, I stare back at him, trying to figure out if he's joking, teasing me. He clasps my hand suddenly, his gaze sharpening to a knife edge. His grip is cool and steely strong.

"Listen, Lara. I *know* that door was locked. Gwen always keeps it locked. How did you *really* get in there?"

"It was *open*," I insist, though I know he doesn't believe me. "I swear it. Gwydion, what . . . what is she keeping in there? What *is* it?"

The grip on my hand tightens until it becomes uncomfortable.

"Let's just say in the case of that carriage, there are some things it is better to be ignorant about." His voice is hushed and full of secrets.

I try to remove my hand from his, immediately affronted, but his grip is tight. "What do you *mean*?"

"Well, you know what they say about a little knowledge."

Actually, I don't, but I sense it isn't good.

"Hey—hey, La?"

Rhys. And the spell is broken. Gwydion releases my hand

like a sprung trap, taking a large glug of his wine and turning to stare blankly out the window.

"Um . . . yeah?"

"Um, Shosh needs our help with something."

This is a lie. We both know Shosh is on lates and is currently sleeping, but I get up anyway.

As I follow Rhys out of the carriage, I can practically feel Gwydion's stare burning a hole in the back of my head.

16

I follow Rhys back to my cabin.

The carriage rocks unsteadily around us as he paces the floor. The space feels restricting, too small to fit both of us as well as all our history. I perch on the chair opposite my bunk.

"Okay, so what's this great revelation?"

Rhys glances at me, a wariness in his eyes as if he's weighing up how much to reveal.

"You know, even without what I'm about to tell you, I think you should stay away from Gwydion. I get the feeling he's bad news. And why was he grabbing your hand like that?"

I'm surprised at how agitated he looks.

"It was nothing, seriously."

He sinks into the bottom bunk and swipes at his phone before wordlessly passing it to me.

It's a newspaper article dated a few months back. I scan the text quickly.

DISAPPEARANCE OF WEALTHY LANDOWNERS

> Fears grow for missing couple, Gryff and Gloria Llewellyn.
>
> Emergency services were alerted to the disappearance of the wealthy couple near Gwynedd, Wales, at around 5:30 p.m. last Sunday. The alarm was raised by their son, Gwydion, aged nineteen, on his return from holiday. The estate the family have lived on for generations was found in a dangerous state of disrepair, with trees damaging both the foundation and the roof of the manor and causing it to partially collapse. Despite a thorough search of the grounds, any bodies have yet to be discovered.

I pass the phone back to Rhys with a frown.

"Okay, that is a bit weird. You're sure it's them?"

Rhys swipes the screen and shows me a photo from the same article. Crouched down beside a fluffy white terrier is a more carefree Gwydion in a green quilted gilet.

"Is that it? Was there anything else?"

He gives me an exasperated smile. "Don't you think that's enough?"

I think hard for a moment. *No.* It's not enough. Missing doesn't equal dead, and even if it does, it doesn't mean Gwen or Gwydion were involved in any way.

"I don't know . . . to me it sounds like the house was a

total dump and collapsed. There's always stuff on TV about stately homes falling into ruin because they cost hundreds of thousands to maintain," I say, thinking aloud. "It's a tragedy. But it doesn't make either of them murderers or suspicious or anything...."

Rhys narrows his eyes. "No? I mean, he never thought to mention that his parents recently disappeared, or that his entire house *collapsed*, during any of your frequent heart-to-hearts?"

The self-satisfied look on Rhys's face is making me quietly furious.

"Why *would* he? It's not *like* that between us. I'm just being professional, like you."

Rhys thinks for a moment. "Okay . . . you're right. I'm sorry. I was trying to look out for you."

I am both unsettled by the article and infuriated by his assumptions.

"I don't *need* you to look out for me. I've managed perfectly well by myself for the past eighteen years—"

"Have you, though? Lara. I hate that it's so . . . so weird between us at the moment...."

I snort despite the unpleasant churning in my stomach.

"Okay—then why are you insisting on making things weirder? Can't we just try to move past this? And if we can't, let's follow your example—you know, like how unpacking stock is more appealing than talking. Because honestly, Rhys, at this point, I *agree*."

And I don't know if he realizes it, but I'm not asking anymore.

I am *pleading*.

He blinks a few times, his emerald eyes pained, and I chew my lip, refusing to break my stare and praying he'll take the hint—that or leave. I don't even know which of the two I'd prefer.

"I want to clear the air." He tries again. "I want to understand—whatever it was that happened with us and . . ."

I close my eyes. I don't scrunch them shut; I don't bury my head in my hands. I am preternaturally calm. I *know* what he wants, but I don't know if I have it in me to give it to him. What I *really* want is to bury it all. The reason I came here was to be born anew on board this train in some far-off country. A Lara-with-no-past. What *he* wants means revisiting that past, digging it up, excavating the very things I want to stay buried.

I coldly correct him—a shield against the truth.

"There *was* no *us*, Rhys."

He laughs, but there's no humor in it. "Uh, there absolutely *was* an us, Lara. We were friends—you were my *best* friend, along with Casey, Ade, and Stevie. You can't just pretend that didn't happen. Then you met"—he grimaces like he's tasted something unpleasant—"*him*, and all of a sudden we didn't exist for . . . what was it now . . . eight months?"

"Oh? Were you counting?"

I'm trying to buy time to *think*, but my words come out way more caustic than I want.

Rhys slumps down on the bunk.

"*Yeah*, actually. Maybe I was."

Rhys and I have always understood each other. From the start, things were always surprisingly, *delightfully* easy between us. An almost sibling-type relationship but with a flirtatious edge that both of us would fervently deny if ever questioned about it.

But as much as I loved his company, I always suspected there was an imbalance between us—a certain smugness about Rhys. Deep down, I felt he denied the depth of our friendship because I wasn't good enough for him—a view I strongly suspect was also held by his family. Because Rhys was *that* student. The one all the teachers adored. Who seized every aspect of academic life with gusto. You couldn't even sneer at him or tease him for it, because it was all *genuine*. And he loved to help others, never minded giving up his time. He was always volunteering to run tutoring sessions, organizing study groups, and setting up how-to blogs for higher math groups. STEM was his thing, but he excelled at *everything*. Effortlessly holding the moral high ground without ever being pious.

I guess I felt forever in his shadow. Silly, bang-average Lara, always goofing around, making bad decisions.

And then along came Beckett.

Older than the rest of us—already out of school, in fact—with a flashy car, a private-school education, a privileged background, and all the messy golden hair a girl could ask for. Someone who *saw* me. Saw me as smart, decent, *desirable* . . . someone who invested in me, wanted to make me the best version of myself.

"Look, Rhys," I say quietly. "I don't know what you want me to say. I was in a relationship, like . . . what did you expect?"

He shoots me an exasperated look. "What did I expect? I *expected* you to still be my friend."

"Yeah, well, things change when you're in a relationship. Maybe one day you'll understand that yourself."

"I have *been* in relationships," he snaps back. "Not that *you'd* have noticed, since I apparently ceased to exist the moment you met him. And yet I still managed to have friends as well. Those things are not mutually exclusive, Lara."

I look up at him, cheeks hot, unable to hide my surprise. The Rhys I knew had always been too involved in his studies to ever date seriously.

"Look, why is this all my fault? It works both *ways*, Rhys," I say, gathering myself. "You *all* decided you didn't like Beckett, so you started avoiding me as well. Don't try to rewrite history and act like this was entirely *my* doing."

His green eyes blaze into mine. "You're right. I didn't—I *don't* like him. You changed when he was around. The way he spoke to you . . . tried to change you. He made you smaller, La—he—he diminished you."

"You met him literally *twice*, Rhys! So I can't help but think there are other reasons why you didn't like him. Perhaps the same reasons why you apparently don't like Gwydion."

I'm just being petty. But I'm surprised to see Rhys blushing, his cheeks coloring as if I struck him.

"Okay, fine, La. Have it your way. You think whatever you want, whatever makes you happy."

I might have won, but there's no victory in it. In the still quiet of the room, I stare at him, the way his dark lashes lie sootily against his lightly freckled cheeks, I recall how he looked talking to Gwen the other night, all golden smiles and glinting green eyes, and how, after everything I've done—everything I've done to *him*, inadvertently or not—it could never, ever be me in her place; it could never be me he looked at like that. I'm not elegant, sophisticated, a *prodigy*. I could never be worthy. Not now, not as I am.

Because the truth is, I'm incomplete these days. And the vital parts of me . . . the parts Rhys liked . . . they're lost now.

Behind my eyes is a rising tidal wave of emotion—black and viscous. Even now I won't acknowledge it, won't face the truth, however tired I am of this violent seesawing between us. He wants to get off and level it; I know he does. But he doesn't know how, and I don't either.

"Look . . . I'm tired," I say, defeated. "That shift was pretty hectic."

And he understands, the way he always does. Still refusing to look at me, he nods, his dark curls tumbling over his forehead. I have the sudden urge to sweep them away.

It's not until the tears drop upon my cheek that I realize I'm crying. Silently, but it won't stay that way for long. Without another word, Rhys leaves, the door clicking politely closed behind him.

I lay awake for hours. I am so *sick* of crying. Beside me, my iPhone clock silently marks off the minutes; occasionally I pick it up and look, surprised at how much time has passed, sometimes surprised by how little. How many more nights will I face the choice between no sleep and my nightmares?

The train's passage is disarmingly quiet tonight, and I'm hyperaware of any movement in Rhys's cabin. My fingertips trace the wall softly as I hope for the secret slide of the vent between our rooms, the soft ping of a message, a gentle tapping against the wall, or even a hushed knock at my cabin door. One final attempt at breaking down this wall. And maybe this time, I'll be ready to help.

But there's nothing. Only silence.

APRIL, LAST YEAR

"Good day at school?" Beckett asked with a smug smile, pushing a glass of champagne toward me.

"Ah, it was all right, y'know . . . pretty boring."

Beckett graduated the previous year and was learning the ropes at his dad's high-end estate agency in lieu of university. Today he closed his first deal, so we were celebrating.

"And your little friend . . . Bryce, isn't it? How's he doing?"

I frowned down at my drink, eyeing the bubbles with suspicion, wondering whether he'd be annoyed if I asked for a Diet Coke instead.

"Do you mean Rhys? Uh, fine, I guess. Why?"

He drained his own glass quickly, refusing to look at me.

A bad sign.

"Oh, I just thought I saw you guys together the other day, that's all. After school."

I shrugged. There was something cold, almost unpleasant,

about his tone that I didn't like at all, as if he were accusing me of something. "Beckett, we're mates, that's all. . . . We walk home together on Friday after class. I mean, you *know* we do." I shook my head with a frown. "Anyway . . . it's *Rhys*."

Why had he been driving past my school? Could he have been spying on me? Trying to catch me unawares? What was I meant to do? Tell Rhys, *Sorry, but Beckett doesn't like me walking with you, so I'll need you to walk home a different route.*

"Well, I've changed my hours. I can pick you up on Fridays from now on," he said in a tone I'd come to recognize as final, busying himself with pouring more champagne, even though I hadn't taken a single sip from my glass.

"Okay, fine," I said, quietly belligerent. I wanted to ask why he couldn't just be nice and drop off Rhys, too, since we passed his house on the way to mine, but deep down, a quieter part of me already knew the answer.

After this exchange, his tone lost its chill, and I was pleased when he headed over and pulled me into a warm hug, relieved my apparent transgression hadn't ruined the evening. We curled up on the sofa with a movie, and things were good again. He was sweet and kind and affectionate, and I began to think Beckett was right about Rhys anyway. Maybe it *was* weird for me to walk home with him now that I was in a stable relationship.

And as the movie ran its course, I found myself recalling the secret thoughts I'd harbored about Rhys before meeting Beckett, and I became surer still, glad the lights in the lounge were low so the heat I felt in my cheeks at this recollection wasn't apparent.

Whether Beckett was right or not, it didn't make it any easier to tell Rhys. I considered just texting him, but I knew that was cowardly, knew that my friend deserved better. I managed to avoid him for most of the week, as we were both caught up in other things—him with his tutoring and shifts at his mum's café in town, me . . . well, with Beckett. But on Friday, when the bell rang for the end of the day, I found him where he always was, leaning by the lockers, waiting for me.

"Hey, we made it," he said, pulling himself off the wall and hoisting up his backpack.

"Yeah, long week, huh?" I replied distractedly, allowing myself a final few moments of appraisal. If I'm honest, I preferred his laid-back style to Beckett's regimentally ironed, checked button-downs, and I liked how Rhys was growing his hair longer on top, leaving it to twist into relaxed dark curls. For one brief, insane moment, before I broke the news, I wanted to ask him, urgently, if I'd imagined everything between us, had imagined the way his hand had closed over mine—

I forced myself to snap out of it. Clearly I had imagined everything, which is why we were in this situation to begin with.

"What's wrong?"

"Nothing," I said brightly, opening my locker and throwing things haphazardly into my bag. "It's Friday afternoon, how can anything be wrong?"

"Hey, I forgot to say earlier, if you're free Sunday afternoon, I've got time to go over the biology coursework if you like? You can come to mine."

I'm relieved he gives me an in to bring up Beckett. My Sunday afternoons were now taken up in the idyllic countryside surrounding Beckett's house, walking Evie, his beautiful Italian greyhound.

"Ah, sorry, I've got plans," I said. "Also, um, I'm getting a lift home today. . . . I meant to tell you, but I, uh, forgot. . . ."

The words emerged robotically, like someone else was saying them, and I expected him to mutter an "okay," stick on his headphones, and walk away. Rhys was King of the Unbothered, Lord of the Nonchalant. But for once, he didn't.

"La . . ."

I hyperfocused on doing up my bag. "Yeah?"

He lowered his voice. "Is—is everything okay with you? Really?"

The lights were on a timer in the school hallway and suddenly snapped off, painting the corridor with shadows. It was a gloomy spring day, rain spattering heavily against the windows, dampening the noise of the world outside.

Steeling myself—I'd been anticipating this—I looked at him wide-eyed. He appeared genuinely concerned. Worried, even.

"Yeah, why?"

He flicked his gaze away. "It's just you've been bailing on us a lot lately. We're all happy for you, y'know, with Beckett and all, but—"

For the first time ever, I felt oddly elated. Like I had climbed some rung above him. Like I was worthy, now that I was part of a pair. And I didn't avert my gaze from his. I brushed my hair back from my face, utterly unbothered.

"Good," I said, pressing the hallway light switch back on and shutting my locker door. "Good, I'm glad you're happy for me."

17

I toss and turn in the small bunk, not for the first time wishing there was some way to switch off the memories that always return at night, unwanted ghosts drawn to my tears as to the scene of a crime. Outside, in the corridor that runs alongside the cabins, I hear quiet footsteps. Cass's voice floats gently over the rumbling of the train, and hastily I wipe my tears away. I begin to get up, remembering I said I'd check on her, when I realize she's with her brother.

"Something's *wrong*, Theo. I mean, why hasn't he answered his phone?" Cass speaks quickly, in a harsh whisper.

"Because he's probably under anesthetic, Cass! He had an emergency tracheotomy—you're not going to be calling your nearest and dearest the day after *that*, are you? Are you finished? We're not even meant to be in here—this area's for staff."

"I know that, Theo, but I feel watched, *listened to*, out

there. I—I don't want *them* to overhear. Anyway, listen. I googled that private hospital he was supposedly taken to, and when I called them, they denied ever having a patient with his name!"

Theo exhales noisily. "Come on, Cass, it's probably just the language barrier! Even you admit your French is horrid. Look, I promise I'll give them a call first thing tomorrow—I've got no bloody signal at the moment. Now I'm going to get to my cabin to get some sleep, and I suggest you do the same."

"Wait—wait, Theo. There's one more thing. Look at this."

Curious, I peer through the peephole. Cass is standing a little way back from my door, tugging up her sleeve viciously and displaying her forearm to Theo. "*See?* It's some kind of . . . of puncture wound. I have no idea how it happened. All I know is I woke up with it yesterday, and it itches like crazy. But *how*? How'd I get it? Normally I'd think it was a mosquito bite or something, but on a *train*?"

Theo looks unhappy and replies in a low, resigned voice. Whatever he says seems to temporarily reassure Cass, because moments later, they retreat back to the passenger carriages.

Almost glad of the distraction from unhappy memories of my past, I climb back into my bunk and think. Something is definitely . . . *off* on this train. That weird statue . . . Xavier's phone (and it *was* his, whatever Gwen might say) lying beneath it, like an offering. Petals in the shape of a *body*. And now that disconcerting news story. . . . People don't just disappear.

But did you see what was coming out of the watering can? Did you see what they were watering them with?

Okay, Rhys was definitely off with that one, but it still nags at me, because Rhys is not at all prone to flights of fancy. I decide to speak to Shosh again tomorrow. Someone needs to take a good look through that flower carriage—for the sake of us all.

I don't see Rhys during breakfast service, and I'm scheduled to spruce up the guest cabins this morning. As I distractedly change the heavy cotton linens, the rare morning sun sparkles off the polished mirrors and elegant walnut surfaces, turning dust motes into gold, and all my late-night fears about petal monsters and owl-beast statues seem frankly ridiculous. Amending my plan, I decide to speak to Rhys before going straight to Shosh. I don't want her to think I'm paranoid or a troublemaker.

Once my shift is over, I hurry to the staff room for the mid-morning meeting, hoping Rhys isn't going to be weird with me after last night's awkward conversation. My heart lifts as he immediately makes his way over to hand me a coffee.

"I heard we might be stopping again this morning," he says by way of greeting.

I accept the coffee gratefully, pleased he's happy to pretend yesterday didn't happen. So pleased, in fact, I'm tempted to give him an impulsive hug.

But I don't.

"Yeah? How come?"

But before he can answer, Shosh sweeps into the room in that imperious way of hers, and we take our seats at the table. She rattles off her usual list of reminders and warnings, but this morning she seems distracted, and her somber eyes don't match her smile.

"Right, guys. Another little bit of good news for you all. Cass and Theo, understandably, have had a change of heart and are canceling their skiing trip to go and see Xavier at the hospital, as they've not been able to speak to him on the phone yet."

"Dude had a *pen* stuck through his damn larynx, and they're worried about not being able to speak to him?" Samira wonders, incredulous.

She has a point. Rhys, looking down at the table, quirks his mouth in a slight smile, while Shosh frowns.

"What I *mean* is, they'd just feel better being with him. That whole situation's gotta have been a bit of a holiday buzz-kill, y'know? Anyway, while they wait for their taxi, you guys can have a couple of hours off, since we're currently well ahead of schedule."

There are murmurs of approval around the table, although no doubt Rhys will find something else on the train to do rather than speak to me—maybe alphabetize the wine selection. So when Shosh calls the meeting to a close and we all file out, I'm surprised when his hand lightly rests on my shoulder, and he inclines his head back to the table.

"I've been thinking," he says once we're alone.

I grin and sit down. "Uh-oh?"

He quietly closes the staff room door and joins me at the table.

"Yeah, all *night*, actually. I'm starting to think there are too many things about Gwen's so-called *organic matter* project that don't add up—don't you?"

I wince inwardly. I mean ye-*es*, and Rhys didn't even get to see the delights of what I've dubbed "petal guy." But the sun is finally shining, the train is stopping in the French countryside, and before long we'll be in Tallinn and I'll be starting a new phase of my life. Every click of the train along its track brings me closer to that. Today sweeping the weirdness under the rug and getting on with things seems so much more preferable to opening this can of rose-scented worms.

"Yeah . . . kind of," I say diplomatically.

"That weird-ass statue aside, the news article I found makes me . . . uneasy."

"Uh, yeah, and let's not forget *Xavier*," I add without thinking.

Rhys gives me a strange look. "What about him?"

Trapped, I give him a quick rundown of the petals-and-vines situation, and he frowns.

"You saw him cough up literal *petals* and didn't think to say anything?"

"No, of course not," I hiss. "All I'm saying is they were spilling out of the tissue he left on the table, so that's what it *seemed* like. Occam's razor suggests he was just cleaning up the mess from one of Shosh's wilting flower displays."

I regret saying this. Rhys looks even more troubled. I bet he's already got a bullet-point list entitled "Weird Shit" on his Notes app. "Look, Rhys, honestly, I think the best course of action is to keep our heads down until we get to Tallinn. It's less than a week now, after all."

But of course, whenever there's the suggestion that something strange might be going down, Rhys is like a puppy with a squeaky toy.

"Right, but hear me out—" He pauses as heavy footsteps pass outside the door, then resumes once they've faded away. Honestly, the fact that he's so concerned puts me on edge. Deep down, I can sense that he's right, but going to Shosh with a lot of essentially groundless rumors about our guests might run the risk of our getting kicked off the train—especially since these two are big tippers—and I *need* the money this job is going to provide me with.

"The assistant Gwen brought on the train was wearing a mask when we saw him in that carriage, right?" Rhys asks.

I nod. A tiny trickle of fear works its way down my spine.

"So what if it was for *protection*? What if Gwen's transporting some kind of plant-based *disease*, like—SARS or the t-Virus or—"

"Rhys, I hate to break this to you, but *Resident Evil* isn't real—"

"You know what I mean, though, and maybe it infected Xavier? You're the one who said you saw vines or something emerging out of his mouth. What if *that's* what happened to Gwen and Gwydion's parents? What if that happens to *us*?"

I exhale and put my head in my hands, watching my dreams of Costa del Sol beaches and whitewashed Greek villages begin to go up in smoke.

"Okay," I say, more to the table than to Rhys. "Okay. So we keep a close eye on them. We don't have enough concrete evidence to talk to Shosh yet, so we watch and we wait until we do. You keep an eye on Gwen, and I'll keep an eye on Gwydion. Agreed?"

Rhys nods. "Agreed." He pauses. "Do you trust him?"

I shake my head. "No. I don't know him well enough, but I think he *wants* to get to know me . . . if you know what I mean."

Rhys gives me a dark look, and I think he's about to say something further but apparently thinks better of it.

The skiing siblings are the first to enter the dining carriage for lunch. Theo supports Cass, who looks paler than ever. I hope she's planning to get herself checked out, too, once they reach the hospital. Theo stands back as she commences a violent sneezing fit, picking up the vast bouquet from their chosen table.

"Hay fever," he declares grimly, depositing them on the nearby walnut sideboard.

As each day passes, the arrangements of fresh flowers placed on every dining and side table and in myriad vases throughout the train grow more and more ostentatious. Shosh must have a supply somewhere that she puts out during the night shift; the thought of Gwen creeping down here every morning before sunrise to arrange them all like some elegant spider is more than a little unnerving.

"You doing okay?" I ask Cass quietly as I take their order.

All she wants is tea.

"Honestly . . . I've felt better," she replies with a gentle laugh, then her expression changes and she quickly waves me away.

I dodge back as she sneezes again, and it must just be water droplets, but in the morning sunlight that slants through the blinds, the spray issuing violently from her lips looks an awful lot like pollen.

18

After we finish clearing the lunch things away, the train begins to slow. I look out the window, surprised. I expected we'd stop in a city or, at the very least, a town, but we are still deep within the sweeping French farmland.

Regardless, as the train eases to a stop and Shosh opens an exterior door, spring sunshine washes over my face, causing the shadows that have been clinging to me for the last few days to shrink away, my heart lighter than it has been for months.

"Right, everyone," she announces, her voice warm, clearly grateful for the break herself. "You've got two hours—basically, as long as it takes for the taxi to arrive. Don't go too far, and *don't* get lost. We've got places to be, schedules to keep to, and we won't be waiting for any stragglers."

At first glance, the station is remote and utterly deserted.

I can't hide my disappointment. Being a big fan of a French accent, I hoped there'd at least be some kind of chic coffee shop where I could sit with a fresh pain au chocolat and a latte and make conversation with someone who isn't from this bloody train. But the door to the waiting room is locked, the paint peeling from the walls, the padlock long rusted, and the only exit from the station is a half-open iron gate, aggressively topped with iron spikes and creaking in the breeze. As I trail my hand lazily along the gate, Gwydion appears behind me.

"Important to keep out herds of wandering cows, I suppose," he muses. "I, uh, think we misunderstood each other yesterday."

Ever since our chat in Domme, he doesn't intimidate me the way he used to—even if I am suspicious of him. Besides, this is the perfect time to find out a little more about his background and what happened to his parents.

I smile at him.

"The creepy warning was a little weird, but you were absolutely right. I shouldn't have been poking around your private carriages."

"Well." He smiles. "Don't worry, I'll keep your secrets."

Through the gate is a semicircle of gravel, where Theo and Cass stand, cases and skis piled beside them, awaiting their ride to the hospital, both hollow-eyed and drawn. Cass has spent the last day or so constantly staring at her phone in irritation, and this morning is no different.

I walk over, giving Theo a polite nod and Cass a tight hug.

"Sorry your holiday's turned out so shit," I murmur, unsure what else to say.

She pulls away and smiles at me, and for a moment, I get a sense of the sunny, generous girl she really is behind all the worry. "Yeah, well. I don't much like skiing anyway. Mother just made me come along to keep Theo out of trouble."

Beyond the weed-strewn gravel of the station car park and through a splintering gray wood gate is a field of desiccated wheat and, beyond that, a flat expanse of meadow that seems to stretch on forever under the cerulean stretch of sky. The wheat is tall and gray, whispering sibilantly in the strong wind.

I drift over to where Gwydion is staring at a now-defunct timetable, the paper yellowed and faded beneath its cracked frame.

"You know, I'm glad they're getting along," he says. "I'm sure you've noticed yourself, but it takes Gwen a while to open up to people."

I follow Gwydion's gaze to where she and Rhys are deep in conversation on a rusted metal bench outside the station, heads bent together as if conspiring. They look like the perfect couple: he rangy and tall, she as delicate and elegant as the flowers she tends. Both intelligent, successful . . .

I remind myself he's just carrying out our plan. Besides, Gwen's a little old for Rhys.

"It's beginning to be a bit of a cliché, but want to keep me company again?" Gwydion asks, giving me a sideways smirk that's best described as devilish and sending an unexpected wash of heat over my body. I smile back. Plan or not, some fresh air away from the dark confines of the train and the opportunity to stretch my legs in charming company seem a welcome prospect.

"Absolutely."

We begin wading through the waist-high rows of wheat, the scratchy husks snagging the thin tights of my uniform, until we reach the broad green meadow beyond, dotted here and there with sweet-smelling shrubs. Idly I take my phone out of my pocket to snap a picture of the first actual view I've seen in days that isn't the interior of a train. Before putting it away, I check to see if I have a signal out here. Dad and Gran must be worried sick, even though I warned them I might not be in contact until I left the train. But irritatingly, there's nothing. Not a single bar. I try dialing Dad's number, but it doesn't even ring—just three short beeps and then silence.

"Do you have any signal on your phone?" I ask Gwydion, hoping he'll let me borrow it if he does. He shakes his head. "Sorry, didn't bring it. Just wanted to enjoy the stillness—revel in the beauty of nature, you know?"

I probably should have guessed. There's this old-school eccentricity about him that's both amusing and intriguing.

We stop at the top of the field, and he whisks off his coat, the lining peacock-colored paisley, and collapses onto it with catlike grace, patting the space beside him. I oblige but feel a little on edge. It's so open here, so exposed. You can see to the horizon in every direction, and of course, that means that anyone can see us, too.

"You don't reckon the farmer's strolling around with a shotgun or something?" I ask with an uneasy laugh. "*Get orf of my land* and all that."

Gwydion chuckles. "No, I do not. It's obvious there's no one around for miles."

This does not exactly ease my nerves. But I can see the station in the distance, most of the others milling about the still-deserted parking lot.

"Do I make you nervous, Lara?"

He lies back, resting on his elbows, smiling inscrutably at the sky.

"Honestly? A little," I admit. "I've never met anyone like you before."

He laughs, an easy, appealing sound, and I relax a little.

"How so?"

I shrug. "You're very . . . confident. Sure of yourself."

"I suppose it comes with the money. There's very little I have to worry about."

I hug my knees and give a small laugh, my questions semi-prepared. "All right for some. So tell me about yourself. Why aren't you at uni or something? And if you're really some Forbes-under-thirty hot shit, how come you're stuck on this train delivering all those plants? If they're that important, shouldn't that be your parents' job?"

It's a deliberate question.

DISAPPEARANCE OF WEALTHY LANDOWNERS . . .

The words spool in my mind like ticker tape.

As he replies, his voice loses its usual edge of permanent amusement. "I've told you; I don't *want* to be here at all. Even though Gwen's older, she's not particularly . . . streetwise. She suffers from terrible anxiety and isn't very good at dealing with people—so I agreed to come and do the people-pleasing. And I'm not at uni because I don't choose to be. I'd rather spend my time . . . making investments instead. As for why us and not our parents, well, our parents aren't around anymore . . . there's *only* us."

I soften my voice. "I'm sorry, Gwydion. Can I ask what happened to them?"

Reflexively, he clenches his hand into a tight fist, then splays it open.

"Of course you can ask, but unfortunately, I don't have an answer."

"Oh?"

"Funny story, really. I was away with some mates on holiday when I got a call from a neighbor saying there was a problem up at the house. They were pretty vague, and I couldn't get hold of my parents on the phone, so being the dutiful son I am, I took the next flight home, and when I got back, I found that the entire place had half collapsed." He gives a bitter laugh. "I mean, whatever drama the tabloids like to make of it, it wasn't entirely surprising; I suspected the place had been slowly subsiding for a while. . . . I kept telling them they needed to cut down some of the trees that surrounded the house, do some basic upkeep. It was the roots, you see, the tree roots. But there was no way my parents were ever going to move. That house has been in my father's family for . . . for generations."

He might call it a funny story, but a tear slips down his cheek as he speaks, his voice softly hypnotic.

"They were listed as missing. And we all thought the worst, at first. But the police ordered a thorough search of the wreckage and, turns out, they simply weren't *there*, you know. And other things were missing, too. A couple of suitcases . . . their passports. It was pure *hell* for the first month or so, staring at my phone, waiting for them to get in contact. They were both charmingly old-fashioned; neither of them had cell phones. . . ." He shakes his head sadly, his glacier-clear eyes staring down at where the *Banebury* waits in the station. "But you can't exist in that state forever. That curious limbo between hope and grief. And as time goes by, your hopes start to fade." He rubs the sleeve of his fine-knit sweater over his eyes, and I feel guilty at having pressed him. "It was pretty clear what had happened, to my mind and to anyone else who chose to look closely. As the months passed and costs mounted—first the roof, then the foundations—the estate got in such a way that there was no hope of saving it. And all the money my parents had poured into it had left them utterly bankrupt.

"But you know, despite it all, they never once touched the trust funds they'd set aside for Gwen and me. And ever since they left"—he sighs, despondent—"that cruel *hope* you feel at every vibration, every ping of your phone . . . even though you know it isn't them, won't ever be them. Because, Lara, missing is so very much worse than dead. You're left with all these *questions*. And while I hate myself for it, I often wish they *were* dead, that their bodies had been found, so that I'd have something to *grieve*. . . ."

His voice catches and trails off.

I stare at him, horrified, but his gaze is locked on the grassy scrub beneath us. "Oh, God—look, I'm—I'm so sorry . . ."

He blinks, sitting up and shaking his head. "Honestly, it's not as bad as I'm making it sound. Gwen and I grew up in boarding schools. We were lucky if they remembered to collect us for the holidays. In a way, this trip has been very good for me. . . . I've needed the distraction."

Gwydion looks at me then, his expression sincere as he pushes a lock of ebony hair out of his eyes, and an unexpected shiver of desire dances through me. "Okay," he says, "now you've heard my life story. *My* turn. Why is someone like you working aboard this . . . ghost train?" He pauses meaningfully. "What are you running from, Lara?"

I'm quiet for a while before answering.

"Okay, well . . . the answer to your first question is in the second." I sigh. "It's been a rough couple of months, to be honest. I—I needed some time out."

He nods as if he understands. "Yes, you have the air of a person escaping. . . . Not all the time but sometimes. Sometimes you let the mask slip."

To my horror, my lip trembles at his words, and I stare at him, horrified he has seen through me so easily.

"You don't have to talk about it," he continues, his voice soft but sure. "Just know that in time, Lara, all things wither and fade. Yes, the good, but happily, the bad, too. You won't feel this way forever, that I can promise."

Wordlessly, he takes my hand, softly holding it in his. His words are soothing in a way I can't explain, and given so easily, so generously, like a well-practiced spell. We sit in gratified silence for a while, listening to the early-spring winds playfully tear about the trees behind us and chase through the cornfield. Brushing away a useless tear, I lie beside him, watching the thick banks of clouds scud lazily across the sky, pulling my thin, work-issue fleece tighter around me. Gwydion settles back down, resting his head on his hand, revealing those neat white teeth, his canines ever so slightly elongated, like an amiable wolf's.

"I still can't decide if you're lovers or enemies," he says. My cheeks heat furiously as I realize he's looking over toward Rhys, now leaning against the gate of the station, talking to Carlos.

"Neither," I say, keeping the regret from my voice. "Just . . . old friends that have grown apart, that's all."

All it was and all it'll ever be.

"That's the way of things, I suppose," he muses, tilting his face toward the sun. "Things fall apart. The center cannot hold, and all that."

"I guess," I reply quietly, not entirely sure what he means.

"I can't say that information doesn't please me, though," he continues, shifting to lean over me in a way that sends sparks shooting through my blood, that screams of pleasant dangers.

"Oh?" My voice sounds alarmingly strangled as his luminous eyes lock on mine.

He chuckles easily, looking away again. Flirting is a game to him, one he's good at. With a shy smile, I close my eyes and relish the feel of the sun on my face.

When I open them, Gwydion is gone. I sit up and see he's wandered away in the direction of a shadowy copse, the trees withered and gray. I remain where I am, flopping back on his coat and closing my eyes, enjoying the sunshine. A few minutes pass, then my eyes flick open at the sound of his footsteps padding through the thick, damp grass. In his hands, he holds a crown of creamy white flowers cleverly laced together with some kind of reed.

"Here. Queen of the Meadow," he announces proudly, sitting back down beside me as I accept them.

"Well . . . thank you," I say, placing it in my lap, a little embarrassed. "It's certainly an improvement on Queen of *Poisons*."

"Ah, so you *have* been talking to my sister."

"Tell me about that third carriage," I say quietly. "Why did you tell me it was dangerous? Why did you warn me about it? Were you—were you joking?"

He turns and considers me for a few moments, his glacier-blue eyes unblinking. "You saw it, didn't you? The artifact, I mean."

A cloud momentarily obscures the sun, darkening the

meadow and lengthening the shadows of the trees, and I shiver. I picture it back on the train, lurking in the shadows, emaciated, decaying, centuries old.

"Yes."

He nods.

"It's old. Ancient, even. Due to the carving on the base, we're pretty confident it depicts a character from a Welsh legend, from the Mabinogion—the earliest collection of Welsh stories. These tales can be traced back centuries, originally collected from bards and storytellers. Her name is Blodeuwedd. These days some call her the goddess of spring or the goddess of flowers."

I listen, entranced, as Gwydion continues, idly picking at the grass as he speaks.

"Blodeuwedd itself means 'Flower Face,' but it's also an old Welsh term for 'owl.' She was created to subvert a curse placed on Lleu Llaw Gyffes—by his own mother, would you believe it—a curse that decreed he could take no human wife."

His cadence changes, slows like a receding tide, his voice deepening and his accent thickening as he begins to recite something: a story, a legend, a spell.

"And from the soft haze of the sun-dappled meadow, the magician conjured a bride for Lleu Llaw. Her skin was the delicate white satin of oak blossom, her eyes the same honeyed gold as meadowsweet petals, her hair the shade of broom, a spill of soft-morning sunshine over pale shoulders. A flower bride, as gentle and as glorious as spring rain, destined to

thrive in sunlight and birdsong. It came as no surprise to anyone when Llaw fell headlong in love."

His words seem to magic images into the air, paint pictures in the scudding clouds. His voice is lazy and singsong, like an incantation. I delicately sniff the crown he has given me. The scent is sweet . . . almost sickly, and not entirely pleasant. I place it on the grass beside me.

"So you're telling me that"—I pause, wondering how to describe it politely—"that statue is supposed to be *her*—this most beautiful woman."

Gwydion gives me an indulgent smile. "In her *final* form . . . yes. The story ends in tragedy. Anything involving curses and fate never tends to end well, does it?"

"What went wrong? Why didn't she love her husband?"

Gwydion shrugs, methodically pulling the petals from a daisy as he speaks. He loves me; he loves me not.

"Perhaps she didn't want to do as she was told? On top of that, I doubt she was very particularly pleased when she realized that the sole purpose of her creation was to live in his cold stone castle and provide him with heirs. Let's not forget there was more of nature about her than anything human. She was a wildflower wilting away in a darkened room. Anyway, time passed, and she fell in love with a hunter, Gronw, on one of the rare occasions Lleu was away—I imagine he guarded her like a rare prize—and together they conspired to kill him."

"And she was turned into that—that beast—in revenge for Lleu's death?"

"Yes. It's an owl. Like any flower, what Blodeuwedd loved best was feeling the sun on her face. Company and warmth and chatter made her feel alive. What better way to punish her than to turn her into an owl, a solitary bird that hunts in darkness."

"Harsh."

"You know, Lara, there's something about you that puts me in mind of her," he murmurs, leaning forward to pick up a strand of my hair and twist it gently in his fingers. I'm aware it's another line, but honestly, I've heard worse. "These golden curls of yours . . ." He makes eye contact almost shyly, flicking his gaze down to my lips, his lashes dark against his flawless skin, and my blood heats to boiling point. "They're beautiful, like buttercups, like primroses in early spring, like meadowsweet. *You're* beautiful. . . ." He waits, and my senses are now full of him; I can see nothing beyond the cold twin stars of his eyes, can smell the spearmint on his breath.

But I have been here before, with beautiful boys spinning words out of gold—those I yearn to trust but don't. And there are still too many unspoken questions in my mind—about Gwydion, about Gwen—for me to let my guard down.

"That's sweet of you," I say softly, flopping back onto his coat, deliberately removing myself from the radius of desire. His lips curve into the kind of wolfish smile that has me seriously reconsidering my actions, but he throws a pleasant-scented arm around me while remaining at a polite distance. We lie there for a few minutes, not speaking, the warm brush of the sun on my eyelids lulling me into a state of drowsiness. Eventually my eyes close for longer than a blink, and for the first time since boarding the train, I drift into a deep and uncomplicated sleep.

19

When I wake, the sun is setting far on the horizon, and I'm alone. I rub my forearms, dappled with goose bumps despite my fleece. It's *cold* now; any warmth the weak sun provided has been entirely leeched from the landscape. The grass beside me is flattened, and both Gwydion and his coat are gone. I struggle up—the ground beneath me is unpleasantly damp—and as I do, something tips over my face. I pull it gently away from my head. It's the crown of flowers; their white petals look like they've been dipped in gold. Where *is* Gwydion? I stagger up quickly, momentarily panicked that the train might be gone, but to my relief, it still waits in the station.

"Gwydion?" I call, although I sense I am alone.

Oddly, though, I have the intense sensation I am being watched.

Giving in to the feeling, I look behind me.

In the growing dusk, the thicket behind me is dark. The

trees seem crowded closer than before, their branches wizened and intertwined. And I can make out the shape of a person within—only a shadow. Is it Gwydion?

I stand. My head feels unpleasantly heavy, like it's too big for my body.

Placing the flower crown back on my head, I walk toward the trees, pulling my sleeves over my hands and rubbing my arms against the chill. My mind is running faster than I like—a low panic, an underlying feeling that the train is going to leave and I will be stuck here alone, miles away from civilization in the very depths of the countryside with no phone signal and no money. My public-school French limited, beyond *oui, non,* and *Où est le Centre Pompidou?*

The copse is up a steep incline. I fix my eyes on the shadows within. I saw someone there; I *know* I did—a quick flash of eyes, a sudden blur of movement.

"Gwydion?" I call again. Louder, my voice insistent, a trace of fear and uneasiness in it that I cannot hide.

I hesitate outside the circle of trees. They are like no trees I've ever seen before. Tall and twisted, with gnarled, bleached branches, huddling toward the dark center like a circle of hunched giants.

"What are you *doing* in there?" I call, but my voice is whipped away by a sudden wind that whistles through the small gaps in the tightly entwined branches.

My foot crunches on dead leaves as I step closer.

Lara . . .

A voice on the wind or in my head?

I am being *watched*.

I whirl around on a whim, half expecting to see someone standing directly behind me. But there is no one. Only the train in the station, its windows glowing merrily in the dusk. The tall rows of corn sway in the wind, their husks entwining, whispering secrets.

Lara...

Come closer.

The voice is coming from the trees. And it's not Gwydion. It is too *high*, too sweet, too lilting.

I take another step toward them, screwing up my eyes, desperately trying to make sense of the darkness within.

Come... closer.

"Who's—who's there?"

It's not what I feared. Not some burly farmer wielding a gun... Not some stranger wearing a fencing mask...

Deep within the center of the trees, I see her. A pair of amber eyes that glow with their own luminescence. I am reminded again of my first night aboard the *Banebury*, of peering through the peephole of my cabin door.

Lara.

Please...

"What—what do you want?"

I want to sound brave, but my voice is pleading, half whipped away by the wind.

I want—

I want to be flowers—I want to be flowers again—I—

There is a loud creaking, a violent snapping within the

scrub, branches breaking and wood splintering. Movement from above startles me. A sardonic low chattering followed by an earsplitting screech.

My nerve breaks.

I turn, the flower crown tumbling to the ground as I run through the waist-length grass back toward the sanctuary of the train. Why hasn't it left yet? Why are we still here? Why hasn't anyone come looking for me?

As I reach the boundary of the wheat field, I stagger to a stop. The wheat is now almost as tall as I am. How is it possible it's grown this quickly? The station isn't far, though—only a hundred meters or so away. I push my way through, the dusty scent of dry wheat filling my nostrils, suffocating me, the husks filling my throat, until finally I emerge, panting, on the road before the station.

But the train is moving.

Footsteps pound behind me, and someone screams my name, their voice rising higher and higher in pitch until it becomes the wretched whistle of the departing train, and then finally, the hungry screech of an owl.

I jolt up immediately, relief flushing through me. A *dream*. That's all. I haven't been sleeping well; it's hardly surprising I dozed off.

Gwydion yawns loudly beside me, and as I sit up and rub my eyes, I hear the sound of someone stolidly swishing through the grass.

"La?"

Smoothing my hair, I look up, flushed and disoriented, to see Rhys looming over us.

"Hey, we need to go back, guys," he says shortly, his face an unusually expressionless mask. "Shosh says we're due to depart in ten minutes."

The sky is darker now, threatening rain, and it's much colder than when we disembarked. Rhys strides ahead, creating a path through the graying husks of corn, while Gwydion ambles alongside me, still talking about Welsh legends in that deep musical voice of his. And as he speaks, he seems to conjure the meadow around us into life. The grass becomes thicker and more verdant. The skinny shafts of corn seem to ripen, no longer thin and gray but fat to bursting. And I must not have noticed before how long abandoned the station is. Ivy and bindweed have claimed it completely, lacing themselves tightly around the gutters, the walls, the opposite bank; green tendrils stretching across the platform and twisting about the rails.

Gratefully I climb back aboard the *Banebury*. Glancing out the window, I notice that the bank on the other side of the platform seems closer than I remember it, the dense shrubbery seeming to reach longingly toward the *Banebury*'s sleek chassis. Above us, trees crowd over the train, creating a natural tunnel. Everything looks so impossibly *green* and alive when it's barely even spring. Curious, I watch as Shoshanna and Carlos hack at the rails with fire axes, removing what appear to be tree roots. After my strange dream, the idea that we might be stuck here makes me uneasy.

But after ten minutes or so, the train gives a violent jolt, and we are off once more.

That evening everyone is in much better spirits after their bout of fresh air. Shoshanna sings as she helps me lay the table for dinner, while I am still busy mooning over my moment with Gwydion.

For dinner Carlos serves up squares of rich moussaka accompanied by a fresh green salad. Even Gwen appears to be in good spirits, joining in with the conversation in her quiet, measured way and even smiling now and then. Only the baroness looks unhappy, glowering at everyone and snapping at us staff.

"So are you going to tell us what exactly you're transporting in those carriages?" she finally asks Gwydion after her ill-advised fifth gin and tonic, her speech slightly slurred. "And *why* are they always kept locked?"

Gwydion looks at her, his grin frozen eerily on his face.

"Organic matter—plants, if you prefer. You attended our charity dinner, didn't you?"

"Yes," she snaps. "And I made a *rather* generous donation, as you are well aware. My question is, don't you think you should unlock those carriages so we can all enjoy them?"

I watch from my position in the kitchen as Gwen quietly puts down her cutlery and pushes her plate away. A dangerous tension has invaded the once-cheery dinner. The baroness turns her attention to Shoshanna.

"Is it legal to transport that amount of plant matter across borders? Has anyone checked? I mean, there are things *growing* in my cabin, dear. Were you aware of that? And Becca's. Hardly an indication of this five-star luxury you promise."

Shoshanna's mouth is set in a firm line. "Is that right? Interesting, because the girls and I clean them on the daily, and we haven't noticed anything growing in them."

"Then perhaps you are not doing as good a job as you should," the baroness snaps back.

"Like what?" asks Rhys, pausing before collecting plates, calm but curious. "What's growing?"

"Well, what do you think? Plants! Moss, on the windowsills, and ivy—or something vinelike—on the ceiling, so you might not notice it at first, especially if you insist on doing a rushed job of housekeeping. But you know, I can *hear* it at night . . . slithering . . . like a *snake*. Sometimes . . . sometimes, when I'm half asleep, I swear I can feel it crawling across my skin, keeping me still, holding me in place. . . ."

A chill trickles down my spine like a drop of ice water.

Shoshanna is not amused, but she speaks kindly. "I think perhaps you might have had enough gin for one night, baroness."

"*Baroness*," she mimics. "You're *staff*, girl; you've no business telling me what to do or when I've had enough of anything. And besides, I rather feel you should be addressing me as 'Lady.'"

"Wow, *Baronesses Gone Wild* was not on my bingo card this trip," mutters Samira from behind me.

"Hey—hang on a minute," begins Rhys steadily, but of course Shoshanna's got this.

"Interesting. . . . I gotta ask, do you want to get into a conversation about things that shouldn't be in cabins?" she asks, steely-eyed. "Because if you do, I'm more than willing to share what I have found in your assistant's, my *lady*."

Becca goes a fiery shade of fuchsia, seeming to sink beneath the table. We've all noticed that unmistakable herbal smell emanating from her cabin, however many windows she opens.

The baroness gives her a sharp, disapproving glance.

She opens her mouth as if she's about to say more but doesn't. Instead, she snaps her mouth closed like a turtle, stands and slams her chair under the table, and totters unsteadily out of the carriage.

"Now, now, Gwen, you really *must* keep those plants of yours under control," says Gwydion, looking hard at his sister.

For once I am enjoying my dream . . . something involving a warm, sunny meadow and the giant bobbing heads of sunflowers. I feel sure that Gwydion is there, too, lying beside me, face turned to the sun, although already the cobwebs of the dream are drifting away, a low, insistent knocking at my door dismissing them.

I sit bolt upright.

"Y-Yeah? Who is it?"

Relief flushes through me as I hear Rhys's voice, low and urgent.

"Hey—La, it's me. C'mon, let me in."

I glance at my phone. It's just after midnight.

"What the hell, Rhys," I mutter, climbing down from my

bunk and pulling a hoodie over my tank top and shorts. I wrench open the door. "This better be good," I complain, stifling a yawn. I squint at him. "Anyway, I thought you said we were *locked in*?"

"I know... I did say that," he replies, looking distracted. His hair is mussed from sleep, and he wears a faded *Jaws* tee and checked pajama bottoms, glasses perched on his nose. He blinks at me for a split second and then awkwardly edges past me into my cabin, closing the door quietly behind him. "So, turns out I was wrong; we weren't *locked* in. Well... not in the way I thought."

There's a strange expression on his face. The pupils in his round, dark eyes are huge; his face is so pale his freckles stand out in stark relief.

It takes me several moments before I realize he is scared.

I rub the vestiges of sleep from my eyes, fully alert now. "Rhys, what are you talking about? What's going on?"

He raises his hands, which I now see are crammed with thick bunches of some weedy green plant.

"It's *this*. This was covering the doors, literally *growing* over both our doors—*that's* why we couldn't get out. What the baroness was saying at dinner about things... *growing* in her cabin got me thinking.... That's why it looked as if the doors weren't locked—they weren't; they were just... stuck."

I stare down at his hands. It is the same stringy green weed with large white trumpet-shaped flowers my granddad is forever pulling from his allotment fence. "Stuff grows like wildfire," he's always grumbling.

What the hell was it doing growing outside our doors? And how have I never noticed it? I took biology in high school. Plants need water, light, and CO_2 to grow. Plants—even weeds—do not just spring up from the carpet in a matter of hours and disappear by morning, especially not on moving *trains*.

I narrow my eyes. "Rhys . . . like, are you . . . are you okay?"

He collapses onto the lower bunk. "I . . . think so. And I get why you'd ask. It seems impossible to me, too."

I sink down beside him, noticing with chagrin how he edges away from me a little.

But then I remember the ivy I discovered that second night on the train, not yet fully grown, only a single thin tendril, but trailing through the entire length of the train. Why did I so easily dismiss it at the time?

I take a closer look at Rhys. He looks *tired*. Concerned. Worried. Stretched too thin. All the things he never usually looks. Without even thinking, I put my hand over his. He flinches slightly but doesn't remove it. He's shaking, I realize. I lower my voice, soften it. He needs someone to listen. "Okay, then, from the beginning. What exactly happened tonight?"

He closes his eyes as he begins to speak. "So . . . I—I couldn't sleep. It's weird. I should have been exhausted, but I was tossing and turning, and even though my window was open, the cabin felt stiflingly hot." He swallows. "So I got up, meaning to go refill my water bottle and grab some ice from the kitchen, but when I tried to open the door, it wouldn't budge again."

He looks at me. "I'd checked with Shosh earlier, brought up the possibility of our being locked in at night, and she'd laughed, saying how that was a lawsuit waiting to happen. So I used the flashlight on my phone to check through the track in the door, and she was right. There was no deadbolt or whatever you call it beneath the latch. . . . The door *should* have opened."

He moves his hand from under mine and runs it through his hair. "So, I don't know . . . some low-level panic set in. I wrenched the door back and forth, but there really was *something* keeping it from opening. Looking again with the flashlight, I noticed something thin crisscrossing the gap between the door and the doorframe, like string or something—so I got my knife—"

"Whoa . . . you have a *knife*?"

He pulls a face. "Just a Swiss Army pocketknife. I only use it for the scissors and toothpick. Anyway, I ran it around the door, cutting through whatever it was, and then . . . then it finally opened."

He swallows. "And outside there was a load of this." He nods to the discarded weeds on the floor, now shriveled and pathetic. "On the floor outside. It's *bindweed*. But it was all around the corridor and"—he lowers his voice and leans forward—"and it was all around your door, too."

I pause, not saying anything for a while.

Because I don't *want* to hear this.

I don't want Detective Rhys and his wild and unnerving theories. I came here to get away from endless mental gymnastics. I wanted a boring, monotonous job, followed by several exciting weeks of traveling through new countries, floating on a pool raft in the Med while sipping on virgin margaritas.

"Look, there's got to be some kind of mistake. . . . This *can't* be true, Rhys," I say, looking him fully in the eye, aware I am giving him a subtle warning. "We can't be . . . locked in by plants. It's—it's ridiculous. It's not even *possible*."

Rhys nods. "Oh, I know that. I appreciate that we're on a bloody train, not in a park. But that doesn't change the fact that it happened, and it doesn't change the fact that it feels like some weird shit is going down."

His green eyes are overbright.

"Gwen is researching *accelerated growth*, remember?" he continues. "And when we stopped earlier, did you notice—granted, you were too busy schmoozing Gwydion, but did you notice what had happened to the train when we went back?"

"I was not schmoozing *anyone*—"

"But did you *see*, La? Did you see how everything had changed? Within only a couple of *hours*."

I am silent for a minute.

Because I *did* see.

It's funny how the mind seems to naturally compensate for things like that—things that *can't* be possible. It tells you that you just aren't paying attention, that you're daydreaming, you're distracted; things aren't that bad, you're exaggerating, you're remembering wrong—

Those springy saplings, silver heads bobbing and bending low over the tracks like contortionists, almost taller than the train. The brown, dusty roots of trees had weaved themselves tight between the train and the track. Shoshanna's concerned face as she and Carlos hacked the tracks free.

Rhys stands up, agitated, his usually relaxed face drawn, malachite eyes almost black. "I'm going to look in those carriages right now. There must be something in there that's causing this. I mean . . . that has to be where these plants are originating from. And if this gets worse, it could be . . . *dangerous*. For everyone—if it isn't already." He opens the cabin door. "So, you coming or what?"

20

As we approach the now-familiar ornate wooden door of the greenhouse carriages, I feel an unpleasant churning in my gut, like worms writhing in compost. It feels dangerous to be here at night, to be here in the darkness. And I start to wonder if we've been shut in our cabins at night for good reason—maybe there *is* something... experimental going on aboard this train that we're not *meant* to know about. Maybe we are being kept in the dark for our own safety. Maybe there are government levels of security going on. And it isn't long before that leads to thoughts of Russian oligarchs tumbling off balconies and special agents found zipped up inside duffel bags—people who had found out what they wished they hadn't—

Intrusive thoughts, Lara, that's all *they are.*

But are they? Because Rhys hesitates before the door, too, running his hand lightly over the intricate wooden carvings.

"It's a face . . . ," he murmurs. "Surrounded by a wreath of flowers and . . . and birds. Owls, I think. I never noticed before."

I hadn't noticed either, had just taken it for some fancy floral pattern. The moonlight slants through the carriage window, giving the etchings a ghostly glow. I try to peer in through the stained-glass windows, but beyond them the carriage is in utter darkness.

"Well, at least we know no one's in there," I say, trying to calm my own nerves. "Maybe we should go back? Investigate in the daylight when we can actually see?"

Helpfully, at this point in time, my mind conjures up an image of Gwen festooned in black spiderwebs. Imagines her lying there, in a coffin, hands crossed over her chest, her cold eyes shut and—

I dig my nails into my palm, cutting off *that* particular train of thought.

"And it doesn't look like anything's growing out of there," I point out, looking around the pristine antechamber. The emerald-green carpet is deep and immaculately clean. The walls have been polished within an inch of their life.

"Maybe something is growing up from beneath the train?" says Rhys. "Like some kind of iceberg situation. Besides, we're here now," he continues. "May as well go in and take a look."

Rhys turns the handle and pushes the door to no avail. "Looks like it's locked again—or stuck," he mutters in frustration. But when I seize the handle, the door swings open smoothly. Rhys gives me an odd look, but says nothing. Beyond the door, the flower carriage is pitch-black. Hurriedly I switch my phone's flashlight on and shine it around. I breathe a half sigh of relief. Things look normal enough in here. Still and quiet. The flowers sway with the soft motion of the train, the intense, sickly scent of lilies permeating the air.

"Seems . . . fine?" I say, giving my light a half-hearted wave about the room, hoping Rhys will suggest going back.

"Mmm . . . don't there seem to be . . . more of them—more flowers, I mean—than there were before?" asks Rhys, frowning.

Honestly, in the weak beam of the flashlight, I can't be sure.

"Perhaps, but Gwen and Gwydion were both up-front about the whole accelerated-growth thing," I murmur. "So, say it's got a bit out of hand . . . ?"

I recall what Gwydion said to me the other day, the day he gripped my hand so hard it hurt.

—especially at night.

That's when she goes hunting—

I now have the overwhelming urge to go back to my bed, happy to let the plants hermetically seal me safely in my room until the next morning, but ahead of me, Rhys has almost reached the next carriage. I curse under my breath.

"*Come on,*" he says in a stage whisper, edging toward the door. "Let's just have a quick look at the next one. The sooner we're out of here, the better."

On that point, at least, I could *not* agree more.

The next carriage is darker still. The branches of the trees stretching over us look white, bleached, and skeletal in the wavering light of our phones.

"Hey, *look*," Rhys whispers, his tone a warning.

At the other end of the carriage, a pool of golden light spills out from under that disguised door, accompanied by a low humming sound, a vibration trembling in the air. "Someone's *in* there."

"Well, let's just look through the keyhole," I whisper, now needing to reassure *myself* that everything is aboveboard, let alone Rhys. "It's probably only Gwen or Gwydion."

"At this hour? And doing what? That carriage is practically empty."

I creep forward slowly, focused on not tripping over anything.

"Wait—*wait*," Rhys hisses, holding up a hand and whirling around. "Did you hear that?"

There is the unmistakable sound of movement in the carriage ahead, followed by a weak groaning.

I stare at Rhys, wide-eyed.

"Turn off your flashlight," he orders quietly. "We don't want to get caught."

"What? *No!*" I hiss back. There's no way I am standing here in utter darkness. I can feel myself starting to panic, losing control of my nerves, watching them scatter to the floor and roll away like marbles, and out of nowhere a memory rises up and takes me.

APRIL, LAST YEAR

"What are you doing here?" Beckett asked, his voice sharp.

I backed away from the door as if the handle had burnt

me. It looked innocuous enough, identical to the rest of the doors in the sunny inner courtyard.

"Sorry. I—I was just looking for the bathroom," I said, a wounded look on my face.

Immediately he relaxed.

"Oh," he said, "it's the next one, babe."

I smiled at him and opened the correct door, but I was lying. I wasn't looking for the bathroom at all. I wanted to look in that room. Because I had been in every single room in his parents' ridiculously ostentatious McMansion but that one. His den, apparently.

"A guy's private space, y'know?"

And I did know. I knew that I should respect his wishes, trust him, and just leave it alone, but since I'd met him, I'd found myself becoming less and less trusting rather than more. Not what I would have expected, but it was the truth all the same.

I think it was the disparity that got to me. I was expected to make my phone accessible to him at all times (*I do trust you; it's everyone else—I just know what guys are like*) while his own was permanently locked with a code unknown to me. I was expected to reply to his messages as soon as humanly possible, including during class, while he could leave me on read for a day, explaining that he'd temporarily lost his phone or something equally unlikely, the banality of his excuses ever more insulting. I was expected to flay myself open to him, show him everything, every secret part of me, while he kept so much of himself hidden.

There was a story that had scared me as a child, called

"Fitcher's Bird," about a wealthy sorcerer who had married many times and whose latest bride is told she can explore wherever she likes in his extensive castle except for this one room.

One single room in an entire castle. It shouldn't have been a difficult promise to keep.

But curiosity has its way of gnawing at you. Always whispering *What if?* and *Why?*

Now, I didn't think for one moment that Beckett's secret room contained the disembodied remains of all his ex-girlfriends, like those the storybook wife found, but I still couldn't shake the feeling that there was something, something he didn't want me to see, in that room.

I flushed the toilet and stared into the mirror, barely recognizing the girl I saw looking back at me with her poker-straight hair and newly cut blunt bangs. I supposed it made me look sophisticated, like he'd said, but honestly, I resented the upkeep. No, that wasn't it. I missed the girl who used to look back at me.

Deep down, I knew it wasn't right. That I was not a doll to be dressed up, not a lump of clay to be shaped into his idea of perfection. But, as I was forever reminding myself, the good outweighed the bad. Everything had its price, and this was a small one in the grand scheme of things. But newer, darker prices seemed to emerge endlessly from the shadows the very moment one was paid.

I knew even then that things weren't as perfect as they used to be, that there was a puncture in this sunshine, a wound slowly oozing poison.

When I returned to the kitchen, Beckett threw something down on the marble countertop and gave me a triumphant smirk. It was a pair of tickets. I picked one up, curious.

"What's this?"

He smiled at me, the giddy excitement in his bright-blue eyes once more reminding me why I fell in love with him, why I was lucky to have him.

"So, to properly celebrate this deal closure, I thought we'd spend a few days in London. Dad's got an apartment there. What do you think?"

The tickets were front-row seats to a musical I'd been dying to see, about Henry VIII's wronged wives.

"We could take in the Tower of London while we're there, maybe even Hampton Court. I know how you love your history."

I smiled, confused, as I took in the date printed on the tickets. They were for the very next day—Friday, Beckett's day off. And while in theory it did indeed sound like a dream trip, there were a couple of obvious roadblocks.

"Uh, that does sound amazing . . . truly, but, Beckett, I've got school tomorrow. I already missed a day last week. They're really strict about attendance before exams. Also, I'd need some time to get Gran to come around to the idea of my staying overnight somewhere—"

Dad and my grandparents knew about Beckett. After all, he was my first "serious" boyfriend. We all had the awkward talk about taking things slow, and while they were pretty liberal, going on a weekend away with him was *not* going to be an immediate yes—

I watched in dread as the grin dropped from Beckett's face with the suddenness of a summer squall.

"The tickets aren't transferable. I know you think money grows on trees around here, Lara, but they were really expensive—"

Okay, but you knew I had school.

But I said these words in my head, not out loud. Instead, I grew quiet, retreating into myself, wishing he wouldn't put me in these situations, wouldn't seemingly create them on purpose. What did he even have to gain from it?

A violent slam made me jump—the door, of course. I was so on edge lately, always jumping at shadows. The tickets lay there, ripped in half on the counter, and I sat in the kitchen alone, having messed things up again.

Lara, Lara, Lara, he would later muse, flattening my hair beneath his fingers, teasing my curls straight.

Am I so wrong?

For wanting to make you into something . . . better?

For teaching you how to make me happy?

For needing to conjure you into perfection?

Meadowsweet—found in ditches, on the banks of foul-smelling ponds.

Broom—black seedpods exploding in the sun.

Oak—leaves riddled with toxins.

I was slow to learn that beautiful things keep their dangers well hidden.

And here I am, outside a door once again.

And just as before, I open it.

Instinctively and without thinking, I push the door to the final carriage open just a crack, barely a centimeter, and peer inside.

The light in the room is wan and flickering—candlelight, I remember; there are no electric lights in here.

The whispering has returned. That voice, soft and insistent—a driving, relentless sound imbued with need.

Meadow . . . sweet. And briar. The blossoms of the oak.

It is as if we've stumbled across some unholy Mass.

The baroness is laid flat on the stone plinth before the idol, where the petals were arranged last time I ventured in here, her arms stiff by her sides, her eyelids sheened pearlescent, her red hair a fiery halo around her pale face. She's wearing a translucent nightdress like some Gothic offering, her skin beneath it waxen, surrounded by melting candles that flicker precariously in time with the train's steady progress over the tracks. Effort has gone into making her comfortable; lavish sage-green cushions prop her up as she lies in what I hope is deep sleep.

Beside her, incongruous amid the natural colors and plants, is a metal IV stand, attached to which is a bag that appears to be half filled with a dark red liquid that can only be blood.

It looked—it looked an awful lot like they were watering them with blood—

A shudder wracks my body as I remember ribbing Rhys about that. Attending to the baroness, adjusting the line in her arm, is a person shrouded in black. Even though they're mostly faced away from us, I can tell they are wearing that odd fencing mask. Is it Gwydion, or Gwen, or is it that hidden figure I saw getting on this train with them and who'd apparently never left?

"What in the hell—?" Rhys comes up behind me.

The whispering persists, soft and insistent. . . . Some recording, I guess—but *why*?

"We have to get out of here, Rhys," I murmur as if in a dream. "We can't stay—we have to *go*."

Not needing to be told twice, Rhys laces his hand through mine, the warmth of his fingers both reassuring and jarring, snapping me out of my strange, dreamlike state. With a shaking hand, I pull the panel silently closed and, heart skittering in my chest, follow Rhys out of the carriage. A sense of doom descends on me like a heavy curtain, leaving me shaky and scattered. There's no escaping it anymore, no more pushing it under the rug. We're not paranoid. Something aboard the *Banebury* is *badly* wrong.

We inch through the carriage of vines, Rhys's flashlight focused determinedly on the ground, creating a thin path of light, then closing the door carefully behind us. I pray it's my imagination, but I am sure I can hear movement behind us, heavy, inquiring footsteps.

"Quickly," I hiss, pushing against Rhys and narrowly avoiding knocking over one of the bird-clawed chairs. Eventually we emerge into the piano lounge, where someone has helpfully switched on the light.

We pause, leaning against one of the tables, catching our breath. Rhys's mouth is set in a grim line, his skin ashen.

"Um . . . guys?"

Both of us whirl our heads in the direction of the voice. Standing at the other end of the carriage, duster in hand and looking mightily confused, is Samira.

21

Samira stares at us, wide-eyed, clearly teetering between amusement and concern. Warily I glance back at the door to the greenhouse carriages. There's no sign of light or movement through the dark windows, but I'm sure it won't be long before there is.

Rhys drops my hand like a hot coal. "Oh, hey, Samira. We were just . . . ," he begins promisingly, before abruptly coming to a halt.

"There was a noise," I say as confidently as I can muster. "Like a weird banging. . . . I went to investigate . . . but I didn't want to go alone, so I, um, asked Rhys to go with me."

Samira's lips curl into a knowing smile. "Oh, is that right? A weird *banging*?"

I am too nervous to even blush at this point. We need to get as far away from this part of the train as we can.

"No, seriously," says Rhys, composure apparently restored.

He begins to make his way through the maze of small tables, and I follow him. "Someone had left a window open in there, and the shutter was making an almighty noise. Surprised you didn't hear it yourself."

"Yeah, I didn't," says Samira, puzzled once more, watching us head to the door of the carriage. I pause, not willing to leave her here alone.

"Hey, it looks *amazing* in here, by the way. You're really thorough! You should probably get some rest now, too. If there's anything left to do, I can help you finish in the morning. I've actually got a couple of free hours." I inject some of the adrenaline coursing through me into my voice, making it steely, and Samira looks at me and relents.

"Yeah, well, I was just about done here anyway." She stretches and yawns. "Well, night, guys."

We follow her silently through the train back to our cabins. The second she shuts her door, Rhys speaks in a low, urgent whisper. "Okay. Okay, so we're in agreement, right? After what we just saw, we *need* to tell Shosh, and we *need* to stop this train."

Rhys puts it out there unequivocally. And there's no denying it after what we just saw. Mentally I wave goodbye to my summer plans, watch my wages go up in flames, but all that is infinitely preferable to being laid before that—that *thing*—and becoming Gwen's latest plant sacrifice.

I follow him toward Shosh's tiny office, starting at every

bump the train makes, every squeak of the woodwork, casting anxious backward glances at the shadows behind me. Shosh often works the night shift, monitoring the CCTV while watching game shows on her iPad, but before we even reach the office, I can tell it's dark and unoccupied.

"Where *is* she?" Rhys asks.

"I don't know," I reply. "But there's no way I'm creeping around in the dark looking for her. Not tonight."

I'm mildly surprised when Rhys agrees. "What about the baroness?" he whispers. "Should we go back . . . ? We shouldn't just leave her. . . . I mean . . ."

He deliberately leaves the sentence unfinished, and I close my eyes, sick and shaky. "I . . . I can't," I confess quietly. I'm no hero; I don't have any reserves of bravery left to draw from. There's something so strange, so *wrong*, about that last carriage . . . I can't face it again, not so soon, and not in the dark. It would be stupid of us to go blundering back in there. I wait for Rhys's impatient insistence, but it doesn't come. When I open my eyes, he's looking down at me with a strange expression, his mouth a firm line.

"No, it's okay . . . I get it. Look, let's—let's get you back to your cabin."

Once there, I slump onto the bottom bunk and stare uselessly up at the springs of the top one while Rhys paces the room in a tight circle.

"Okay . . . *okay*. We need a plan," he says with quiet and reassuring authority. And for the first time, I am desperately grateful he's here. Yes, being reminded of my recent past wasn't ideal to begin with, nor was constantly encountering the slowly moldering corpse of our friendship, but I forgot how brilliant he could be in a crisis. Firm and unshakeable, like the city walls of Carcassonne. "We'll find Shosh first thing in the morning," he continues. "From what I could see, it looked like whoever was in there was taking the baroness's blood for some reason. So what could that reason be? Do you reckon there's any way it could have been ... aboveboard?"

I put my hands over my eyes, mind made up. "No. I *highly* doubt it, especially after that earlier conversation at dinner. And I think we might already *know* the reason. You saw it, didn't you?" I realize with growing unease. "The first time I showed you those carriages—through the window."

Rhys doesn't say it aloud but pales as he realizes what I mean—the watering can full of blood. Guilt seeps through me at not believing him.

"Think about it: if you were drugged, you wouldn't really notice anything was wrong the next day. You'd be a little weaker, I guess ... depending on how much blood they took. Might have some bruising ... you probably wouldn't even notice the puncture wound—"

I think of Cass and how she appeared paler and more fragile every day, how she rolled up her sleeve and displayed her arm to Theo that night. Had they done the same to me, to Rhys, without our even knowing?

"*God*, I don't even think she's the first," I murmur, explaining to Rhys what I overheard Cass say. "And didn't you say

Gwen invited you to her cabin the other night? Maybe she was planning to do this to you, too."

Rhys frowns. "Do you think Gwydion is involved?"

I think hard.

Fact is, I don't know. I think of his silent tears in the countryside, the way he easily removes the mask he wears when we're alone, and I don't *want* him to be. I want to continue our light, uncomplicated flirtation until we reach our final destination. But that doesn't mean he isn't. I know better than most how wolves can disguise themselves with flashing eyes and charming words.

"I don't know," I reply honestly. "Possibly. But when we were alone the other day, Gwydion was saying something about Gwen being . . . *different* lately . . . since she started her research. Like, they'd grown apart. There's the chance he isn't involved—that he could even help us, be an ally—maybe he suspects something, too."

Rhys runs a shaky hand over his face. "God, I feel terrible about leaving her in there . . . she's old and frail, what if she—" He picks up his phone and stares at it in frustration. "But I don't know what else to *do*. . . . At least it's clear *now* why we were being locked in. Problem is, we don't know what we're dealing with or how much danger we're in. And there's never any fucking cell *service*!"

I pull my phone out of my pocket. It's the same as his— just a blank line where the signal should be. But even if we could contact the police, what would we tell them? And how could they help us when our location is literally changing by the minute?

"What do you think Shosh will do—when we tell her?" I ask quietly, staring wistfully at the moonlit sky flashing past the window. The train is as silent as ever. If we'd stayed in our rooms as intended, we'd never know any of this happened. Quite the double-edged sword.

"Well, when we tell her exactly what we saw—an old lady having her blood taken, possibly without her permission—even if it *was* with her permission, it's still likely to be illegal. For starters, that carriage doesn't exactly look *sanitary*. I expect Shosh will contact the authorities and kick them off the train. What else would she do?"

A thin tendril of uneasiness creeps about my spine as I remember how Shosh so easily gave up Xavier's phone to Gwen.

But what if she already knows?

What if telling her what we saw is a massive mistake?

"Can it be real?" I ask quietly, more to myself than to Rhys. "*This*, I mean. It seems like something from some old monster feature . . . plants that thrive on blood."

Rhys finally sits down on the chair opposite, his head resting on his arm.

"I have no idea. My initial reaction is '*no*, what the fuck,' but then how else do we explain what we saw? Then there's that article—about their parents disappearing on an overgrown estate. . . . I hate to say it, but it kind of . . . fits."

I sit up, chewing this over. "Gwydion told me about that. . . . And the way he explained it, it didn't seem as . . . sinister as the article made it sound."

"Oh?"

"Yeah, he said the estate was proper old and his parents had long neglected the grounds . . . the house already subsiding thanks to some tree roots. You know, that happened to my neighbor's wall—some old bamboo shoots started pushing it up from beneath. *And* he said things were missing from the home—passports, suitcases."

Rhys is silent for a few seconds, and I sense the tension in the air, sense the uncertainty in his voice, testing the waters. "La, look, I know you wanted a break after everything—"

"After *what*?"

He stands up, exasperated. "You *know* what! God, I am so *tired* of tiptoeing around you all the time, Lara. But the truth is, to me, it sounds more like you *want* to believe Gwydion more than you actually do."

"Okay, but you weren't there, you didn't hear what he said!"

"I don't need to *hear* anything from him, I know what I *saw*! You can keep burying your head in the sand if it makes you feel better, but you need to ask yourself if your need to not derail your summer plans is worth putting yourself in danger."

I exhale slowly, tears springing to my eyes. If Rhys notices, he doesn't say anything.

"Do you really think we can *trust* Gwydion?"

I wipe roughly at my face. "I don't know . . . he's different when we're alone. More himself. More . . . normal, and less showy. But honestly, I don't know him well enough to give a definitive yes."

He looks away for a moment, his pleasant features oddly twisted. "Looked like you knew him pretty well earlier."

I stare at him. There's no way he could be jealous.

"Sorry," he relents, running a hand through his hair. "I'm sorry. It's been a long night. Just be careful, though, La. It seems unlikely he's completely unaware of what's going on."

But there was only *one* person in that carriage with the baroness.

"We should try and get some sleep," he continues. "I might try and look for Shosh again now—"

"No!" I say without thinking, casting a dark glance at the door. "Don't go. Not tonight. Promise me you won't."

The words come out unbidden, but the look of surprise on Rhys's face forces me to explain more. "It—it could be dangerous for us to be separated. Whoever was in that room knows we saw something. They could come looking for us. Please . . . stay here."

"You want me to stay in here?" clarifies Rhys, slowly. "With you."

Why does he have to make it sound like it's a fate worse than death? It isn't like we haven't slept in the same room before, same *bed* before.

"Jesus, it's not like I snore," I say, annoyed. "Just until it gets light and we're sure . . . whatever's gone on tonight is over." I lower my voice. "*Please.* I don't want—I don't think we should be alone."

He shrugs in an overly casual way and looks at the bottom bunk, where I'm still sitting. "Well . . . sure."

It's probably just my imagination, but I can't help feeling that some nerve-tinged electrical charge is seeping into the atmosphere. If we weren't both so on edge and if it wasn't *Rhys*. I mean, in a sexy there's-only-one-bed situation, he's the type who would firmly insist upon the floor.

I haul myself up onto the top bunk, pulling off my hoodie, balling it up and deliberately aiming it at his head in a bid to dismiss the awkward tension. He aims it back at me, then lies, fully clothed, on the bottom bunk, the weight of his rangy form shaking the cheap frame.

"Night, La."

I murmur goodnight back and, comforted by his presence, slip straight into an uneasy sleep.

MAY, LAST YEAR

There came a turning point. A point where I really began to acknowledge, for the first time, that I had made a mistake.

Beckett was away with his father on a golfing trip to Scotland, and with five boyfriend-less days at my disposal, I had time to catch up on all Stevie and Casey's messages. Happily, I agreed to meet them all at the Cozy Cuppa after school. I was looking forward to it.

"Oh my god—she's alive! Where have you been!" shouted Stevie dramatically the moment I walked into the café.

I winced as the entire room turned to look at me, including Rhys, who I clocked making lattes behind the counter. A guilty part of me had hoped he would be here. He'd been the reason I'd nonchalantly suggested meeting here, in fact.

Truth was, I missed him.

I sat down and was immediately dissected by my friends.

"Oh my god, you look so . . . different—love the hair," squealed Casey. "I can barely ever find you at school these days!"

I guess I did look different. Even when Beckett wasn't around, his influence clung to me like a cloying upmarket fragrance. My hair was straightened, and bouncy bangs now framed my face. I felt uncomfortably overdressed in a tartan skater skirt and a tight black sweater. Stevie was wearing pajama bottoms, Crocs, and a smiley face sweater, while Casey was wearing a satin vintage slip dress over a mohair knit. Casey and I had shared a similar style before Beckett, both of us always poring over Pinterest and pinning our favorite looks and designers, and I felt a momentary pang of regret, because this "different" wasn't truly me, and Casey knew it.

"So how's it going, lovely?" continued Casey. "Still all loved up in Loveland, population two?"

I smiled. Beckett might have his faults, but it made me feel mature to be with him. Older. Lent me a sophistication I'd never had before.

"Yeah, it's going good, thanks. Beckett's away with his dad this week—"

"Ohh," remarked Stevie with a knowing look. "So that's why you've been allowed out."

I blinked and was about to respond when Rhys rolled up to the table with our tray of drinks.

"Hey, La," he said coolly. Too coolly. I began to think this meeting might have been a mistake.

"Hey, how's it going?" I asked, matching his tone as if he were a mere acquaintance. Not someone I used to spend three out of five weeknights with, studying or, more often, playing *Baldur's Gate*.

"Busy, actually," he replied once we'd taken our drinks, and gestured to the rest of the café, which was, contrary to Beckett's strident opinions, absolutely crammed with customers. "Guess I'll have to catch up with you later."

"Jeez, what's his problem?" I muttered once he was out of earshot, with an uncomfortable grin. No one smiled back. In fact, Casey looked decidedly uncomfortable, while Stevie had her over-it look on.

"Look, I'm just going to come out and say it," said Stevie. "This whole thing with Beckett has happened crazy fast, so fast we didn't even get to talk to you about it or him or anything!"

I blinked at her and robotically took a sip of my coffee.

"He's not got the best rep," explained Casey diplomatically. Good cop, bad cop. Like they had planned this. An ambush. Wasn't I meant to be their friend? Beckett had mentioned that some people had it in for him back at school. Jealous, he'd explained matter-of-factly. There were a few salty ex-girlfriends he'd mentioned, too. Crazy girls who'd gone psycho once he'd broken up with them. His words, not mine, although after listening to some of his stories about them, I was kind of inclined to agree with him.

"What do you mean?" I asked slowly, but even as the words came out of my mouth, I regretted them.

"We tried to tell you—after the party," continued Stevie. "But it was like you didn't want to hear."

I stared at her, incredulous. I knew she wasn't jealous, not as Beckett insinuated Casey might be, so what was her angle?

"Hey, is this some kind of setup?" I asked with an exasperated laugh. I wanted to catch up, to have fun, maybe even to plan some stuff together. I loved being with Beckett, but there was no denying I missed my friends. I glanced over to where Rhys was violently bashing about the coffee machine. "I thought we were hanging out?"

"Okay, yes, but why can't we hang out when your guy is in town, though? We miss you," said Stevie, staring fixedly down at her drink, not even looking at me.

"We can," I said, throwing a desperate glance at the exit. It felt as if the whole café was looking over at this point, judging me. I even caught a glimpse of Rhys's mum, of all people, trying not to stare while spraying down an empty table.

Stevie rolled her eyes. "Lara, you know I love you, girl, but you also know I don't fuck around with the truth. I kick myself again and again for not being clearer with you that night you met him, but that guy is known to be poison."

"That guy is my *boyfriend*," I said, my chair squealing across the tiles as I stood. "And I thought you were my *friends*."

* * *

Unsurprisingly, I don't sleep well for the remainder of the night. My brain is trapped in an unhelpful cycle of strangling vines and choking leaves, of unpleasant, emaciated owls with hungry amber eyes; of Beckett's golden smile as he strides purposefully toward Rhys, of the baroness, waking in fright, pale and disoriented, of monstrously large sunflowers and cornfields the height of skyscrapers.

Why didn't we do more to help her?
What if she's dead?

A soft creaking from outside my cabin shakes me out of my half sleep. Could it be Shosh?

"*Rhys?*" I whisper into the darkness.

But I'm met with only his soft, even breathing. Not wanting to wake him, I climb carefully out of my bunk and over to the door, treading softly. Cautiously, I look through the peephole.

The corridor is empty.

Then I hear it, the unmistakable sound of someone turning a key in a lock, a soft, certain *clunk*. Then follows a soft creak as a door swings inward. The noise is coming from the cabin immediately to my left.

Rhys's cabin.

Fear grips me as the sibilant sound of slow, careful footsteps emanates from the vent in the wall. Whoever it is, is trying hard not to be heard. I hurry over to Rhys, crouching down and giving him a gentle shake. "Hey . . . hey, Rhys. Wake up."

He looks so untroubled in sleep, his dark lashes lying against flushed cheeks, that I feel guilty for waking him.

His eyes flicker open, the pupils huge and dark. "Hey . . . you. What's up?"

His voice is thick with sleep. I put my finger to my lips and whisper: "Listen a sec. . . . Can you hear that?"

He struggles up, whacking his head against the top bunk. "Ow. . . . Jesus. Like what?"

I bite my lip in frustration. "*Shh.* . . . Like . . . footsteps." I gesture at the dividing wall. "I think there's someone next door . . . in your cabin. *Listen.* . . ."

We must make a weird tableau, him sitting, rubbing his head, me half crouched before him, my heart thumping in my chest like a piston. I think once more of those eyes I saw that first night, staring thirstily at my cabin.

That's when she goes hunting.

Not a single sound emerges from the cabin next door. It's as if whoever is in there is listening, too. Waiting for us to dismiss them.

"You might have been dreaming." He lowers his voice. "It's normal to be a little on edge after . . . y'know."

Reluctantly, I climb back onto the top bunk and lie there quietly, staring fixedly at the ceiling. A strained silence grows and grows in the darkness, like an unchecked weed, until Rhys finally breaks it. "Are you—are you okay, Lara? Do you . . ." He hesitates, softly clears his throat. "Do you want me to come up there?"

This, this offer from Rhys, is almost more shocking than

anything else that has occurred tonight. And I allow myself to picture it. His familiar shape in the darkness, climbing up, the creak of the ladder, of the bunk, the shift of it all as he settles beside me. I imagine moving over, politely making room for him, here beside me. The narrow space of the single bunk forcing us close together, the softness of his worn T-shirt against my skin, the idea of lifting it— The sudden thought is unexpectedly, almost violently, thrilling, wrenching me clean out of my fear, those footsteps now forgotten. Would he hold me—put his arm around me—pull me close to him? I think of the way his hand felt earlier, strong fingers laced tightly with mine—I think of those few seconds in his bed a century ago—and the way I had read too much into it. A friend simply trying to comfort a friend becoming something so monumental in my head that I'd ruined—

"La . . . ?"

"No," I say, much louder than I intend. "No, no. I'm fine. I'm—I'm just imagining things . . . that's all. I'm sorry. Please—please go back to sleep."

22

As dawn breaks, I dimly hear Rhys return to his cabin, and after I catch a few more gray hours of restless, dreamless sleep, I'm woken by a lazy rap at the door.

I open it to find him on his knees, patting along the doorframe.

"It's almost all gone," he says in wonder. His hair is standing up at haphazard angles, and I resist the urge to kneel down and smooth it. He stands, opening his hand to reveal a few shriveled strands of bindweed. "But it was there, all right. You good?"

As we knock at Shosh's cabin door, I feel nervous. Like a kid having to rouse a teacher from the staff room, but she readily admits us into her cabin—much less of a sardine tin than our own, and more of a suite. The room is almost suffocatingly heady with the scent of flowers, thrust into vases, jam jars, and pint glasses on every available surface.

"Gotta keep the displays somewhere," she says with chagrin, gesturing for us to sit on a pink sofa, clearly an escapee from the Dahlia Bar. "So, guys, what's the emergency?"

I let Rhys do the talking; I am so tired, I'm struggling to concentrate. And if I was worried Shosh was going to be glib, or skeptical, or drag us directly before Gwen to explain ourselves, my fears were thankfully misplaced.

To my relief, she looks entirely unsurprised, nodding along to everything Rhys says.

"Yeah, I don't want to start off with giving you guys a warning," she says soberly. "But it's really bad form for staff to be wandering around guests' private cabins at night. I mean, I shouldn't have to tell you that."

I open my mouth to protest, but Shosh just puts up a hand. "Imagine those cabins weren't part of some scientific research, but someone's private chambers. Imagine that end carriage, in particular, was a *bedroom*. Would you still feel justified about wandering around in there late at night?"

Rhys looks down, chastened, but I'm not about to let this go. "Okay, granted, we were in the wrong," I say. "But can we stop talking about *hypothetical situations* and start talking about the fact that a frail old lady—also one of our *guests*—was having her blood siphoned out of her body last night?"

Shosh is still admirably unmoved. "Context is everything, Lara. And, not being someone with a master's degree in botanical research myself, I can see how it might appear to anyone *snooping*. But rest assured, everything is aboveboard, and

I am fully aware of what is going on in those carriages as are all the people involved."

To my annoyance, Rhys appears to relax a little beside me, a noticeable lessening of tension in his shoulders. He's always been such a rule follower. Bet he would have been there at Yale, pushing Milgram's dial all the way up to eleven, no questions asked.

"Okay, what about those plants—the bindweed—growing around our cabin doors, preventing us from getting out at night?" I push. "C'mon—that's flat-out dangerous. What if there's a fire on the train or something and we're trapped in our rooms?"

At this, Shosh frowns. "Yeah, I'll admit that was alarming. There have been a few issues with some of those plants being a little too *abundant*, shall we say, but rest assured, guys, none of this is news to me, and we're working to get everything under control. Gwen's fully aware—she's the one who first brought it to my attention—and she's working on a solution. It shouldn't happen again—I'm monitoring the situation."

"And the baroness? How can that be aboveboard?" I ask, although less confidently than before.

Shosh taps the side of her nose. "I understand how it might have appeared to you guys, but unfortunately I'm not in a position to discuss our guests' private arrangements with you." She then pats the sides of her armchair decisively. "Y'know, I'm pleased you've trusted me with your concerns, but stay out of those carriages until we get to Tallinn, and everything will be good. Capisce?"

We watch wordlessly as she stands, checking her watch. "Now, if I'm not mistaken, I'm pretty sure there's somewhere you both need to be."

Blearily, I lay out the usual buffet breakfast on the dining carriage counter, my mind buzzing, a dangerous nest of poorly insulated wires. Should I ask the baroness about last night? If everything is as legit as Shosh says, then surely she won't mind explaining—

"Aha, there she is. Our beautiful hostess. Good morning, Lara."

For the first time, instead of brightening my mood, Gwydion's voice sends a distinct chill down my spine, an uneasy ball of dread lodging in my gut.

I don't turn immediately. Images of last night crowd into my mind, making me almost afraid to. Could he be about to offer me my own midnight invitation? His sharp gaze locks on mine, sparkling, *well-rested*. Okay, it doesn't *look* like he stayed up all night draining old ladies of blood—quite the opposite.

"Good morning," I say politely. "How are we both doing?"

Because, of course, Gwen is by his side. Silent and knowing. Gwydion gives me that dazzling smile that always leaves me a little flustered. I think back to him lying in the meadow, his Artic-blue eyes shining into mine.

But is there some sly intent beneath it all? How much does he really know? Not for the first time, I wish Gwen wasn't present. Alone, I'm sure I could get him to open up, to confide in me, and then—

"Fantastic, thank you! Carlos tells me we should be crossing into Germany later today. Have you ever been through the Black Forest? It's quite the sight."

He chatters away amiably as I serve them coffee and toast, and I keep my eye trained on the carriage door, hoping to see the baroness walk in, sprightly and demanding tea.

After what feels like years, the siblings get up to leave, and I am still unable to say anything to Gwydion; Gwen's cold death stare prevents me.

The moment I get the chance, I knock gingerly on the baroness's door. Becca answers it, her sullen face tipping into annoyance once she sees me. She opens the door a crack. The room behind her is dimly lit, the drapes still shut.

"Yeah?"

"I . . . uh, I came to see if her ladyship needed anything?"

"Well, that's nice of you, but if we wanted room service, we'd ask for it."

"It's just . . . it's just you guys didn't turn up for breakfast this morning, so I wondered if you wanted a cup of tea or something."

"Look—we've already had your lanky mate knocking at some ungodly hour, and now you—"

"Oh, I'd *love* a cup of tea, dear," comes a familiar voice behind her. Becca rolls her eyes. I'm dismayed to hear that the baroness sounds weak, her voice barely a croak, but still, she *is* alive. And she does sound tired—not scared, like a person who was unwillingly sapped of blood.

"Fabulous! I'll fetch it right away," I say, raising my voice and narrowing my eyes at Becca, who immediately shuts the door.

"You already checked on her, then," I say to Rhys as I begin the laborious process of making her tea back in the kitchen.

Rhys is spooning cereal into his mouth. He looks as tired as I feel. "Yeah, course—first thing. She seemed okay. A little pissed off, I'd knocked that early, but I was so relieved she answered the door I could have hugged her—I didn't. Anyway, I made up some lie, said I thought I'd heard shouting—"

I shoot a wary glance at the kitchen door. We're still alone.

"Did you ask her? About last night?"

"I tried to. I asked her if everything was all right, and she insisted it was. She looked a little paler than usual, more tired, but I couldn't just ask her outright if she was aware her blood was being taken last night without coming across as a complete weirdo."

"What do you make of what Shosh said?"

His expression grows serious. "Honestly, I *want* to believe her. It would be a lot easier, trusting that we're all perfectly safe and that everyone knows what's going on. But . . . but something doesn't add up." He lowers his voice. "Look at Cass. . . . You said she had a puncture mark in her arm and didn't know why. What if what happened to Xavier happens to her—and to the baroness—and we just left her? I wish I'd gone back last night, but—" He looks around, almost guiltily. "I was *afraid*."

"Hey, so was I," I say quietly, wanting him to know there's no shame in being afraid of shady midnight medical practices involving poison plants, faceless beekeepers, and needles. "Her explanation about the bindweed makes no sense," I continue. "Gwen's plants being 'a little out of control' doesn't explain why plants are targeting people's cabin doors, keeping them locked in."

"Preventing them from seeing what's going on down there at night," Rhys agrees. "And by the way," he continues, his voice lower still, now scrutinizing his cereal intently as if it were communicating a hidden code, "when I offered to come into your bunk last night, I only meant—"

"Yeah, I know," I say immediately, saving us both the embarrassment. The damning knowledge that I am forever stuck in the friend zone is the perfect finale to this wonderful morning. "Sorry I woke you up. I was just . . . you know, spiraling. I'm going to speak to Gwydion. Alone. He must know *something*. And he's different from Gwen. I mean, she's his sister—don't you think it's weird that he doesn't seem to *like* her? Sometimes . . . sometimes I even wonder if he's scared of her." I shake my head, unwilling to meet Rhys's eyes. "If I'm right about this . . . then I think he might open up to me if I can get him alone. And remember, *he's* not the one who tried to recruit you to his plant-based blood drive. That was Gwen."

"Be careful" is all he says. His look says more.

* * *

I'm on break until dinner service, so, remembering my promise to Samira, I head down to the piano lounge. Passengers don't tend to use this lounge during the day. Sure enough, a STAFF CLEANING IN PROGRESS cone has been placed outside, and I can hear the sound of hoovering.

Samira grins when she sees me and unplugs the vacuum.

"Carlos treated everyone to a little concerto after dinner last night. Who knew he could play like that? The floor's covered with crumbs, but I got it now."

"Sorry," I say. "I came as quick as I could."

Samira nods, then sinks down at one of the small circular tables. I join her, sensing she has questions.

"So . . . about last night? Something you want to get off your chest? Maybe about what you and Rhys were getting up to in those carriages?"

She gives me a wicked smile, but there's uncertainty in her eyes, and it's my duty as a friend to warn her.

"It wasn't like that—unfortunately," I confess. "Samira, there's something strange going on aboard this train—and in those carriages specifically."

Samira frowns but doesn't seem as shocked as I anticipated. Maybe she's sensed something, too?

"Last night Rhys woke me up because he found out there were these *weeds* growing up all around the door and keeping us from leaving our cabins," I continue.

"*Weeds?*" Samira's eyebrows shoot up.

I nod. "Yeah. You should check tonight, see if they're around your door. It only seems to happen at night. By morning they're gone. I think they're meant to keep us in, to stop us snooping around in those greenhouse carriages."

Samira shakes her head. "Come on, Lara. If you and Rhys want some private time down there, you don't need to spin me stories. I'll mind my business. Just don't let Shosh catch you. I meant to tell you, but she was saying something the other day about you and him being in and out of each other's cabins."

I lower my voice: "I'm *serious*, Samira. I think there's something going on in them—specifically at night—that's dangerous. Maybe even deadly. I think it's linked to what happened to Xavier—"

"Xavier choked on his dinner or had an allergy. We were told."

"Yes, but told by *who*?"

Samira frowns and lowers her voice as well: "What exactly are you saying—are we in danger? Have you guys reported this?"

"I've tried to tell Shosh, but she keeps insisting everything is fine—but it's not and I'm sure it's not. Just promise me you'll keep away from the greenhouse carriages for now. Don't go in there for any reason."

Samira nods. "I mean, with my hay fever, I wasn't planning on going in there." She pauses. "So what *is* in there?"

I shake my head. I don't even know. Something more than the sum of its parts, though, something more than fast-growing flowers and an old statue, *that's* for certain.

"I'm not sure yet, but I'm trying to find out. Please, just promise me you'll stay away?"

Samira duly warned, and with an hour of my break remaining, I figure now is the perfect opportunity to speak to Gwydion.

Outside, the weather is miserable. Gray spring rain streams down the windows, turning the view into streaks of dark paint. Overnight the landscape has changed dramatically, and the vast open plains of the French countryside have given way to dense coniferous forest, darkening the close corridors of the train even further.

I wander down the rocking train, now practically deserted. There's no sign of Gwydion in the dining carriage, nor is he in the Cedar Lounge, and it's too early for him to be troubling the bar.

I know where his cabin is; I've straightened it a couple of times. It's a weirdly personal thing, tidying someone else's private space. The fact he is fastidiously tidy, leaving everything, including the bathroom, in pristine condition, leaves no clues to his personality.

Outside the rain worsens, spattering aggressively against the glass as mile after mile of fir trees flash past, some mere meters from the train, giving the carriages a gloomy aspect. All the lights are already switched on despite the early hour. I enter the narrow passageway where his cabin is located and knock gamely on his cabin door.

He opens it, looking as if he has just woken up from a nap,

his usually neat black hair in disarray, his blue shirt untucked, the top unbuttoned.

"Lara," he says, a curious glint in his eye. "What a pleasant surprise. Please, come in."

I step into his cabin. The heavy velvet curtain that separates the sleeping area from the living area is pulled right across, obscuring his bed and swaying with the movement of the train. Still, nothing seems amiss in here. He gestures to an empty chair, and obediently I sit.

"I'm glad you're here," he confesses in a low, intimate tone. "I wanted to talk to you at breakfast, but I wasn't sure how to get you . . . alone."

"Oh?" I say blandly, not wanting to give anything away, while my stomach churns with a complicated mix of uneasiness and desire.

"Yes, I want to talk about last night," he says without preamble. "About what you saw." His clear eyes are like mirrors, betraying nothing except my surprise.

I gasp a little but then relax. If he truly were involved in something dark and monstrous, surely he'd go to greater lengths to hide it.

"Yeah," I say, sounding bolder than I feel. "That's why I'm here. There are all kinds of things occurring on this train lately that are . . . strange. I mean, was that you last night? All masked up?"

Gwydion frowns. "*Masked up?* And no, I wasn't there. At breakfast Gwen told me she caught you snooping around the greenhouse again while she was 'carrying out a treatment,' as she put it." He gives me a searching look. "I'm curious—what exactly *did* you see?"

I give Gwydion a hesitant rundown, unsure of how he'll react to what I'm about to tell him. About how we saw the baroness lying beneath that hideous effigy, her blood slowly pooling into a bag while she lay there unconscious, her skin tinged a worrying shade of gray.

As I speak, he nods soberly in understanding, then gives a ragged sigh.

"Yeah. It's not the first time this has happened."

I lean forward, energized by his casual admission. "I didn't think so. But why does Shosh think it's all aboveboard?"

Gwydion pinches the bridge of his nose and exhales. "Gwen must have convinced her. You see, she's been framing this as some sort of advanced beauty treatment. I didn't know anything about it until—until Xavier. What was it she said, now . . . ? Something to do with the accelerated regeneration of facial skin cells—linked to the plants, you see. She assures me everyone's consented." He gives a distasteful shake of his head. "But you know, I don't buy it."

So it *was* Gwen—or her assistant—with the baroness last night.

"Okay, then what *is* she doing?" I ask, my words tumbling over each other, desperate to be heard. "Is it dangerous?"

Gwydion's mouth thins to a worried line. "I don't know, exactly. I didn't *think* it was—not at first. I thought it was what she said, some shady but essentially harmless treatment—but ever since what happened to Xavier . . . I've been . . . well, on edge."

"Why?" Now that someone other than Rhys thinks there's something untoward going on, the questions pour out of me like a torrent. "Did Xavier sign up for this—this treatment? Do you think that's why he got sick?"

Gwydion gives a rueful smile. "One question at a time. . . . Like I already said, Gwen's research is based on this *accelerated growth*—and from what I understand, that part's legitimate enough; it's signed off on and funded by several eminent universities. But the thing about Gwen is, she's the kind of person who never knows when to *stop*. Whose interest in knowing *more*—always knowing more—has the potential to lead somewhere dangerous."

I shiver, and the scant reassurance Shosh's words offered me earlier disappears into vapor.

"She told me the reason she started this little side hustle," he continues, "is because our trust funds aren't going to last forever, especially now the estate has gone."

"Okay, so what exactly was she *doing* to the baroness? I mean from what I could see, it looked like Gwen was taking her blood, or carrying out a transfusion. Is what happened to Xavier going to happen to her?"

Gwydion shifts uneasily. "I don't know, but I plan to find out. You know, I was a big supporter of her work at first. Who could argue with it? Accelerated growth in crops is game-changing, *world*-changing—think of how it could benefit drought-affected areas—and I was incredibly proud when her research was given the green light. But lately . . . lately, I've been concerned. I know you thought my reasons for accompanying her were a little flimsy—and you were right. The truth is, I've come to—well—*watch* her. Like I said, this research of hers . . . it troubles me."

I lean forward, entranced. Because he is correct. Whatever Shosh might say, there is something wrong about this. And it starts with those carriages. They are not the modern facilities a research scientist, a scientist who's proposing they can cure famine, would be working in. They're not the kind of sterile environment that supports patients on IVs, or even the most basic beauty treatments. There is, in fact, nothing modern, nothing scientific, about them at all.

Gwydion reaches forward, placing a cool hand on mine. "Lara . . . I've said it before . . . but that carriage contains something very old and very strange. Something sly, and sentient. Something that gives Gwen the impression she's in control, when in actuality, I don't think she has any idea what she's really dealing with."

And I know what he's talking about. It would sound like madness to anyone who hasn't been in that dark, windowless carriage. Who's never looked upon what it contains.

"And do you?" I ask.

He shakes his head. "Not yet. But believe me, I'm planning on finding out."

"Whatever's in that carriage has nothing to do with *science*, Gwydion," I whisper as the room darkens around us. Unnerved, I glance out of the window as the train clatters on through a low gray mist.

"No," he agrees, his voice hushed. "You're right."

"Is there anything I can do to help?"

Removing his hand, he shakes his head. "I don't think so. At least, not yet. I think at present I have it under control."

I look at him; his eyes intense in the gloom as the dark forest flashes past behind him, his cabin silent apart from the soft squeaks of a room in perpetual motion, the quiet clatter of the train over the tracks, and at that moment I want nothing more than to trust him. To believe he does have all this strangeness under control.

But for once the warning voice in my head is louder. The voice past-Lara never used to listen to. The old life-is-for-living, capture-the-moment, seize-the-day, YOLO Lara. Because I am beginning to understand that if life teaches you lessons, it's foolish not to learn from them.

23

Once I'm done cleaning up after lunch service, I head dejectedly toward the Azalea Coffee Lounge in search of stray glasses.

The moment I enter the opulent carriage, Rhys makes a beeline for me. "Where have you been?"

"Sorry—I've been speaking to Gwydion, and guess what—"

"It's *Samira*," he interrupts. It's then I notice how agitated he is, pacing the small space, the books behind him tussling in sympathy. "She's missing. She's not in her cabin, and she hasn't turned up for her shift."

"I spoke to her this morning," I say, confused.

Rhys frowns. "Shosh says she's disappeared."

"Disappeared?" My anxiety heightens, as I somehow already know where she is. I warned her off those carriages. Why would she ignore me?

But I know exactly why. The same reason I searched for

the key to Beckett's den. The same reason that left me standing before that hideous statue. Curiosity can be a terrible thing.

Rhys looks as concerned as I feel. "You know how chill Shosh usually is, right? Well, she seems genuinely worried about her. She's asked to carry out a full search of the train. Now."

For reasons I can't put into words, other than some odd pulling sensation, a morbid sense of destiny, I tell Rhys I'll start my search in the Llewellyns' carriages. I stand outside the greenhouse carriages, my heart beating feverishly. The carving of the woman's face stares out at me wistfully, a study in longing, her eyes deep gouges in the wood.

My hands are shaking. There's something terrible within these carriages. I don't know *how* I know this, only that it's inescapably true. It's in the unnatural stillness, the muted sounds of the train, in the way the very molecules of the air are arranged. It's a barrier—a warning. Beware, beware, *beware*. That beautiful face, stern, telling me, *warning* me, that there are things that, once seen, can never be unseen.

And I have been here before. Standing before locked doors I promised not to open. Rooms I've promised never to enter.

Samira, I remind myself. I'll open the door for her.

With a deep breath, I twist the handle, and just as before, key or no key, the door swings smoothly open.

The first carriage is eerily still. The perfume of the roses, the lilies, is overpoweringly sweet today, with an undertone of something richer, darker beneath. A scent that makes my stomach churn.

I know that the smell is blood, earthy and raw, the coppery tang hitting my lungs like a glut of pennies before I'm even halfway across the second carriage, and immediately I stop, tears welling in my eyes, not wanting to go further, needing to stop my straying footsteps, needing to run back and alert everyone *else*.

Because I don't want to see this. But nevertheless, something propels me into the following carriage, dark and damp. The sound of the rain is amplified here, spattering on the glass roof and streaming down the vast windows.

"Samira?" I call softly. "You in here?"

It's strange. I can practically feel her presence, the soft violet notes of her perfume lingering in the air. Up ahead, the door to the final carriage lies half open. Beckoning me forward.

"S-Samira?" This time I say it quietly. I already know she's beyond hearing.

The candlelight flickers up ahead, almost mockingly. And for once, that sibilant whispering is curiously absent.

Samira lies on her back before the owl beast, her head leaning at the foot of the statue, the rest of her body sprawled over the stone plinth at its base. At first, I think she must have changed clothes before coming here, swapped her crisp white day shirt for a black evening one, until I realize the once-white material is darkly sodden with blood. Thick tendrils of briar extend from behind the owl like thorny tentacles, encircling Samira's wrists, her ankles, and, worst of all, her neck. Her eyes are wide open with blank surprise. Sharp thorns puncture her skin in a thousand places; red rivulets tiger-stripe her skin. Blood congeals in a dark, sticky puddle beneath her, dripping slowly from the plinth and pooling on the floor.

From the gray color of her skin to the blue tinge of her lips . . . I know she is dead. A fact utterly undeniable that settles in my gut like lead.

But worst of all is the expression on her face. Her unseeing eyes, wide with fear, lips slightly parted as if she's praying for deliverance.

I gag as thick, salty bile floods my mouth, and I whirl away, retching violently. My brain is pounding a discordant warning—*Get out, get out, GET OUT*—and I stagger back through the carriages, stumbling wildly in panic. I find I can't *speak*, let alone cry out, and my hands won't work, my fingers too thick and shaky. I push blindly through razor-edged palm fronds and thick, obstructing branches. As I reach for the door that will take me out of this place, something latches tightly about my ankle—a hand, a vine, a bramble, I can't tell. With an almost otherworldly strength, I'm wrenched backward, my head hitting the cold stone tile first, and as I blink wildly up at the white sky, the world dims and quiets around me.

MAY, LAST YEAR

I slammed the coffee shop door behind me, leaving its bell jangling madly. To my horror, Rhys was out front, leaning lazily against the window and scrolling through his phone.

"Lara?" he said, pulling himself up the moment he saw me.

"I *thought* you were busy!" I spat, storming past him, brushing furious tears from my eyes. "Or was that a lie, too?"

"Hey—hey, wait a minute." He jogged to keep up with me. "Lara—La."

Gently he caught my wrist, and I whirled around, wrenching it away.

"What! Oh, wait—I guess it's your turn to lay into Beckett now."

"I have no interest in talking about him, believe me," replied Rhys. "I want to talk to you . . . just about school and stuff. I've gotta finish up my shift right now, but I'm free later this evening."

I hesitated—with him, I couldn't help it—and he pressed home the advantage. "Please?"

I relented. I couldn't ignore everyone, and other than Casey, Rhys had always been the easiest to talk to.

"Fine," I snapped. "If that's what you want."

Back home, when I cautiously told Beckett what had happened over the phone, he was immediately sympathetic, telling me exactly what I'd suspected. That my friends had grown jealous of us, jealous of our closeness, confiding once again that Casey used to have a crush on him, something I wasn't sure of before but that seemed to make sense now. I didn't tell him anything about meeting with Rhys later, though. It was an entirely innocent affair, but Beckett just wouldn't see it that way.

I walked to Rhys's and was warmly welcomed in by his mum. If she was surprised to see me, she didn't say anything. And it was strange being back in his room. It had been a month or so now, but everything was cozily familiar; nothing had changed at all. Above his desk still hung a poster of the periodic table, of all things, and collecting dust on a shelf was the same lineup of Pokémon plushies. But if his room was the same, things between us were not—they were stilted. Where before I would have immediately flopped back on his bed, now I stood like a stranger, clutching at my pricey handbag, not quite knowing what to do. Rhys didn't comment on my appearance, on my straight hair, gold highlights, my skater skirt, the necklaces of gold stars looped about my neck. Instead, he nodded at my bag.

"How'd you fit all your books in there?"

"Uh . . . I haven't brought any," I admitted.

He'd messaged me earlier, reminding me to bring my science textbooks so we could work on the latest piece of coursework I was lagging behind in, but I had no intention of studying. I wanted to know what was going on between us all, why no one could accept Beckett and me. Why I had to choose between him and my friends.

"Is that what you think's happening?" he asked once I'd vocalized it, his expression intent, sitting in his gaming chair, glasses on. "That we're making you choose?"

"Yes!" I exclaimed. "Every time I do meet up with you guys, you're always banging on about what a terrible guy he is."

"Well, to be fair, we don't meet up very often anymore," said Rhys, his calm demeanor beginning to irk me. "Would you even be here, La, if he wasn't out of town?"

Sinking down on the edge of his bed, I pretended to think about this, although I already knew the answer. It was hard to explain to Rhys in a way that made sense, though. He didn't know about Beckett's trust issues, issues he assured me had nothing to do with me—he trusted me, but he didn't trust other guys. Told me he knew what they're like, knew what they think about.

But not Rhys. Beckett didn't know Rhys. The whole reason I was there was because I absolutely did trust him.

"You're right." I sighed. "I know I shouldn't have cut you guys off the way I did, I *know* that . . . but that guilt feeds into the avoidance thing, and it's now this fucked-up negative-feedback cycle, and I don't know how to make it better. . . . It's just, outside of school, I only have so much time—"

"And you owe it *all* to Beckett?"

Rhys had turned away, busy typing something into his browser as if this conversation wasn't important to him.

"No—*no*. It's not that—"

I didn't *owe* it all to him, but maybe I simply wanted to *give* it all to him. Someone who finally saw me. Someone who didn't simply *act* as if they cared about me, listened to my deepest fears and regrets, and then, when it mattered most, just . . . blanked me. The unwelcome memory of that night at Cecily Hunterson's sixteenth made my mind up for me. I took a shuddery intake of breath.

"Look, I think this is a mistake, actually—I'm sorry you all hate my boyfriend, but we're together now, and you guys are just going to have to deal with it."

I stood, beginning to put my coat back on when Rhys spun around, and I got tangled up in his gaze. Concerned, sorrowful, and something else—something intense and dangerous that I sensed he was trying to hide.

"Lara. . . . Just answer me this, then. Are you . . . are you happy?"

It was so weird, so bizarre, how much that question threw me. I was happy, *so* happy, back when Beckett "chose" me. It was like basking in the heat of some glorious sun, all its warm rays stretched out toward me.

But *was* I happy now?

"Because if you are, then I'll—we'll—leave you to get on with it . . . if that's what you want. If that's what makes you happy," Rhys continued.

I sensed the importance in his words. This was a choice for me. A crossroads.

Did these clothes make me happy? Did straightening my hair every morning make me happy? Did ignoring my friends' messages make me happy? Did being expected to answer my phone at regimented times make me happy? Did getting a lift home on Fridays make me happy? I used to look forward to those afternoons, the school week over, kicking through the leaves, laughing at whatever dramatic events had happened in class that week as we made our way to the café for a hot chocolate. Now I'm whisked away from everyone the moment the bell rings to Beckett's clinical mansion.

Was I happy? Was I truly?

"No."

The word vomited out of me, shaky, almost pleading, and I flopped back on the bed as the tears came, exhausted and lonely and lost. Tired of pretending. Tired of convincing myself I'd made a good choice. I masked my face with my hands and forced my breathing to steady, feeling like an absolute fool. The bed creaked as Rhys settled on the end of it, and my heart began to thud hard in warning. Not because I was in any way anxious or afraid of him, I could never be afraid of Rhys, but because this was the exact moment when I realized the extent of the mistake I had made. I might have loved Beckett, or at least that's how it felt during the good times, of which admittedly there had been fewer of lately, but Rhys—Rhys was entirely different. The way I felt about Rhys—unrequited as it might be—took my breath away. And I'd thought it would die in the dark spaces of my heart, unfed and unwatered, but now we were alone here, I discovered it had grown, despite my neglect, my forced ignorance of it, into something monstrous.

"Oh, Lara. I'm sorry."

There was no pity in his voice. Only sadness and regret. And the tears came harder at the truth of it, spoken into life. My breath came clean away when the silence grew too thick and he finally folded, lying beside me and wrapping his arms around me like I was something precious, his green eyes soft and sorrowful. And he felt so safe and so strong and smelled so good—a clean mix of laundry detergent and citrus—that, impulsively, I nuzzled closer, wanting to somehow burrow into his chest and become one with him, as if it would somehow take us back to when it was good between us. Besides, it was too painful, too difficult, to look at him with my every emotion painted clear on my face, written large in looping script. And though we were both fully clothed and both above the sheets and it was all very sensible and Rhys-like, the moment I confessed, "I've missed you," in his ear, the words leaving my lips as honestly and effortlessly as breathing, there was a cataclysmic change between us, like the first clap of thunder on a close summer day. His strong fingers tightened about my upper back as my lips brushed his ear, and as he pulled me crushingly close, as my leg twined through his, both of us needing to be closer. And I finally knew it wasn't some unrequited crush I had, knew that this was something fierce and honest and absolutely real.

I tilted my head up carefully, meeting his eyes.

Then my phone went off, shockingly loud in the silence. I knew without even looking that it was Beckett, and guilt speared through me, fierce and fast; it was as if his eyes were staring out of the damn phone. The moment Rhys caught sight of his name on the screen, he pulled away from me so quickly he nearly fell off the bed, pretending to bend over and search in his rucksack for something.

"I'm sorry," he said again, kindly and not without regret. "You should probably answer that."

24

When I wake, I'm in my bunk, the sheets pulled up to my chin. The charnel stench of blood is gone, replaced with the fresh fragrance of spring blossoms. A soft wave of relief washes over me as I listen to the patter of rain at the window and the steady rocking of the train.

Thank *God*.

It was just a dream—or, more accurately, a *nightmare*. I'm overtired, maybe even sick, but no one's dead, least of all Samira. We wouldn't still be on this train if anyone was actually *dead*—

"Ah, Lara. . . . You're awake."

Shosh's voice is unusually shaky and thick, which sets alarm bells clanging noisily in my head. I scramble up, staring over at her in horror at where she sits in the armchair, her iPad on her lap. With a sickening, cold wash of dread, I see I'm still clothed, lying on the bottom bunk, still wearing my uniform from earlier. And then finally I understand that what happened wasn't a dream. That I really did see Samira . . . lying there . . . dead—eviscerated by *thorns*.

"Here." Shosh passes across a bottle of water, which I hurriedly drain. My head whirls and throbs unpleasantly as I push the sheets aside and attempt to stand, before immediately giving up and slumping back down on the lower bunk, sweaty and disoriented.

"S-Samira—?"

She shakes her head softly. "I'm sorry to have to tell you this. She was already gone when you found her." Shoshanna reaches across the space between us, squeezing my hand in sympathy. "There's nothing you—or anyone—could have done for her. I'm sorry—*so* sorry you had to see that."

I stare at her, my mind a mass of jumbled puzzle pieces, nothing making sense.

"No. Wait—*how*? Shosh, how could that have happened? All those—the *thorns* . . . how is it possible? And what *happened* to her? What is going on in there, in those carriages? We're—we're *all* in danger! Why the fuck are we still moving? Why haven't we *stopped*?"

Shoshana looks at me, her gaze hardening.

"Lara, calm down. Losing your temper is not going to help an already tense situation. Right now, things are under control." She flops back into the chair, squeezing her eyes shut. "Why couldn't you guys *listen* to me? I *told* you not to go into those carriages, I told you they were private—restricted. If you'd done as I'd said . . . If Samira hadn't been snooping around . . ."

She trails off, shaking her head, and I look at her in horror. "*What?* No! How is this in any *way* under control? Rhys and I *told* you what we saw—we warned you what was happening, and now Samira is dead! There's no way you're saying it's her fault?"

Shosh swallows and I notice how badly her hands are shaking. It's as clear as day that she's never had *anything* under control.

"Look, Lara. For your own safety, you need to take it down a notch. You slipped and hit your head pretty badly. We're taking turns sitting with you, to check you're okay. And as soon as we're able, of course we're going to stop the train."

Gingerly I pat the back of my head, wincing as I discover an enormous lump that pulses painfully at my touch. Well, that part, at least, is true.

"As soon as we're able," I mutter. "What do you mean, as soon as we're able? We need to stop *now*. Shosh, Samira is dead! We need to tell the police! Tell her family!"

Every time I shut my eyes, I see her lying there. I will never, *ever* get that image out of my head. I know this with utmost certainty. There was something dark, something almost ritualistic, about the way she was killed. The thorns circled thickly about her neck like some torturous rope, around her wrists, her ankles—the utter disbelief and fear in her eyes. The desperate look on her face.

"Did you see her? Shosh, we are *all* in danger! Seriously, what the *fuck* are you even talking about?"

Shosh stands with a frustrated sigh. "Look, Lara. I know you're in a bad place right now, but you need to watch your language. You're in danger of sounding hysterical—delirious, even—when it's important we all keep our heads. Also, maybe think about taking some responsibility here."

I'm in a bad place? No shit.

Outraged at this, I once more attempt to stand, but the room swings violently around me and a crushing pain throbs in my brain. I fall back down.

"My suggestion—no, actually, my *order*—is that you're to stay in here until you're fully recovered. We're on the way to a station where there'll be help, and Gwen's already working to fix things on board. She's assured me none of us are in any danger—"

A wave of nausea sweeps through me as she talks. More false promises. More minimizing. More *lies*. I am so *sick*, so tired, of this narrative.

Lara, Lara, Lara . . . you're mistaken. Lara, honey, everything's fine.

I didn't hear your calls, babe! I must have accidentally switched my phone on silent.

No—no, you're completely misremembering that message—she's only a friend!

You never told me it was your gran's birthday; I'm sure she won't mind your missing it just this once.

Without warning, hot bile floods my mouth, and I stagger into the bathroom, where I relieve myself noisily of my breakfast. When I reenter the cabin, Shosh stands outside the bathroom, regarding me with concern. She's regained some of her composure and hands me the water again.

"Sorry," I mutter, taking a grateful swig.

She shakes her head. "Jesus, don't apologize; you've been through something truly *awful*. . . . And on top of that, there's a good chance you might be concussed."

She takes my shoulder, gently leading me back to the bunk.

"Look, take this opportunity to rest. You've had a terrible shock. Gwen's checked you over; she doesn't think your head is anything to be overly concerned about. . . . It's more the . . . psychological fallout. You know, coming to terms with what you saw."

I shake my head, immediately regretting it as the room drunkenly lurches around once more. The idea of Gwen "checking me over" makes me shudder. But the truth is, I'm decidedly not with it; my eyelids feel unpleasantly heavy, and I'm so dizzy I can barely stand.

Shosh helps me back into bed and somewhat awkwardly attempts to help me get comfortable, plumping my pillow and placing a fresh bottle of water by my side. From her pocket, she pulls a white blister pack of pills.

"Here," she says, passing me a couple. "Take these."

I eye the packet suspiciously, and she rolls her eyes. "Jesus, Lara. They're only *painkillers*. For your head. Worst they'll do is make you drowsy."

Feeling stupid, I swallow them with a glug of water.

Shosh is about to speak when we both realize the train is beginning to slow. I sit up and crane my neck to look out the window. Although it's only late afternoon, it's almost dark outside, the clouds hanging thunderously low, but thankfully, the rain has relented. Yet there's no sign of any station, and no platform visible. We are still deep in the forest.

With a queasy lurch, the train stops.

Cursing under her breath, Shosh bolts out of the room.

Any relief I might feel at the train stopping is quickly dissipated the second I hear Shosh locking my cabin door from the outside.

"Shosh? Hey! Shosh!"

But I hear her footsteps already pounding down the corridor. Swallowing, I force myself to stand and try the handle. The door is really locked.

I rattle it. The door itself is flimsy, like a bathroom stall door, and I could probably force it open if I needed to. Is everyone getting off the train? What if they forget I'm in here, locked away in my cabin—what if I'm left here and—

An unfamiliar, elegant female voice breaks into my thoughts: "Would all passengers please return to their cabins and listen carefully for further announcements."

It's a prerecorded message. It plays a couple more times, and I hear footsteps pass my cabin. I consider calling out, but I am *so* tired, it's an effort keeping my eyes open. Without warning, the train starts up again. Perhaps there was something momentarily blocking the line. I wait for another announcement—for Shosh to return and explain the stop—but there's nothing, only the silence outside my door, until the pain medication fuzzes my thoughts and the familiar motion of the train pulls me into a deep and dreamless sleep.

Muffled voices sift like sand into my dreams.

"*Why* can't I speak to her, though? After everything that's gone on, I just want to check she's okay."

Rhys.

"Um, after what you pulled earlier, you're lucky you're still on this train, my friend!"

And Shosh, sounding extremely displeased. They must be standing directly outside my room.

"Oh, is that right? So getting off is an option now? Because the fact that it hasn't been is the exact reason *why* I pulled the emergency cord!"

Despite everything, I muster a smile. So, that explains why the train stopped earlier. Nice one, Rhys.

"Rhys, you cannot just stop the train in the middle of nowhere! I don't know how many times you need that explained! All you're doing is *delaying* our journey. If you pull a stunt like that again, you'll be confined to your cabin for the rest of the trip."

"What, like Lara? Is she being punished, then?"

"Listen to yourself—of course not! She's taken some strong painkillers to help with her head, and they've probably made her drowsy. She needs to *rest*. A good friend would want her to get better, not wake her up to offload their paranoia. Now, Carlos and I are going to—for want of a better word—de-*weed* the antechamber by the greenhouse carriages and get them all locked up. I know it's not one of your regular duties, but we could use your help."

Shosh is using her firmest tone, her words biting and final. There's no arguing with it.

"Rhys," I try to say. "It's fine, I'm okay." But my words are thick and slurred, like Dad's when he comes back late from the betting shop, and before long I tumble back into unconsciousness.

25

The next time I wake, it's fully dark. The curtains in my cabin are still open, and I'm observed by a bloated yellow moon. Disappointment seeps into my bones at the realization we're still moving.

Feeling lousy, I sit and chug a bottle of water and debate whether or not to visit the staff room. Then I remember, I'm locked in. It was probably a bad idea anyway—I can't face another confrontation with Shosh right now, and to be honest, I don't have the bandwidth to talk to anyone, not even Rhys. It's hard to wrestle with the fact that Samira—her joyous smile and infectious laugh—all of that's *gone.* My fond memories now replaced by the smell of congealed blood and the mottled, purplish color of her flesh. Lying back in my bunk, I stare up at the ceiling, my breath coming fast and shallow, signaling the imminent arrival of a panic attack. Focusing on my breathing, I force my mind back to happier times:

Granddad's garden, with its sharp smell of woodsmoke and its orderly rows of staked green beans. My weekly dates with Casey at Shake Shack, busy chatter all around us as we catch up on that week's gossip, the taste of ice-cold mint chocolate chip on my tongue. Stevie and I screaming at Rhys's rugby games on Saturdays, our breath like dragon smoke in the sharp morning air, the field glittering with rhinestones of frost—back when I was *able* to go—before Beckett—

And now I *am* distracted, not by the warm glow of past memories but by a fierce rush of anger. Those memories, the ones I cherish, are so much fewer since I met Beckett, since I allowed myself to be gradually metamorphosed into something smaller, something quieter—a butterfly entering a cocoon and emerging as a caterpillar.

The soft clunk of Rhys's cabin door closing interrupts my thoughts. At first I assume he's finished his shift and is going to bed, but then my ears prick up at the unmistakable low rasp of Gwen's voice. What is she doing, visiting his cabin this late? Is he in danger? The next recipient of her sinister "beauty treatments"? I can't hear exactly what she's saying, but she sounds agitated. I sit up, wondering if I should call out to him, check if he's okay—indicate to Gwen that we're on to her—when Rhys replies, his voice low and soothing and not at all scared. At this point, I'm reduced to awkwardly wedging my ear against the open vent between our rooms. I'm dismayed, not to mention embarrassed, when moments later, the other side of the vent is snapped shut.

Their dull mumbling is infuriating, so I cross the room to grab one of the tiny bathroom glasses and press it against the wall like I've seen on the vintage cop shows Dad loves.

Disappointingly, it barely makes a difference, but I do catch a few words. Both my name and Gwydion's are thrown out, as well as Samira's. I wrench myself away, blood heating, half of me tempted to hammer on the wall and demand to know why they're talking about me. But their voices quiet further, to almost a whisper, and a thin, electrified terror creeps through my every vein.

I've heard Rhys's voice like this before: kind and authoritative. And I know exactly how he is looking at her as he uses it. Typically, my default response to this rare version of Rhys is to roll my eyes, but secretly I love it. Because it's a voice that has offered me everything I've never had, everything I've sought out—and poorly—elsewhere: reassurance... stability, the promise that things might not work out how I want, but they *will* be okay.

Suddenly I'm struck by an image of them sitting together on his bunk, their shoulders, their thighs touching. Her glossy, expensive black hair tickling his face, her beautiful ice-blue eyes framed with bashful dark lashes.

I jam a pillow over my head.

The soft mumbling conversation continues, and I wedge my AirPods into my ears, burying my head once more beneath my pillow, praying I do not need to listen to any suspicious silences. I "accidentally" bang my elbow against the wall and give a loud fake cough, all to remind them of how incestuously close we are. Eventually I drift away again to a playlist of ambient sounds.

MAY, LAST YEAR

Rhys called me before I even got home—well, tried calling me. But I just felt so *stupid*. The moment I saw his name, I rejected the call. Hadn't I proved I was just as bad as all of Beckett's terrible exes? Going round to some guy's house, lying on his *bed*—I didn't even have any excuse, hadn't even brought any books with me—

He sent me a message in the end. And, of course, it was an apology. A sweet one, a sincere one. Eloquently explaining what had happened. Apologizing if it had seemed as if he was taking advantage of my tears, because that was the last thing he wanted—

The *last* thing he wanted?

I couldn't read any more. I clicked Delete, and I didn't reply.

And when Beckett returned, I'd never been so relieved. It didn't take him long to pick up on the fact that something was wrong. I was shocked by how angry he got, pacing the room, calling my friends every name under the sun. I wanted to defend them, did so in my head, but found I couldn't correct him, didn't want to make him deflect that anger toward me, because wasn't I the architect of all this?

When he'd walked through the door, he'd been so happy

to see me, like an excitable puppy. A bouquet in one hand, Nando's takeout in the other. But after I came clean, he asked me to leave, his eyes glistening with unfallen tears, asking why he was always the last of my priorities, why I considered everyone's feelings except for his.

Lately I'd taken to keeping my phone on silent when I was with him. If my friends called—and after that disaster of a meeting, they'd been calling a lot—he'd invariably make some cruel, disparaging comment about them. Though I told him, gently, to stop, that they meant well, that he didn't know them as I did, the sight of a message from Casey or Stevie, even an innocuous "you okay, babe?" immediately soured his mood.

Deep down, I knew things were coming to a head. My studies were suffering, for one thing, exam season was approaching, and my tutors—and I—were becoming increasingly concerned that I wouldn't now make the grades needed to get into the universities of my choice. Another thing Beckett seemed to choose not to understand. After all, he hadn't needed to bother with university, deposited straight into a well-paying job in his father's office, forever rejecting the notion that I actually enjoyed learning, that I actually needed a degree to get a decent job in something I was actually interested in. I'd tried to keep on top of my studies, but the nights seemed to get later and later, and on Beckett's days off, he'd suggest I skip school so we could mooch around town. The days leading up to my finals began to slip away from me, sand through my fingertips.

The day of his return, I'd stupidly left my phone on Beckett's kitchen countertop while I used the bathroom, and of course, that was the very moment another message from Rhys arrived. I'd considered blocking his number—it would certainly make my life easier—but I couldn't bring myself to actually do that to him. Plus, while he never messaged me about anything deep, the occasional, bizarre Pokémon memes he sent never failed to make me smile.

The moment I came back into the room, I sensed the change in atmosphere, some primal instinct blaring a silent alarm, like an animal backing away from a murky watering hole, crocodiles lurking silently beneath the surface.

Beckett had moved from the sofa to sit at the kitchen counter. His head angled down into his hands, pretty golden hair shining in the pendant lights above the island.

"Hey, what's up?" I'd asked warily, and rather than reply, he viciously slid my phone across the smooth marble of the island. Instinctively I caught it. The screen was unlocked—as he insisted it always was *(Lara, you know we don't have secrets between us)*—and a large wall of text was visible on screen. As I began to scan the message, my heart plummeted. I immediately knew who it was from. The polite, almost formal cadence. The proper punctuation. Rhys messaged like a bloody teacher.

La, I know you're wrapped up in a relationship at
the moment, and I want you to know this is not
any kind of judgment on that, but our head of year

asked one of us to message you, and I drew the
short straw, I guess. He's really worried about your
attendance. You've missed a lot of classes and he
thinks you'd benefit from being back in class full-
time, but if for whatever reason you can't do that,
there are online classes you can take. He's tried to
leave messages for you and your dad but says no
one's replied. He wants to arrange a meeting so
the school can help you fix things. He's asked you
to give him a call.

Then, a second message, a few seconds later. An after-thought.

La, I also want you to know we all miss you. I keep
hoping you'll drop into the café one day for a chat,
but you never do.

I looked over at Beckett, alarmed in all manner of ways. Not least of all, at the sight of a tear dripping from Beckett's sculpted cheek onto the polished countertop.

"I knew it" was all he said.

And for a moment, I stupidly thought it was all going to be okay. Beckett had read the message and finally understood the importance of this time of the year for me. He was upset to know I was struggling with my studies, and I could feel the beginning of my own tears and even a bright streak of hope. That he would start to be supportive, that I could go back to school without receiving an interrogation before and after. I let out a long breath.

"I knew I couldn't trust him—or you. Tell me why it's okay for a guy to keep messaging you, telling you he *misses* you. How is that okay, Lara?"

I immediately sucked my breath back in, sharply. His eyes weren't full of sorrow as I'd thought; no, they were glittering with pure rage. I shook my head, incredulous.

"*That's* what you took from that? Beckett, I am fucking up my exams! Potentially, my life!"

He scoffed. "Oh? And that's my fault, is it? Maybe if I could trust you, maybe if you didn't want to keep disappearing off to this guy's café—which I have on good authority from my dad is severely struggling, by the way—maybe you'd have attended more classes!"

"If you could trust me? When have I ever done anything to suggest you can't? When?"

"*I miss you . . . hope to see you at the café,*" he mocked in a high, grating voice. "Lara, a guy is texting that he misses you and you expect me to be okay with that? Seriously?"

"It says *WE*! *We* miss you! He means my friends, Beckett! You know, the ones I'm not allowed to see anymore—"

He slammed both hands down on the countertop, making me jump.

"Stop trying to change the subject, Lara. Do you miss him, too? Answer me. I deserve to know."

I bit my lip. There was a dangerous energy crackling in the room. And a dark, rebellious part of me wanted to scream at him, YES, actually! Yes, I DO miss him. More than I ever expected to. More than I even *want* to. I miss his involuntarily pink-flushed smile at my terrible jokes. The way his eyes look when they catch the late-afternoon light. Even if he never saw me the way I wanted him to, it doesn't even matter anymore, because what I miss most of all is his *friendship*, his kindness, his lack of judgment—

"No! I already told you!" I lied, and the very act of doing so seemed to damage my heart, hardening it to stone with every denial. I *deserved* Beckett. We were equals in deceit, in cruelty, it seemed. "I haven't seen him in ages. He's literally repeating what a teacher told him to tell me. Why's that so hard to understand?"

Without warning, Beckett whirled around and slammed his fist hard against the wall, cracking the plaster, and I gasped, backing away toward the doorway, toward the front door.

"He's asking you to meet him at a café, Lara!"

"So what if he is?" I yelled back. We were in tandem, a wild tango, with me taking one step back as he took one forward. Beckett had never hit me, and I'd never imagined he would, but he had hit other things before in frustration . . . walls, doors. "He's just a *friend*, Beckett!"

Another lie. It's like I couldn't stop myself. Rhys was only my friend because he never wanted anything more. That was why Beckett and I deserved each other. That was why Rhys was right not to choose me. He probably sensed something lacking in me from the start, something dark, something that was always going to align me with Beckett's orbit.

Beckett stopped moving toward me, his eyes glinting like a fox's in the darkness of the hall. He thrust out his hand, beckoning.

"Let me message him back."

This wasn't a polite request; it was a demand. And this wasn't going to be any kind of message I'd ever choose to send. I could see the trap he had set for me. The final closing of the circle.

"Why?" I asked pathetically. "Just tell me what you want me to say, and I'll message him. I'll do it right now. You can watch."

He gave a sardonic snort. "Are you going to let me or not? If you're not, you may as well just get out now and not come back. If I can't trust you, Lara, we both know there's no point to this relationship."

I should have taken the chance. I should have run and never looked back. I should have gone directly to the café and apologized to Rhys, to everyone, for how I'd treated them. But it felt impossible. I was too tied up now. There were too many threads binding me tightly to Beckett. Too many secrets he was keeping for me, too many lies I'd told to keep him happy. There were photos I'd agreed to send in the fevered flush of a new relationship, things I'd told him about my dad in a fit of anger. It was like trying to escape from a sticky spiderweb: the harder I tried to set myself free, the more caught up I became.

Swiping tears from my face, I handed him my phone with a shaking hand. But as I watched him type in his poison, his lies, to an unsuspecting Rhys, a sick smile on his pretty face, for the very first time, I felt those threads that bound us together so tightly start to loosen.

This was an undoing.

I don't know how much time passes before I wake.

Snapping open my eyes, the single AirPod that remains in my ear still hissing rain noises, I take in my surroundings.

What was it that woke me?

Then I hear it: a slow, irregular thumping coming from the wall—Rhys's cabin—from Rhys's *bed*.

My cheeks grow hot with embarrassment, but I come to my senses. There's no way, no *way* on this earth, that Rhys would be in there, doing . . . well, *anything* . . . let alone with *Gwen*. I check the time. It's three a.m. The witching hour, as my gran would say. The time when everyone should be asleep, not dry-humping bioterrorists.

Lara, come on—

Fumbling for my other AirPod, I flip the hood of my dressing gown over my head, now more angry than anything else. This job is proving to be an utter nightmare in more ways than one. Before I wedge the AirPod in, the thumping comes again.

This time, something about it makes me pause.

There's something about the noise that's *wrong*.

I'm no expert, but it doesn't seem to me like the rhythmic motion of someone getting into it—it's almost eerie—faint and intermittent—*weak.*

I sit up.

Fuck's sake, Rhys, don't you dare judge me for this.

Clearing my throat loudly, I climb into the lower bunk and knock on the adjoining wall. "Hey, um, Rhys? Could you keep it down in there? It's three a.m."

I almost snort at my voice. I sound like an overly formal air steward.

There follows an expectant silence, and despite the cool of the night, despite the fact that I'm completely alone, I feel my skin slowly turn scarlet.

The sound comes again—a slight scratching this time, and then a longer, slower slide.

The fuck?

"Rhys—I'm sorry to, uh—interrupt or whatever—but you're kind of freaking me out right now."

I say it quietly—but loud enough for whoever's next door to hear. I wait to hear something in response—a murmur of conversation, an embarrassed laugh, a muttered apology—but there's nothing, *nothing at all.*

"*Rhys?* Are you okay in there?"

The thumping becomes a scrabbling, louder now, almost desperate.

"Rhys? Seriously? What's going on?"

I scramble for my phone, charging on the small table under the window, and fumble for the flashlight, ready to slide open the vent between our rooms and fully yell. But what I see chills my blood.

The vent is already open, and thin green stems coated in sticky, translucent fur emerge from the slats, twisting their way down the wall, touching the sheets.

I tumble backward off the bunk ladder, shuddering, not even bothering to throw on a hoodie, and rummage through my uniform for my staff keys. Next, I force the door. The adrenaline surging through my body gives me the extra strength I need, and within seconds the door flings open, bouncing off the wall. I notice with chagrin that the bindweed has returned. Ripping tendrils away from Rhys's door, I hastily unlock it, not even bothering to knock.

I don't know what I expect to see—but either way, I expect it to be bad. At first I can't even take it in.

There's a familiar (and, of course, lone) bulk on the top bunk when I tiptoe in, and I think I've made a mistake, that Rhys is just asleep and I'm an overreacting loon. But it's the *smell* that alerts me. I raise my flashlight and look closer.

It *is* Rhys—but it's also not.

It takes me a few seconds to recognize what he's covered in—the stench of it, revoltingly thick and green. Goosegrass. My gran's dog—a perky Jack Russell terrier—is obsessed with eating the stuff, sticky and rough-skinned and *everywhere* in our garden come summer. It's has a hideous texture, like Velcro. But it covers every inch of Rhys, and in the darkness, it looks oddly like it's *moving*.

I can barely see Rhys beneath it all—which part of him is up and which part is down. All I can see is a thick mass of writhing green, and all I hear is a hollow sound—an awful sound—a furry, viscous choking, a terrible *rasping*.

He will DIE, La.

He will die unless you do *something.*

That's when the shaking starts. My entire body shakes—my hands especially. My teeth chatter, my ears ring—I have no idea what to do—no idea how to save him—all I'm capable of is *looking*.

Lara, think—THINK.

Then I remember: he has a knife.

Wrenching open the single drawer of the tiny dresser, I snatch up the knife, almost dropping it several times as I try to figure out how to extract the blade.

I haul myself up to the top bunk and begin carefully sliding the blade beneath the weeds, pulling it upward with all my might, starting by the pillow end, next to what I *think* is his face. I steady myself as much as I can, trying to move in time to the swaying motion of the train. The weeds spring away from my hands with surprising ease, seeming to almost shrivel at my touch.

And he's breathing—he is *breathing*—and yes—yes—we can get through this—*I* can do this—

I move further down, whacking my head against the ceiling with such force the whole room throbs violently around me, my vision blurring for a terrible few seconds. The moment I can focus again, all embarrassment forgotten, I climb over him, his body beneath mine, familiar but cold in its thick carapace of weeds.

Soon I see his eyes, dark and fearful, as I continue to wrench away entire armfuls of the stuff, freeing his chest, then his arms, so he can assist me.

And when we're finished, there is an entire garden on the floor.

26

I climb back down from the bunk in shock and collapse onto the chair, staring in horror at Rhys. "Shit—what—what *happened*? What's going *on*?"

He remains sitting up in the top bunk, throwing handfuls of weed onto the floor, his face haunted, his hands shaking.

"What happened . . . ? La, I . . . I think you just saved my *life*."

I stare at the pile of weeds on the floor, terrified they might start moving again, like slender snakes slithering toward me, encircling my wrists, but instead they seem to wither and brown beneath my stare.

"Who—who *did* this to you? What happened?"

He shakes his head. "I—don't know how it happened. All I know is that when I woke up, they were already starting to cover my face. I started pulling it all away, but it grew so *quickly, so fast,* and I couldn't keep up with it, couldn't *breathe*—I—" He gives another shaky sigh, and I realize he is trying not to cry. *"Fuck."*

"Gwen," I say darkly. "I heard you guys in here earlier. Why the *hell* would you let her in here, Rhys? We *know* she's the cause of all this—Shosh pretty much admitted it."

He looks down at me, and I notice a slight flush to his cheeks. "She came to tell me she has an idea of how she might stop all this. She wants to talk to you about it, too."

"Okay, but why does she always insist on talking to you in the dead of night?"

He pauses, thinking carefully before he answers. "She didn't say as much, but I think she's afraid of her brother, or wary of him, at least. I don't think she wants him to know she's talking to us."

"Afraid of *Gwydion*? Come *on*. Her plants, her research, her mistake—her *fault*," I say sharply.

Rhys says nothing for a while, just stares down at the swiftly shriveling weeds that still litter the floor. He clears his throat. "Lara, how . . . how did you do it?"

I look up at him, confused. "Do what?"

"How did you do it? Get them off me, the weeds, I mean."

"You saw. I used your knife."

He shook his head. "Okay, but I'd been trying to pry them all off for a minute or so before you came in. . . . They just—just immediately grew back, like out of nowhere. Then you walked in, and they all seemed to . . . to shrivel up the moment you touched them. It was—"

"Weird?"

"Amazing."

I say nothing else, because I don't have an answer for him. It is absolutely weird, but so are a lot of things right now. I'm only grateful I could help.

"We need to find Shosh immediately," he says, climbing down and brushing the remainder of the weeds away. When I realize he's only wearing a T-shirt and boxers, I immediately turn to face the door, blinking and hot-faced. He continues talking unabashedly as he struggles into his joggers. "Once we tell her that we've *seen* it, both of us—that these things nearly *killed* me; once we're saying exactly the same thing, how we're *all* in danger—she'll *have* to listen. She has no choice. She'll have to stop the train right now or at least forcibly detach those bloody carriages."

But thinking about the last time I spoke to her, I'm not sure I possess the confidence in Shosh that Rhys does.

The narrow corridor outside our cabins is darker than usual. Thick ropes of bindweed and ivy wind their way up the doorframes, latticing the lamps and limiting their light. I wrench a handful off the wall in frustration, pleased at the way it shrivels from my touch.

"It's everywhere," says Rhys, looking uneasily at the dead weeds in my hand. "It's getting worse."

"Yeah, we can't carry on like this," I agree. "Rhys, if Shosh doesn't listen to us, what are we going to do? We can't just keep waiting for her to come around."

Rhy's mouth thins to a concerned line. "Honestly, I'm not sure, La."

It takes us several minutes to peel away enough of the weeds to be able to open the door of the adjoining carriage. Even in here, weeds crisscross the ceiling lights and thin branches stretch from dark corners.

We find Shosh sitting in the staff lounge, staring blankly into space and picking at her nails, and even though we've not even started talking yet, I already feel hopeless. Beneath the table, a thick, springy moss has started to carpet the floor, and nettles weave themselves tightly around the handles of the cupboards, trapping their content.

Shosh's eyes are ringed with dark shadows, and she pinches her forehead tightly in her hand as we join her at the table. When she speaks, her words contain as much sincerity as an automated voicemail: "I don't know how many times I need to tell you, but I have the situation under control. Gwen is working on something right now to contain it all. The greenhouses are all locked up, and we've all just gotta keep our nerve and sit tight until we—"

I dump the bag of weeds we collected from Rhys's cabin on the table. "Sit *tight*? Shoshanna, a whole load of these were strangling Rhys in his sleep! Locking the greenhouse hasn't made a bloody bit of difference. Samira is *dead*! She was bled out by *thorns*! Xavier might be dead—not everybody saw, but I swear he was choking on something that looked like . . . like a vine. I mean, take a look around you! *We need to stop the train!*"

Shosh shakes her head, like a blade falling, the sword of

Damocles descending, dooming us all, our deaths now awaiting us around every corner.

"We *can't*," she says dully. "Haven't you been paying attention, Lara? Haven't you *seen* where we are?"

"I don't care where we are!" I shout, my voice cracking, my head throbbing unpleasantly in time with the rhythm of the train. "We need to get off this train *now!* We need to get help. Can you—can you radio someone?"

"She's right," says Rhys bluntly, searching for my hand beneath the table. And despite my face flushing violently, I grip it back gratefully. "We need to stop the train and alert the authorities, and if you don't listen, then we're going to contact the driver and get *him* to stop the train ourselves. If you won't see sense, then I'm sure he will once he catches a glimpse of this."

Shosh shrugs in such an indifferent way it *chills* me. Drains me utterly of hope.

"Go ahead. Try and stop the train. You have absolutely no authority to do that, but if you're hellbent on *killing* yourselves, I'm not going to stand in your way. I'm curious about where you're planning on going when we stop, though." She gestures to the darkness beyond the windows. "We're deep in the Black Forest right now. You gonna wander through the woods with a trail of breadcrumbs?"

Rhys sighs defeatedly.

"Why *haven't* you called for help yet?" I ask her quietly, looking her directly in the eye. "What's really going on, Shosh?"

Shosh casts me an irritated look and chews at a nail. "Don't you think I've already done that? Jesus, Lara, how negligent do you think I am?"

I decide it would be wise not to answer this. "Look, you can keep minimizing this all you want, but one person has been hospitalized—possibly dead. Samira *is* dead! And if I hadn't heard him bashing away against my wall, I'd be telling you Rhys was dead tomorrow morning." I shudder involuntarily as I say those words. "What makes you so sure it won't be you waking up with a noose of ivy tightening around your neck? And if you somehow manage to survive, how are you planning on explaining the fact that all this happened on your watch and you just blithely refused to stop? I have to ask. . . . Are you *involved* in this?"

Shoshanna looks rattled, darting a glance behind her, as if afraid she's being watched. "Don't be so ridiculous, Lara. We *are* stopping! I radioed ahead the moment I saw what had happened to Samira. We are heading direct to Cologne—the next major station. I am absolutely stopping this train. Just not here, in the middle of nowhere!"

"And how long will that take?" presses Rhys. "Don't you sense it, Shosh? We're running out of time." He gestures to the pile of dead weeds that lies between us on the table like a bag of dead snakes. "Why is it so important that we stop at Cologne? *Any* station would do."

Shosh stands abruptly, the shriek of her chair legs making me jump. "I don't have time for this," she says, turning away from us and supporting herself at the counter, head bowed. "You don't know the full story. All I can tell you right now is that we are getting to that station and we're not stopping beforehand." She turns back to us slowly, her dark eyes glittering with intent. "Not for *anything,* understand? Not for anything."

27

Rhys and I go back to his cabin, too dejected to even speak. He sits on the bottom bunk, still fruitlessly trying to get a signal on his phone while I perch on the armchair, knees drawn up to my chest, as I try to make *sense* of all this. It's like trying to stack a slippery house of cards.

"Do you believe her?" asks Rhys. "Do you believe she's got a plan?"

"No." I snort. "It's pretty clear now that Shosh is getting a big fat paycheck to ensure that this train gets to its final destination."

He nods, brow creased. "And we're all just collateral damage."

Collateral damage. I think of Samira and shudder.

"Fuck *sake*!" exclaims Rhys, tapping violently at his screen. "How is there nothing? Not a single bar of signal, no 3G, 4G, 5G, *anything*? I can't even Google stuff, let alone call anyone."

"And what exactly would you Google?" I ask. "WikiHow to escape a fast-moving train of killer plants?"

He casts me a dark look and tosses his phone on the small fold-out table in frustration. "*Not* helping."

Ignoring him, I stare down at his phone, my eyes widening, and nod in its direction. "Shit, Rhys—*look*."

The back of his phone has slid off, revealing a furry patch of green. With a shaking hand, he picks it up, entirely removing the case. The insides of the phone are coated with a slimy green moss. The sim card is destroyed, blackened, partially dissolved.

"What the *hell*—"

Swallowing, I pull my own phone from my pocket and immediately peel off the case, pulling out the sim tray. It is the same situation. The sim is sticky and smells dankly of weeds. The phone is basically useless.

I stifle a gasp with my hand as Rhys sighs deeply, staring up at the ceiling.

"Well, I guess that explains *that*," he murmurs.

"We're trapped," I whisper. "There's no way this is an accident. They don't *want* us to call anyone; there's no way we can get help—"

"Who?" says Rhys urgently, like I've solved the riddle of the Sphinx. "Who's *they*?"

I snap a glance at Rhys, irritated that he's expecting some sort of revelation from me. "I don't know *exactly*. I mean, do *you*? What *were* you and Gwen talking about earlier? You know, an hour or so before you almost *died*? Shosh already admitted that Gwen was indirectly responsible for Samira's death, thanks to her little shop of horrors down there, but you decided a little late-night one-to-one with her would be a good idea?"

He shifts uncomfortably, clicking his phone back together and shoving it into his pocket before looking up. "I already told you. She asked how you were—and, Lara, she seemed genuinely worried—and told me to hang tight, that she was working on a fix. Right now, with Shosh acting as she is, it looks like that might be our only hope."

"A *fix*?" I snort. "And you believed her? Rhys, she's behind all this! Who do you think is paying Shosh? I mean, did you not consider there could be a link between your meeting in your cabin with a crazed botanist who studies out-of-control killer plants and then nearly dying minutes later, in the same place, from said plants? Wow, guess your hookup really wasn't all that, Rhys."

He wrinkles his nose. "Jesus, Lara, we weren't *hooking up*. She's like three years older than me. Where the hell did you get that idea from?"

"You closed the vent."

"*Gwen* closed the vent. I think she's the only one on this train, other than us, who understands the severity of the situation we're in—the only one left who might be able to stop all this. And it isn't you she's worried about; it's Gwydion. I think she thought you might tell him we were speaking before we could talk to you. You said Gwydion seems scared of Gwen—I think it's the other way round."

I sigh, my anger diminishing. "Do you think he could be behind all this?"

Rhys looks me in the eye. "It's worth considering. I don't know, she sounded genuine—and genuinely concerned. She didn't tell me much; like I said, she insisted she wanted to speak to us both together, when you were up to it."

"Okay, it's just from my side it looked like you were keeping her secrets. How long have we been friends?"

His expression darkens. "Um, well, if we're talking in recent months, apparently not at all."

I still remember the look on Rhys's face when I told him it would be better if he didn't wait for me after school anymore. The surprised hurt and how quickly he hid it. When I asked him to stop messaging me . . . Worst of all, I remember his face at the summer party. I deserve the dig.

There is a dangerous atmosphere in the room now. Like the gloves are off, all bets are off. I want to see how far he'll go, how far I can push him. There is a sense of release, too— how long have we both wanted to have this out but have been too afraid to, too polite, too worried about what will be uncovered?

"All I'm trying to say is, we need to stick together," I say quietly. "And that means not having late-night chats with Gwen, of all people."

"Why do you even *care* what I do in the privacy of my cabin?"

Why is he so deliberately missing the point?

"I *don't*!"

He looks down to face me. We are inches apart now. I stare into the moss green of his eyes, his returning gaze thunderous. His voice is low, accusatory. "Sure *sounds* like you do."

"Wow, Rhys. You sure have a high opinion of yourself, don't you?"

He shrugs and folds his arms, mirroring me. Neither of us will look away.

"Okay, but at least it's deserved," he said. "Good friends, loyal friends, don't *deny* each other three times, like some kind of fucked-up apostle, now do they?"

And then, just like that, I don't want to do this anymore. All my anger rushes out of me like air from a punctured balloon. Because I realize that there's no way I can win this one. I *was* a shitty friend. I *did* deny him again and again. I work my tongue around my mouth, bite my lip, and subtly tilt back my head, because I don't want to cry. I'm so done with crying, but the tears come anyway, scalding down my cheek.

All the fight immediately leaves Rhys, too. He blinks away the fierceness in his eyes, one hand slipping to my shoulder.

"Fuck—La, I'm sorry," he says. "And I know you're sorry, too. I didn't mean it; I know it wasn't you—not really. It's just this situation . . . it's making both of us tense."

With his other hand, he gently brushes away a tear with a considerate swipe of his thumb. I catch my breath at the feel of his skin against mine, forget to release it as he stares at me, sorrow turning to curiosity as his thumb continues to trail down the curve of my heated, flushed cheek, moving inward to trace my bottom lip. Softly I part them, only a little, my gaze traveling down to his lips, slightly parted, the top one a pretty cupid's bow.

"La . . . ?" he says, his voice barely a whisper, careful fingers tilting my chin.

A quiet tap at the door causes us to spring apart as if caught in some nefarious act.

Mortified, I immediately turn away from him and fumble with the door. Maybe Shoshanna has come to her senses, realized she's not, in fact, immortal and is ready to offer us some help.

But instead, Gwydion stands there, dressed in an old-fashioned green smoking jacket.

"Look, I know eavesdropping is bad form and all that," he says as I glance over at Rhys, whose cheeks are bright pink. "But I couldn't help but overhear some of the earlier conversation you had with your esteemed leader, Shoshanna." I notice he looks at me as he speaks and not at Rhys. "And while she might not believe you . . . I do know my sister. And while I may not possess her expertise, I do have *some* idea about what's happening on this train." He pauses. "I also think you're both right. . . . I think we are *all* in real danger."

28

As we leave the sanctity of Rhys's cabin, I can immediately tell that things have gotten worse.

It's darker, for starters. The beautiful glass globe lights that line the passenger sleeping car are inexplicably weaker, dimmer—as if the plants have somehow leeched their power.

We follow Gwydion silently through the cabin carriages, our feet sinking into the soft pile of the carpet, mottled here and there with thick patches of lichen, until we reach the Dahlia Bar. Once there, Gwydion reaches over the marble countertop, helps himself to a bottle of red from behind the bar, and pours himself a large glass, proffering the bottle toward us.

I shake my head distractedly. Things here are weird enough without adding alcohol to the mix.

"This has been a fucking rough night. I need to be on breakfast service in a few hours," mutters Rhys.

I shoot him an incredulous look, but Gwydion laughs out loud, and it's then that I realize this isn't his first glass of wine.

"*Service?*" he says in disbelief. "My friend, there's no one *left* to serve. Things have fallen apart."

"Where's Carlos?" I ask.

"I had to help him to bed an hour or so ago. He'd made *quite* the dent in the bar stock. Seems like you two aren't the only ones affected by what's been going on here."

"Okay, so start talking. What *has* been going on here?" asks Rhys, who, to my surprise, helps himself to a bottle of Corona.

"Well, for a start, we have a dead body on board. I mean, I'm not the most frequent rail traveler, but I feel that's *fairly* unusual."

His casual dismissal of Samira as a "dead body" makes me shiver, like cold water splashed on a hot pan. Rhys takes a swig of his drink and settles back onto one of the plush couches. "Look, enough of the arch comments. We're here and we're listening. What do you have to tell us? What can we actually *do*?"

I perch on the edge of a barstool, cracking open a cold can of soda, and wait.

Gwydion takes another glug of wine before he begins to speak: "My family owns a large quantity of land in North Wales, a little north of the Snowdon range. Do either of you know the area?"

I certainly don't. I've lived in London for most of my life. And is now really the time for Gwydion's life story?

"Yeah," Rhys says, "and we already saw the article. The mysterious disappearances of your parents." He adds acidly, "Only now it doesn't seem so mysterious."

Gwydion ignores him, training his icy gaze on me. "It's an area long steeped in mythology. Damp and bleak and surrounded by rugged mountains. A hard land for a hard people. We can trace our estate back centuries, ancestor to ancestor; the land has always been in our family."

Gwydion pauses, glancing at Rhys, who I notice is slowly and methodically ripping up a napkin between deep gulps of his drink.

"Several months ago, after receiving a rather generous windfall from a deceased distant relative, my father appointed a team of landscapers to start the deforestation of one of the wilder parts of the estate, close to Caer Tylluan—a ruined fortress. My mother had an idea to build some bougie flint cottages for B&B purposes—the estate is expensive to maintain and doesn't pay for itself.

"As usual, there was commotion from the locals. Apparently, this particular wood contained trees that were thousands of years old—as if we didn't already know. On top of the eco protestors, we also had a lot of issues with trespassers, new age hippie tourists—you know, the type obsessed with yoga and worshipping the moon and recharging their crystals in there. All that kind of shit."

I raise an eyebrow. Already something seems a little off about his story, but I can't quite put my finger on what.

"So Father paid for increased security, ringed the area

with fences, but it took much longer than anyone expected to clear the site. The trees there *were* old. Ancient, even. Oaks and elms; their roots went deep, deep down into the earth, stretching far into the distant past. To add to the difficulty, the whole area was thickly wreathed in briar and brambles."

He wrinkles his nose, as if disturbed by the memory, then continues. "Weeks later, in the midst of it all, as the excavators were finally digging down into the remains of the roots, we discovered what looked to be the ruins of an old stone circle that had been hidden within the trees and entirely covered in plant matter," he says. "Druids were thought to have used them in worship, and at the center of the circle, as if caged within it, was the statue you've seen—the artifact that stands in the last of the greenhouse carriages."

"The owl thing," I clarify.

Gwydion nods. "Exactly. So the landscapers immediately called my parents to show them. Mother rather liked it, so she found a new home for it on the front lawn. She has a few Goldsworthys, Hepworths, and the like. . . . It seemed a good fit."

He peeks at us both in the dim light of the carriage, the rain once more pelting against the glass, as if to check that we are enraptured, as he'd hoped. We are. He's a master storyteller. It's his voice, I think. Lyrical and deep, as if reciting an incantation.

"It was only a day later when we began to suspect that something was . . . *wrong* with it," Gwydion goes on. "Dad came storming in that evening, downing a whiskey and cursing the gardeners to high heaven. Apparently the grass on our east lawn had grown to knee height overnight. And not only that: the statue we'd recovered was wreathed in thorns, as if they'd grown out of the thing."

My throat grows dry as he goes on. "Gwen was home from uni at the time and was immediately captivated. Started doing all these obsessive scientific observations, such as recording time-lapse video of the area, taking soil samples, and so on. I was interested, too, at first. It seemed like . . . magic of some kind to me . . . something enchanted and ancient, causing everything around it to *grow*."

His eyes sparkle with the recollection.

"A few days later, my father had to pay the landscaping team extra to clear the lawns. It was really quite the sight—mother's rosebushes had become particularly rampant. Later that same day, the boss turned up at the door. Both Gwen and I suspected something was up. I remember hiding in an alcove off the entrance hall as he spoke to my father. The landscaper's voice was hesitant . . . reluctant. But I *heard*. I heard it all. Once they'd ripped up all the briars, trimmed back all the nettles, they found something scattered all about the base of the statue . . . bones."

"Bones?" I repeat, the small hairs on the back of my neck standing up.

Gwydion nods. "Small bones—a rabbit's, perhaps, or a bird's. We didn't think anything of it at first . . . but then, the very next day, Grumble disappeared."

"Grumble?"

Gwydion gives a long sigh. "Mmmm. Our dog. . . . Honestly, he was a nightmare anyway. Hideous, yappy little thing that took chunks out of both Gwen and me when we were toddlers. That same day, despite the hard work of the landscapers, we realized that the growth on the lawn was now genuinely out of control. You can guess what we found when, once again, the area was stripped."

Rhys takes a long swig of his beer. I wonder if he's thinking about his own dog.

"Mother was devastated and demanded we destroy the statue, crying out again and again that it was cursed. I was more than happy to, but then Gwen stepped in. Using Father's contacts in the pharmaceutical industry, she'd managed to get hold of some laboratory in Eastern Europe. She'd sent them her videos, her careful recordings, all her data, and it turned out they were willing to work with her and pay her a quite unbelievable amount of money to examine the artifact. So that is what we are *really* carrying on board. Several million pounds' worth of apparently cursed Celtic artifact."

"Blodeuwedd . . . ," I whisper.

"Quite." Gwydion turns to look at Rhys. "It appears you already know the next part of the story. Needing to get away from all this nonsense, I took a trip to Mykonos with some friends when Gwen returned to uni. When I got home . . . my parents had gone, and the estate—well, as you read in the article, it was in a bad way."

He shakes his head in apparent sorrow.

"I wanted to *destroy* that thing, had this gut feeling it was responsible. But Gwen went berserk at the suggestion, saying it would be unethical, that we had a duty to use whatever was contained within the artifact—magic, or some unexplained science, whatever side you fall on—for good. That we could create a charity, harness its abilities to help countries suffering from famine or drought. And like a fool, I listened to her. Yes, Gwen's my sister, but truly we've never been close. We've attended separate boarding schools since we were in preschool. I've never *really* had the measure of her."

He pauses, his expression darkening.

"But still, I took to the idea, liked the thought of being involved in a charity—and let's face it, with the collapse of the estate, we needed the money. Everything was arranged, and we managed to book this train to take us there. Gwen said it was imperative we choose a quiet train in case anything . . . went wrong—I should have known something wasn't right then. We had the carriages custom-made with the deposit Gwen had been granted from the lab, and I volunteered to accompany her as a sort of unofficial spokesperson for the charity. Everything seemed like it would be fine—better than fine. Naively I thought we might be about to do some real good in this world. Until the night I saw her disappear into those carriages, accompanied by Xavier. . . . And last night, when she left her room," he continues, his eyes flicking to Rhys, "last night I found the documents she was hiding. Found out what she *really* did. And what she's planning on doing . . . unless we can stop her."

Rhys and I both stare at Gwydion, fully spellbound.

"You see, the place the artifact is heading to right now, as we speak, isn't a research center at all, not in the way *she* made it sound. No. Gwen *has* sold the artifact for a life-changing amount of money, should they approve the sale, should she show them it works. . . . But not to any research center—she's sold it to a major bioweapons facility."

"Wait, wait—*wait* a minute," I say, my voice preternaturally calm. "So we've got a magical woo-woo artifact that controls plants and is going to be sold as a bioweapon by your nefarious sister? *Please*, Gwydion. This isn't the latest episode of *Black Mirror.* Jesus."

I give him a slow clap, looking over to Rhys for encouragement. "I mean . . . come *on*. As stories go, that's got to be the biggest load of bullshit I've ever heard, right, Rhys?"

My skin itches the moment Rhys doesn't immediately back me up. He seems to be turning the idea over in his head in a way that is making me increasingly anxious.

"How?" he says, leaning forward. "Say we believe you, say what you've told us is true . . . how exactly can it be used as a bioweapon?"

Gwydion's lips curl in a slight smile. And I'm annoyed that now he seems more invested in Rhys believing him than me.

"Use your imagination. You've already seen what she can

do in these close confines, stuck aboard this ridiculous train with only a few common plants to play with. Imagine what she can do left unchecked. When fully *fed*. Back home, while she was feeding on the occasional woodland creature, it still took the gardeners a full month to clear that copse. Every day the greenery had grown back, thicker and stronger and . . . worst of all, *stranger*."

I swallow as the unbelievable truth of his words sets in. "Okay, say this is true. What exactly are *we* going to do?"

Gwydion nods as if he's already thought of everything, something I find desperately reassuring. "As soon as I discovered the documents, I met with Shoshanna and the driver—we agreed to keep things low-key so as not to cause panic. We're currently on a diversion to the next major city, a hundred miles outside the Black Forest. There we can all alight safely, and Gwen will have the authorities to deal with. You can understand that Shoshanna didn't want to cause any more alarm."

I inhale sharply. Any more *alarm*? A friend of mine has *died*. Only a few hours ago, *Rhys* almost died. I force myself to breathe. Despite everything, it's a relief that Gwydion is a few steps ahead of his sister and has put a plan into action.

Maybe everything *will* be all right?

Rhys clears his throat. "Out of interest . . . how *is* it activated? The artifact. You mentioned finding bones . . ."

Gwydion narrows his eyes and then sighs. "I have the feeling that both of you already know."

"I *knew* it! That first day in the carriage," says Rhys, his voice husky with disbelief. "I *saw* it. It's blood, isn't it? God, like some kind of *monster.*"

Gwydion gives a short shake of his head, his eyes widening in an odd sort of reverence. "She is no monster. She is Blodeuwedd."

"The lady of flowers," I say. "Flower Face. I remember the story. But wait, why would she be . . . *killing* people?"

Gwydion steeples his fingers. "At the end of the myth, she is cursed by the magician who created her to transform into an owl, cursed to haunt the night skies, never to bask in the sun again. So she is angry, I think. She thinks her punishment was unjust—and rightfully. I believe she wants revenge."

He gets up and steps before me, almost uncomfortably close. "But don't you *know* this already?" he whispers. "Don't *you*, out of all of us, feel it? Her pain. Her anguish. You *hear* her, don't you? She speaks to you."

I stare at Gwydion, confused.

No, not confused . . . *scared.*

"What? No? I don't know what you mean."

But I do.

That strange whispering I hear whenever I'm in the greenhouse carriages. That fever dream I had out in the field that day. Was that *her*? Can Gwydion really be speaking the truth? How is it he knows?

"She was conjured of flowers—meadowsweet, oak blossom, and broom," I say, remembering. "She was the most beautiful woman ever to live. But she didn't want to be a wife—at least not Lleu's. The magician's plan had failed, his loyal friend killed by her lover, so he *cursed* her. He turned her from flowers into an owl—a predator."

Gwydion's eyes gleam like glaciers in the low light. "Oh, indeed . . . so we must not be surprised when she goes hunting."

29

Gwydion looks unusually shaken, *haunted* by what he's shared. His hand trembles as he places his glass on the bar. If he is making this up, he is a fine actor.

I release a shaky sigh. "I don't want to believe this, but after everything that's happened, everything I've seen—I do," I admit, grimly.

Rhys rips the label from his beer bottle, his brow furrowed. "So we're all stuck here with that thing for—what did you say—a hundred miles?"

Gwydion nods. "More or less. We need to stick together and keep safe until we stop."

I turn this over in my mind. A simple enough plan, but something still scratches at my brain, something that doesn't quite make sense.

"Let's talk to the driver, then," I say, quietly calling his bluff. "Find out exactly how long we're stuck on this hell train for."

"Good idea." Gwydion nods. "While you do that, I'm going to see exactly what Gwen is up to. She's been locked in her room for hours . . . it's worrying me."

Silently we watch him go.

"Well, you know him best. Do you believe him?" asks Rhys once we're alone, his emerald eyes boring into mine.

I give a sudden, uncontrollable shudder. I still don't trust Gwydion, but a lot of what he said makes absolute sense. And strange events are born of strange things, aren't they? And I've never seen anything stranger than that statue . . . somehow alive and yet not alive—nothing like the bland and blind effigies that line museum walkways. No, whatever is in that carriage is something else entirely—beseeching, hopeless, and terrifying all at once.

I clear my throat before answering, my words considered: "Ordinarily . . . I'd think he was having us on, or that maybe he was struggling with mental health, to put it politely. But that's before I saw the things I've seen here. What's happening aboard this train . . . it's not . . . logical. . . . It's both oddly natural and yet *not*, if you know what I mean. *Supernatural*."

Rhys nods efficiently, then gets up. "Yeah, I do know. Enough's enough. I don't give a damn what Shoshanna says. We need to speak to the driver. I don't pretend to fully understand what's going on, but staying on this train with that *thing* for another hundred miles is madness."

I follow him, my mind busily whirring like a hummingbird's wings, past Shoshanna's tiny office, barely more than a cubicle, to the driver's carriage, the door to which is always kept locked.

Rhys hammers on the door with a violence that startles me. It's the action of someone on the very edge.

"Hey!" he shouts. "Hey, driver, can you let us in? We need to talk to you. It's urgent; we need to stop this train as soon as possible."

I look warily out the window. The darkness of the forest flees swiftly past. It's barely dawn. The moon is still high above us, a bright, sardonic yellow.

Rhys commences hammering again, and I pull his arm away. "Hey, *hey*—wait. Think about it. If Gwydion is telling the truth, if we even believe half of what he said, then maybe Shosh is right—especially if she's working with Gwen and knows what the artifact is capable of. *Do* we want to stop in the middle of a deserted forest? A place crawling with all kinds of . . . greenery and plant life? Does that honestly sound like a good idea?"

Rhys slumps against the door and follows my glance out the window and into the dark crowd of immensely tall fir trees. "Okay, okay. Point taken. But still, if Gwydion has explained the situation to the driver, then why aren't we ditching those carriages?"

The driver's cabin remains ominously quiet.

Rhys pushes open the door to Shosh's—thankfully empty—office and returns moments later with a fire extinguisher. He then proceeds to bash it repeatedly into the driver's door, causing some significant dents.

"Are you okay in there?" he yells, his voice strained and raspy. "Can you *hear* us? We need to decouple some carriages—urgently! We're in trouble!"

It's weird. There's no sound coming from the driver's carriage at all. And rather than slow at the commotion Rhys is causing, even if only because there appears to be a madman battering away at the door, the train appears to speed up.

The truth crawls unpleasantly over me like tendrils of poison ivy. "Something's wrong, Rhys . . . something's *wrong*," I moan quietly. Because if I say it any louder, it might be true. "Something's *always* been wrong, and we've all been too busy, too wrapped up in our jobs, our shifts, in that stupid greenhouse, to notice."

Rhys turns to me, dropping the extinguisher and pushing back his dark hair, his eyes wild. "What? What's wrong? What do you mean?"

"The *driver*. Where are they? *Who* are they? Where have they been this whole time? Have you ever seen them at dinner? Any trace of them in any of the cabins? Have you ever fixed them a drink? Could you tell me what they looked like?"

"*Shit*," breathes Rhys, flopping back against the wall. "Shit. You're right."

I slip into Shoshanna's office and snap on the three ancient monitors above her desk.

"What are you doing?"

"CCTV," I murmur. "I don't know why we didn't think of

it before. Maybe there'll be evidence of what happened to Samira."

Rhys gives a shake of his head. "Those are their own private carriages, remember. The train won't have CCTV in there."

The monitors flicker on. Currently the screens show the kitchen, the Cedar Lounge, and the corridor to the passenger cabins. They are all deserted.

"How do we change camera?" I murmur, looking at the antiquated walnut control panel. I see three identical dials and set about twisting them. The pictures flicker and begin to change. There's the Dahlia Bar—movement there, Gwydion once more troubling the wine. The sight makes me uneasy. I know what some people can be like when they overindulge. My own dad's an eternal example.

The second monitor shows the piano lounge, the camera trained on the greenhouse door. I swallow as I notice it's slightly ajar. And the third monitor appears to show an . . . an out-of-control *garden*—a view inside the greenhouse, I assume.

I gesture at the screen with a nod. "Hey. You said the greenhouse carriages wouldn't have cameras."

"They wouldn't—Oh . . . Oh no, oh *God*," mutters Rhys, backing away from the monitor, his face drained of color. "*Shit.*"

The plethora of plants on the screen means it takes me a little longer to figure out what's wrong.

That image, the black-and-white square that looks like

an overgrown area of the greenhouse, is actually the driver's cabin. The space is small and confined, the world rushing past the windows, and every available area is covered in leaves as broad as dinner plates and garish monstrous blooms, their petals starkly blue, white, and navy in the old-fashioned monitor. But that isn't what frightens me the most; that isn't what makes my hands begin to tremble uncontrollably.

On closer examination, a figure in uniform is sprawled upon a seat facing the controls, their head forced unnaturally back. Giant twisting tendrils erupt from their mouth, splitting their jaw wide open like a marionette's, the tendrils even now writhing toward the windscreen and twisting around the control panel. The driver's eyes are forever unseeing, the sockets crammed with dark blue blooms.

"We. Are. *Fucked*, aren't we?" I cry, tears dropping helplessly from my eyes. "Whatever happens, we're *fucked*. There is no one *driving* this train. No human, anyway; there's been no one driving it for God knows how long. We're going to smash into another train soon . . . a station . . . maybe any second now . . . and we're all going to die. . . . We're—"

Rhys grabs hold of my hands and draws me toward him. "La, listen to me. *Listen.* We're going to be okay. The train isn't going all that fast, not in the grand scheme of things, and remember what Shosh told us when we boarded? We're using mostly out-of-service and disused lines. We're going to be okay. If we can break the door down and—"

I shake my head. "And what? Miraculously learn how to

drive a train? Pray there's a copy of *Train-Driving for Dummies* stashed in the dashboard?"

Rhys gives an exasperated sigh and turns back to the monitors, looking for the off switch. "Look, I'm sorry I don't have all the answers," he says quietly in a way that hurts my heart. "I wish I did. I'm just doing my best."

I'm about to apologize when he jumps back from the switch in shock. "What the hell?" At this point, he sounds more resigned than surprised.

I follow his gaze. Tendrils of ivy are now creeping through the plug sockets.

"Do we risk pulling the emergency cord anyway? Force this thing to a stop?" I ask, trying to disguise the wobble of fear in my voice.

Rhys shakes his head. "Already tried. It's been disabled—probably by Shosh," he adds with a dark look back at her office.

This is not what I wanted to hear.

"Okay," I say. "Okay . . ."

"Let's gather everyone together; explain that we need to stop the train ourselves—and now. Maybe someone else will have more of an idea of how we can do it."

I'm doubtful. "*Everyone?* Even Gwen? After everything Gwydion said?"

"Yeah, I've been thinking about what he said," Rhys says thoughtfully. "And I don't buy it, not all of it. I mean, okay . . . so he doesn't want whatever the hell is in the end carriage to reach this lab—that makes total sense. *But . . .*"

He trails off. And once again I understand that there are lies in the story Gwydion told us, that he has tripped himself up somewhere . . . but my brain is too harried to see how.

"But?" I press uneasily.

"Well, why not divert to *anywhere*? The first safe place. Why a major capital city? I was more or less with him until he said that—it seemed *off* to me. The obvious thing to do is to decouple the carriages. Plus, the way he said it made me feel like it was more performance than the full truth." He pauses. "And there's something Gwen said earlier that I haven't been able to forget."

"Go on."

"Well, it's actually more what she *didn't* say. Since they boarded, she's been so worried about Gwydion. You've seen it yourself; she barely lets him out of her sight—like some kind of obsessed babysitter. Is that the action of someone eagerly delivering a cash-on-delivery weapon? What if, rather than being worried about him, she's worried about what he'll *do*?"

We both jump as branches rattle and scrape at the window beside us.

There's a soft sifting sound from the office behind me, and I yelp as something stings my ankle. A slim green stem is wrapped around it—nettles. They now carpet the floor of the office, the soft down of their serrated leaves unfurling as the seconds pass.

I kick it away, and Rhys follows my gaze grimly. "Let's go to the library. It's safer there," he says. "We can figure out how we want to break the news to everyone. Here, I just feel . . . I don't know. Overheard."

I'd prefer the quiet privacy of my cabin, but he's right; they're now too near to the rapidly growing morass of briars. I imagine being trapped inside, thorns forcing their way through the door, shutting us in before they wind their way around our necks.

We slip through the train like mournful ghosts, and I hesitate before entering the quiet space of the Azalea Coffee Lounge, locking the door behind us.

The library is deserted and one of the few places on the train not yet overcome by foliage. I follow him around the bookcases to a quiet corner and collapse onto an oversized leather couch while Rhys leans against the window, deep in thought. "If only there was some way for us to decouple those carriages—"

I shake my head. "Even if we could, I think it's too late. Those plants, they're everywhere. . . . Rhys, we're trapped. And we're running out of time. What—what if we don't survive this? We've run out of options. What if we're just waiting it out—waiting to *die*."

My lips tremble at that word, and I wait for reassurance from the usually stoic Rhys, but it doesn't come immediately, and dark seconds tick by.

"No way. The Lara I know would never give up without a fight," he finally says with quiet determination.

I shake my head in quiet desperation. "Yeah? Well, maybe I'm not the Lara you know anymore."

"Nah. You're still the same old Lara I remember. From . . . before."

The Lara you didn't want, I think bitterly.

A strained silence stretches out, and I can almost *see* the unspoken words floating in the air between us, begging to be said. Rhys won't look at me, and when he finally speaks, his voice is low and shaky.

"If—if we are in trouble," he begins, stuttering a little, "serious trouble, I . . . I want to be honest with you about something. About what happened between us. I don't want to have regrets . . ." He trails off, leaving the sentence dangling there between us.

"What regrets?" I murmur. I now have the distinct feeling I'm walking into a trap. Rhys looks down for a moment, as if losing his nerve, then immediately raises his head, pinning me down like a struggling butterfly with his solemn green gaze. "You *know* what it is I regret, Lara. We both do—how long are we going to keep pretending otherwise? At . . . at the party. And everything that came after."

I run a clammy hand over my face. I don't know if I can handle this right now. I want him here with me, desperately, but I also want him a million miles away. I want him to fix all our problems, everything that's broken between us, but I don't want to speak about it. And I want—

I want *him*.

I do—I *do*—it's inescapable. Despite everything that is happening, it's just some exasperating biological fact. And instead of the feeling being quelled by the stress of the situation, it's somehow heightened by it—by the knowledge that we are running out of chances, running out of *time*. Unlike me, Rhys hasn't changed at all. He's always been himself, steadfast and annoyingly . . . honorable. And I want to make him *dishonorable*. I want to grasp his unruly dark curls with both hands and force his knowing gaze away. I want to reach for him, smear my mouth against his, and desperately I wonder if he wants this, too. If I take this chance, this last possible chance, will he kiss me back? Will his kiss be as hungry as mine? As desperate? Did I imagine everything between us that day in his room, how his body felt against mine, hot and wanting? Surely not.

I choke down a sob of frustration. Even if what I feel in my heart is right, even if Rhys wants it, too, I know he won't do any of that, anything I want, anything *he* wants—not without sensibly talking things over first.

But the one single thing I don't want to do is *talk*. The guilt, the shame—it's still all too big.

"Look—Lara . . . I know you don't want to talk about it, but—"

My stomach churns painfully, my heart thumps hard against my ribs. "Rhys . . . Please. I just . . . I can't. Listen, you *know* I'm sorry," I say, the words bursting out of me. "You *know* I feel terrible about what happened with you and him. Yes, I made a mistake, a massive mistake. I freely admit it. . . . What else is it you want from me?"

Rhys is quiet for a whole minute. Then he shakes his

head. "No, it's not about that—what we need to talk about. It's about . . . about what happened before. Before . . . him."

I stare at him, for once speechless.

To my horror, Rhys buries his head in his hands and sobs. Just once, a harsh, desperate sound. Then, removing his glasses, he wipes a hand roughly over his eyes. "Look. . . . I've thought about it a lot, and probably more than is healthy, but if you . . . if you can't talk to me, honestly and openly, then if we ever do manage to get off this bloody train, then we should . . . stay away from each other. And . . . and for good. I—I don't think we're good for each other anymore."

His voice shakes as he speaks, and my heart splinters.

"Rhys—?"

"I've tried so hard to do what you want, La. To bury it all. To forget it. To pretend it didn't happen. To admit I fucked it up and move on. But being here . . . alone with you . . . well, the fact is, I *can't* pretend anymore. Fact is—it *hurts*."

I get up and sit beside him, gently pulling his hands away from his eyes.

"Oh, Rhys. I've just been—" And now it's my turn to cry. Silently, though, grateful that the dim light in here doesn't make it obvious. "So *ashamed*. Of how I treated you. How I treated Casey, Stevie—all of you. But most of all, I'm ashamed of how I let *him* treat *me* . . . how *stupid* I was to allow it. How *weak* I was to go along with it all. I ask myself a million times a day why I didn't leave earlier. Because if I had, then maybe—"

"You're *not* stupid," he says fiercely, pulling me toward

him so we're face to face now and there's nowhere to hide. "And you're not weak. You have *nothing* to be ashamed of. He was *abusive*. *Stop* saying sorry, because it wasn't your fault. You have nothing to apologize for. *Lara, none* of it was ever your fault."

30

In the quiet of the library, he stands, not letting go of my hands, pulling me up and into him, melding me against him, my head against the warmth of his chest. It feels oddly familiar, breathing him in, all clean laundry and salt sweat, as his hand tentatively strokes my hair, his wandering fingers curious. It's a restless kind of embrace, both of us craving more, one hand slipping to my waist to hold me closer.

"None of it," he repeats, softly but firmly, into my hair. "And you know I've never been angry—and certainly not with you. *Never*. But lately . . . I just—I just don't know how to *be* around you . . . La. Not without its being obvious that I want"—he swallows, his voice a low rasp—"what you don't want."

What I don't want?

Despite everything, a breathless laugh escapes me.

What *I* don't want? How has he got this so wrong? I have

never wanted anything more. But I can't say this—can't even form words at this unexpected revelation. Instead I reach up, tangling my hands in his curls and pulling his mouth down to mine.

And *finally* we kiss—properly—and it's nothing like I could have imagined and unlike any kiss I have experienced before. The sweetness of it astounds me; I am sinking into a meadow filled with buttercups, blissfully drowning in golden sunshine. It is slow and considered, gentle and explorative. It is everything I've ever wanted and never, ever had.

"Lara," he whispers against my mouth, his voice soft with wonder, his eyelashes lying darkly against his cheek as our lips meet again and again, each kiss gradually, welcomely, becoming less and less polite.

The couch gives an alarming creak as he clasps my face in both hands, uttering a low sound as he pulls me down onto his lap, my arms weaving about his neck, tentatively meeting his tongue with mine, him initially coy and considerate but swiftly giving up the pretense, his kisses soon as heated as mine. And for the first time since I boarded this train, my mind is fully elsewhere, delighting in him, so familiar and yet this version of him so very *unfamiliar*. It is Rhys undone, his breathing heavy and fast, his body heated, his heart thumping hard against mine.

"Lara, wait," he whispers raggedly, and I pull away, stroking his face, mildly exasperated.

"Why? Don't you think we've waited long enough?"

He doesn't answer, only smiles, one hand tugging gently

in my hair, pulling me down to him and kissing me again, and it is longer, deeper, teasing and mysteriously skillful, and I wonder briefly, *jealously,* about Rhys and what he has been doing in these lost months and who with, but moments later I'm lost in him, my thoughts trickling away like sand, my body moving instinctively against his, my hands desperate to know all of him so much better.

He catches my wrist, pulling away with a breathless laugh. "*Way* too long. But I want things between us to be special," he says softly, sitting back, his green eyes glinting up at me in the dark. "I don't want them tainted by all this—by this train."

And I relent, because he's right. I sit up, too, and he smooths down my hair, giving me another brief kiss, thoughtful this time, distracted.

"I'm sorry to interrupt," says a quiet, expressionless voice from the doorway.

Gwen stands silhouetted in the soft light from the window, wearing a stained lab coat. One of her eyes is noticeably swollen, already turning a gruesome shade of purple. She steps fully into the carriage, closing the door behind her.

"Jesus, who hit you?" I ask, scrabbling up and going over to her.

"Who do you *think*?"

The obvious answer is like a knife to my gut. *Gwydion.*

"Oh, Gwen," says Rhys, his tone gentle as he approaches her. "What happened? What can we do?"

My heart hurts for her, but there is something about her that still unnerves me. Her ice-blue eyes shine too brightly, and she wears a too-wide smile, like a mask. Both siblings have always worn masks. I imagine what their true selves might have looked like, boarding the train, shorn of Gwen's chic, chilly armor and Gwydion's over-the-top joie de vivre.

"He's already told you, hasn't he?" Gwen says. "Told you a story, at least. He's always been good at that." She wanders through the carriage, picking up a book at random and casually leafing through it. "And you believed him, didn't you? I mean, it's getting harder and harder to deny, isn't it?" She nods toward the window. "I thought I knew what I was doing. . . . No, that's unfair. I did *know*." She looks at Rhys, her glacial eyes astonishingly beautiful in the dawn. "I knew, because I'd been *so* careful . . . all my observations, all that data, all my research . . . I could account for everything, explain everything. But now?" She gives a bitter laugh. "Now it's all for *nothing*. I should have thought harder about what he was up to. We should *never* have traveled in the spring. You know, it's always been my favorite season—the time everything starts to blossom and grow . . . including her."

I'm hoping it's just the old stretch of track that we are on, but it does indeed look like the forest outside is creeping ever closer as the sun rises, green saplings brushing at the glass, the dark trees now interspersed with a multitude of colors, blossoms falling from branches like confetti.

"Gwen, this *thing*," says Rhys. "How can we put an end to this? Neither of you is getting to your destination now, you realize that, right? You're not selling anything, you're not even leaving this train, if we don't stop it."

Gwen lets out an abrupt, hysterical cackle that makes me jump. "So *that's* what he's told you? Let me guess . . . *I* am some evil genius who wants to sell the artifact as some kind of weapon? Gwydion always was a fantastic liar, comes with the storytelling. It's *him, you know*. All of it. *He* sold it. He lied to me to get me to come along, told me he was interested in my research and wanted to help me use it to create a charity—the same bullshit he's probably told you—but I quickly learned it was all lies. Another chapter in his book of fairy tales. He has only *ever* served himself."

She almost spits out the words, then laughs again, the sound like broken glass, making me flinch.

"I suppose he also told you that it was just rabbits and stuff that he experimented with—you know, to see how their blood increased the . . . the *yield*. And, like all the best stories, this contains a grain of truth—it was, to begin with . . . but then he got *ideas* . . . became curious, became greedy. . . . Goodbye, poor old Grumble. And it wasn't long after that before people started disappearing . . . gardeners, postal workers . . . even our parents."

"He killed them?" I ask, shocked. "Your parents?"

"Not *outright*," she says, her voice unnaturally light. "He's not stupid. He didn't do it in any kind of obvious way that could be pinned to him. And he pulled the same trick here, on the train. Subtle. Clever. No one knew what was happening to Xavier, to Cass, to the baroness—to Samira—until it was too late. You see, she needs to be kept fed or her power, her influence, wanes. None of us are safe. Although *you*—" She tilts her head, looking at me wide-eyed. "He quickly latched onto the fact that *you* are a different matter altogether."

Those plants, browning, shriveling back from my touch, that strange whispering I hear in the greenhouse carriages—insistent, and ever more demanding. Yes, I have an inkling of what she means.

"It was easy enough; you're a captive audience. That's part of the reason he chose a train: sitting ducks all the way. He drugged the passengers, then used their blood to feed her. Just a little, to the point where they'd wake up feeling less rested than usual, a little woozy, a little weak, but with nothing demonstrably wrong. Maybe you're even thinking it wasn't that bad—I mean, don't people donate blood to hospitals all the time? But we quickly discovered that the process isn't as harmless as it seems. You see, she takes your blood, but you, in turn, take something of *her* back into your body. It begins with a cough or a cold, but it isn't a virus, not in any usual sense. She's invading your body, turning your insides from mammalian to plant. You see, she makes you like her—she makes you *flowers*."

A terrible understanding dawns on me. The blossom body lying supine beneath the artifact. Poor Xavier coughing up petals, choking up vines, thorns bursting from Samira—

Oh my *god*. "You knew all this, and you didn't try to *stop* him—didn't think to tell anyone?" I breathe, incredulous.

Gwen shrugs. "People always believe him over me. It's been a pattern our whole lives. Why would this time be any different?"

"Gwen . . . what—what can we *do*?" asks Rhys, an edge of desperation in his voice.

"Yes," I say, a thin ray of hope penetrating the darkness. "There must be something we can do—some way of stopping this, right? If anyone knows, it's you."

That she doesn't immediately say no bolsters my hopes. Gwen has been studying this thing for months. Arguably she knows more about it than Gwydion. "Gwen," I press. "If you truly mean well, you need to *think*—you need to help us."

"Yes," says Rhys decisively. "Let's get everyone together. And you can tell us how we can put an end to this."

Rhys and I rouse everyone from their cabins and direct them into the Cedar Lounge. The fear and uncertainty in the room is palpable. The baroness looks like she's aged a decade since I last saw her, her usually neat perm frazzled, reminding me of Alice's Red Queen. Becca is quieter than ever, watching us all with dark, mistrustful eyes, her earphones for once absent. Shoshanna sits militantly straight, still valiantly attempting to give the impression that she knows what she's doing, but her ragged manicure and bloodshot eyes tell a different story. At least she's given up on the idea of trying to lock me up, I guess.

Carlos is collapsed on the sofa, looking like crap and clutching an almost-empty bottle of whiskey to his chest like a talisman.

Gwen enters last, frayed around the edges, her hair now pulled back in a scrappy ponytail, her usually crimson lips chapped and bare.

"Where's Gwydion?" I ask.

Rhys frowns and gives a brief shake of his head. "I couldn't find him. He wasn't in his cabin."

Behind us, in the direction of the staff quarters, there's an odd rumbling, scratching sound. A deep, violent writhing, like the vibrations of a terrible worm.

"What *exactly* is going on?" interrupts the baroness, her voice querulous. "If we're all in danger, like that poor dear service girl, then why on earth haven't we stopped yet?"

Shoshanna speaks up gruffly: "We're on course to stop at Cologne. Until then I sincerely suggest we all go to our cabins and lock the doors until the train reaches its destination."

"That's all?" Becca asks warily. "What about all these . . . plants?"

Shosh says nothing more.

It's Carlos who speaks up. "C'mon, Shosh. They deserve the same honesty you've given me. Perhaps tell them that one of us here has supposedly struck a deal with a bioweapons lab and we're all in fucking mortal *danger* because of it?"

The baroness gasps and then immediately launches into a violent coughing fit, burying her face in her arm, her red eyes watering. I watch in silent horror as blood-red petals drift from her lips.

I'm trapped in a living *nightmare*.

Becca speaks next: "Yeah. There *is* something wrong," she says quietly. "Not just all these plants, but there's a . . . a *sickness* on board with us, too. Xavier had it . . . and I think . . ." She swallows. "I think we've got it, too. There's a scratchiness in my throat. But it doesn't feel like any virus I've had before; it doesn't feel like a cold. No, it's like . . . like . . . *thorns*. Like something is wedged in my throat and won't come out . . . and is . . . is *growing*." She runs a pale hand over her vulnerable pale neck. "And this whole train *reeks* of some horrible, sickly perfume. . . ." She turns to Shosh. "What have you done to us? Are we going to die? I want off this train—and now!"

Shosh nods in apparent understanding, ready to launch into the same old lies Rhys and I have heard a thousand times. "Clearly, we have a . . . uh . . . situation aboard this train. This research—those plants we're carrying have become a problem. But as I've already explained to you all, we've rerouted and are due to stop at the next station—"

"Oh Lord, Shosh, spare us," I interrupt angrily.

"Excuse me—"

"You heard me. You're not in control anymore! In fact, you're partially responsible for our being in this situation to begin with."

"Has anyone spoken to the driver yet?" asks the baroness, her voice thin. "Surely he has an opinion on all this. I mean, what does he think is the safest course of action?"

Who's going to tell her our driver is now a literal *plant*?

The baroness tries to stand, but Becca pulls her back

down with a sober shake of her head while Gwen collapses into a chair, head in hands, looking almost catatonic.

That sound comes again, an unpleasant writhing noise that vibrates through the train, followed by a sudden, rough scraping at the door that leads to the passenger cabins.

"What *is* that?" Becca wonders aloud.

"Shosh, come on. What will we do? Uncouple the carriages, or stop the train? We're not going to just sit here," says Carlos, standing. We all surround her in a semicircle, waiting for her response.

Shosh frowns, wavering for a minute. "Do you know what? I've had enough of this!" she snaps, and with such determination I almost feel a spark of hope. "They're only *plants*, for God's sake. And we're so close to our destination. But if you're all determined to stop this train, then you know what? Good luck to you all."

And with that, she storms from the room.

Seconds later, the screaming starts.

31

Carlos, Rhys, and I immediately run in the direction of the screaming, out of the lounge, through the dining and sleeper carriages. At the end, Carlos stops dead: ". . . the *fuck*?"

Reluctantly I step forward to see what he's looking at.

The *entire* carriage that used to house the staff cabins is crammed with vicious-looking thorns, more like an enormous tangle of razor wire than anything from nature. It stretches from floor to ceiling and is completely impenetrable. From within its dark tangle comes that low, writhing noise. The thorn mass is *growing*. Second by second.

Shosh sits on the floor a few feet away, leaning against the wall. Her face is crisscrossed with scratches, a particularly nasty one just below one eye. One of her trouser legs is soaked in blood, while the other is rolled up, her calf puffy and swollen from what looks like nettle stings.

"It . . . it *moved* . . . ," she croaks. "Hooked itself around my leg and just . . . *tore* at it."

I reach forward to touch the morass of thorns. The grayish tendrils snake forward and writhe around my wrist like curious snakes, and I snap back my hand, wringing the sharp pain away and sucking my finger. On the now-withered branch is a single ruby-red drop of blood.

Pale-faced, Rhys and Carlos help Shosh up.

"Don't you see what it's doing? It's not only taking over the train," I say with a hushed breath. "It's pushing us all closer to the greenhouse. It's pushing us toward—toward *her*."

The branches are close and tightly packed, each one dotted with teethlike barbs. I can barely see the door behind it. Soon they will take over the passenger cabins, too.

"It's pyracantha," says Rhys quietly. "My dad grows it in the front garden to stop people sitting on our wall and having a smoke while they wait for the bus."

"Don't suppose anyone happens to have a chain saw?" asks Carlos with drunken nonchalance.

"Gwen," says Shosh, wincing as Carlos and Rhys help her up. "There's no way of stopping the train—none. It won't stop until it reaches Cologne. Gwen's our only hope to reach there alive."

The baroness shrieks as she catches sight of Shosh's bloodied leg.

Ignoring her, I turn to Gwen, sick of her silence. "Come

on. It's time to speak up. What about this 'fix' you were meant to be working on—or was that a lie? Have we got any chance of making it to Cologne alive?" The questions tumble out of me, unable to be contained.

"All I can do is . . . apologize," she says quietly, above the low, fearful chatter. We all stop and look at her. She raises her chin proudly, if only for a moment. "What I initially hoped would be a noble cause . . . has . . . has—*ah.*" She coughs, doubles over, and moans.

I stand up. "Gwen?"

"Yes," she says, trying to center herself, eyelids fluttering, white hands shaking like windswept lilies. And all at once, I see it. How did I ever miss it? All along I've seen her as stuck-up and distant, when all she really is, is *scared.* I go to her side, speaking quietly: "It's okay, Gwen. We're listening. What can we do?"

Her eyes flick to mine, and she nods determinedly, swallowing. "This is not a situation I have under control," she admits. "I am trying—I am trying my best, but there are *variables.* To those who don't understand why we can't just stop the train . . . the driver's cab is . . . out of action. . . . "And even if we did manage to stop the train, with this growth period currently unchecked, stopping in the middle of a forest or any overgrown area would be *suicide.* This whole train would likely be . . . swallowed."

"*Swallowed?*" says Carlos in disbelief.

"What do you mean, *variables*?" asks Rhys.

"It wasn't always dangerous," continues Gwen, staring

ahead, almost talking to herself. "The artifact, I mean. Before we got on this train, I had a tight handle on everything, knew exactly what I was doing. But when you introduce new variables, new *stimuli*, to carefully controlled experimental environments—"

She stops and looks at me. I run a hand down my face. Speculative science isn't what we need right now. We need to know how to survive until we stop.

"Are you able to make some kind of . . . I don't know, plant killer or something?" asks Rhys in desperation.

Gwen shakes her head. "I'm not sure it's possible to kill it altogether—but I might have an antidote. It'll stop . . . it'll stop whatever it was that happened to Xavier happening to anyone else. I need a little more time. Let me go back to my cabin, check my research. . . . Maybe there's something I've missed, something else I can do. There has to be some way of slowing it, at the very least."

I look over at Rhys, my expression skeptical, and shake my head, because I have no intention of waiting around for Gwen, of all people, to get us out of this.

JUNE, LAST YEAR

The end-of-year school party, and the final time I saw Rhys before meeting up with him on the train, was held in the vast Victorian greenhouse of a local museum that had once been the manor house of an eccentric collector.

I'd wanted Beckett to come at first. God knew it had been so long since I'd properly talked to any of my friends that I would need him there strictly for the conversation. But as our relationship progressed (or rather, deteriorated), I became more and more worried about the scene he might create.

"It's only for a couple of hours, okay? You can pick me up early if you like. We'll arrange a time to meet."

He'd smiled, but in that thin way I'd come to know was a warning. "Oh, cool. So I'm not invited to this, then? No boyfriends allowed, is that it?"

"You wouldn't want to come anyway," I reassured him—tried to reassure him. "It'll be proper studenty. Frozen buffet food and terrible music. Not your kind of thing at all."

On the night, I was nervous about entering. But I'd made a promise, and anyway, Casey was there waiting for me as she'd said she'd be, lounging by a case of dinosaur fossils in a shimmering green jumpsuit. Catching my eye, she headed directly over.

"Yes! You made it! Oh my god, Lara—it's so good to see you! Er, don't look so worried."

I grinned at her in relief. It felt weird to be alone, without Beckett beside me, as if I were missing a limb.

"Casey," I said with a relieved smile, taking a large swig of the soda she passed me. "Oh my god, how've you been?"

She yanked me into a tight hug. "Stevie said you wouldn't come, but I knew you would. How are you doing? Oh my god, you look so bougie! What have you been up to? My mum literally had to call your grandma last week to see if you were alive!"

"Yeah, sorry," I mutter. "I've just been so . . . busy."

Busy almost flunking my classes—even my precious history class. Busy being cut off from all my friends. Busy being someone else. Someone I didn't even like.

Casey lowered her voice. "So . . . uh, you gonna talk to him or what? I have to say, he was kind of hurt by your text."

I knew exactly who she was talking about. Had already clocked him standing in a circle of classmates, looking relaxed as ever in a red plaid shirt. I'd always been envious of how comfortable he was in his own skin. It had been a while since I'd spoken to Casey but even longer since I'd spoken to Rhys. And after that message Beckett had sent him, I very much doubted he would ever want to speak to me again.

But before I could make a decision, like *leave*, because clearly it had been a mistake to come, Casey was already waving him over.

He froze as we locked eyes. The relaxed smile on his face instantly faded.

I took a deep breath, the words I'd been rehearsing since I agreed to come circling my brain. "Rhys," I said as cheerily as I could. "Um, how are you doing?"

He frowned at my delivery, and I felt like a complete ass.

"La . . . ? Hey. I didn't expect you to be here. Are—are you okay? We've all been worried about you. We've not seen you for weeks—"

"I was just saying how we've all been trying to call her," added Casey sternly.

The words burst out of me: "Rhys, I never sent that

message—they weren't my words. But I'm sorry you had to read it."

Even then I saw it. Black text on green. Two blue ticks beside it. Read. And no response, no response ever again. The words floated before my eyes at night, neon green, a dark, flashing warning.

Pervert. Stalker. You're so obsessed with me it's embarrassing. Don't you EVER talk to me again.

The mere thought of those words shamed me even then, the fact there was no way to unsend it, delete it, or even apologize for it. Until now.

But to my surprise, Rhys blessedly shook his head as if it had never mattered at all.

"C'mon, La, I never thought for a moment you did. But what's going on with school? The attendance officer says he's met with your gran but won't say anything else. We wondered if you were ill or something . . . like, seriously. I mean, I called. A lot. . . ."

I began to feel upset—cornered again.

"I know, like I said, I've been . . . busy." I gave a nervous laugh. "What's with the third-degree, guys? It's been ages since we were all together—can't we just have a good time?"

Rhys shrugged. He still looked confused, as if he were trying to do some complicated equation in his head.

"Sure . . . as I said, I've—we've . . . missed hanging out with you, I guess. We know you and Beckett are serious, and that's great—we're happy for you—but we're still your friends, y'know?"

I had nothing left to say—no more defense to offer.

Casey stared at us both as the awkward silence grew and grew until it became almost tangible. Then, to my relief, she linked her arm in mine.

"C'mon, then, Lala. Stevie and I have contraband vodka. Catch up with you later, Rhys."

32

Instinctively, Rhys and I shadow Gwen down to her cabin. Thick stems of ivy loop overhead, while a thicket of nettles has grown over the floor. Gwen curses under her breath, brushing thistle burrs from her coat as we stomp through them.

"You're planning on watching me?" she asks impassively, stepping into her suite and heading directly to the desk, upon which stand several test tube racks and a centrifuge.

"Just making sure you're doing what you say you are," I say, not too unkindly, as I linger in the doorway.

My gaze is instantly drawn to the corner of the room. Gwen's "project" has grown to a disgusting height, the lip of it now brushing the ceiling. How is she still feeding that thing with just *flies*?

"How long do I have? Does anyone know how long it will

be until we stop?" asks Gwen, fiddling around with petri dishes.

Rhys shrugs. "Shosh should know. Let me go find out."

As he heads back to the Cedar Lounge, I notice that the door to Gwydion's cabin down the hall is ajar. I peer through the crack, but the room is deserted. His betrayal should hit me harder, but it doesn't. I've almost been expecting it. Or maybe I'm immune to it all now. People can be so *fucking* disappointing.

"Gwydion told me that you entered her room . . . alone, and without the key." It takes me a second before I realize what Gwen is talking about.

"I guess you must have left the door open."

Gwen shakes her head. "I never leave the door open. *Never*. He thinks you're connected to her in some way. . . . Are you? It might help."

I bite my lip, thinking of the whispering, the way the statue seems to stare at me, the way my hands fit perfectly into the door mechanism—

"No," I say abruptly. It's a lie, but my instinct is to deny any link I might have to that—that *thing*. Truth is . . . I'm afraid to examine the connection. "It's nonsense. Where *is* Gwydion, by the way?"

I don't know why I even bothered to ask. I already know where Gwydion is. Where else could he be?

"I always thought it was the plants whispering to me," continues Gwen, as if she hasn't heard me. "I've always spoken to them—we're meant to, aren't we? To help them grow. And

I thought for once they were answering back...." She gives an unpleasant little giggle. "The things they'd *say*, Lara... I should have guessed it was *her*.

"She doesn't like him, you know. She doesn't like Gwydion at *all*. She told me so." Gwen puts down the dishes and looks at me. I don't like her expression. In the dimness of the room, it looks almost vulpine, hungry. "But you... I think... I think you'd have a chance, Lara."

I can't put my finger on why, but this conversation is making me extremely uncomfortable, as is the sight of the giant pitcher plant towering over Gwen. Plus, there's a distant scratching sound coming from the other end of the carriage. I poke my head through the door and look nervously down the corridor, but it's empty, thankfully.

"What do you mean, a chance?" I ask quietly. I don't want to get drawn into this conversation with Gwen, but if there's anything—anything—I can do to help everyone, I can't just ignore it.

"You could speak with her. Try to reason with her. Discover why she's so angry."

"I don't know what you mean," I say despite knowing exactly what she means but not wanting to hear it.

"Perhaps even *destroy* her," Gwen continues. "If you'd like my complete honesty, Lara, I don't think we have much time."

Gwen has stopped whatever she was doing at her desk and is staring at me intently with those frosty blue eyes. But I am afraid. So very afraid about going back into those carriages alone, facing up to whatever ancient power resides there. And then there's Gwydion—

"Um, I'm going to see what's taking Rhys so long," I mutter, breaking eye contact and quickly heading back in the direction of the others.

Rhys, Carlos, and Shosh have relocated to the dining carriage. Shosh sits at a table, pale-faced and shaken, while Carlos has rolled up his sleeves and is busy wrenching a large fire axe off the wall.

"Is your radio not working?" Rhys asks Shosh urgently. "If we could let *someone* know the situation here . . ."

Shosh flushes a guilty shade of red and pulls it from her belt, brushing off shriveled plant matter onto the table as she does so.

"It's not worked since yesterday. . . ." She presses the Talk button, but there is only silence. "I think something's growing in it."

"We need to chop through that shit and get into the driver's carriage," says Carlos, weighing up the axe with both hands. "It's the only way. Are there any other axes on board?"

The fact that by now the thorny morass Carlos wants to chop through has spread across two entire carriages in under an hour does not give me much confidence in this plan. Before I can say this, Rhys takes me by the arm, pulling me gently away from the others, into the kitchen. Despite my slow-burning panic, a charge of dark excitement still runs through me at his touch. Not for the first time, I pray we all escape unscathed.

"La . . . remember back in my room . . . how those plants wilted away when you touched them?"

I give him an odd look, then nod in the direction of the vicious, thin branches crammed with thorns emerging from further up the carriage.

"Yes, but it's not like I have some superpower. You just watched me touch that shrub earlier. Okay, it wilted a bit, but there's no way I can fix all this myself." I show him the bracelet of scratches about my wrist.

He nods impatiently. "I know, but if we told Gwen what happened, then maybe between the two of you, you could come up with some plan, some idea. I'm just thinking about what she said back in the lounge. About—about variables—"

I reflect on what Gwen said to me just now, while we were alone. And imagine Gwydion's face, eager and hungry, as I stand before the artifact—before Blodeuwedd—and I know exactly what Rhys means. *He thinks you're connected.*

The idea that getting out of this mess might rest on me is terrifying—but if that's the only way . . . My hands shake at the thought of having to enter those carriages again, having to face that *thing* again—

"You—you might be right." I release a shaky sigh. "Let me go back and speak to—"

From the next carriage comes a series of rapid, high-pitched, breathless screams, followed by a violent shaking that briefly rocks the train. Swallowing my own scream I rush back down the corridor. The door to Gwen's suite is now shut, and the screaming has stopped as swiftly as it began.

The moment I push open the door, I immediately know something terrible has happened. The room is in utter darkness, and the revoltingly sweet smell is now laced with an acrid stench of vinegar in a combination so powerful it physically knocks me back.

"Rhys..." My voice is strangled. I don't want to go in the room alone.

"What—" he begins, until he, too, is silenced by the stench, covering his nose with his sleeve. He switches on the light. It is a mistake.

It's her plant. Before, it touched the ceiling, topped with a delicate gold-red leaf. But now it's broken and torn, the bottom part of the sac rent open, revealing a pair of legs that end in Gwen's expensive ballet pumps. But her legs end at the knee, finishing at a shockingly white knob of bone, and the rest of her...

Steam rises from the purplish remains, glistening silkily in the lamplight.

I bend over and noisily vomit, ruining the plush carpet. Beside me, Rhys stumbles backward and falls into the corridor. I follow him, slamming the door behind me.

"What the *fuck*?" I take a breath. "What in the actual fuck? We *have* to get out of here. This can't be real... this is *insane*."

Losing it, my breaths coming short and harsh, I head to the nearest external door and yank the emergency cord.

Of course, nothing happens.

Panicked, I pick up a fire extinguisher and hammer at the window.

"What the *hell*, Lara?" says Rhys, his face cheese white. "You're planning to leap from the broken window of a train moving at around fifty miles an hour?"

"Well, okay, genius, what else are we meant to do?" I sob. "We're fast running out of options! Soon that stuff is going to take over every single damn carriage on this train."

Lara—

Then I hear it. Her voice is more vital now, stronger; no longer a whisper but a silken song directly in my ear.

Yes, there is a way out.

Lara, I am waiting—

And it's not off this train; it's through her.

Throwing the extinguisher to the floor, tears falling uselessly down my face, I walk, head down, in her direction, as if I'm heading to my execution. And it isn't just her I have to face . . . it's Gwydion, too.

"Lara, where are you going?" Rhys calls, but I ignore him, hoping he has the sense to keep himself safe until this is over.

Weeds wind their way up through cracks in the parquet flooring. Ivy obscures the windows of the usually light and airy viewing carriage, cracking its vast picture windows like spring ice.

The Cedar Lounge is thickly carpeted with moss, and creepers hang from the ceiling. I have to rip away nettles and thistles, scratching and stinging my hands, before I can even get close to the door of the piano lounge.

I think back to Rhys, staring at me in horrified wonder in the dark of his cabin.

How did you do it?

Because, despite their protestations, despite the way they seek out my skin, circle my wrists like poison restraints, the plants do wilt back at my touch, gradually shriveling and becoming more pliant, brown, and floppy. I hear hurried footsteps behind me, but I don't want to wait; I can't wait, or I'll lose my nerve.

Lara...

It's always the same voice, either in my head or on the periphery.

Lara... please...

People have pleaded with me before, and I always thought I knew better. *Lara, please answer your phone. Lara, please go back to class. Lara, please leave this guy. You don't know the rumors about him.* I realize now that I didn't know better. Turns out, I didn't know *anything*. Not ever listening to those who care about you isn't brave or rebellious. . . . Mostly, it's just stupid.

If there's anything I can do, any way I can prolong this, pause this, distract her, until we're able to stop, then isn't that my duty? I've spent so long being scared, ashamed, guilty... I find I am almost desperate to seize this chance to be brave. With every footstep, I feel stronger, clearer in my head, bolder. Here is a chance to prove who I really am, the me I was before I got buried beneath the weight of other people's expectations.

I reach the piano lounge. Here things are desperate—blistering hogweeds tower to the ceiling, crisscrossed with knotweed. I push my way through, feeling, for the first time in so long, *powerful*.

I reach the greenhouse. I place both hands on the door and say her name loudly, answering her call.

33

The moment I step into the greenhouse carriages, the door slams violently shut behind me.

Seconds later, I hear the handle rattle as Rhys tries and fails to get in, his voice so distant it may as well be a continent away. This carriage is madman's floristry now. Enormous pink-and-white lilies sprout from the corners, while purple foxgloves tower over me like colorful sentinels. Blossoms drift thickly from the ceiling, and flower upon flower blooms before my feet, creating a path through the carriage. Roses twist and writhe through the vegetation, their thorns scratching painfully at my ankles as I push my way through. The scent is sickening, saccharine, stickily coating my throat and lungs like honey. Around me, the world sways and lurches, distant then near again, like waves breaking on the shore, as I breathe in the thick, golden motes of pollen like gold dust. I fasten my once-useless red scarf over my mouth as I clamber through another immense rosebush to the door at the other end, my skin now a jigsaw puzzle of scratches.

I used to find the next carriage colder, almost eerie, but now there's a reprieve. The thick cords of ivy, the snaking vines, the razor-edged palms, all seem flattened back, creating a narrow corridor of verdant green, a peaceful sanctuary, gratefully silencing all noise, all dissent.

Beckoning me closer.

I start when Gwydion looms out of the hidden alcove ahead. "Lara, I was hoping you'd come."

I'm looking at a different Gwydion now, his gilded mask disintegrating and falling apart. Beneath the eloquence, I see he is sly, and calculated, and watchful, his pale eyes shrouded by dark circles.

"Samira . . . ," I say as I approach him and that final door. "Is she . . . is she still—"

Gwydion gives a brief, distracted shake of his head.

"Don't worry," he says. "She's been moved. The area's all cleaned up."

Another tell. As if she never mattered, this beautiful, clever, laughing girl.

"Sorry—*what?* By *who*?" I ask, outraged. If we do ever get off this bloody train, Samira's death needs a proper investigation; her family is *owed* one.

But Gwydion only shrugs. "Your exalted leader or her lump-headed chef, who knows. I do wonder exactly how much my sister's paid her."

It's obvious he can't be bothered to put any effort behind his lies anymore, and there's no reward in my exposing them.

"Why are you here, Gwydion?"

"I wanted to speak to you. Alone. And you—*you're* here because she invited you to come . . . extended her invitation. Isn't that right, Lara?" he asks, lowering his voice. It is a different voice, the charm now melted away, leaving only the smoke, the darkness that has always been there, beneath it.

I *want* to scoff. Want to ask him what the hell he's talking about.

But he's right. He *knows*. And her voice has never been stronger.

That whispering—alternating between the names of those flowers and a different language, unknown and ancient—becomes louder still, lapping at me like subtle tongues of flame, *nagging* at my consciousness, tugging me toward her.

"What does she want from me?" I murmur.

But Gwydion has turned to face the door.

I gaze ahead with trepidation. I don't want to go any further, and it is so dark in there, so *strange*, like some ancient place of worship, a temple of flowers. And even without Gwen's warning, I know Gwydion is not to be trusted, am being reminded even now, the knowledge prickling at my skin like poison ivy.

The owl on the panel stares at us both, its golden eyes solemn and foreboding.

Gwydion turns to me. "Open it," he says brusquely, his eyes bright with a feverish impatience.

"Why?"

"*Open the door,*" he repeats more slowly, like I am stupid.

I look at him, eyes blazing. I want to say no, I will never do a thing he says again, but it isn't him that I am listening to anymore. It is something far stronger. Something that I sense has as little time for his cheap parlor tricks and gaudy lies as I do.

I place my hands on the panel, pushing exactly as I did before. It is unusual how precisely they seem to fit.

The latch releases with a wooden click, and the door creaks open.

"I *knew* it," he exclaims, his voice giddy. "I knew it. Oh my god, Lara—Lara—"

I back away from the door, my eyes directly on him, immediately suspicious.

"I knew it *all* along. Ever since that day we spent in the meadow. When I saw what happened while you slept—"

"Knew *what*? *What* happened while I slept?"

"Come on," he says, ignoring my question, his voice gentle once more, regaining a lick of its former glory. "Come through and meet her. Meet her *properly*. She's been waiting for you."

I brace myself as I enter, the sight of Samira forever etched in my memory. But the carriage is as sparse as when I first entered it, practically barren compared with the previous ones. Above, the candles blaze away in their sconces, and Blodeuwedd stares at me, her baleful eyes glinting in the flickering light. Beside her, in their neat stone troughs, the worst of the plants grow quietly: belladonna, poison hemlock, monkshood.

But now that I'm up close, I see she is different now, less of an owl shape . . . more a crumbling monolith of stone. A pile of rubble lies untidily at her base.

"What's happening?" I ask. "What's happened to her?"

Because she is a *her* and always has been. "Have—have you been trying to destroy her?" I add, hopefully, guiltily. "Might that help?"

Gwydion smiles slyly, and once again I am put in mind of a calculating magician—a purveyor of false hope, a conjurer of lies.

"Oh no, she's not *damaged*. Quite the opposite . . . Lara . . . she's *changing*."

In here, the throbbing in my head has intensified. The atmosphere is so dense, so close, so inexplicable—as if stepping into this carriage is stepping into an entirely different age, different *world*, even.

"What do you mean . . . changing . . . ? Into *what*?"

"You, of all people, should know," he says. "Go ahead. *Touch* her."

It's difficult to look away from her. The parts that are revealed beneath the rocky carapace are both intensely female and also *not*. Vines emerge, thick and green, from beneath the cracked stoneware, like something trying to climb out of its own skin.

"I . . . I don't want to."

But weirdly, I *do*. Am almost desperate to, compelled to.

Not because Gwydion wants me to but because I can feel her looking at me, almost pleading, her eyes glinting a beseeching gold in the candlelight.

Touch me. Make me corporeal. Make me flowers.

It's hard to wrench my gaze away from Blodeuwedd—the longer I'm in her presence, the more I am awed and the less I am afraid—but I do, whirling to confront Gwydion.

"I know what you did . . . to Xavier . . . to Samira. I know *everything*, Gwydion. I know exactly what you are."

Gwydion tears his gaze away from the statue with the same apparent difficulty and blinks at me as if surprised I'm even here. There's an emptiness, a vacancy, in his expression now that scares me more than anything else I've encountered on this hellscape of a train ride. It's as if whoever Gwydion used to be is now hiding somewhere, locked away, replaced by a dark shade. I back away to the door.

He laughs. "Oh? And what is that? Do you know, Lara, you've always struck me as a girl overly concerned with *defining* people. I'm not a bad person per se . . . more of an opportunist.

I don't want to play his game. "Fuck off. You punched your sister. Jesus—you murdered your own parents! You're a *monster*."

Sometimes it really is that simple.

"So I'm a monster through and through?" A sly, slick expression slips across his face like a waning moon. "I mean, let's look at a little example, shall we? What if someone ends up getting punched due to the machinations of another? Who's truly at fault in that situation?"

I stare at him wordlessly, my mouth dropping open. There's no way, no *way*, he could know this unless someone—unless *Rhys*—unless—

"You should know Gwen's *dead*," I counter bluntly. "So I guess you really were planning on killing us all? Even your own sister."

Gwydion gives a harsh laugh. He steeples his fingers, and I notice a single tear trace a path down his marble features, down his sharp nose, to drip off the end.

"It is regrettable," he says, running a swift hand over his face. "But there was no other option. She practically offed *herself* with her insistence on growing that hideous thing in the first place. Of all the beautiful plants available to experiment on, why choose a pitcher plant? Revolting things. Unfortunately, it would have been an excruciatingly painful, slow death. The body of the plant is filled with digestive juices. They *dissolve* their prey."

He gives a nauseating little smirk.

"You disgust me," I spit.

The smirk widens into a sick little smile. "I haven't always."

"It's her," I say, nodding over to the statue. "She's the cause of all this, right? We *have* to destroy her. Else we're *all* dead. Even you. Can't you see that?"

Gwydion looks comically shocked. "*Destroy* her? Are you *mad*? *She*, as you so eloquently put it, is going to make me extremely wealthy . . . and you, too . . . if you'd like."

I ignore this. "What is she, really, Gwydion? She's not a goddess . . . she's so much worse, isn't she? She's—she's a *monster*."

He shakes his head. "No, not a goddess, not a monster, not even a woman—merely a *conjuring*. An attempt to create the perfect partner for a man who was cursed to take no human bride. She was made to be beautiful, compliant, kind, and loving. Everything I suppose a wife should be. But the spell failed. She never loved her husband and was unfaithful to him . . . and now she calls to you. *Abyssus, abyssum, invocat.* Like calls to like."

"You can't *create* the perfect partner," I say, more to myself than to Gwydion. "You can't make them in a lab; you can't conjure them with a spell. That's *not* how it works. That's why it failed. Why it *always* fails."

Don't you want to be better?
Don't you want to be perfect?
You're mine now . . . improved.
My own creation.

He arches an eyebrow, smiling at me. "Regardless of that, you *have* answered her. I suspected the moment you said you'd been in here. You see, the door doesn't open for just anyone. You appear to exert some kind of . . . influence over her. . . . It's extraordinary. But then, so is she. It's also why I'm willing to factor you into my little plan."

"I'm *not* interested," I say firmly, wondering why, in all my newfound confidence, I didn't think to bring something that I could use as a weapon, or at the very least use to defend myself. At this point, I am reduced to trying to push Gwydion over.

"The mythology around it doesn't matter to me, really,"

he continues airily, like a demented Bond villain. I scope out the room, hoping to catch sight of a stray spade or rake. "The hows and whys of it all—why she's hungry, why she favors you, of all people—none of that's important. All that matters is that she *exists*. And I have an incredibly generous offer from someone who wishes to purchase her."

"What for?" I ask, although I already know.

"I told you—it's a weapons manufacturer," he says matter-of-factly. "One of the biggest. I'm not exactly sure what they plan on doing with her, and to be honest, I don't much care. But once I deliver her, once they see what she can do, I'll be a very rich man leaving in a private jet. You're a sweet enough girl, Lara. Why not come with me? We could be perfect for each other."

I can make you perfect—

"What do you mean, see what she can *do*? You said she needed blood for her to . . . to make things grow. You're happy for more people to die?"

Gwydion shrugs. "So? People die all the time. It's not exactly unusual."

"You *are* mad," I murmur, backing away. "Literally insane."

"No," he says loftily. "Not insane, not at all. Just an orphan with a very large estate to rebuild, alone now, it seems, and a rather useful lottery ticket."

"But—but this could change the world," I say, still trying to figure it out in my head. "For the worse. People could be . . . be executed or imprisoned to feed her, to cause this—this growth, and—and what is she really capable of? Gwydion, in the wrong hands, this would be devastating—this could starts *wars*."

Gwydion waves his hand dismissively. "As I say, once she's out of my hands, I don't care what's done with the damn thing. Would you be interested to know the sum I'll receive? It may change your mind."

"No," I reply, still backing away, my hand reaching for the doorknob. I have no idea where I'm going or what I will do next; all I know is that Gwydion is more dangerous than I thought.

"Not so fast," he says, swiftly stepping toward me. "She won't let you leave, not so soon. Besides, I'm not quite finished with you yet."

I watch in horror as thick veins of ivy spring up from the floor and immediately paper over the door behind me.

"And as they say," he continues, nodding in the direction of the artifact, "if you're not *with* us, I suppose you're *against* us. And we can't have that. Not with what *you* are capable of."

I open my mouth to protest, but all that comes out is a strangled wheeze. A thick branch of ivy wraps tightly around my throat like a thuggish hand, its tendrils creeping toward my mouth, silencing me with a noxious green taste.

And quickly the world recedes away.

34

JUNE, LAST YEAR

"La, I don't think you're okay. None of us do."

Later at the party, Rhys and I were standing in a quiet corridor by the ancient Egyptian artifacts. His voice was low and concerned and authoritative in that way I hate. It was a bold statement he was making. And it wasn't until someone finally voiced it that I realized how true it was.

I threw my hands up in exasperation. "Why do you have this constant, pressing need to . . . to mother me? I don't need it, Rhys; I've told you already, I can look out for myself."

We locked eyes. There was sorrow in his, but I was relieved to see no sign of pity—not this time—only uncertainty mixed with a quiet determination.

"Believe it or not, I don't have a pressing need to look after anyone, least of all you. And I know full well that you can look after yourself. But—"

"But what? Why can't you mind your own business?" I interrupted. "Why don't you let me make my own mistakes? You know, Rhys, in your own way, you're as bad as he is, wanting to control what I do and—"

Rhys smiled, but there was no triumph in it, only sadness.

"So you admit it, then? La, he's toxic. Since you met him, it's like you're a different person. And I'm not only talking about how you look. You've stopped coming to class; he's isolated you from all of us—from your friends..."

I looked at him then, really looked at him. And I knew he wasn't telling the whole truth. Everything about him that night was overthought. The way he was standing overly still, as if trying to compensate for the fact he might have had one drink too many. He knew I would be here, and he came with a plan, a mission. I looked him directly in the eye. He might have been able to see through me, but he needed to know that that worked both ways.

"From all of them, or from you?" I asked quietly. "I mean, what are you most worried about, Rhys? Be honest."

It was a cruel thing to say—which is why I said it—and I watched the hurt that flickered briefly in his eyes with a certain feeling of victory.

I don't know how long I'd suspected it. How long he'd buried it; carefully, politely hidden it. There were precious moments when it had flashed to the surface, moments I replayed in my darkest hours. Those long hours spent in his kitchen, his mum cheerfully making us endless cups of tea as he patiently, determinedly, coached me through some impossible math equation, his hand covering mine, warm and reassuring, when I finally understood and quietly cried with relief. That day I came to school hollow-eyed and yawning after Dad had spent all day in the pub, returning home in the early hours of the morning, crashing into things and stumbling, and Rhys had insisted we bunk off and go to his house while he played video games and I got some much-needed sleep in his bed.

There in the cool, quiet museum corridor, the pulsing music from the taxidermy hall miles away; there, where ancient things were once excavated and brought to light; there, where we stood among precious artifacts lit by golden lights. There the truth was finally unburied.

And I was suddenly forced to confront so many things at once. Like how much I had grown to despise Beckett. Like how much I hated myself lately for knowing, deep down, exactly what he was and forever making excuses for it. And most of all, how much I hated *Rhys*. I hated him for always being right and for knowing what I wanted more than I knew myself—hated him for being the cause of all this. And now the final truth was revealed, as the low fire of vodka pulsed through my veins, because in that moment, I was conscious of wanting Rhys more than I'd ever wanted anything before.

But if I was expecting some lovelorn confession from him, I was very much mistaken. Instead, all he did was shoot me a disgusted look and turn to walk away. But I grabbed him by the upper arm, pulling him back to me.

"No, wait—you don't just get to walk away again—"

"Why not? I get it. You've moved on; you're too good for

us now." His voice was still soft and controlled, but he was angrier than I'd ever seen him, his green eyes flashing. I softened my voice and lowered it, afraid of what I was about to confess.

"Why not?" I exhaled softly in defeat. "Because—well, because I don't want you to."

His eyes stared into mine, and the only thing I cared about was the infinitesimal amount of hope I saw reflected there.

Triumph burst within me.

He *did* want this.

He stepped closer.

"But why didn't you ever say anything?" I asked, my breathing suddenly unsteady, tears slipping silently from my eyes. "That night at Cecily's party, I waited for you—you *know* I was waiting for you—and you never did anything. Why? Why didn't you say something? *Do* something?"

He didn't kiss me, instead, he wrapped his arms around me, pulling me into the tightest bear hug I had ever known, walking me back against the wall in the shadow of a stone sarcophagus, and I was helplessly shuddering against him, trying to regain my composure. But it felt like the solar system was sliding away from me, the world was tilting, the planets were careering out of gravity, and I knew it was mainly the vodka Casey slipped into our glasses in the restroom, but I had never needed anything like I needed him right then.

He didn't smell divine or expensive—didn't smell like salt air and cedar. He smelled like his dad's borrowed aftershave—a little oceany—mingled with sweat, but, most important, familiar. Safe. I pulled away slightly, aware of my breathing hastening the closer we'd gotten, and he pulled back, too, his hand sliding down my face, tilting my chin—

"You're drunk, La. We need to get you home."

But I was not about to let him leave me again. "Yes, okay, yes. But you'll come with me, right?"

He hesitated, his eyes blazing into mine, confused and hopeful, and that's all it took. I pulled him into me, my arms sliding around and up his back as his hands found my waist and he bent down, his breath stuttering and shaky, and our lips brushed sweetly, and I knew he was being purposefully cautious because he knew I was drunk and he wanted me to be sure, wanted to make sure I wanted this with a clear and sober head, but I just *wanted,* and I wrapped my arms around his neck, slipping my tongue into his mouth, desire careering through me as he groaned into my mouth—

"I *knew* it."

Beckett's voice ricocheted down the corridor, thick with gloating triumph.

"I took a chance and trusted you, and look what happens."

I had been caught.

I don't know how much time has passed when I wake. I'm still in the greenhouse, strapped tightly by ivy to the stone plinth. I am utterly trapped, like a patient under anesthetic; there's little point in moving. I blink several times, moving my head as much as I can to try to take in my situation.

Gwydion stands before the artifact, although it doesn't look like an artifact any longer. Yet more stone has cracked away, revealing something slender and smooth and green within, like a sturdy sapling.

He's mumbling a string of words over and over again—Welsh, I think—his hands raised, his head lowered.

As if sensing that I'm awake, he turns his head to look at me with a wolfish grin. "She's *changing*, Lara. It's almost time."

"You need me," I say quietly. I have no idea why, but I know it's true. It's why I'm here, and it's also why I'm not yet dead.

"I'm going to release you now," he says. "There's no point in trying to run away. All the doors are locked, and besides"—he gives me an unpleasant grin—"you've seen for yourself: she won't *let* you leave. She wants you here."

But before he even leaves his chair, I feel the pressure around my wrists and ankles lessen as the ivy falls away to wither and die. I notice his surprise. He quickly stands. I stand, too, and, ignoring him, approach the statue as if walking in a dream.

The closer I get, the more stone crumbles away, falling to the ground in clumps with a soft crack. I begin to realize that she has wanted me here all along. That all the shrubs, all the bushes, all the ivy, the nettles, everything forcing us all to this end of the train, were in fact only for me.

It was a summoning.

"What do you want?" I ask her quietly. "What is it you want me to do?"

I brush at the remaining stone, which easily falls away at

my touch, disintegrating to powder—a hollow casing revealing something extraordinary beneath.

And as the final piece of stone, the piece covering her face, falls away, I breathe in sharply.

"Blodeuwedd," I gasp. "*Flower Face.*"

Standing before me is a woman of around my height and age. I say a woman, but everything about her is utterly unearthly—or, to be more accurate, entirely *of* the earth. Her skin is the color of winter moonlight and glitters in the darkness. Her eyes are a honey gold and glow like sun-warmed amber. Her hair is a riotous concoction of white and golden blossoms that tumbles past her waist, tiny petals drifting before her like moondust.

Behind me, I sense Gwydion bowing down on one knee in silent worship.

"You're free of him," I whisper to her. "You're *finally* free."

35

JUNE, LAST YEAR

The flashing blue lights and the whine of a siren didn't seem totally alien amid the golden glow of the party lights.

And even though most people had left, I was still there, my head fizzy and pounding with champagne bubbles and corner store vodka, my beautiful gold party dress spattered with an almost artistic spray of crimson.

Rhys's hand was clammy and still as I clutched it in mine; his face, swollen and unrecognizable, one eye alarmingly purple. Still, his pulse beat steadily in his wrist as he lay obediently still. I stared in disbelief at my miserable tears plopping steadily onto his shirt. And all I could think was that it should have been me lying there, not Rhys, because I'd driven Beckett to this. *I* had caused this.

Deliberately or not, I'd hurt them both.

I rode with Rhys to the hospital, never once giving up his hand, my phone endlessly buzzing with Beckett's messages and calls and WhatsApps and emails, to the point that the paramedic quietly but firmly told me to switch it off.

His parents had arrived before me. His dad, silent and ashen faced, immediately followed his son through the hospital. His mum turned and stared at me as I went to follow—her usually smiling face, the same tawny-green eyes as her son's, now stricken with hatred.

"You stay right there," she hissed. "You were never good enough for him, never. And now look what you've done."

Wordlessly, I drifted out of the hospital and over to the taxi stand, where I gave the driver Beckett's address.

I couldn't stay with Rhys as I'd wanted to. Not without his mum ripping into me—and justifiably. And I couldn't go home. Dad would have been there, probably drunk, acting stupid and asking all the wrong questions.

Besides, I needed to confront Beckett. Needed to end this. And to ask him why. Why do this to Rhys, when all along, up until tonight, the night I had finally seen Beckett for what he was, I had always chosen him, always put him first.

But his house was dark and empty.

I took the key from beneath the large urn to the left of the door and opened it, quickly shutting off the alarm.

I called his name softly into the darkness.

No one answered.

Where could he be?

There was one place. And even if he wasn't here, it was

time, I decided, to find out what he'd been keeping from me—the person who was never allowed a single secret of her own.

I took the key. I opened the door.

Within his den, there were no dismembered dead girlfriends, no bizarre taxidermy, no serial killer articles pasted to the wall, no weed farm—all the increasingly bizarre things I'd imagined I'd find in here. Instead, the room was blandly innocuous—a disappointment. I'd wanted to find something in here to *humble* him. Wanted to uncover his dirty secrets. To whisk away his carefully curated facade, like a ballroom entertainer with a tablecloth. But all along, it seemed he'd been telling me the truth.

Chewing my lip, I debated whether to leave or to risk a closer look.

The room was just a den. A large TV dominated one wall, beneath it a desk with multiple monitors attached to a PC and several gaming consoles. So far, so predictable.

There was a small couch, a bookcase crammed with graphic novels, a set of weights, and a lifting bench.

Nothing out of the ordinary.

I experienced the sinking realization that there was nothing wrong here, no dirty secrets, no hidden sins, the fact that it was just a private space for him finally hitting home.

Tears began to prick my eyes at the unfairness of it all. At how I was always the one in the wrong. How Beckett was, in the end, hiding nothing. How he was rightfully angry because he caught me kissing someone else—hadn't he been right to be suspicious of my intentions? All he'd ever wanted was for me to live up to his ideals, to be the perfect girlfriend, but I couldn't do it. I would never be perfect. Not for him, not for Rhys, not even for myself.

Not for anyone.

"She's magnificent!" gasps Gwydion from where he's kneeling on the floor. "I could never, ever have imagined how beautiful she is. She's . . . she's unearthly. She's perfection."

Blodeuwedd stands still, not blinking, not even appearing to breathe. And the more I look at her, the more I realize there's more about her that is flower than anything resembling a human. Her limbs are strong and sinuous, twisted like spring saplings, and her eyes, the color of summer honey and haunted by sadness, bore into my own.

Around her, the room seems to ripple and distort. Roses blossom, their thorny branches stretching across the floor; the air is filled with the sickeningly sweet perfume of lilies; while behind Gwydion, the carmine-belled foxgloves grow monstrously tall. One by one, as they are overtaken by foliage or branches, the candles snuff out, until we are all left in the dark.

But I am not as afraid as I might be.

Lightly she takes my hands, then holds her palms against mine. Her eyes are luminous in the darkness, spilling soft golden light. I expected them to be full of rage at how she has been used, but instead, they're filled with something softer—not quite sorrow. . . . I think . . . I think what I see is understanding.

I'm reminded of her story. Created by a magician only to serve, to be *used*. A plaything for a man cursed never to take a human bride, nothing more than a vessel for an heir, a tool to cheat his fate. Created to be placid and pleasing and *perfect*. To do as she was bid, whether she wanted to or not. Conjured from an image in a man's head, never allowed to be who she truly wanted to be.

It has taken me too long to understand that trying to mold yourself into another's idea of perfection brings nothing but unhappiness. It's the very definition of being set up to fail. All the styling, makeup, designer clothes, and expensive jewelry in the world would never have made me what Beckett *really* wanted.

It's taken me too long to realize that the price of always prioritizing someone else's happiness, someone else's needs, someone else's pleasures at the expense of your own, is a price too high. A price that leaves you wanting, a price that begs the question, when you're alone in the dark, *Is this what you really wanted?*

Was it worth it?

"I'm sorry," I say to her quietly, her hands still touching mine, her skin petal soft. "I'm so sorry for what happened to you."

Does she understand what Gwydion is planning? Is there any way we can stop it? I hear footsteps behind me in the darkness. He's attempting to leave. He curses in the dark, and I hear him ripping away at the foliage covering the door.

Something silken whispers over my skin. My first instinct

is to pull away, but her hands grip mine more tightly, and I cannot. The scent of freshly cut grass envelops me as the feeling continues. It's like being swallowed within a rosebud, smothered beneath a secret midnight garden of ferns. Time slips away. The noise of Gwydion cursing behind me fades, and I am—

I am back in Beckett's house.

Back in his den.

Soon he will come home, his car pulling up erratically in the driveway, spilling gravel. By that time, I will be sitting in the doorway, a sobbing, apologetic mess.

He will storm past me, uttering words of disgust, opening the door and slamming it behind him.

And he will never open it for me again.

But for now—

I turn to leave but jump as I see someone standing in the doorway—someone who's both there and not there. She is beautiful in a way I cannot describe. It's like looking at the reflection of the sun on water, all refracted light, a splintered spectrum. An image so unworldly, you cannot hold it in your head.

She points to the wall beside the door. The one that in my distress, in my haste, I miss the first time, the time before.

The wall is covered with photos, each one beautifully, carefully framed. And the subject in each picture is the same.

They are of a girl around my age. A beautiful one. She

has long, poker-straight blond hair, soft, overly long bangs, and arresting dark eyes, her perfect features accentuated by a delicate cat eye and blush-pink lipstick. In each picture, she's dressed like an epitome of some preppy upper-class girl in polite shades of beige, white, navy, or black.

A shrine to an ex?

It takes me a while before I realize.

They are not all the same girl.

I squint, confused.

I notice because, in a few of them, the girl is standing beside Beckett and it's impossible for her to be three different heights. Close up, I can see the slight differences between the shapes of their faces, their complexions, their builds.

What the fuck, *Beckett?*

You could be so perfect.

I back out of the room, and as I do, I knock over another photo.

I recognize her even though she's looked so different lately.

Because this one . . . this one is of me.

36

Blodeuwedd looks at me, her hands still holding mine, the light from her eyes spilling like molten gold, illuminating the carriage. And in the dim light, I see that she is changing again. Her limbs are stiffening—no longer the silken silver-green they were before but drying, turning rigid and gray. The downy silver-gold blossoms of her hair start to shrivel and brown, drifting to the floor.

Thank you. . . . I have waited so long for someone to listen.

She doesn't exactly *say* it—her lips don't move—but I hear it in my head all the same, like the chiming of a delicate silver bell.

Now, you must put an end to this.

Before me, she continues to shrink and diminish, shriveling down inside herself, from springy green to brown, mottled and decayed and finally brittle gray, until the woman has gone and all that remains is the blackened stump of a tree.

And now I know what it is I need to do.

The only way I can explain what happens next is that it's like I am sleepwalking, or clinging to the webs of a dream in those still hours of the morning when you can still bend and shape the path of it to your will. Everything around me is hazy, misty, and unclear and seems to be moving so much more slowly than before, even the train itself. It's as if I am sheltered deep within a chrysalis, shaken delicately by the slow motion of the carriage, cushioned by plant matter. Around me, all is dark, the lights have gone out, and I shouldn't be able to see a thing; the logical part of my brain understands that, but it doesn't explain why I can see the fuzzy golden outlines of my surroundings, why I am free to move.

Gwydion has managed to escape to at least the next carriage. A ragged pile of weeds is scattered about the floor, and the door is half open. I stand hesitantly before the entrance. In there, nature holds dominion. There's nothing to see but dense branches and foliage. But on closer inspection, a small tunnel appears to have been hacked out of the middle, low to the carriage floor.

I reach out, instinctively brushing the nearest branch, and it cracks and blackens at my touch, falling to the floor.

Swallowing, I stagger through the cabin—the plants and leaves here all wilt before me, parting like green ocean waves.

In the first carriage, the riotous blooms brush past my hair, caressing my skin with their farewells before they parch and die. I can hear them whispering, exhaling sadly as they release themselves from life.

My touch, even my gaze, withers them all.

And through the door, in the next carriage, in what used to be the piano lounge before it became a narrow tunnel of evergreen fronds, are Gwydion and Rhys.

They're grappling with each other. Gwydion is a little taller, but Rhys is a little stockier.

The words are ripped out of me, my vision sharpening. *"Stop it!"*

Rhys whirls around in surprise, his face a mask of relief. "Lara?"

Rhys is distracted for only a split second, but Gwydion uses it well. He whirls around, grabs the fire axe from its mounting on the wall, and, with both hands, hurls it, not at Rhys, but at the window behind him, which shatters completely, letting in a rough night breeze that stirs the fronds of the trees that have taken root.

"Well, we can't do this *here*, can we?" he says coldly. "Lara's put paid to that."

Rhys turns toward the window, but there isn't time to warn him. I watch in horror as Gwydion hauls him up by his shirt with both hands, shoves him hard through the jagged gap, and then, to my surprise, jumps out after him.

* * *

There's no time to scream.

I lean out of the window, instinctively knowing what I must do, and at my silent command, tree roots erupt violently from the ground, enveloping the track, the train, its wheels, and finally bringing us to a creaking, shuddering halt. Cursing, I thrust open the nearest door and tumble down from the train onto a mossy bank lined with gargantuan conifers, where Gwydion kneels over Rhys, punching him repeatedly in the head.

No.

Not *again*.

I won't allow this to happen again.

Gwydion screams, wild and high, as two thick lengths of briar explode from the slope and loop around his wrists, fastening tightly and wrenching him away from Rhys.

Good, I think as I hear the sound. Thinking of Samira. Of what *he* did to her.

He whips his head around, staring at me, his face a mask of both hatred and fear. And in it I see Beckett, his lip curled into a wicked sneer. The same delicate, fine veneer hiding the savagery beneath. God, how could I ever have cared for him—

Gwydion manages to rip one hand free from the briar, scrabbles for the axe, and clumsily frees his other hand.

"What is *wrong* with you?" I shout as he lurches monstrously toward me, blinking away the blood dripping from a nasty scratch on his forehead. Behind him, Rhys gives a pained moan and attempts to get up.

"All this . . . all this *death*, and for what? Just for money? Even your own *sister*? Your *parents*? Gwydion, what do you have *left*?"

He stops and looks at me, a curious glint in his eyes, accompanied by, I'm pleased to see, a faint glimmer of fear. "What *are* you?" he whispers. "What . . . what did she *do* to you?"

Truthfully, I don't know. But if we are speaking of metamorphosis, I do know that something has turned Gwydion from a selfish little boy, only interested in money, into something much more frightening.

"It isn't about money at *all*," he continues, wiping a distracted hand over his bloodied face. "I knew you wouldn't understand; even now, even with everything you know, everything you have at your disposal, you still don't understand. Don't understand what you could do if you wanted to." He shakes his head. "It's nothing to do with money; it's all about *power*."

"You wanted to unleash her on a city," I say, understanding now. "You needed to prove what she was capable of before you were able to sell her. You were planning on killing hundreds, maybe thousands, of people."

To my utter disbelief, he only smirks. "*Now* you're thinking like the smart girl I took you for. The more, the better, frankly. I wasn't going to make much money from a couple of unfortunates on a train, now was I?"

He sighs, weighing up the axe in his hands. "But I should have planned more carefully. Should have thought about the fact that Blodeuwedd was never a goddess; never had any true power to steal. She was created in the image of a woman—and like you, she was *weak*. Weak in power, weak physically, weak in intelligence, and, as the legend goes, weak in *morals*."

I stare at him in utter disgust.

"She wasn't weak. She followed her heart. And look what it got her . . . punished by someone like you . . . someone who only cared about controlling her."

He shrugs, that cold glimmer in his eyes again. "It doesn't matter anymore. Everything's fucked thanks to you." He pauses, glancing swiftly behind him. I follow his gaze, my heart heavy. Rhys is lying still on the ground.

"So," he continues, "I suppose the only thing left to do . . . is clean up all this bloody . . . *mess*."

Before I realize what's happening, he whirls the axe behind his head with both hands and brings it down toward me.

The blow glances my forehead, and I topple to the ground. Warm liquid pools rapidly in my eyes. There's a violent flap of wings and a creaking, shifting sound that seems to come from deep beneath the earth. From my position on the ground, in the hazy moonlight, my vision partially obscured, I don't fully trust what I see. Swirling around Gwydion, there's a tornado composed of vast torn roots, ropes of ivy and nettle, thorn-speckled roses, and purple thistle. It encircles him, envelops him, swaddles him in fecundity, drawing him to its center, pulling him closer and tighter, until it is a pulsating cocoon of plant matter. Seconds later, it bursts open with a screech that pierces the night air and a deafening flap of wings.

An owl flies into the darkness of the forest and is gone.

And moments later, so am I.

Gratefully slip-sliding into the quiet dark.

37

Finally I see it.

I am Lara Bethany Williams, and I have always been good enough.

And everything, everything else, is flowers—

His voice is low but unsteady, his breath hot and sweet in my ear, like the perfume of lilies—but Gran says lilies mean death, and, well, that's surely where I must be after—after—

"La, *La,* listen, please—you have to stay awake. You have to stay with me until help arrives . . . you have to *listen* to me, okay? Stay with me and—and—let me tell you a story.

"So it was Cecily Hunter's sixteenth birthday party, the one with the stupid Gatsby theme; you know how much I hate that stupid book. But I went anyway because *you* were going. I know you think I'm made of stone or whatever, but all damn year I'd wanted to do *something*. Something about . . . about *us*. Well, okay, you know me, more like *say* something. I guess all told I'm a man of words, not action. Anyway, everyone was telling me that I should, that you wanted me to—that there was a chance I might not be as friend-zoned as I thought, and of course, *I* wanted to. I didn't need anyone to tell me that—I *knew*. I always knew. Since the first time I saw you, sitting in the library trying to study from some outdated textbook, it was like everyone else was in black-and-white and you were the only thing in color. And I don't know what I was scared of that night— But . . . no, that's not right. I know exactly what I was scared of—"

Together we hasten into the glade beneath boughs of oak and briar, the grass twinkling with yellow meadowsweet blossoms like little stars, and I know it is spring, but all around us, it is like snow is falling . . .

But it isn't snow; it's cherry blossoms, magnolia blossoms, apple blossoms, falling from the sky, a silken confectionery, a sweet-smelling blizzard—

"I was afraid of rejection—obviously, from you. I thought it was better not to know than to try . . . and get it wrong. I couldn't have taken it if you'd laughed or . . . or been disgusted or . . . if I'd ruined our friendship . . . And now I know that all it really was, was cowardice."

The glade is quiet and secluded. He chose it well. The air is delicately laced with fragrance—the cusp of spring sweet in the air—

"I messed *up*. La, I was so, so nervous. And I drank too much, and yes, I flirted with—god, I can't even remember her *name* now; it was so *stupid* of me. All I wanted was for you to notice me for once—to *see* me—in the way I'd *always* seen you. To see that I wasn't *just* reliable old Rhys but that I could be wanted, too. I began to act like I'd already *been* rejected, when the truth is, I hadn't even been brave enough to *try*. And you seemed so quiet that night—"

These three vows I will make to you:
She shall not be made of mortal flesh.
She shall be more beautiful than any flower in the meadow.
And she shall love you perfectly.

"Then the lights went down, and I couldn't see you anymore. I began to panic. I was running out of time, and it felt like this was my last chance, my *only* chance, and I didn't even realize at that time how true that was—"

—and when the magician sees her fully whole, he can barely believe his artistry. Delicate flower made delicate flesh; pearlescent petals in her downy hair, and the glade is alive with birdsong—

"And then I finally saw you, alone, looking at me. Like you were waiting. And I knew, if there was ever a chance, it was *now*. The last song of the night was playing; I'll never forget it, some cheesy old eighties tune. And without even speaking, I walked over to you and . . . and we danced. La, your hands were in mine, and you looked into my eyes and smiled, your eyes like stars, and I'd never seen anything more beautiful. And it was *so* perfect, you know? Like it was meant to be—"

As they step out of the clearing and into the meadow, he

wonders how it is possible that she is somehow more beautiful than everything that surrounds her, her eyes brighter than the cerulean ribbon of sky above; her skin as soft as spring buds—

"Then the song ended, and you looked at me expectantly, and I knew it was time. Like the clock striking midnight in *Cinderella*, chiming like some doomsday warning, the sand in the hourglass slipping swiftly away, the wrecking ball swinging . . . *Time, gentlemen, please.* . . . But I couldn't do it . . . I couldn't *say* it. It was impossible. At that moment, it all seemed too . . . *big*. The cold realization that if I messed this up, if I'd somehow got it wrong, not only would all the things I'd been dreaming about since the moment I met you be whisked away forever, but likely you would, too. The second you left, I came after you, but when I found you, you were getting into his car. And then, La, you'd gone . . . and he—well, he never left."

You're way too pretty to be crying over some guy. . . .

"And I've regretted that night every day since, and worst of all, I've always thought I was responsible. Like it was all my fault . . . what happened . . . after. Because . . ." He sobs, a harsh choking noise, and I wish I could hold him, tell him I have never blamed him, not once, but I cannot speak.

"Because I was too scared to say anything when I needed to, and afterward, when I began to see how you'd changed, how quiet you'd become, how *different*, I was worried, but I didn't know what to do or how to make it better. I thought you'd say I was jealous—and in all honesty, I was. And then, when he hit me at the end-of-year party, you don't understand, but I was—*glad* he did—I felt like I deserved to be punished for my cowardice."

La—a musical note—my name on his lips.

"God, La—please, *please,* wake up. I don't know what to do...."

A tear falls on my cheek, warm. A face is pressed against mine, warmer still. I hear a shuddering of breath.

"La? Please. I—I—couldn't bear it if anything happened to you. I've—I've always, *always* loved you."

My eyes open, and his stare into mine, wide and unbelieving. I blink rapidly, then reach up and pull his face toward me. Our lips meet, hot and tentative and so very brief.

He pulls back immediately, the shock evident on his face. "Oh, thank *God*! Are you okay?"

"Why do you always have to be so sensible?" I murmur, sitting up and wincing. There is a sudden throbbing in my head, so vicious I worry I am about to projectile vomit and entirely ruin this moment.

"Are you for real?" He narrows his eyes. "Lara, I thought you were dead! Or . . . worse . . . that you'd changed into some . . ." He trails off. "I . . . I thought you'd changed."

He takes my hands and envelops them in his own.

"You know, Rhys, I *have* changed," I say quietly. "But it's been a long time coming."

* * *

We climb back onto the now-stationary train, exhausted and bruised.

Now there is not a single trace of a plant anywhere on board. Even in the greenhouse carriages, all that is left is a series of empty, dusty planters and, in the very last carriage, nothing but a tiny pile of powdered stone.

Carlos is sitting at the kitchen table, a dazed expression on his face, and, alerted by the slamming door, the baroness and Becca emerge cautiously from their cabins.

We gather in the Cedar Lounge, the five of us. "Where's Shosh?" I ask, glancing about nervously.

"I locked her in her suite," says an exhausted-looking Carlos. "I was concerned she might try to . . . alight early. I don't want to be the one left trying to explain all this to the cops."

"What *are* we going to say?" I wonder quietly.

"The truth?" suggests Rhys. Of course he does. But I'm not even sure what the truth is anymore.

Beside him, Carlos nods darkly. "Yes. It was those passengers—the Llewellyns. I thought there was something shifty about them the moment I received their first breakfast order. What happened to the guy? I found a working phone in his luggage—that's how I managed to alert the cops."

"He, uh, had an unfortunate accident," I say quietly. "We don't need to worry about him anymore."

Carlos shrugs. "Can't say I'm sorry for his loss. Poor Samira . . . poor Terrence. And Shosh has got herself some explaining to do. . . ."

"I think she was in a difficult spot," says Rhys diplomatically.

The baroness clears her throat. I'm relieved to see she's already looking better, her eyes clear, her hacking cough gone.

"I . . . uh, don't suppose there's any chance of a cup of tea while waiting, is there?"

"I've got it," I say with a smile.

EPILOGUE

The evening sun sparkles off the communal swimming pool below the hostel balcony. A rose sits, wilting, in a cheap bathroom glass.

Last night, as we ate tapas and watched flamenco in the town square, Rhys bought me the ridiculously overpriced flower from a vendor at the restaurant, and we both collapsed into laughter after my initial look of terror. Then, holding my face in both hands as if it were some priceless treasure, he kissed me. Later we sat on the beach and watched the sun slowly melt into the ocean, my head on his shoulder, his arm around my waist.

This morning the rose's petals are all but gone.

I think of a beloved fairy tale where love slowly blooms even as the petals of an enchanted rose fall. I think of a woman made of flowers tethered to a person she didn't love, and I absently brush the stem with my fingertips.

The rose blooms anew.

ACKNOWLEDGMENTS

Of all my books to date, this one feels the most personal. I am always keen to gush about horror and how I love to be scared—but the scariest things, the true horrors, can be the hardest things to talk about. Writing about these experiences has proven difficult, too. I'm grateful to live in a time when coercive control is much more openly discussed, where just because a relationship doesn't contain violence doesn't mean it isn't abusive.

On to the thank-yous! I'm going to keep it concise!

I am forever thankful to my world-changing superstar agent, Claire Friedman. Three books in, and I *still* can't believe I get to do this. I'm eternally grateful you took a chance on me and my spooky books. Here's to more!

Equal thanks to my fabulous editor (and, by the time this book is published, fellow author), Lydia Gregovic. You continue to be such a wellspring of confidence and encouragement—and the way you understand my characters and bring clarity to my stories is a wonder. When I started out, I was a little worried about what working with an editor might entail, but you are truly a joy to work with!

Thank you to everyone at Delacorte Press who had a hand in bringing this book to publication, including Krista Marino and Wendy Loggia for their championship of me and my work, Tamar Schwartz, Colleen Fellingham and the copyediting department, Liz Sutton in production, Cathy Bobak for the interiors, Sarah Lawrenson for being the best publicist I could ask for, Judith Haut and Barbara Marcus, and the entire RHCB Sales and Marketing teams, who are the very best in the business. And thank you to Dawn Yang for the gorgeous cover artwork, and to Trisha Previte for her skillful design!

A big thanks to Louise Lamont at LBA, my UK agent, for ensuring my books were published in the UK—so my friends and colleagues stopped thinking I was making things up if they couldn't find my debut in bookshops.

As ever, thanks to my family, particularly Neil. Thank you to the librarians and booksellers and to the bookish community. I endlessly appreciate how you spread the word about the works you're passionate about.

And thank you, lovely reader. You're truly the reason I get to do this.

ABOUT THE AUTHOR

AMY GOLDSMITH grew up on the south coast of England obsessed with obscure '70s horror movies and antiquarian ghost stories. She studied psychology at the University of Sussex and, after gaining her postgraduate certificate in education, moved to inner London to teach. Now she lives back on the south coast, where she still teaches English and spends her weekends trawling antiques shops for haunted mirrors. She is the author of *Those We Drown*, *Our Wicked Histories*, and *Predatory Natures*.

HAVE YOU READ?

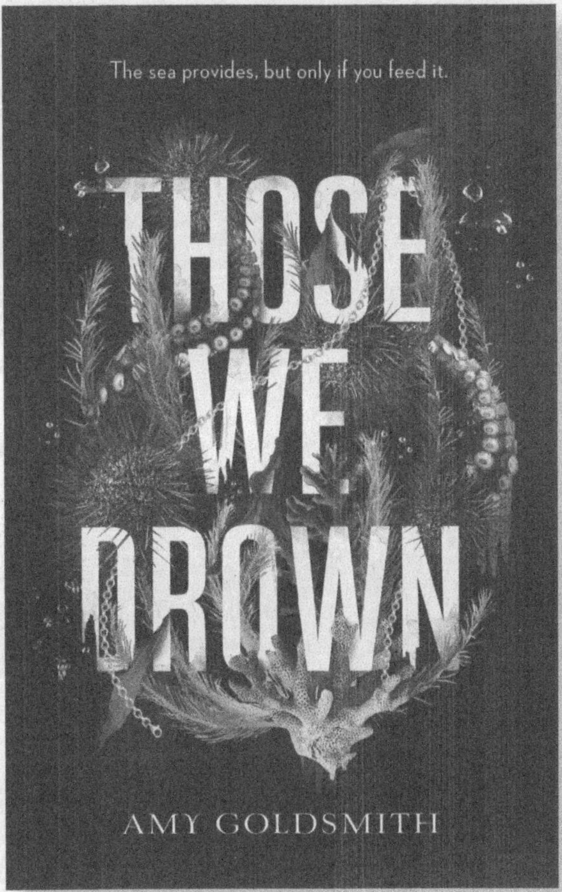

THOSE WE DROWN

The sea provides, but only if you feed it.

AMY GOLDSMITH

HAVE YOU READ?

Thank you for choosing an Ink Road book!

For all the latest bookish news, freebies and exclusive content, sign up to the Ink Road newsletter – scan the QR code or visit Ink.to/InkRoad

Follow us on social media:

bonnierbooks.co.uk/InkRoad